# FAMILY SINS

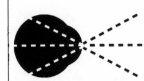

This Large Print Book carries the
Seal of Approval of N.A.V.H.

# FAMILY SINS

## David Compton

**Thorndike Press • Waterville, Maine**

Published in 2005 by arrangement with NAL Signet, a member of Penguin Group (USA) Inc.

Thorndike Press® Large Print Core.

The tree indicium is a trademark of Thorndike Press.

The text of this Large Print edition is unabridged. Other aspects of the book may vary from the original edition.

Set in 16 pt. Plantin by Liana M. Walker.

Printed in the United States on permanent paper.

**Library of Congress Cataloging-in-Publication Data**

Compton, David.
    Family sins / David Compton.
      p. cm.
    ISBN 0-7862-7141-8 (lg. print : hc : alk. paper)
    1. Organized crime — Fiction. 2. Irish Americans — Fiction. 3. Lotteries — Fiction. 4. Informers — Fiction. 5. Clergy — Fiction. 6. Large type books. I. Title.
PS3553.O48395F36 2005
    813'.54—dc22                     2004059814

*To Dan and Jane O'Donovan*
*for their friendship and hospitality*

**National Association for Visually Handicapped**
-------------------------- *serving the partially seeing*

As the Founder/CEO of NAVH, the only national health agency solely devoted to those who, although not totally blind, have an eye disease which could lead to serious visual impairment, I am pleased to recognize Thorndike Press★ as one of the leading publishers in the large print field.

Founded in 1954 in San Francisco to prepare large print textbooks for partially seeing children, NAVH became the pioneer and standard setting agency in the preparation of large type.

Today, those publishers who meet our standards carry the prestigious "Seal of Approval" indicating high quality large print. We are delighted that Thorndike Press is one of the publishers whose titles meet these standards. We are also pleased to recognize the significant contribution Thorndike Press is making in this important and growing field.

Lorraine H. Marchi, L.H.D.
Founder/CEO
NAVH

★ Thorndike Press encompasses the following imprints: Thorndike, Wheeler, Walker and Large Print Press.

# Chapter 1

The Spanish mission church of San Xavier de Bac shimmered like a mirage in the late-afternoon desert heat. Father Michael Driscoll, parish priest in the Papago Indian community south of Tucson, Arizona, squinted at the stark white confection of domes and arches as he passed through the spartan garden courtyard, and entered the church through the weathered mesquite doors.

His footsteps echoed around the empty nave. He picked up a candy wrapper off the floor, straightened a row of chairs, scraped candle wax off the sanctuary railings with his thumbnail. The weariness of a day that had begun before dawn had not completely dulled his senses. He lifted his eyes up to the glorious interior of the church, drank in the polychromatic-painted walls and altars, the gold gilt on the saints' statues glittering in the sun's

7

rays coming through a lofty window. The old Franciscan friars had designed the mission church as a showplace in the New World, to demonstrate the glory and power of the Catholic Church to the natives. Two hundred years later, a simple parish priest was still awed.

He was finally alone. A few precious moments to himself before preparing for the evening Mass. He knelt on the cool tile floor in the transept, the Chapel of the Sorrowful Mother, and closed his eyes to pray.

"Blessed Mother of God . . ."

A thousand thoughts from the day rushed in to fill the inner silence. The school fund-raiser for the children. The endless restoration of the two-hundred-year-old church buildings. The deceptively placid face of Bishop Ferdinand, his superior, to whom he still owed his monthly reckoning of the parish's financial accounts. The giggling junior high school girls in his confirmation class who whispered behind his back, referring to him as Father What-a-Waste, a reference to his good looks, his housekeeper had assured him.

He drew a deep breath to clear his mind and began his prayer again.

"Blessed Mother of God . . ."

Suddenly there was a mournful, piercing wail that startled him, a woman's cry of such desperation and complete sorrow as he had never heard before. Father Michael froze in place.

The woman's voice cried out again, even as he was on his feet, rushing to the back of the church to find who was in such agony. The sound seemed to be coming from the choir upstairs. He rushed up the steps, but was mystified to find no one there.

There was a pitiful sob of gathering intensity, and a low moaning that made him think of funeral grief, coming from some indeterminable place. Then the wail began again, bouncing off the barrel-vaulted ceiling and walls, filling the interior of the church. It was loud enough that he had to cover his ears.

Just as suddenly as it had begun, the woman's voice was silent.

He was too disturbed by what had just happened to finish his prayers. He walked briskly back to the church office, stopping along the way to inspect the baptistery, small chapels, and other niches of the church, failing to find any sign of the woman in distress.

"Father," he heard a voice say.

He flinched at the sound of the voice. Consuela, a third-generation Papago housekeeper for the priests of San Xavier, held out the telephone. The look on her face gave no evidence of her having been the miserable voice.

"Didn't you hear someone crying out just then?" Michael said.

"I'm sorry, Father. I heard nothing but the telephone."

He saw the receiver off the hook on his desk.

"A woman for you," Consuelo said somberly. She left his office, closing the door quietly behind her.

"Father Michael," he said.

"Michael! You've got to come — immediately!" It was a shock to hear the familiar voice. She was hysterical. "They've taken Daniel and they're going to kill me!"

"Lydia," he said. He hadn't heard Lydia Jellicoe's voice for over four years, since just before he had begun seminary. "Where are you?"

"In Dublin, in my mother's old flat," she said breathlessly. "Michael, you've got to stop them. You've got to get Daniel back. You're the only one they'll listen to!"

"Lydia . . ." His mind raced, trying to

10

make sense of what he was hearing. It was almost too much, hearing from *her* after so long, and hearing her distress. "I'm a parish priest now. I can't just drop everything and jet off to Ireland. Have you called the police? What's going on?"

Instead of an answer, all he heard was a crashing sound. Then Lydia's scream.

"Lydia?" he shouted over the phone. The line went dead.

Through his office window under the sign DRISCOLL COMMERCIAL BUILDING, Aiden Driscoll stood watching his elder brother, Kevin, open the door of his car and help their father out. The old man, Brian Driscoll — not all that old, just seeming that way — held on to Kevin's arm for balance as they walked up the sidewalk to the unremarkable entrance of the two-story 1950s flat-roofed building overlooking the Boston docklands. Aiden read his father's lips as he cursed his son, had a violent coughing fit, then spat into the bushes. Kevin held open the door. He resembled his father: slim, dark-haired, with a permanent menacing look on his face. But whereas the father's threatening facial features had been set from a lifetime of professional bullying, the son's were an

11

accident of genetics. Two bulky body-guards, a couple of Aiden's own men, followed behind, smirking at his nursemaid brother. A third man, Ger O'Keeffe, rolled out of the driver's seat and locked the car.

"Jaysus," Aiden said to himself, shaking his head.

Aiden smoothed back his hair, hiked up his tailormade trousers, and prepared for his father to explode into the office.

The old man said as he entered the office, "There's got to be a million fucking dollars just lying around the streets, ready for us to scoop up." The bodyguards waited outside. Ger, a holdover from his father's days in the business, came in and took a seat on the couch. He dressed a lot like the old man, slacks and sport coats.

Brian said, "We drive in through the South Side and the niggers and Puerto Ricans have taken over. They're pimping and lending and making book and setting up their own protection. You tell me why we aren't getting a piece of that."

"Nice to see you, Dad," Aiden said.

"Don't fucking try to humor me." He banged his morning newspaper on the desk as he sat down. "I don't know what the hell you do here all day. I built up a nice business by getting out on the streets and working the neighborhoods, and you sit in here on your ass all day pushing paper."

"Dad . . ." Kevin warned, sensing Aiden's growing anger.

"Bad night?" Aiden said. "Wet the bed again?" He spun toward a mirror and fixed the dimple in his tie.

Kevin tried to interject: "Aiden —"

"You just don't want to dirty your hands, get involved in the business at the street level," Brian said.

"Right, Dad. Anything you say." He turned to his brother. "Remind me why the hell you brought him here?"

Kevin shrugged.

"I was thinking maybe I'd start coming in every day again," Brian said. "See about putting the old organization back together. We'd get control of the South Side, then the rest of the city."

"Dad, who's in charge?" Aiden got right in his face and said loudly, "Who is in charge?"

Brian Driscoll wheezed, coughed, spat into his handerchief. Kevin snapped his fingers, ordered one of the men outside to get a glass of water.

"Take it easy on him," Kevin said quietly.

"We were fearless in my day, isn't that right, Ger?"

Ger nodded glumly.

"I did four years in prison," Brian said. "For what? For the business. For the family."

"Aw, fuck it," Aiden said. "You can't have it both ways, Dad. You can't retire, hand over the business to us, then show up here to play the boss again. Plus you're sick."

"I just have a bad cough."

"Do you know how much money we make? Do you?" Aiden pulled out a piece of paper from a file cabinet and threw it in front of his father. "Bottom line, after taxes, over thirteen million dollars last year. That's the family's money."

"But you're paying taxes. You have all these other businesses you have to screw around with to move the money through. Everything's too complicated. I don't understand what you do. You're playing games with stocks. What's that all about? It's all funny money. You've got a room full of people scamming retirees. Hell, in my day, everything was done in cash. I never paid a cent to the IRS."

"Yeah, and that's what the Feds got you on. Who cares anyway, Dad? After taxes, we're still making ten times what you did."

The old man ignored him. He snapped the sports pages flat in front of his face.

"Will you please get him out of here," Aiden said. He flung the door open.

Brian spoke as he looked at the baseball scores. "You think you're so goddammed smart."

"I have a business to run," Aiden said. "Do something useful." He shoved a bowl of bridge mix hard across the table to his father, spilling it. "Go to the park and feed the ducks, Dad."

# Chapter 2

Father Michael Driscoll found Bishop Ferdinand deadheading his beloved tangerine-colored roses in the tiny garden oasis behind the bishop's Tucson residence.

"Ah, Father Michael. You've brought your monthly financial report."

"Not exactly, Your Grace."

"Then you've brought me more problems from that glorious desert church of yours." He snipped another withered bloom, let it fall to his feet.

"I need your advice."

"That's always what you say when you are about to tell me something you have already made up your mind you are going to do. What is it, another restorer for your temple of gold? Our people are impoverished, and now you've hired someone to cover the toilet seats in gold leaf? You will bleed this parish dry before you are gone."

Bishop Ferdinand pricked himself on a

thorn, sucked the blood from his finger. Michael could not help but smile to himself.

"I need to ask for a short leave of absence."

"Is this a church matter?"

"It's a personal matter."

"I see." Bishop Ferdinand bent to pull a weed that had ensnared a small statue of Saint Francis. "And who will take over your duties at San Xavier while you are away?"

"I've already spoken with Father Douglas from my seminary class. He could come for a week or so."

"Or so."

"I need to go to Dublin right away."

"That would not be Dublin, Ohio, or Dublin, Georgia."

"No, Dublin, as in Ireland."

"And how does a poor Franciscan priest who has taken a vow of poverty fund a jet-setting lifestyle such as that to which you aspire?"

Michael did not answer.

"Hmm?" The bishop had still not looked directly at Michael. "And this advice you come seeking. You've obviously made up your mind on the matter before coming to me. It's really a plea for funds, isn't it?"

"I own nothing."

"And neither do I." Bishop Ferdinand encompassed the modest rectory and garden with a sweep of his cassocked arm. "All you see is the Church's, and the Church's, God's."

"I've already made a plane reservation to leave this evening."

The bishop considered that. "When you came to us you knew what you were taking on. There is so much work to do in your parish before you leave us in the fall. I also fear that this sabbatical of yours will negatively impact your responsibilities at the mission church in Peru you have committed to. You seemed so enthusiastic about going there."

"That hasn't changed. It's only that I need a small amount of time to sort something out."

"And a small amount of money." The bishop turned on a garden hose and filled the birdbath in the center of the brick courtyard. "You came all the way here from Boston to make a clean break from your sinful past. Tell, me, Michael: Does this sudden need to rush off to Ireland have anything to do with what we talked about before you took your priestly vows?"

Bishop Ferdinand had received Michael's confession before he had been ordained a priest. Michael had bared his soul, confessed everything.

Michael said nothing.

"So is it your family's business . . . or that woman?"

Michael drew a breath. The sound of the water splashing drew a brilliant turquoise finch. The bishop looked at Michael directly for the first time as the water spilled over.

"Both," the bishop surmised. He shook his head and sighed. "I know there's nothing I can do to hold you back. We've lost so many good priests. You've done exemplary work with the Papagos. I sincerely hope I'll see you again one day."

"Of course you will. I'm sure this will just be a matter of days."

Bishop Ferdinand shrugged. He cleared the fallen blooms from the brick courtyard with the hose spray. "You heard a voice from your past. Resist, Michael, resist. 'The devil goeth about like a roaring lion, seeking whom he may devour.'"

"You're not making this any easier."

"That's exactly the point. As you are hurtling across the Atlantic at thirty-five thousand feet, I want you to think back on the people you served in your parish home, the people who need you, rely upon you for spiritual guidance. The poor Indians you are deserting."

"I'm not deserting anyone."

"I know it is a difficult choice to make: the squalor of Lima, Peru, versus the dazzling boulevards of Europe." Bishop Ferdinand embraced him. "God bless, Michael. I'll be praying for you."

"Thank you, Your Grace."

"Praying that you will be so overcome by feelings of guilt and self-loathing that you will hasten back to us."


"There's one for you."

A man nudged his female companion, her skin just like his own — as white as the dazzling beach on which they lay. The woman to whom her attention had been directed was removing her bikini top. She adjusted the towel behind her and reclined against a dune. Oblivious to the two people propped up on their elbows only a stone's throw away, she rubbed baby oil over her long legs, her flat stomach, her breasts. She glistened in the high September sun.

"Eyes on your work, Sergeant," Burke said.

Deputy Inspector Claire Burke and Detective Sergeant Hurley, both of the Garda Síochána, the Irish police service, scanned the beach from behind cheap dark sunglasses purchased at the ice-cream kiosk near the car park at the other end of the mile-long beach. This far down the Long Strand, usually the only people stretched out on this remote section of West Cork coastline were gay couples and nudists.

A young family walked toward them through the shallow surf, the little boy dragging a plastic shovel behind him, the little girl dripping ice cream in the sand. The mother, plain of face and utterly un-remarkable in her leggings and sweatshirt, was apparently reading text messages on her mobile phone as she pulled an ice chest on large wheels. She chose the spot for them. The father pitched a large beach umbrella to protect the infant he had been carrying.

"Beats the hell out of Dublin," Sergeant Hurley said, as he followed a wave breaking on the vast beach.

"Thank Maeve O'Driscoll and her gang. If they didn't have someone from the po-lice in West Cork on their payroll, we'd be back in the city, soaking up bus fumes."

"That's exactly where my wife thinks I am. Sitting behind a desk on Harcourt Street."

"So how are you going to explain your savage tan?"

"Lobster bake, more like it."

An hour passed. A haze drifted in from the sea and hung over the beach in the late afternoon. The little girl held on to her mother's hand and splashed in a pool left by the receding tide. Despite what she had told the sergeant, Inspector Burke had herself been distracted by the virtually nude woman as Hurley dozed off.

"Hey, wake up," Burke said. "Watch what she's doing."

Hurley pursed his lips as the topless woman reapplied baby oil. "God, I don't know how much more of this duty in West Cork I can stand. She's fucking gorgeous."

"The other woman. The mother."

Hurley squinted to see. "She's reading text messages, looks like to me."

"That's no mobile phone. That's a GPS," she said, referring to a global positioning system device that would indicate a exact latitude and longitude within a few yards' accuracy. "What's the father doing?"

Barely visible behind the umbrella, the father was busy working on something, watched over by the little boy. While the two detectives had been distracted by the sun and surf and the oily topless woman, the father had taken the shovel his son had brought and dug over a dozen holes at the base of a sand dune. Large, deep holes.

"He's loading the ice chest. This is it."

"For God's sake, it's just a family out for the day."

"They must have been given coordinates when the heroin was buried the other night. They're using the GPS to locate the shipment. I'm calling in help." She spoke quietly into a two-way radio hidden in her towel as the father took down the umbrella and picked up the baby.

"I think you're right. They're packing it up."

"Let's move!" They both scrambled to their feet, grabbed their beach towels, and caught up with the family as they set off in the direction of the car park.

"Cute baby," Inspector Burke said to the man.

"Thanks."

Claire Burke saw a stirring in the scrub at the top of the dunes; the snipers were in place. She put her finger around the trigger of the semiautomatic handgun hidden in her towel, reached for her Garda Síochána shield inside the pocket of her shorts. She saw a flutter out of the corner of her eye: the sunbathing woman shaking out her towel. She turned; the father smiled stupidly at her. Claire realized too late that the flutter was a warning signal; the bathing beauty was one of *them*, a decoy. In the instant she was distracted by this thought, her partner spun around and fell, struck by a bullet to his chest. The children screamed and Claire closed her eyes and cringed, expecting to take the next blast. She heard the noise, but felt nothing. With a single shot, one of the police snipers felled the topless woman, who had just seriously wounded Claire's partner. In a blaze of cross fire, Claire managed to take out the father himself, left dead with a gun in his hand.

A helicopter popped over the dunes, kicking up sand in the rotor wash, ready to take the dead and wounded to the hospital.

A band of police in street clothes guarded the mother and children as Claire tore off the lid to the ice chest. There was nothing but remnants of lunch meats and empty beer cans. "Bloody hell," she said.

The mother screamed hysterically at her. The children clung to their mother's legs and cried. Claire kicked the ice chest, turning it over. Out spilled the ice, the garbage. And a half dozen tightly wrapped packages the size of bricks.

She could barely raise a smile. She left the forensic team to photograph and collect the evidence, then boarded the helicopter. "We got them, big fella," she told her wounded partner. "Beginning of the end for the O'Driscolls." The medic lifted the oxygen mask from Hurley's bloodied face.

"Good day at the office," Hurley said heroically before he stopped breathing. The medic slumped in his seat, removed the blood pressure cuff from the dead man's arm. There was just too much blood.

Father Michael spoke to the airline's reservations representative from a gas station pay phone near the bishop's residence. "I don't even own a credit card," he said, barely concealing his irritation. She told him his only alternative was to pay cash at the ticket desk to confirm his reservation and guarantee a seat. "And surely there's some kind of emergency fare you can give me," he said. Michael listened impatiently. "I understand what your rules are for bereavement situations, and I don't have a death certificate, but I also happen to know the plane is only half-full." Not getting the answer he wanted, he slammed the phone down.

Back in San Xavier, he tried finding Lydia's Dublin phone number but was unsuccessful. Directory assistance was a wasted effort, since the number was "ex-directory," unlisted. He heard Consuela shuffling worriedly in the hall outside his door. Time was running out. He had a packed carry-on bag and an unconfirmed reservation on a flight that departed in less than four hours. But he had no ticket.

He emerged from his office to find a tray covered with a fresh dish towel. Beneath it was his lunch. The soup was cold to his touch, the coffee tepid, but he had no appetite anyway.

He found Consuela polishing a brass collection plate in the sacristy. "Why don't you go home early?" he told the housekeeper. He saw her to the door of the church, then locked himself in.

Set upon the table at the back of the nave door were pamphlets and postcards about the church. There was a collection box to accept donations for the restoration of the church. San Xavier had welcomed three tourist buses earlier in the week. The visitors were always generous to a fault as they left the splendid church.

Michael rested his hands on the box for a moment, took a deep breath. He knew he was guilty of rationalizing.

*I'm doing this for Lydia,* he told himself as he removed the lock from the box.

He counted the bills and left the loose change. Someone had even left a lottery ticket. There was just enough cash to get him from his humble parish home to Dublin.

Clutching the money to his chest, Father Michael knelt at the front of the church and prayed for forgiveness, then prayed for Lydia. He had stopped praying for her over a year earlier, finding the vision and memories her name summoned to be too intense for a Franciscan priest who took seriously his new vows of chastity. Now he felt that no longer praying for her safety had been a mistake.

A final prayer — a promise to repay the church every penny. Plus interest. He hadn't the slightest idea how he would do that, but he would. No matter what it took.

*So help me, God.*

# Chapter 3

All across the rugged Irish landscape of West Cork, ten squads of O'Driscoll family gang members rode silently in cars through the nighttime countryside in different directions, speeding through villages, past darkened farmhouses, skirting ditches and dilapidated dairies.

At precisely two a.m., ten men would be torn from lovers in back alleys, pulled from their beds, or ambushed as they staggered home from the pub.

Before the end of the night, ten men would be tortured, and confessions — real and contrived — secured.

But only one would have betrayed the family. Only one would have tipped the police off to the heroin shipment buried on the beach. As long as the cancer was cut out, it didn't matter how crudely it was done or how much of the body was mutilated in the operation. Ten sacrificed to save the whole was not too many.

"Let it be a sign unto them," Maeve O'Driscoll had pronounced upon returning home from Saturday-night Mass, when she had sent her son, Liam, and his most trusted soldiers out to do their wicked deeds, delivering a warning to the weaklings in her own clan at the same time as she did to the meddlesome authorities. Her daughter, Noreen, stood beside her as the order was given, arms crossed in an Irish blessing of sorts.

At the dawning of the day — by farmers on tractors, church wardens on their way to unlock doors for early worship services, deliverymen speeding from the city with their truckloads of Sunday newspapers — ten bodies would be found in different parts of the countryside, hands nailed to wooden fence posts, legs broken with spikey baseball bats, a shotgun blast to the head.

Magpies sat on their chests and pecked their eyes.

In the name of Maeve O'Driscoll — and her bastard brood of hooligans.

"So what's the scam, little brother?"

Aiden Driscoll considered the question, offered Kevin a beer from the refrigerator.

29

The wives gossiped at the dining room table and lit up cigarettes, the scraps of Sunday's pork roast pushed aside to make way for elbows. The children rushed through the kitchen to the backyard, where old man Brian was already sleeping in the hammock, his ragged woolen flat cap pulled down over his eyes, arm dangling, cheap cigar still burning.

Kevin handed Aiden a file folder. Aiden turned up the radio, leaned against the counter so he could keep an eye on both his father outside and the women in the dining room.

"No scam. It's legit." Aiden leafed through the papers, a list of businesses — ownership, addresses, telephone numbers.

"Bullshit. What did you have me get all this information on freakin' convenience stores for sale in West Virginia for? And run the list of owners through a database of criminal convictions?"

Aiden flipped pages, sipped beer as he read. He closed the folder. "Listen," he said smoothly. "Right now what I need you to do is make sure Dad stays out of the way. Keep him busy. Take him to the movies weekdays until his nap time."

"You think I'm nothing but your errand boy? I know what you're trying to do.

You're trying to keep me tied up. Cut me out of the business. You don't tell me shit about anything anymore."

Aiden drew a breath and watched the children rocking the hammock, swinging his father in ever-widening arcs. A Jack Russell terrier nipped at their heels. The old man held on in postlunch alcoholic terror.

"Kevin, of course I need you involved," Aiden said reassuringly. "Things are about to happen. I can't do it without you. Just be patient."

Brian Driscoll had had enough. Muttering something about a nap, trailing grandchildren and a yapping dog and the stink of Irish whiskey through the kitchen, he pushed through his sons into the den, where children and dogs weren't allowed.

"Into the shrine," Aiden said. He shooed the kids back outside.

Aiden sipped beer and read the paperwork.

"Come look at this," Kevin said, cracking the door to the den.

The curtains were drawn, the room illuminated dimly by a fragile lightbulb on the wall, its filament a tiny cross, the kind of light placed beneath framed prints of the Sacred Heart certifying that the house had been duly blessed by a priest. Every inch of the room was filled with mementos from Brian Driscoll's childhood in Ireland, back before he had dropped the "O" in front of his surname, as so many other immigrants had done: A section of an Ordinance Survey map of the land where the old shite damp house was located from which he had fled in his youth. A piece of the auld sod in a bogwood box on the coffee table. First-communion pictures going back four generations. Over the couch where he now lay in near coma was a framed print of young men in their Gaelic Athletic Association uniforms, standing, squatting for the parish team photograph taken after the 1933 county championship. Brian Driscoll's breath rattled in his chest as he dreamed of swatting a ball over the goalpost with his splintered ash hurley.

"He's practically an invalid," Kevin said, quietly closing the door. "You shouldn't be so hard on him. He drinks like that because he's in pain. And because he misses Ma. And Michael."

"Our sainted mother, our sainted brother," Aiden said in a mock West Cork accent as he pantomimed crossing himself.

"I wish you could hear yourself sometimes. If Michael were here he'd be so ashamed of you."

Aiden scoffed. "And what good's a priest in the family if he's not around to heap burning coals of shame on our heads? Michael gave up his right to any say-so in our affairs when he rejected his family, took his priestly vows, and fled to the desert, holier than Jaysus. He hasn't even bothered visiting his poor old da. You wrote him he was sick, didn't you?"

"Maybe he's not allowed mail. Or he's busy at the mission."

"You sound like your mother. Always making excuses for her eldest boy."

"Forget Michael. I'm just thinking of Dad. He's harmless. He makes a lot of noise, that's all. Can't you give him something to do in the office a few hours a day? Make him feel useful?"

"No!" Aiden said fiercely, smashing his fist on the counter, rattling cups in their saucers. The women stopped talking in the dining room to listen. "That asthmatic old man can still cause a lot of trouble. Especially if he finds out we're working a deal with our West Cork cousins. He'd go ballistic and ruin everything. He's still holding family grudges from thirty years ago."

"What exactly the hell are you up to?

Does this have anything to do with the convenience stores in West Virginia?"

Aiden realized he had said too much, too soon. He said calmly, "Just keep him away from the office the next few weeks." He dug a pair of twenty-dollar bills out of his wallet. "Go down to the liquor store and get him some more Jameson tomorrow morning. Make sure he doesn't wake up for the next few weeks."

"You're a runny cunt."

Aiden stuck a finger hard into Kevin's chest. "That's why I'm Mr. Big now, and you're not. Big brother."

A priest in Temple Bar at seven in the morning was an uncommon sight. Father Michael remembered that Lydia's Dublin flat was less than a ten-minute walk from the city's principal entertainment district, but the recollection was dimmed by five years' time and the two bottles of wine they had shared that particular night when she had led him to her mother's pied-à-terre in the city.

The cobblestone streets where the taxi had dropped him off were filled with vans unloading newspapers and fresh bread and flowers for the stalls. A host of pigeons descended to devour whatever fell from the crates being unpacked by the vegetable vendors. Michael turned a full circle, looking for orientation. He followed a whistling tradesman, striding purposefully, until he was free from the maze of shuttered restaurants and pubs and boutiques.

He wandered the streets around the Castle, pushing against the flow of bankers and solicitors and civil servants and shop girls on their way to the city center. He caught his reflection in a plate-glass window and saw that the sleep-deprived, unshaved, windblown priest passing by must have looked to the Dubliners giving him wide berth on the sidewalks like John the Evangelist in search of lost souls in the evil city. But the only soul he was seeking was that of Lydia Jellicoe.

When he saw Saint Patrick's Cathedral he knew he had gone much too far. He doubled back toward the city center, then fell in step with a gang of university students heading toward Trinity College at the bottom of the wide boulevard.

The street with the row of elegant red-brick Victorian buildings looked familiar. He saw himself walking with his arm around Lydia's slim waist, saw her fumble for the front door key as he pushed aside her thick blond hair and kissed her neck, slid his hand beneath her sweater. Saw her pull him inside the doorway to the flat upstairs above the Chinese restaurant where daughter, like mother, fled the wilds of West Cork and took her lovers.

Up the street, a group of boys in school uniforms blocked the sidewalk. Police cars blocked the street. Even before he got there, Michael could see the fuchsia flowers in the stained glass window above the door, a design Lydia had created herself. Already Michael was full of dread.

"The detective asked my dad if he had heard anything Friday night," Michael overheard one of the youths saying. "He told them just the usual screaming and cars racing up and down after the pubs let out."

"I saw them taking her out," another of the boys said excitedly. "I could see everything from my bedroom window. They had her on a gurney."

Michael felt a lump in his throat, fought a wave of nausea.

"But the bag was zipped. She was dead, all right."

The police were taping a notice to the front door, sealing the house.

"What do they do with them?" the first boy said.

"Come on," the other answered derisively. "Everyone knows they take them to the city morgue. They cut them up, then weigh their organs. Then they pack their guts up in a bag like a turkey at the butcher and sew them back into their bellies."

Michael grabbed hold of a railing to steady himself.

# Chapter 4

Maeve O'Driscoll's shrill voice rang out like a tribal war cry in the hills above Carnmore House with the sound of her grown children's names: "Noreen! Liam!"

The sound carried easily through the dense fog that enveloped the sixty-acre estate bounded on one side by a lake and land running down to the sea on the other. The weather blowing in from the Atlantic Ocean rarely settled there, though, and a patch of brilliant blue was already spreading to the west.

"Noreen! Liam!"

Like many other landed families in West Cork, the O'Driscolls considered themselves to be fishermen or farmers first, and wage earners second. Life revolved around the routine of setting out to sea in the morning, caring for the cattle or sheep in the evenings.

A head count that morning after breakfast revealed the loss of three ewes that had recently been covered by the ram. Before any other business could be conducted, the sheep had to be found. But the children had been out in the damp mist for two hours already.

Liam's whistle to the border collies was as distinct as Noreen's. Maeve heard her son driving the sheep down the hills on her left. Her daughter was farther up, calling for the dogs in a lower treble, invisible above the clouds, up where she would be able to see the ocean. Sometimes the sheep got spooked by the fox and ended up falling off a cliff.

Even in the middle of September there was a roaring fire in the library of the grand Victorian country house that was at the heart of the Liss Ard estate. Maeve O'Driscoll sat at her massive oak desk in the window looking out onto enormous rhododendrons as old as the house. She stubbed out her cigarette in a seashell and lit another. She shook the damp from her ginger hair, cropped short since the birth of her firstborn, Liam, twenty-eight years earlier.

The children entered the room together, smelling of heather and lanolin, faces bright with wind. Liam fell heavily into his chair next to the fireplace, stirred the glowing stones with the poker. Heir to half of Maeve O'Driscoll's fortune, he would never inherit the high-backed seat from which she ruled her kingdom by the sea. He was a male and he was muscle, and was thus useful. One day he would present her with a simpleminded male child like himself. He was happy taking orders and pulling lambs. Someone trustworthy had to oversee mending the fences and filling the rutted driveway on the estate. Then a jar at Noonan's in the evening with the lads, a few quid in his pocket to place a bet on the dogs running at Curraheen Park.

Noreen stretched out on the hearth rug, crossed her long legs, smoothed her hair, as black and sparkling as the coal fires. She unself-consciously ran her hands over her high breasts, enjoying a brief autoerotic moment. No woman of her age and intelligence and extraordinary beauty could fail to know the secret envy she aroused in her mother, the twinge of dark lust in her brother.

"I've made a decision," Maeve pronounced. "We are officially out of the import business. The incident at the Long Strand confirms we no longer enjoy the protection of our friends at the local garda station. We can continue to distribute Ecstasy we get from Dublin, but outside detectives have taken over our case, and it's far too dangerous now to bring anything into Ireland ourselves."

"Would be a lot easier now that we're no longer burdened by a traitor in our midst," Noreen said.

Liam had seen to that. He sat impassively listening to his mother and sister discussing how he had killed ten men in one night. Liam had bought the box of tenpenny nails himself at the farmers' co-op and distributed them accordingly. The lads brought their own claw hammers and Louisville Sluggers. As a point of family pride, Liam had delivered the *coup de grâce* to the heads of each with a hand-tooled boxlock ejector ten-bore pheasant gun, traceable back to the retired English doctor from whom it had been stolen a week earlier.

For Ma.

Maeve drew on her cigarette, read his mind. Murder was a thrill: a fast gallop on horseback on the beach after a snort on a brilliant morning, the greyhounds streaking across the hard wet sand alongside.

"We can't live off trailering a few dozen lambs to market," Liam said. "Our inter-

41

ests in the pubs and fish-processing plant won't exactly pay the bills to run this place. We've got one more shipment coming in from Amsterdam we've already fronted three million in cash for. We can't walk away from that."

"There's no way we can land that here after what's just happened," Maeve said.

"I'll find a way," Liam said.

Liam had a good mind for numbers. And the spilling of human blood was a useful vice, unlike the other ones Liam thought his mother knew nothing about. But she knew everything: the family profits going up his nose, into his arm. Another reason to exit the drug trade.

"What's going on in Boston?" Noreen asked.

Boston meant their cousins in America. Aiden Driscoll and his starched-white-shirt organization.

"There's our future, children," Maeve said. She brushed cigarette ash from the desk. "There's no shame in working with them in return for the kind of money we could be seeing. Fifty percent of a couple of hundred million dollars will buy a lot of hobby sheep and Burberry handbags. We pull this off and we'll be set. For generations. And untouchable by anyone."

"I still wonder if we really we need them," Noreen said. "There's got to be some way we can do this ourselves."

"We need them, just as they need us," Maeve said. "We both find the arrangement distasteful, but this would be impossible to carry off otherwise."

Just how distasteful working with Brian Driscoll's family was the children would never know, Maeve mused. The thought of that awful old man filled her with more hatred than she felt toward anyone else. She had, after almost thirty years of animosity, only just been able for the sake of business to put aside the murderous thoughts she had toward Brian Driscoll. At least she wasn't having to deal with him directly, but only his sons.

Maeve continued. "There are legal considerations, issues relating to ownership of property by foreign nationals over in America that would overcomplicate the operation — and slow it down. Time really is of the essence. We simply can't be seen as having an interest in the business. The police would not exactly be sending a very friendly referral if the American agencies conduct a routine criminal background check."

Noreen wasn't happy with that answer.

"The idea was *ours*," she said.

"The idea was Declan's," Maeve corrected. "And we should be grateful that he brought it to us, rather than taking it directly to Aiden Driscoll" — she said the name with an American accent — "which he could have easily done, but he still considers himself to be more West Cork than New York. I talked to Declan yesterday. He's not ready to move, but soon. No one under this roof possesses the expertise that Declan has, or a reliable, clean way to buy the kind of business required that Aiden has. For now, we tend to our sheep, we mend our fences. We wait. We maintain total secrecy. Declan will let us know when it's time."

"It's the middle of September, for chrissake. Don't you ever take the Christmas decorations down?"

Declan O'Driscoll sat alone in near darkness at the long bar of O'Shea's Pub in Manhattan's West Village. The shabby garland, plastic poinsettias, and silver-tinsel Christmas tree were early seventies kitsch. Half the colored minilights strung over the mirror behind the bartender were burned out.

The pub owner was tending bar. Paul, a

44

wiry old Kerryman, topped off a glass of Murphy's Irish Stout and set it in front of Declan. Declan marked his place in the book he was reading with a beer coaster, and smiled at the perfect pint. "I'm still in the Christmas spirit," Paul said. "Now feck off."

They laughed quietly.

A cloud of steam enveloped Paul as he took a rack of glasses from the dishwasher. He got busy drying them. Declan savored his first sip of the beer. "So how's the world treating you out there?" Paul asked.

"No complaints." There was still a clearly discernable trace of Ireland in his own voice.

"Still at that big accounting firm?"

"I haven't been fired." Sip of beer. "Yet."

"You keep bringing that boss lady of yours in here and hand-feeding her peanuts like that, you're going to be gone, lad."

"They're filberts. You know this is the only Irish bar in Manhattan where I can get filberts? Anyway, all I do is offer her the nuts. I can't help it if she wants to suck the salt off my fingers."

"Doesn't anyone ever suspect what you're up to when you take two-hour lunches together?"

"I'm a bad corporate citizen. What can I say?"

"Say *sayonara* to your big job in the Big Apple."

Declan swallowed a mouthful of beer. "Not so big. I'm a lowly computer geek working in the auditing department." He waggled his fashionable punk-nerd black-framed glasses for emphasis. "An anonymous cog in the great machine that is Whitehall-Cogburn."

"One day I'm going to throw on all the lights in here when the two of you are having a snog in the back booth. What if one of your clients came in here and saw you two going at it?"

"I can confidently say our clients would *never* leave an audit trail running through *here*."

"You have single-handedly lowered my opinion of Trinity College Dublin graduates. I figured you must have had some smarts if you got a degree from there in computer science. Was I wrong or what?"

Declan shrugged. "It's all zeros and ones, Paul. Easy-peasy. Numbers are my friend. Numbers have no conscience."

Paul shook his head in disgust as he dried the last glass. He leaned against the wall and picked up a copy of *Ireland's Own*, a treacly-sweet collection of stories from the motherland set in garish graphics. Declan watched him flip to the "Pen Friends" section in the back of the weekly magazine and become engrossed in the lonely-hearts ads — old bachelor farmers still looking for wives, widows desperately seeking men who could keep up the pace of a jig at the annual Irish Country-women's Association dances.

Declan propped his book on the bar and found the angle of light from the bare low-wattage bulb overhead he had been using to read by earlier. He read a chapter and ordered another pint.

"What the hell's that?" Paul asked, looking at the spine of the book.

"Game theory."

"Like running football plays?"

"Like probability and statistics."

"You're a sad case, Declan. You come into an empty bar after work and read a math book? You need to get out."

"I *am* out," he protested.

"I mean out of here. Tell you what, let me at least do this. My wife's got an old collection of *Reader's Digest* Condensed Books going back to nineteen-fifty-some-thing."

"Pass, thanks." Declan dug a ten-dollar

bill out of his pocket, laid it on the wet bar.

"Did I say something to offend you?" Paul said, faking hurt.

"I come in here to remind myself exactly why I left West Cork. Now I remember."

"Ya feckin' eejit."

Declan drained the glass, winked at his friend. "See you later, Paulie."

"Order you another case of filberts. *Slan.*"

The Dublin City Morgue is presently no longer conveniently located adjacent to the city's main bus terminal. Several times a month, a late-middle-aged couple will arrive from the country, step out of the station into the bewildering bustle of streets just north of the Liffey, invariably ask directions from some sharpie rushing by on his way to an important meeting, and walk the few yards to a contemporary building nearby. This is not the morgue, but the Store Street Garda Station. The policeman on duty informs them that while the city's new state-of-the-art Medicolegal Centre awaits development, the state pathologist's facilities have been located several miles away. They take a taxi to an address off the Malahide Road, circle around back of the Fire Brigade's Training Centre, and pull into a small car park in front of several one-story prefabricated buildings. They are met by a sympathetic policeman outside who explains what is about to happen during the identification process. He will, as he had done on the telephone, tell them that their son had been living rough by himself on the city streets. To spare their feelings, the garda may also tell them that the boy probably died of exposure or heart failure, though the coroner's verdict will have to wait several months, and the family won't bother making the trip back from the country to the Coroner's Court for the pronouncement. If they did, they would hear the autopsy report read out by a state pathologist, the wasted liver and a lethal cocktail of drugs in the blood and urine samples drawn from the cadaver telling the true tale. The couple weep on each other's shoulders, but if they knew any better, they would fall to their knees in the mortuary's viewing room and thank God their son died a relatively peaceful death. Because in the cold storage drawer in the next room lies someone else's dead son, not as lucky, evidently homicide. As the country has virtually outlawed guns, murder tends to be especially savage, done with bare hands or weapons of convenience, usually involving horrific knife wounds or bludgeoning of the head. Often the face is so mutilated that the deceased can be identified only by fingerprints, dental records, or DNA samples.

It was just after such a couple exited the low building — by the looks of their hands and faces and by the whiff of cattle in their clothing, a farmer and his wife — that Father Michael stood at the door and knocked. A policeman sat in his car with another uniformed officer and made notes as the man and woman drove off in their taxi.

"I'm Father Michael Driscoll. I wanted to know" — his words caught in his throat and skipped like a badly scratched record — "a woman . . . would have been brought in this morning. . . . This is the morgue, isn't it?"

A man in civilian clothes who Michael surmised was a technician listened and looked skeptical. "You didn't have an appointment, did you?" he asked. He took notice of Michael's clerical collar. "Were you making inquiries on behalf of the family, or are you a relative?"

"You see, I don't even know if she is here. I'm afraid there might have been a murder."

Without replying, the technician walked over to the police car and spoke through the window. The police got out of the car and joined Michael on the steps as the technician went back inside.

"Morning, Father." They took turns talking.

"You say someone's being murdered?"

Michael recognized their jovial demeanor as a ruse, normally effected to keep a suspect calm.

Good Lord, he thought. The idea that he might be considered a suspect had never crossed his mind.

"I received a phone call the other night under highly suspicious circumstances," he said. "A woman I know was in trouble and asked me to help. I went to her flat, but apparently I was too late."

"You're in a Dublin parish, are you?" The American accent had thrown them.

"No, I was just visiting —"

"This woman who was murdered?"

"Yes, but I came *after* the murder." A bit too defensive, he thought. More calmly he said, "My parish is in Arizona. Look, I don't even know if there has been a murder; it's just that I suspect something awful has happened. That's why I'm here."

"You left your parish in America and

flew all the way here because some woman called you from Dublin?"

"Yes."

"What's this woman's name?"

"Lydia Jellicoe. Is she here or not?"

The name registered on both their faces.

"There's someone we'd like you to talk to." It was an order, not a request.

# Chapter 5

"You say you came directly from the airport to the city center today?"

"Yes."

"Then you'd still have your passport with you."

"Of course."

"May I see it, please?"

The man with short-cropped red hair had introduced himself as Detective Chief Superintendent Charlie Brady. It had taken him only five minutes to drive to the pathologist's facilities. He was a head shorter than the two police officers now standing on either side of him on the steps.

Michael showed him the passport. The stamp from Irish immigration at the airport would clearly show when he had arrived. Michael knew instinctively the way Brady's mind was working: *Perhaps this priest standing in front of me was actually here before this woman was killed?* The standard tourist visa he had entered the country on would exclude Michael as a possible suspect in any foul play. Then they could get to work finding out what had happened to Lydia.

Brady seemed satisfied with what he saw. "That's fine, thank you. Let's go in there to talk, why don't we?" he said. They went into a narrow doorway, and Brady asked the technician if they could use the viewing room for a few minutes. The two police officers remained outside and Brady closed the door.

The viewing room in the prefab building had been transformed into a faux funeral parlor. Recessed lights, carpeting, wallpaper. The body the farm couple had been in to identify had been taken away. All that remained were a half dozen chairs along the wall and a small table in the corner.

"Sit there," Brady said.

Michael sat next to the table, Brady on the other side.

"Mind if I record our conversation?" Brady said, setting up a cassette tape machine.

"No. Do you mind telling me what's happened to Lydia Jellicoe?"

Brady pressed record on the machine. Michael felt the eyes of someone from behind a small mirrored glass set in the wall.

"Feel free to help yourself to some water," Brady said, opening a bottle of water and pouring some for himself. Michael did the same. "So what brings you to Ireland, Father?"

"As I was telling the guards outside, I got a call from Lydia Friday night, asking for my help. She's an old friend."

"A good friend, I take it."

"Yes."

"What exactly did she say on the phone?" He began taking notes.

"She said that someone was trying to kill her. She said that only I could help her. And she said they had Daniel."

"Who's Daniel?"

"I don't know."

"Go on."

"The last thing I heard was a crash and a scream; then the line went dead."

"Did you try phoning back?"

"I didn't have her number."

"Did you try calling her family?"

"Her parents died a few years ago. She doesn't have any siblings."

"Friends? Coworkers?"

"It's been a long time. I've completely lost touch with anyone she might have known in West Cork."

"Exactly when was the last time you saw her?"

"About five years ago."

"Isn't that a long time to let pass in seeing a friend? Someone who felt she could phone you from across the Atlantic and that you would come to her rescue?"

"I live in America. She lives here. I'm a priest," Michael said, as if that would explain everything.

"So you say. That reminds me: You wouldn't have any credentials on you to prove that, would you?"

"Probably so."

"The phone number of your superior to confirm your employment would be helpful, as well."

"I'd rather not get my bishop involved."

Brady nodded, underlined something in his notes. "Okay. The last time you were with her. Where was it? What were the circumstances?"

Michael had not revisited that day with any emotional depth for years. Now it all came back to him — Lydia's tanned and slightly windburned face, the deep blue eyes, lightly freckled nose, full lips; the puff of warm air through the hills that carried with it the savory tang of ocean spray and the sweet coconut smell of the gorse in

May bloom; a flutter of baubles, scraps of paper covered with prayers, a tinkling glass Christmas ornament suspended from the outstretched arms of the Blessed Virgin Mary; Lydia's long fingers intertwined with his own, palms tightly cupped, running his thumb over female flesh and bone. He had leaned on those memories like the walking stick he took on their hikes.

"A grotto in West Cork near Lough Ine, a shrine in the hills."

"And you talked about what?"

"I told her I was going to seminary. I wouldn't be seeing her or Ireland again."

"But you are our guest once more. Something draws you back. A woman, no less."

"I know what you're thinking."

"I've seen it before, Father. Even the clergy have women problems."

"It's not like that at all."

"It never is. You told the officers outside that you went to her Dublin flat early this morning, but you were too late. I thought you said she was living in West Cork?"

"Her family lived in West Cork, but they owned a flat in the city. When she phoned me she said she was in the Dublin flat. I assumed it was the same one."

"You'd been to it before."

"Yes."

"Exactly what were the circumstances in which you were last in her Dublin flat?"

Michael sat back in his chair, ran his hands over the stubble on his face. He had never imagined that he would be sitting in what amounted to a police interrogation room, explaining to a stranger the details of his personal life prior to entering the priesthood to a stranger. *Inevitably*, he thought, *it comes to this*. He answered: "We were lovers."

"I assumed so." Brady flipped through the pages of the passport again, turning it this way and that to read the stamps. "By chance, do you have relatives in Ireland?"

"Yes. Well, cousins in Cork. Second cousins, actually."

"So you had grandparents living here?"

"Yes. They've both passed on."

"Do you also have your Irish passport with you, Father?"

Michael realized he should have seen where that line of questioning was heading. If he had grandparents native to Ireland, he would have qualified under a special program the government ran for dual citizenship and an Irish passport.

"No, I don't."

"So it's just possible you could have entered the State on your Irish passport prior to Friday night, left the country the next morning, then returned on your American passport this morning, thus making it appear as if you had not been here during the period in which you claim there was a murder."

"That would be very clever of me, wouldn't it?"

"You're an educated man. We'll have to make inquiries. I'm afraid it *will* be necessary to speak with your bishop. Sorry." He pocketed the passport.

"What are you doing?"

"I'll get you a receipt for this. You cannot leave the country until this investigation is complete. And if you travel out of Dublin, you must first report to the garda station on Harcourt Street."

"If there's already an investigation, you must know something about Lydia Jellicoe. Was she murdered?"

"Grab your Bible, *padre,* and come along with me."

A woman was waiting for them in the pathologist's autopsy room. The cut of her clothes and cut of her straight blond hair was more company director than forensic pathologist or even senior police. Her perfume was a subtle voice among the din of disinfectants and preservatives.

"Father Michael," Brady said, pulling out a pack of cigarettes. "This is Detective Inspector Claire Burke."

"Father." Claire nodded, her hands in latex gloves. Her smile was pleasant, detached, but she engaged Michael with her eyes, held them a fraction of a second longer than he had expected. "Would you mind taking a look at this woman? I'm afraid this might not be easy."

"Okay."

Michael felt suddenly woozy. He had been in morgues before, spent long nights sitting with family in funeral homes as a priest, been the first to discover the dead and dying in various states of decay. This was different. This was — he expected — someone he had once loved more than God and life itself.

Brady fumbled with a cigarette, grimaced at the NO SMOKING sign, and put it away. Claire nodded to the technician. Michael had hardly noticed him standing in the corner of the room wiping surgical instruments. The technician opened a door to a refrigerated unit and pulled out a trolley with a body under a sheet. Claire pulled back the cloth, folded it down over the cadaver's chest.

"Do you know who this is?" she asked.

The face was hideously deformed, the damp blond hair still in a ponytail. The head had been meticulously cleaned of blood, which only made the extent of the injuries more horrific. A dim sum of skin, muscle, bone. It could have been an answered prayer — someone he didn't recognize — except for the tiny asterisk of a scar on the cheekbone. His fault, having lost control of the tool he was using to ratchet taut the barbed-wire fence around the horse paddock that last summer they were together. There was more blood and more raised voices then than now. A sponged-off, aseptic silence. As horrible as her injuries were, Michael could not force himself to look away.

"Lydia," he breathed.

"Lydia Jellicoe?" Brady asked.

Michael nodded.

Claire covered the face.

Brady asked, "May I see your hands, please, Father?"

Michael stretched out his hands, palms down. Brady examined them, then turned them over.

"No cuts, no scratches, no bruises," Claire said.

"No calluses," Brady added. "A priest with soft hands. What a surprise."

"Inspector, being a priest is what I do. It's not the totality of who I am. Can you tell me what you know? Do you have any leads? Anything?"

"We don't discuss ongoing investigations with the public. Certainly not with a potential witness."

"Or a suspect?"

"Are you putting yourself into that category?"

"I've come a long way to help a friend who I believe was in serious trouble."

"You used the word *murder* earlier. That would be serious trouble."

"I could be useful to you."

"I seriously doubt it."

Michael had been struggling with whether or not he should say anything about his past before becoming a priest. He had worked so hard over the past few years to put that part of his life behind him, shut it out of mind so he could focus on his pastoral duties, and now he wondered if he should volunteer the one thing that might demonstrate his credibility to the Dublin police so that they would let him help figure out what had happened to Lydia.

"I was an undercover detective with the Boston Police Department before I became a priest," Michael said.

"Ah," Brady said after a beat. "Now *that's* useful. But is it true? Claire, when will that background check on Father Michael be completed?"

"Preliminary information tomorrow morning. Detailed in a few days."

"Interesting," Brady said to Claire. "We have an ex-lover, ex-detective priest who appears the day a body is brought in here, and he offers to help solve her apparent murder. Very tidy. As juicy as this all might look to the uninformed, I frankly don't think you were directly involved in any murder, Father. We found a small quantity of heroin next to the body. She died with a tourniquet on her arm, and enough needle marks on her body to indicate she was a regular user. Perhaps we'll find something more of interest after we've completed our detailed technical examination of her flat, but I doubt it. What we have here is a woman who died with a needle up her arm. She ran into some trouble with her dealer and he beat her to death. The autopsy will bear me out on that point."

A cell phone rang, its polyphonic synthesized pop tune completely out of character with the present surroundings and the matters being discussed. Michael expected Claire to answer the call, but Brady dug the bleating phone out of his suit coat pocket and answered.

Brady listened for a moment. "Now?" he said impatiently. He rang off, swore to himself, pointed the phone at Michael. "Thanks all the same, Father, but we'll not be taking you up on your very kind offer. Claire will undoubtedly have more insightful questions for you than I did. She won't be so easy on you. After all, she's made it her job to get my job. But first she needs to solve a major crime." He arched his eyebrows at her.

Brady pocketed the phone, lit up a cigarette on his way out the door, tossed the match into the corner. "Though I'm afraid the beating to death of a heroin addict by a street dealer does not qualify."

Brady left a wake of pungent smoke.
"I'm sorry about all that," Claire said.
"It's all right."
Claire avoided his eyes now, tugging her gloves snug. "She has no close family?"
"You were watching from behind the two-way mirror in the interrogation room, weren't you?"

"Yes. Does she have any children?"

The thought had never occurred to him. "I'd be surprised. I'm sure not."

"May I show you something?" She pulled back the sheet down to Lydia's pubis. "Classic cut, C-section. A cesarean. I'm sorry to have to ask, but did she have this when you knew her?"

"No." Michael looked away, watched the second hand on the wall clock. "That must be Daniel."

"The child's name?"

"She said something about their taking Daniel when she phoned me."

"There have been no reports of any missing children found. We didn't have a name, and we still don't have an age."

"Good Lord."

"Do you know who the father is?"

Michael could barely comprehend the reality of Lydia's death, yet alone the fact that she had a child. He shook his head slowly, letting his words flow without thinking about what he was saying. He shrugged. "I assume a cousin in West Cork. I had heard she had taken up with someone in the family after I left. But I really don't know."

"Could we get a name of who the father might be?"

Michael laughed weakly. "There are so many. You'd have just as much luck by phoning every O'Driscoll in the phone book down there."

Claire cocked her head as if she hadn't understood him correctly. "What did you say the family name was in West Cork?"

"Same as mine. Well — O'Driscoll. Why?"

She looked at him hard. *What was she thinking?* he wondered.

"You said you haven't been in touch with your family down there for some time."

"That's right."

Claire nodded thoughtfully. "Getting back to Lydia. You heard she had taken up with someone in West Cork?"

"Letters from home while I was at the theological college. Any foul rumor that made it from Cork to Boston. My parents despised her. I stopped reading my mail from them."

"Why did they despise her?"

"She was from an prominent Anglo-Irish Protestant family. My mother thought she was pulling me away from my faith, my family, my profession, my country. Small things like that."

"Was she?"

"Yes. For a while."

"And your father?"

"He had to listen to my mother complain."

"I know this must be difficult."

"It is."

"Something else I wanted your feedback on. The pathologist is certain she was tortured before she was killed. There were cigarette burns on her body, burns on her skin as like electrical shocks." Claire started to roll Lydia over to expose her back.

"I've seen enough."

"I'm sorry." She covered the body, and the technician who had been hovering in the corner wheeled the trolley back into the refrigerated unit, then left them alone. "Do you have any idea why someone would do that?" Claire asked. "Did she have some valuable information?"

"Not that I know of. But it's been a long time."

Claire pulled her gloves off. "One more thing."

Michael drew a deep breath. "Yes?"

"There's something else I wanted to show you." She went into an adjoining room.

While she was gone, Michael saw a folder on a desk. On its cover was a case number. Checking first to make sure no one was watching, he looked inside. There were pictures, apparently of the crime scene in Lydia's flat. He flipped quickly through a series of all the rooms. At the back of the stack were the pictures of Lydia's body lying on the floor. Taken in the harsh light of the camera flash, they seemed even more gruesome than seeing her in the morgue. He heard Claire returning from the other room and was about to close the file when something struck him as odd. The tourniquet on Lydia's arm looked out of place. Another moment and he realized it was knotted in a way impossible for Lydia to tie herself. He closed the file just as Claire was returning with a large clear evidence bag.

"Take a look at this," she said.

Michael closely examined the object inside. It looked like a thick, curled horn, clotted with blood.

"The suspected murder weapon," she said. "A ram's horn from a whitethorn walking stick, I'd say. Judging from the thickness of it, I'm guessing it was large, more of a staff, really. No fingerprints. We think she was struck so violently that the top end broke off. Apparently she was beaten and gouged with the long end. Have you ever seen this before?"

"No." Michael couldn't be absolutely sure, but in his heart he felt he was telling a lie. He hoped it did not show on his face.

"Are you all right?"

"It's warm in here."

"It's freezing in here, actually, but I know what you mean."

"I need to get outside."

"I understand."

Claire escorted him to the front door. She recommended a bed-and-breakfast on a major bus route just out of the city center.

"Yes, okay, you can reach me there," he said. "Tell me the truth: Is this investigation going anywhere?"

"My boss has pretty much made up his mind and doesn't want to waste department resources on it."

"And you?"

"I have a very large mortgage on a nice flat in Ballsbridge within walking distance of St. Stephen's Green."

"There's a child missing."

"I'm sorry."

Michael left her standing on the steps outside the prefab building as he walked along the drive to the Fire Brigade's Training Centre entrance. He caught a bus on Malahide Road back to the city center, then struck out on foot toward St. Stephen's Green. A stiff wind on the bridge over the Liffey smeared the tears on his face. Anonymous amongst the lunchtime shoppers, he tore the clerical collar from his shirt and threw it into the river. As it hit the water, he allowed a little hardness to settle into his heart.

*Better a cop than a priest to solve a murder and find a missing child, right?*

He had to keep walking. He decided he would give himself the twenty-minute bus ride from the city center to the B&B in Rathmines to mourn for Lydia. He would cross himself as he passed the churches along the route, like the old people still did down in the countryside; then he would begin to figure out why his favorite custom-made whitethorn walking stick that had gone missing five years ago had suddenly reappeared, and why it was used to kill the only woman he had ever truly loved.

# Chapter 6

Aiden Driscoll's big Mercedes came to a complete halt in the fast lane of 93 south of Boston. News radio was reporting a jackknifed tractor-trailer rig blocking eastbound traffic four miles ahead. He imagined the mess forty pallets of spilled olive oil would make across four lanes of interstate and how long it would take the fire department to mop it up. Maybe even longer than normal if it were deemed a biological hazard. Aiden set the parking brake and pulled the file folder marked *West Virginia* from his briefcase on the passenger seat.

He propped Kevin's sorry collection of convenience-store prospectuses in his lap against the steering wheel. The profit-and-loss statements inspired both awe and disbelief: awe in the amount of retail business that could be generated from selling pork rinds and Slim Jims; disbelief in the turnover of natural gas canisters to fire the stovetops and water heaters of so many double-wides set up on cinder blocks. Tampons, quarts of oil, hot dogs, air fresheners, frozen pizzas, Liquid-Plumr, cigarettes, milk, bread, beer, and bait — the lifeblood of any rural community.

From the back of the folder he pulled a list of the West Virginia independent convenience-store owners who also had felony convictions. The associated prospectuses were held together with a bulldog clip. He had already sorted the reports and pulled out the top one — a net loser that looked promising. The income side of the statement was respectable, all things considered. Almost eighty-five thousand dollars in the last year. Not bad at all for a rural convenience store. But the outflows were killing the business: cost of goods, utilities, taxes. The albatross was the mortgage on the building, financing to purchase and remodel the store, accounting for some pretty awful financial ratios. Someone had paid a substantial premium for the place only the year before. Someone who must have considered himself a damned marketing genius. Not smart enough, apparently. Overoptimistic and overextended. It wouldn't be long until the local bank would be the proud owner of DeVry's

Quick Mart in Snapeville, West Virginia, population 438, unincorporated.

Aiden read down the list of DeVry's vendors and contractual relationships. Everything as he would have expected. His eyes settled on one entry — exactly what he had been searching for. The reason for the premium paid by the business's owner, listed as Dwayne DeVry, with a local address and telephone number. The State of West Virginia. It could only mean one thing.

The midnight-blue car was soaking up the late-afternoon sun, and the engine was beginning to overheat. Aiden rolled down the windows, cut the engine, felt the heat roll into the air-conditioned interior. He pulled a Churchill from the leather cigar tube in his suit coat pocket and lit up. Reclined the seat a bit. Got a good half inch of ash on the tip of his cigar. Tilted his face to the sunshine, sunglasses filtering out all the haze over the Boston skyline, the bullshit detector set to filter out all the crap he was about to hear. Now he was ready to do a deal.

Aiden got DeVry with his cell phone on the second ring. He heard the smooth-sliding bearings of a commercial meat-cutting machine and a customer telling DeVry testily she wanted it "thinner, thinner."

"Hell, yes, it's a great little business," DeVry said. "I got them waiting three-deep 'cause I'm on the phone with you."

Aiden introduced himself as an investor. He explained that he got DeVry's name from a business broker.

"I really hate to sell the place, Mr. Driscoll. But like I told them fellas, I'm getting too old to work the counter twelve hours a day."

"How old *are* you, Mr. DeVry?"

"Forty-three. But I have a heart condition. The stress is killing me."

Aiden imagined that the Cheez Whiz on Ritz crackers and the foot-long beef stick he whittled on throughout the day with his greasy pocketknife didn't help. Actually, DeVry might very well have been a perfect specimen of health.

"Tell me about where you're located." Aiden pulled a road atlas from the door pocket, flipped to West Virginia, found Snapeville at the foot of the Alleghenies.

"Couldn't be a better location. We're right at a busy crossroads just outside of town. Truckers and motorists coming in and out of here day and night."

*Motorists.* A term from another time, another place. From rural West Virginia stuck in the early 1960s. Aiden smelled a lie. The interstate had bypassed Snapeville by more than five miles. The secondary roads in and out of town would be full of vacant motels with cracked cement swimming pools in dire need of chlorine, pawnshops full of dusty power tools and Mother's silver plate. The nearest fast-food franchise was forty-five minutes away on winding, potholed roads littered with dead possums and squirrels.

"Hear that cash register humming?" DeVry said. Aiden imagined the phone was being held next to the machine. "It's a cash cow."

Aiden saw in his mind DeVry holding the void button down, letting the tape spill onto the floor. "Hell of a business you got there. But it's fairly rural in those parts, wouldn't you say?"

Without a trace of indignation, DeVry said, "The whole goddammed state is rural, Mr. Driscoll."

Aiden enjoyed a long draw on his cigar and smiled at that one. "Tell me, you get any visitors from Harrisonburg in there?"

"Tourists? Sure, loads."

"I was thinking more in terms of people from state government. People nosing around your business."

"Got ya." His voice dropped. "No, we

75

ain't seen no one from there. Not since I owned the place, anyway. We're too far from a Shoney's breakfast bar and not far enough away from the county dump to end up on the revenuer's audit list. My books are clean, though, and I only keep one set. The financials you got on me are what it is, warts and all. Just keep in mind, this business is prime for development. Only way to go is up, up, up." He sounded like a cheerfully optimistic terminally ill patient knowing he had, in reality, only a few more months at most.

"Thank you for your candor." Aiden suspected the candor ended where the sticky finger on the till began. It didn't matter. He wasn't interested in becoming the convenience-store king of the Alleghenies anyhow. "Oh, by the way, I was curious. I see you have a contractual relationship with the state. I assumed that means you have a license to sell state lottery tickets."

"That's right. The lottery's a real magnet."

"But if I'm not mistaken, convicted felons aren't eligible to own businesses that sell lottery tickets. What's that all about?"

DeVry finally stopped talking. The woman getting her wafer-thin turkey loaf was gone. Maybe that sound Aiden heard in the background was the fan on the wall blowing the Pabst Blue Ribbon banner over the door. Maybe it was DeVry nervously tapping his chewed-up ballpoint pen end over end onto the counter. But it sure as hell wasn't the sound of customers swarming the store.

"You're alone," Aiden said.

"You're a sharp one, Mr. Driscoll."

Aiden flipped to the back page of Kevin's report on the business and its ownership chain. Credit history, legal judgments, criminal records. "Let's be honest, Mr. DeVry. You bought that piece-of-shit store in the middle of nowhere from someone who had previously acquired a license from the state lottery commission. You paid top dollar. You took out a large bank loan, counting on every redneck in the county coming into your place to buy lottery tickets. Problem is, you've got a felony conviction for installing illegal slot machines in backwoods bars from one end of the state to the other, and convicted felons can't become licensees with the state for the purpose of selling lottery tickets. Even if you did do your time. You should have done your homework. You're in deep, Mr. DeVry."

"Yep."

"You're on parole, aren't you?"

"Yep."

"Filing a false application for renewal of the lottery license you took over is a felony offense, isn't it?"

"Yep."

"So if you happened to be convicted of doing something that fucking stupid, that would be a violation of your terms of parole, wouldn't it?"

No answer.

"You're a lucky man, Mr. DeVry."

"I'm outta luck. I'm out of the gaming business. I just want to sell up and move down to Florida."

"Live the dream, Mr. DeVry. In the meantime, don't have a heart attack over it. My lawyers will be in touch."

The place to start was the African fetish on the mantel.

Michael walked slowly along South Great Georges Street, brushing shoulders in the midmorning bustle along the sidewalk, confidently inconspicuous in the modestly fashionable clothes he had bought near the B&B at Oxfam, the secondhand charity stores where the hip and homeless shopped. Free from his clerical collar and black suit, he looked at the world through different eyes. He felt like a wholly different person, better than his old self, better even than his priestly self. Yes, now he had the perspective of the pulpit and confessional. But for the first time in five years, he saw people look back at *him*, not at the uniform of office, but at the man. And if they had bothered to look into his face for more than a passing moment, they would have understood that here was a man of absolute resolve. His life's purpose was not merely to solve a crime or save a sinner, but to bring Lydia's killer to justice. Someone had killed the only woman he had ever loved. It was only after seeing her again — even lying dead in the morgue — that he realized how much a part of his life she had been, even after they had parted.

Another thought passed through his mind, but he quickly pushed it aside so he could focus on what he was doing: Was it justice he was seeking, or was he being driven more by the need to assuage his own guilt for having left her? He couldn't help but think that if they had remained together, she would still be alive.

Just as he had cleared these thoughts, the image of Lydia's missing child took their place. He felt a pang of desperation.

How much time was left to find her son before he, too, was harmed?

A horn blared, bringing him back to the moment. He stopped on the sidewalk and evaluated his position on the street.

Exasperated by his inability to get a good long look at Lydia's flat above the Thai restaurant without drawing unnecessary attention to himself, he popped into a men's clothes boutique across the street. He must have felt up, sniffed, examined the lining of every hand-sewn leather jacket on the racks as he secretly scoped out the windows and doors to the opposite building before he could see the solution to the problem that had been bothering him since awaking before dawn.

The dilemma was that the mantel was in the flat, and the flat was sealed by the police. But the commotion of the streets was his ally. The noise of cars and Guinness trucks, bottles being thrown into the bins behind restaurants. The best time was soon approaching — after the midmorning tea break but before lunch, when the builders had again fired up their pneumatic jackhammers, the pile drivers were ramming the earth, and the streets were even more crowded with post-school-run mothers shopping and people on their way for an early bite to eat.

The perfect setting for a convincing day-time burglary of opportunity.

Michael took a seat near the back of the Thai restaurant, ordered the daily special from the blackboard. The last time he had been to Dublin it was Mandarin, a takeaway convenient to the Jellicoe flat, almost pleasant enough for a sit-down meal if it hadn't been for the dozens of superior restaurants within a few blocks of where he was sitting. Only the menu seemed to have changed. A narrow room, reception desk and cashier at the front, glass-topped tables with the same vases filled with plastic freesia. Kitchen down the back hall, lavatories, emergency exit where the cook and waitstaff went to sit on empty beer kegs and smoke. The Great Wall of China wallpaper still wound around the room, presumably all the way to Bangkok now.

He leisurely ate the chicken satay as the restaurant filled to capacity. He used the time to reassure himself that what he had just committed himself to do was also the morally correct thing to do. Claire Burke had made it clear that solving the murder of an apparent drug user was not going to be a high priority for the police. From his own experience working in law enforcement, he instinctively knew that trying to work with the Dublin police would be a waste of time. Clues to the murder were growing stale by the hour. He also knew that the longer he was missing, the less chance there was of finding the child alive, a fate about which Claire seemed even less interested. Now he owed it to Lydia to do everything in his power to find the boy. If there were going to be justice for Lydia and resolution of his own feelings of regret, remorse, and — realistically, he admitted — revenge, he would have to act decisively. And on his own. Even if it meant bending a few rules, maybe even breaking the law.

He paid and went back toward the lavatories, looking through a beaded dragon curtain into the chaotic kitchen. Everyone was busy at the one p.m. lunch crush. He passed the lavatories, slipped quickly out the back door to a small cement courtyard full of kitchen exhaust, rubbish bins, and beer kegs. One of the wheeled bins had the address of Lydia's flat. It was empty.

Michael pulled on a pair of gloves, set one empty keg on top of another, then put a third next to them as a step up. After he stood up, a curse entered his mind, but did not pass his lips: the window to Lydia's flat was still out of reach.

Back down on the ground he looked around for help. He untied a nylon line running diagonally over the courtyard where kitchen towels were hung. He stuffed a couple of the greasy rags into his back pocket. He doubled the line, threw it up over a stout pipe projecting from under the eave where a satellite dish was attached. The dish wobbled when he tested the line's strength, but held firm.

From atop the beer kegs he wrapped the nylon line around his hands and began pulling himself up, climbing the side of the wall, inching his way closer to the window. By the time he was halfway there, the satellite dish was not just wobbling, but bouncing, and the pipe was starting to bend downward under his weight. With only inches left to go, the line slipped dangerously close to the end of the pipe. Certain he was about to fall, Michael held on to the line with one arm while he wrapped the towels around his free hand and smashed the lower windowpane, cleared the shards from the mullion. From his trouser pocket he removed the table knife he had taken from the restaurant, thrust it under the window lock. His arm was shaking from the strain of holding himself in position as he worked the knife, trying to lever up the screws holding the lock into place. Just as he and the satellite dish were about to collapse to the ground, the lock finally popped free. He lunged upward, pushing the window open, got a hand over the windowsill, and hoisted himself inside.

Michael stood breathing hard in a bedroom illuminated by the soft gray Dublin sky from a skylight in the ceiling above. The curtain of the window he had just come through fluttered in the wind, carrying with it the smells from the kitchen below. He figured he safely had about five minutes before the police turned up, if a neighbor had seen him break in. And the forensic team could show up at the front door anytime. From what Michael had learned from Charlie Brady and Claire Burke, at least the police hadn't gone over the place in any detail, so there might be clues for him to discover.

By the look of the clothes hanging on the back of the door he was in Lydia's room. He took off his gloves and felt the material of a short black dress, more sumptuous even than his liturgical vestments. Perhaps it just seemed that way because it was a woman's. More precisely, because it was Lydia's.

Michael didn't have a moment to waste. He felt the old adrenaline kick he used to get going undercover for the Boston Police Department. The time pressure, informants' lives on the line. His own life on the line.

There was nothing remarkable in the bathroom or the hall. He walked into another bedroom, flipped the light switch. The duvet on the small bed was printed with a pattern of moons and stars. On the pillow was a stuffed toy, a small bear in a Harrods sweater, the kind tourists bought in the duty-free shop at the airport. At the foot of the bed was a pile of folded laundry. Michael picked up a small pair of denims, guessed the child's age to be three or four years old.

The apartment was compact but opulent. The main rooms were filled with museum-quality art, bright paintings from contemporary artists, nineteenth- and early twentieth-century sculpture set among antique furniture, predominantly Georgian. In the eat-in kitchen, two untouched place settings were arranged neatly on the table, a bunny napkin ring above one plate, a tortoise above the other.

In the sitting room, as viewed through a porthole cut into the kitchen wall, blood congealed on the carpet and was splattered on the wall.

Michael had seen the worst of it at the morgue and in the crime-scene photographs, but the sight startled him, and he shuddered. He had seen it dozens of times before as a detective. This was where Lydia had been murdered. It was so unreal.

The sitting room was dark except for the shaft of light through the porthole. Using a handkerchief and being careful not to leave fingerprints, he tried to turn on a floor lamp but it didn't work. Only when he switched on a table lamp at the end of the couch did he discover why, as his legs became entangled in an electrical cord running from the wall outlet to an adjacent chair. The end of the cord was snipped, the green and yellow wires pulled apart, the copper ends exposed. It would have been a very effective means of eliciting information.

In the few minutes remaining, he needed to focus. He already knew how she died. What he had come here for was to find clues as to who had done it. By the time the forensics team had made a sweep of the flat, they might have accidentally destroyed what could have been the only evidence of her killer. They would have hours; he had only minutes.

What looked out of place? It had been five years and he had been there only once before. He tried to remember. Nothing struck him as particularly unusual.

*Keep asking questions,* he told himself.

Was there a man living there with her now? There was no evidence of that, either in the bedrooms or the bathroom.

Against the wall adjacent to the fireplace, a human figure moved. Michael jumped. A tall man with a weapon in his hand, his shadow cast by the light through the fluttering curtains in the open bedroom window. The form was strangely familiar; then he realized it was the fetish on the mantel, an African tribesman with spear and shield.

In his concentrated efforts to get into and explore the flat, he had almost forgotten — the fetish, Lydia's dope stash. The hardest drug she had ever done was some pot, which she kept hidden in a secret compartment in the fetish's distended belly. He opened it and found nothing. Even if she had been using heroin, this was where she would have kept it.

What else? *What else?* The ticking of the clock on the wall heightened his anxiety.

A couple of burned matches ground into the carpet, but no candles anywhere to be seen. Lydia didn't smoke, although he recalled the faintest smell of cigarettes in the curtains as he had come in the window. Michael looked at the room through his detective eyes, searching for details, something incongruous with the immaculate, well-ordered apartment.

At the back of the fireplace, among the stones left by a coal fire, a charred cigarette butt. He lifted it out and examined it. The word *Carabello* was printed on the paper near the filter. He was unfamiliar with that brand. He wrapped it in newspaper and stuck that in his pocket, too.

He noticed that the trash cans in the rooms were empty, except for the kitchen. The wheeled bin outside would have been full if Lydia had been taking trash out, so she must not have been there for very long before she was killed.

*There must be more,* he told himself. Something he could use to unravel the mystery of her death.

In the kitchen he noticed some gritty substance underfoot. He knelt down and determined it was sugar. More sugar on the counter. He opened a large canister. Inside, buried in the sugar, was a bag.

Even before he opened it he knew it was the heroin, but it was much more than a user would have stashed away. He couldn't even consider the possibility that Lydia was somehow involved in drugs like that. Brady's technical examination people would have found the drugs in the canister. Michael had other ideas. After seeing the picture of the tourniquet on Lydia's arm, he suspected her drug use wasn't credible. Perhaps the drugs were a plant, the whole overdose scenario staged? He slipped the bag into his coat pocket.

It struck him as odd that there were no pictures of the child, although there were photographs of Lydia in the flat. He took a small framed picture from the bookshelf, a photograph taken of her in West Cork against a large fuchsia shrub in full bloom. By looking at it, a person would never know that he had been standing beside her when it was taken. He had been cropped out of the picture as he had been cropped out of her life.

The glass in the frame caught the reflection of flashing blue lights out the window. Michael saw two police cruisers coming up the street. They had their sirens turned off. That would be for him.

He was out of time. He pulled the plastic

shopping bag serving as a trash-can liner out of the bin in the sitting room and wrapped the frame in it, then stuffed it into his back pocket.

He hung from Lydia's bedroom window-sill and dropped five feet to the cement courtyard. As he fell he saw the vigilant old shut-in sitting in the window of the building behind him who must have reported the burglary. She had phone in hand again, dialing 999, the emergency number. With her glasses thicker than the leaded windows of St. Patrick's Cathedral, he doubted she could see his face.

Back inside the crowded restaurant, he hid in the men's room until he was sure the police who had been coming in the front door of the establishment at the same moment he had been coming in the back had passed him by.

He walked casually to the front of the restaurant and grabbed a complimentary mint at the cash register on the way out.

# Chapter 7

With a critical eye, Maeve watched her daughter set up a shot on the approach to the fifth hole of the Skibbereen Golf Club. Maeve caught her mobile phone in midring before Noreen brought her club head down.

"I've gone as far as I can without access to the rest of the system." It was Declan, calling on his lunch hour from a phone booth near his Wall Street office.

Maeve shaded her eyes as if calculating the distance to the next green, and squinted through the pines separating them from the adjacent fairway. Creeping along the road skirting the rough was an unmarked van, no doubt packed with cameras and equipment to intercept their electronic communications. The police had turned up the heat, openly following them whenever they left the Carnmore compound.

She had left Liam behind the wheel of

their car in the car park of the small cinder-block clubhouse to secure the car from any attempt to plant a listening or tracking device. He had been happy to spend a couple of hours reading the grey-hound racing forms and napping in the late afternoon sunshine while his mother and sister got nine holes in. She was un-aware that, instead, he was engaged in a fierce staring contest through his window with a couple of police officers who had parked so close to the car that he couldn't even open the driver's-side door.

"Ah, sure," she said. "Tear the feckin' thing apart if you have to. It's no use to me broken down in your shitehole of a garage."

"I just wanted to let you know I'm waiting on parts. I can't do a thing till I get the parts."

Declan wouldn't risk calling unless there was a serious problem.

She heard the anxiety in his voice: "And if I don't get them by next week I can't promise you you'll have everything fixed before you go on your holiday. We're running out of time. Do you understand?"

He was worried their timetable was slipping.

"I understand."

"The only thing I can suggest is that maybe you can call the parts place yourself. It's out of my hands now."

"Excellent suggestion. Thanks a million."

Maeve pulled her cart to the green, tapped her ball in, and plucked it from the cup. She faced away from the van on the road as she cleaned her ball.

"You need to book a flight out tomorrow," she told Noreen. "Cork to Prague, Prague to New York. Hire a car and lose whoever is following you on your drive up to Boston. Your cousin Aiden needs some attention."

"I've got that meeting Wednesday night. I *have* to make it."

"Liam can go in your place."

"I'm not sure that's possible."

Maeve narrowed her eyes. "Don't contradict me, daughter. Declan says it's time to go, but he hasn't heard anything from Aiden yet about getting us a convenience store. We need to push him, get him to make this happen. We're in trouble if we don't, but we can't afford to let him think we're desperate or he'll eat us alive."

Noreen chipped in a shot from the edge of the green. "Shall I take the Ritchey nippers?" She flexed her hand as if working the sheep castration tool.

Maeve smiled wickedly. "You'll never get them through airport security, m'dear."

Noreen stood hands on hips, hair blowing in a fresh breeze. A local musician who had composed a song about her sang her praises in the local pubs: *"No fairer lass than she, south of the River Lee."* Indeed.

"I'm sure your arrival will be a pleasant surprise," Maeve said. "Slay him with your charm."

"Failing that?"

"Have you ever had a man refuse you anything?"

"Sounds vaguely incestuous."

Maeve's mood darkened, the thought of one of the other family members touching her daughter filling her with disgust. "Be careful," Maeve said. "Just make sure he understands that if he screws this up, he'll have more West Cork O'Driscolls swarming the streets of Boston than during the Great Famine emigration."

In the shelter of a doorway Michael unwrapped the framed photograph he had taken from Lydia's flat. It wasn't the picture that interested him as much now as the plastic bag with which he had padded it. Stretching it taut in his hands, he read the name of the newsagent from whom it had been obtained — then used as a bin liner — a shop only two blocks from Lydia's flat. He removed the photo from the frame.

The cramped, narrow store was floor-to-ceiling candy on one side, newspapers and magazines on the other. Cigarettes and mobile phone top-up cards behind the register. The candy bars were on the racks, penny piece candy in straw baskets down near the floor for young children. Just a small mom-and-pop operation. The man leaning over the counter reading a tabloid newspaper looked as if he had been in that same position for several decades.

Michael showed him Lydia's photograph. "You remember seeing her?"

The shopkeeper barely moved his head, glanced over his glasses, resumed scanning the newspaper. "I'm not in the habit of discussing who I see and don't see with strangers."

Michael reached over and got a copy of the *Irish Times*, laid it on the counter along with the correct change. The storeowner put the money into the till, turned the newspaper page, otherwise ignored Michael.

"Okay," Michael said, "so now we've just

conducted a transaction. We have a relationship. We're no longer strangers." He
smiled engagingly.

The man looked at the picture in Michael's hand. "Haven't seen her for a few
days."

"Did you remember her ever saying anything about what she was doing in
Dublin?"

"Look, boy, I sell her some sweets for the
kid. She was a nice girl, but we didn't
stand around gabbing."

"Was she ever in here with anyone?
Other than a child?"

"I never noticed. It's a busy place here,
as you can see."

There was no one else in the shop but
Michael.

A woman stepped silently through a
door at the other end of the shop. She laid
her hand on the man's back the way a wife
would as she moved past him in the tight
space behind the counter. She studied Michael's face carefully as she took a magazine from a pile of periodicals held back
behind the counter with people's names
written on the covers. She gave him a copy
of the child's comic book *Beano*.

"When you see the little boy, will you
give him this?" she said. Then, gently re-

buking her husband: "You old fool."

Michael read the name on the cover, said it out loud: "Daniel."

"Danny's a sweet lad," she said. "His mam had asked us to start holding back a copy of *Beano* for him every week. But they never came in to pick it up Friday like they usually do when we get it in. I knew she was from West Cork, and just figured they had gone home for a spell. But I didn't want to throw it out. Just in case."

Seeing the boy's name, knowing that whatever had happened to him, the child would never see his mother again, Michael was almost moved to tears.

The woman stooped over and put some of the piece candy into a bag. "You think you might be seeing him soon?" She didn't wait for an answer. "Give him these, too. He always loves the Gummi Bears." She showed him the open bag. "See? I've picked out all the green ones. He says he thinks they taste like 'paddy the frog.' Do you know what that is?"

"No."

She smiled broadly. "*Pâté de foie gras.* Isn't that cute? I can hear him saying it in his little baby voice. Now how many four-year-olds know what that tastes like?" She laughed.

"How much do I owe you?" Michael said, barely able to contain his emotion.

She pressed the bag and magazine against his coat. "Nothing, dear. Just tell them both we miss them in the shop. God bless."

Michael paid the taxi driver and stepped onto the sidewalk in front of the stately but peeling Georgian house overlooking Belgrave Square Garden. He climbed the steps to his B&B and rang the buzzer to the bright red lacquered front door and waited for a member of the house staff.

Instead, he was greeted by a surprise.

"I can't decide if you are virtually naked or virtually invisible without your collar, Father." Detective Inspector Claire Burke blocked the doorway. "I would say you were trying to blend in with the common folk. My mother would say that a priest out of uniform always looks like he's on a cheap holiday to the Canaries. Especially easy to spot in the city." She looked down at his feet. "You're not wearing sandals, are you?"

Michael's hand felt in his coat pocket. "What are you doing here?"

"I'm afraid this isn't a social call."

"I'd like to get to my room."

"You don't want to go there just yet. Especially if you are carrying anything with you that might be problematic."

Michael held fast to the bag of heroin. He saw the men behind her bustling in the reception area, carrying what looked to be evidence bags. "I take it it's not just because the bed's not been made and the toilet swished."

"I'm sorry. Brady went behind my back and got a search warrant." She closed the door behind her and joined him on the steps. "I told him he was wasting his time, but your cleverness grates on him, and although he frankly doesn't give a damn about the murdered woman, he doesn't like being made a fool of, especially in front of me. It's legally sanctioned intimidation. And since you took your collar off, you've lost all moral authority. Why don't we go for a walk?"

Mothers played with their children on the playground in the center of Belgrave Square Garden. Ignoring the sign posted on the gate prohibiting dogs, a woman let her springer spaniel off the lead to run across the expanse of green. Michael and Claire had the footpath around the perimeter of the park to themselves.

"Brady had me put on a mike before you

99

came down to the morgue. That's why I appeared to be so unsympathetic after you and I were left alone."

"And you're not wearing one now?"

Claire held her suit coat open. "Care to search me? I happen to disagree with Brady about the motive behind Lydia Jellicoe's murder. Despite the preliminary evidence, I don't think she was directly involved in drugs in a major way herself. Just a gut feel."

Michael glanced back at the B&B. A camera flash backlit the curtains in his basement room. Claire led them at a leisurely pace, giving her associates plenty of time to go through his belongings, he figured.

"So," she said, "what was it that drove you to the priesthood? Lydia Jellicoe?"

"No, not Lydia." He was irritated. "Why do so many people have a hard time understanding that sometimes a man is drawn to the religious life, and not running from something?"

She looked at him for further explanation.

"Everyone comes to the priesthood in his own way. Sometimes it's a lifelong journey there; sometimes the impetus is a person, sometimes an event."

"I'm guessing it was an event. It must have been traumatic."

"You could have been an inquisitor on the bishop's seminary candidate review committee."

"Perhaps the answer will be self-evident when the Interpol query hits my desk later today. Or should I seek the answer in your service record with the Boston Police Department?"

"It's personal. And it has no bearing on Lydia's murder, which is why I am sitting here on a park bench in Dublin talking to you."

"It was that bad, was it? Enough to make you forsake your family and the woman you loved? How could you leave someone you claim was the love of your life? Perhaps she didn't love you."

Michael voice did not quaver: "*She loved me.*" He stood up quickly, faced away from Claire, breathed in the warm summer air, blinked away tears. "She loved me enough not to stop me. I loved the Church more than I loved her."

"And now maybe you think you were wrong," Claire said softly.

"I grew up in the Church, but I wandered, as many do in their youth. I later joined the police force. Working as a detective gave me a new perspective on life and death. I finally acknowledged to myself that I was a deeply spiritual person and was drawn back to the Church." Michael considered what he had said for a moment. "No, it was more powerful than that. I felt compelled to a vocation in the Church."

"And at what point did Lydia Jellicoe figure into this?"

"I had known Lydia almost all my life from the summers my family spent over here. Our love developed gradually; then one summer during college I knew she was the one. She would come to Boston when she could, and I used all my vacation time to go to Ireland. We ran up the phone bills in between."

Michael was thinking of those blissful summers spent with Lydia. Setting out into the waters of Baltimore Bay, picnicking on an island beach on local smoked Gubbeen cheese, crab sandwiches, tart apples, white wine they had saved from a short trip to France the previous month. Then making love below on cabin cushions damp with sea air before raising the sails and returning home.

"Tell me what she was like," Claire said.

Michael had never had to describe Lydia to anyone before.

"What made you fall in love with her?" Claire pushed.

He took a mental step back and tried thinking of Lydia and his relationship objectively. "She was, quite simply, the most incredible woman I had ever known — even apart from her great beauty. She was intelligent and funny and sexy and a very talented artist."

Claire looked around her. "Any big city will have hundreds of women that fit that description."

"Are you fishing for a compliment?"

"No, I just want to understand. What was it that made her the great love of your life? What was so special about Lydia Jellicoe?"

Michael closed his eyes and brought up her image. He was watching her sketch a landscape in an artist's notebook as she sat on a stone wall on the back side of a hill near Lough Ine. She was so intent on what she was doing that he was able to watch her for a full ten minutes without her even knowing he hadn't taken his eyes off her. The sky above them was dark, but in the distance over the ocean, the sun shone onto the water and islands. The beauty of the scene was breathtaking. Her own beauty was sublime. There had never been a more perfect moment for him. He thought then that they would always be together in West Cork. She would paint. He didn't even know what the hell he would do, but it didn't matter. They would get an old farmer's cottage and fix it up. They would have children. That was the first time he had ever had those kinds of thoughts about any woman.

But he had walked away from all that. He felt a pang of sorrow — despair for his own life now, as he mourned for Lydia. Feelings he had suppressed suddenly surfaced. He admitted to himself that he might have regretted leaving Lydia for the Church. No — at that moment he *did* regret leaving Lydia for the Church.

Michael said, "To try to put into words who she was and how I felt about her would be to diminish her and what we had."

"But something happened that changed your life."

"Something happened," Michael echoed. The sudden mental transition was jarring. He took another moment to collect his thoughts. "One night I was working a murder. It must have been three in the morning. There was a large group of us there at the scene, interviewing witnesses in a tenement, collecting evidence. It was apparent the dead woman had been beaten, then killed. It looked like she had been strangled, but there was blood everywhere, floor to ceiling, and we couldn't figure out where it had come from. Everyone else reckoned she had put up a fight and it was the murderer's blood, but it didn't feel right to me. My supervisor gave me the order to close off the scene and leave; then I discovered a bloody laundry bag under a kitchen cabinet."

Michael watched a child climbing the playground bars. He was a boy, about the same age as Daniel must have been.

He continued. "Somehow I knew what it was even before I opened it. It was at the same moment that the priest assigned to our precinct showed up with coffee and sandwiches. He kept a police scanner in his bedroom and had heard about what was going on. I had gone through a rough period professionally and he and I had ended up talking informally about that, which led to discussions about my spiritual life and where it was going. At first I didn't see him enter the room. I was already on my knees to pull the bag out from the cabinet. He watched me pray over the bodies of two babies who had been brutally slashed. I opened my eyes and saw that he was kneeling beside me praying. He told me right there, amidst all the blood and confusion in the middle of the night, that I had another duty. And somehow I knew what he meant. The next week he and I visited the bishop and started my road to becoming a priest."

"Fair enough." She guided them to a bench opposite the playground where they sat. "Did you find anything in Lydia's flat this morning that I need to know about?"

Michael watched a flock of pigeons swarm on the horizon and didn't flinch.

Claire continued: "When I told you that the technical examination team had not yet been into the flat, I told you that as a professional courtesy. I didn't expect you to take advantage of that information and break into the crime scene beforehand. Did you take anything while you were there? Did you leave anything — like fingerprints?"

Michael wasn't going to answer her. His mind was still turning over the problem of the murder weapon, his walking stick. Many times, as he had hiked out into the desert around Tucson, he often thought how useful it would have been to have it so he could beat off the sidewinders and gila monsters. He had given it to Lydia when they parted. That was the last he had seen of it. Never did he think he would find it again under the present circumstances in Dublin.

Claire Burke must have sensed he was holding back about more than just the reason he had left the police force to become a priest, as she interrupted his thoughts. "I understand how upset you are about Lydia Jellicoe. If you want me to help you find out what happened to her, you're going to have to be forthcoming with me. You have my word I won't betray you. Talk to me. Help me bring resolution to this tragedy. Tell me everything you know."

*Not yet,* he thought. *Not quite yet.*

They saw the plainclothes police officers leaving the B&B on the other side of the park and climb into a van with their evidence bags. As he turned to watch it speed off, she dared to take advantage of the moment to lay her hand on his arm.

"Michael . . ." she said. "I'd really feel more comfortable just calling you Michael."

She was shameless. How many more solved murders did she need for her next promotion? He knew what she was doing.

He felt angry, used. Why did women think priests were so susceptible to a woman's caress in a private moment?

But finally turning to look into her eyes, he immediately felt he must be mistaken. He had always been a good judge of character, even now with this well-groomed careerist in a skirt. She was no longer the chilly police bureaucrat he had first met at the morgue. Looking up at him now was simply another human, a woman, feeling empathy for the loss of his lover. He'd give her the benefit of the doubt, but not the information she sought. No, not yet. Just in case his instincts were wrong.

"I think I'll just go back to my room for a quiet evening in," he said.

"I understand. Call me tomorrow if you want to talk, okay?"

"Of course. And thank you."

There was a moment of awkwardness as neither could decide whether to shake hands or not. He kept his hands in his coat pockets and she left him.

Michael waited in the park until Claire had made it to the street in front of the B&B. He was somewhat surprised when she strapped on a helmet and drove off on a motorcycle.

Instead of walking back to the B&B,

however, he walked three blocks to the Swan Centre, a small mall on the main street running through Rathmines.

He phoned directory assistance, wrote down a number. In front of the pay phone he decided he couldn't quite fake a West Cork accent anymore, but he could manage a decent Dublin one.

"I don't know anything about Lydia or Daniel," a man at the Liss Ard number told him in reply to his question about how he could contact them. Michael was almost certain it was his cousin Liam O'Driscoll. Michael pressed the point, assuming the identity of a pediatrician in a town near Skibbereen who was returning Lydia's phone call about school immunizations for the boy. "I don't know why she gave you this number," Liam said. "Try Brendan O'Driscoll, her partner. He's in the phone directory."

*Well, at least now I know which one of my cousins she took up with.*

Michael got Brendan's number from directory assistance. He let it ring until he was cut off. He tried two more times. Just as he was about to give up, Brendan answered, sounding half-asleep at six in the evening. Michael tried a different ruse, same Dublin accent: "I had talked to Lydia a while ago and she said you might be able to arrange fiddle lessons for my son. Our boys are about the same age."

"Yeah, I teach group lessons for the kids," Brendan answered groggily. "He might be a bit young, but bring him to the Wednesday-night group. There's a room behind the petrol station on the Castletownshend road. We'll see how he gets along."

"By the way," Michael said, "we haven't seen Daniel for a while and we were wondering if we could get the kids together. I'd be happy to come by and pick him up and take them to the park for a couple of hours. Would this afternoon be okay?"

"They're not here." Brendan sounded confused. "Who did you say you were?"

"Should I try back in a day or so?"

"Sure. What did you say your name was? I'll get your number. Hang on, let me find a pencil."

"I'll just get back with you. Thanks."

Daniel wasn't in Skibbereen. And he no longer had a mother. Most likely he was somewhere in Dublin, a scared little boy about to spend another night in the big city.

# Chapter 8

Aiden Driscoll walked the length of the wooden pier jutting into Boston Harbor and stood watching an elderly Asian man bait a crab trap. If Noreen O'Driscoll had arrived as promised, she would have seen him by now. Among the tourists and lunchtime businesspeople crowding the pier, Aiden saw through his dark sunglasses none of the pale Irish skin, none of the distinctive O'Driscoll clan facial features. The bitch was twenty minutes late, and he sure as hell wasn't going to stand in the hot summer sun waiting for a broken meeting that he didn't want to attend in the first place.

The Asian lowered the crab cage over the pier rail. Aiden put his glasses away and leaned over the rail to watch a second trap being pulled from the murky water, three large crabs still picking at the bacon fat tied inside.

*Enough,* Aiden said to himself, and turned to leave.

At first he thought the hands slipping around his waist from behind were going for the holstered SIG Sauer semiautomatic hidden under his suit coat. He spun to confront the would-be attacker, but instead found himself embraced by a woman looking at him as if they were old lovers. She pulled him closer and kissed him deeply, in a way his own wife would have been embarrassed to do.

"Hello, cousin," she said. "Bring back memories of the boathouse loft?"

"You're late."

"*You* are still the best French-kisser in the family. I'm sorry. I wanted to make sure I wasn't being followed. And if anyone is watching you, now they think I came here to seduce you, not kick your ass."

Aiden walked away. Noreen caught up with him in the relative privacy of an arcade. Aiden paid for a chance to knock down ducks and chickens with an air rifle at a shooting gallery.

Noreen watched him firing away, racking up the points toward one of the large plush toys on the side wall. "How's your father?" she asked.

"The same miserable old man as the last

time you saw him. Only older and more miserable."

"Kevin? Michael, that other dishy brother of yours? Who's in the family business?"

"Kevin's with me. Michael's still out in the desert collecting manna for the Indians. What do you want?"

"There's been talk. Some people are beginning to wonder out loud if your organization is more a help or hindrance to our operation."

"Who's talking?" Aiden said angrily. He squeezed the trigger harder, beginning to miss. "You? That donkey-brains brother of yours? He must be taking a real beating on his greyhound betting."

Noreen stood behind him with her arms crossed, head tilted to gauge his aim. "The subject came up because of the extreme time urgency. Do you realize that if you don't close that convenience-store deal in the next weeks that we've completely missed the window of opportunity? Declan is adamant: He's got one shot at this, or we can flush a quarter of a billion dollars down the toilet."

Aiden squeezed off the last few rounds, just missed a good enough score for any prize at all. "It's rigged," he muttered in mock disbelief.

The attendant took more money from him, enough shot for two gun stations, then returned to his position by the loud boom box against the side wall. Noreen took up her position, carefully sighted her target, and began firing alongside her cousin.

"You know, Noreen," Aiden said, "the difference between your family and mine is that *we* evolved. We emigrated, we cleaned the muck out from under our fingernails, we got an education, and in two generations we built up a nice, tidy business. You're still just a bunch of culchies scamming the local football lotteries and shooting up on the weekends."

Noreen put her gun down and stood over Aiden. "Yeah, our hands are dirty," she said indignantly. "We crucified ten to make sure the one traitor was eliminated. All for our little partnership we've got going here. What have *you* done?" She resumed firing at the targets.

Aiden was unmoved. "*Plenty.* But I don't go shooting my mouth off. That's always been a problem with how you people run your business. I told you from the beginning you needed to compartmentalize everything. I'm not the least bit surprised you had a leak in your organization. The whole fucking pub doesn't have to be let in on what we're doing, you know."

Noreen said calmly, forcefully, "Look, Aiden. You said you could deliver on the convenience store and we took your word for it. My message to you is that if you can't deliver, tell me now, and I'll make alternative arrangements. We'll bring in a new partner. I'm here in the States until this issue is resolved one way or the other." She handed him a piece of paper. "Here's my number at the hotel."

The game ended, the scores improbably stuck just below prizewinning levels.

"It's rigged," Noreen said.

"Don't even think of threatening me," Aiden said, standing erect. "I'm not going to be pushed by around by a bunch of street thugs, cousin. I'm talking to you because it's good business, not because we share the same grandfather. I'll make alternative arrangements of my own, if I have to. You're beginning to sound a little desperate. Everything's just fine on my end. You'll get your redneck convenience store. Just make sure that Declan is ready when the call comes. I'm used to working with professionals, not a bunch of wankers from West Cork."

A foul acid rain fell from the black sky.

Earlier in the night, drug dealers and low-rent prostitutes had moved into position in the Dolphin's Barn area near the train station. Michael knew his way through the neighborhood. So had Lydia.

Michael confronted a figure in a greasy anorak with a permanent address in a filthy doorway. Everyone on the street knew him simply as Joel.

"I sell happy times, relief from boredom, escape from a grim life," he was telling Michael. "I'm not in the security business."

The hood of his anorak hid his face like Death's cowl. The only feature visible was his jaw, and the crooked brown teeth glistening with saliva under the street lamp as he shifted from foot to foot.

"She never bought anything from you? Heroin?"

"No, no. Like I said, all she wanted was a safe place to hide out in the city. She said she couldn't stay where she was, that someone was after her. I don't know why she came to me. I can't get personally involved in the problems of my customers, you know."

Michael gave him the bag of heroin he had taken from Lydia's flat. Joel licked his fingertip and tasted a few grains. "Whoa, not mine," Joel said. "This smack hasn't even been cut."

"Where'd it come from?"

"I don't know. Somewhere way up the chain from me. Like at the top. Nobody I know gets stuff this pure."

"Before Wednesday, when was the last time you'd seen her?"

"Oh, Jesus, that was a long time ago. With you. When you two came looking for that fella from West Cork."

"Brendan?"

"Yeah. The one who tried to trade me his fiddle for a bag. What am I going to do with a fiddle? Typical. You know, last week a carpenter brought me his compound miter saw. I hate it when they get down to selling the tools of their trade. Then they can't earn money to buy from me much longer. They end up stealing, then eventually get caught; then I'm at risk of being fingered when they are bargaining for a lighter sentence. He was your cousin or something, wasn't he?"

"Distantly. Has Brendan been back to you since then?"

"I lost one of my best customers when you took him away. Of course, he'd be dead by now at the rate he was going."

There had been a time — actually the

same chaotic summer of Michael's announcement of his intentions to leave the police force — when Lydia and Michael had come to Dublin to rescue Brendan, who had moved from one addiction to another. The drink had destroyed his career as a top professional musician; the needle had destroyed the man. Michael loved them both, though his other cousins were hoping Brendan the man would be swallowed up by Dublin. As much as the family enjoyed his music, West Cork was full of competent fiddlers.

"Did she bring a little boy with her?" Michael asked.

"I don't know if it was a boy or a girl. The kid was wrapped up, asleep in her arms. She must have been pretty desperate to bring him out to a place like this."

"Did she say who was after her?"

"No, and I didn't ask. I didn't want to get involved. And I still don't. I hate to rush you, but if you're not going to buy something, you need to leave."

Michael saw figures moving among the shadows on the other side of the street. A kind of loose queue was beginning to form the length of a city block.

Joel made a sudden move and Michael flinched. In one hand was a dirty syringe.

Michael thought Joel was going to stab him, but he was only sorting things in his pocket.

"Jumpy?" Joel said with a wicked laugh. He held out a small tinfoil packet from his anorak pocket. "Go on, take this. On the house. You know, before I got into this business I used to hand out chocolate bars to shoppers on Grafton for one of the candy shops on the street. Taught me the power of sampling. Who knows, maybe I'll see you coming back as a new customer. And this is so much sweeter than chocolate."

Michael refused the offer.

"Go on," Joel breathed seductively. "Something to make you forget all about her."

Michael wondered if that was true.

In Aiden Driscoll's office, a tailor was on his knees fitting Aiden for new suit trousers. The phone rang, the caller ID flashing a number with a West Virginia area code. *Perfect timing*, Aiden thought.

"Hang on, Sal," Aiden said.

Aiden got a fat envelope off his desk, pulled out the papers his lawyer had just sent over on the convenience-store purchase. Aiden hit the speakerphone button and assumed his position so Sal could keep working.

"Mr. DeVry. How are things down in your part of the world?"

"Couldn't be better."

Aiden immediately noticed the difference of tone in the man's voice. Was there even a hint of cockiness there? Understandable — after all, here was a man relieved to be having the burden of crushing debt lifted from his scrawny shoulders.

"You got the copies of the contract from my lawyer this morning, I take it."

"Got them right here in front of me."

"And we can get this turned around in the next day or so, right?"

"Everything pretty much seems to be in order."

Aiden suspected a gambit. "Pretty much?"

A moment of silence. "I was thinking."

"Don't think, Mr. DeVry. Sign."

"Not so fast, Mr. Driscoll. I need time to go over these papers. I think I should have my own lawyer go through them with me."

Aiden drew a calming breath. "What's the real issue, DeVry?"

"It's like this. There's a local fella here who's been after me to sell him the place. I sort of feel obligated to let him have a go at it."

"We have a deal. I assumed your word was as good as mine."

"This ain't anything personal; it's just business. I have to look after my own interests. I think I might have been a bit hasty. I'm sure I can get this worked out in a few weeks."

Aiden angrily waved Sal away. The tailor stood up and fidgeted with a suit coat hanging on the back of the door. Aiden stormed behind his desk and leaned over the speaker. "The deal you agreed to was that the sale had to be concluded by the end of this week. That's day after tomorrow. Time is of the essence. You're trying to change the material terms of our agreement. That *ain't* gonna happen."

"I'm really sorry."

"What is it, more money?"

"I know what you're paying me isn't a whole hell of a lot for someone in your position. I think adding a zero might help smooth things out on my end. It shouldn't be any problem for your lawyer to make the change and overnight me the paperwork in time for you to meet your deadline."

Aiden thought for a moment. "And

what's to stop you from trying to jack me around again and again?"

Silence.

"Tell you what," Aiden said. "I'll be there tomorrow morning. I'll make up the difference in cash, so we won't need to waste time bothering the lawyers with making any changes. Go on and set up an appointment with your bank for late afternoon so we can sign the contract and get everything notarized. Agreed?"

"I'll have to see." He sounded doubtful.

"Well, I'll be there regardless. We'll get things smoothed out on your end, no worries."

# Chapter 9

Michael couldn't recall the exact function of the Dublin bureaucrat his West Cork cousins used to rely on to help clear their contraband forty-foot metal containers in and out of Dublin port. Ostensibly they were shipping processed haddock to France, importing tulip bulbs from the Netherlands, but Michael knew better. It all seemed so long ago, and he had never been on the inside of the family's business on either side of the ocean. All he remembered was a nickname said with a knowing laugh and a vague memory that the man examined import documents.

Before he had taken a desk job with the Irish Customs Service, Sean "Knuckles" Fahy had lost the first two joints on the fingers of both hands while coupling coal cars for Irish Rail. The Irish crime world seemed to make more use of nicknames than did the Italians. Fahy was easy enough to find from asking a few blunt questions in the halls of New Custom House. Everyone in the building seemed to know Fahy, even by his nickname. He was in the commercial section and had an office on the third floor on the Liffey side of the building. An eager young government functionary stopped Michael as he approached Fahy's office. He took outside appointments only from nine-thirty to ten-thirty on Tuesday and Wednesday mornings. It was Friday and Michael couldn't wait. Where was he now? On afternoon break at a coffee shop across the road.

The coffee shop turned out to be a dingy workingman's pub, reeking of spilled beer and cigarette smoke. Knuckles was expertly rolling his own cigarette with his stubs, manipulating the loose tobacco in the paper, folding and licking the flaps sealed in place. He lit up, then knocked back half a glass of a whiskey and water. Michael watched it all from the bar, then set another glass of whiskey next to the newspaper Fahy was reading through thick, dirty glasses, and sat down across from him.

"I'd expect a man of your means to patronize a better class of bar," Michael said. "And to dress a whole lot better." The seams along the shoulders of the bureau-crat's cheap suit coat were splitting. His shirt collar was frayed and his cuffs were dirty. "This is quite an act you put on."

"I'm a customs official, sir," he said wearily. "You must have mistaken me for someone else."

"I know all about what you do to earn some cash on the side." That was only partly true. He had heard only rumors.

"Feck off. I go on pension at the end of the year." He turned in his seat away from Michael, snapped his newspaper in front of his face

"Pension, my ass. You getting a flat rate per container you clear for them or a percentage of the value?"

Fahy lowered the paper, drained the last of the whiskey. "What do you want?"

"Who's bringing high-quality heroin into the country?"

"If you believe the papers, everyone is. Personally, I wouldn't know anything about that."

"Glass of whiskey says you do."

Fahy pointed to an article in the newspaper. "You can read just as well as I can. The police know. The journalists know. The public know."

Michael showed Fahy the picture of

Lydia. "Somebody killed my friend and planted heroin on her."

"I'm sorry for your troubles," he said with feigned sincerity.

Michael fought to control the urge to reach across the table and shake him. He took a slug of whiskey, felt it hit bottom. "You must be worth a small fortune by now. What do you do with all the cash? Coastal property? Cars? I mean, how many holiday homes and Range Rovers does one man need? One phone call to the Criminal Assets Bureau and your game is up. They'll find everything you've stashed away over the last twenty years in a matter of days. Instead of working on your tan on a beach in Málaga next year, you'll be turning a whiter shade of pale as a lifelong resident of Mountjoy Prison."

Fahy moved in close enough for Michael to smell the stale whiskey on his breath. "I haven't been involved in anything for months. The police have been cracking down, making arrests, making it stick this time, all the way up and down the line. I don't want any trouble. All I do is stamp customs forms."

"Give me a name."

Fahy wiped a lock of hair from his eyes, took a full measure of Michael. "I don't deal with names. I deal with numbers, yeah? In almost twenty years I've never had a direct conversation with anyone."

"All right, give me a number. A telephone number. An address. Anything."

Fahy hesitated, finished his cigarette before he wrote down a number on the corner of the newspaper, tore it off, and slid it across the table. "You really *don't* want this. This goes someplace from which few have ever returned."

Michael read what Fahy had written. "What is it?" It was too short to be a telephone number, too ambiguous for a street address.

"The taxi queue at St. Stephen's Green every night from midnight til ten a.m. Find the cab with that registration number. And for fuck's sake, don't say you got it from me, though I suppose someone will figure it out anyway."

"A courier," Michael surmised. "The guy who moves the drugs around the city. And how you get paid, I assume." He finished the glass of whiskey in one swallow. He pocketed the number. "If this is wrong, I'll be back to see you again."

"If I were you, I'd be more concerned with if it's *right*. Because there's an excellent chance you won't be able to come back to see me again, even if you wanted to." He shrugged. "It's a moot point in either case."

Fahy adroitly straightened his tie with his mangled fingers and stood up.

"What do you mean?" Michael asked.

"I'm going home to pack my bags. I just decided to take an early retirement. Before you've finished your taxi ride, I'll be on that plane to Málaga. Good luck, mister. *Adios.*"

Maeve O'Driscoll threw a bucket of fireplace ash into the rhododendrons at the back of the house. A few embers smoldered brightly in the thick, wet undergrowth. The smell of the new fire she had just lit in the sitting room filled the cool, clear air. Overhead, too high to be heard, a jet crossed from west to east, coming upon the Irish coast after it had crossed the Atlantic from America, leaving a contrail in the last light of day.

*Noreen should be on that plane,* Maeve thought to herself. *Back in the safe confines of Liss Ard, feeding her flock sheep nuts in the walled garden. Why hadn't she phoned?*

Noreen had been the one to whom Declan had first confided his idea. At the time — when Declan had returned home

to Skibbereen for his Christmas holiday —
it had been more of a boast of his, a bit of
accounting and computer trickery that he
saw as an intellectual puzzle he had solved.
It took Noreen to realize the genius of the
scheme. She was the one who figured out
how to make it actually work, and approached Maeve with a plan. Liam lorded
over his drug empire. Noreen wanted a
piece of the action for herself, but cleaner
and bigger. She felt personal ownership in
the elegant design. Maeve should have
taken her at her word when she said that
she wasn't coming home until she had resolved the issue of the convenience store
with Aiden Driscoll, or cut him out of the
deal altogether. Now Maeve was worried.
Aiden was as evil-tempered as Noreen was
stubborn and beautiful. They were both
young and greedy.

Maeve heard the anxious barking of
Liam's greyhounds. Money and drugs were
his greedy addictions, the dogs his obses-
sion. Rounding the kennel, she saw that
one of the dogs, Feldspar, was missing.
Liam had raised and trained the dogs himself and they were now ready for their first
coursing season. Paying a price that he was
more embarrassed than boastful about to
Ireland's preeminent breeder, Liam had

bought a pair of puppies at the same time, since raising one alone would have resulted in a greyhound that was too docile for the aggressive sport. Feldspar had proved to be the more promising of the two.

She followed the barking to the front of the house. There, along the left-hand side of the lake, her son was restraining a fawn-colored greyhound by a lead with both hands. At the opposite end of a narrow path running straight for a hundred yards stood Peter O'Sullivan, Liam's right-hand man, and the only person her son trusted enough to help with the dog's training. Peter bent over, dragged a real stuffed hare back and forth across the ground, tempting the dog.

Maeve joined her son. It was all Liam could do to hold back the powerful animal. "Watch, Ma," he said with a wink. Peter clapped and called the dog's name. The greyhound strained against the special quick-release coursing lead, the muscles in his back and haunches and legs tensing; then Liam gave the dog free reign.

Feldspar was immediately away, rapidly picking up speed toward Peter's clapping hands. It took only a few seconds for him to run the distance. Peter stepped aside so that the dog wouldn't knock him over, then rewarded him with a scrap of pork from their dinner the night before.

"The first trial's next week," Liam said, referring to the greyhound racing in the countryside. The goal there would not be merely to run the distance, but be the first of a pair of greyhounds to "turn" a hare on an open course. In the last few years the owners had begun using muzzles to appease the blood-sport protesters.

"He looks as if you've got him in good shape," Maeve said. "You've put a lot of work into getting him ready for the season." Peter was rubbing the dog's muscles briskly with liniment as if the animal were a boxer after a well-fought sparring match. "All the more reason you needn't worry yourself about the phone call I just got from Amsterdam."

Liam's face went immediately dark. "What's up?"

Maeve had hoped to avoid this conversation, but knew Liam would find out on his own soon enough. "The skipper of the trawler with that shipment we bought is refusing to leave port. He's saying the weather will be too bad."

Liam looked at the clear sky. The first stars had appeared in the twilight. There was barely a breeze. "Fucking hell!" He

131

smacked the dog lead hard against his leg, then started walking quickly down the training path toward Peter and the dog. Maeve followed.

"Let it go for now, Liam. It can wait a week. I'm sure he knows what he's talking about. I heard on the shipping reports on the radio that there's a major storm headed in from the Atlantic."

"What a coward. Wait till I find out who it is! It's a storm, for fuck's sake. That's what good skippers do, sail through storms. We can't hold off for a week, Ma. There's no place to store the shipment for that long. We have to get it out of port before the Dutch police find it."

"We're under enough pressure as it is with the police here. I don't think now is a good time to be bringing that shipment in anyway."

"So what are we supposed to do? Just dump three million euro's worth of heroin over the side? We've already paid for it. We can't walk away from that kind of money."

"We have to learn to walk away from it. For the family's sake. This was going to have to be the last shipment anyway. We're getting out of the business."

"I'll bring it back myself."

"Jaysus, *no*, Liam," Maeve said sternly.

"It's not worth the risk."

Maeve needed Noreen's help. She was the only person who might be able to coyly dissuade Liam from his destructive tendencies. An addict wouldn't listen to reason. The money was too much of a temptation. All Maeve could do on her own was attempt to manipulate his emotions.

"You'll miss Feldspar's first trial," she said.

Liam looked to the hills above the house and calculated the timing. "I can catch a flight over to Amsterdam tonight, be on the ship in the morning. I can just make it back in time, even allowing for a slow crossing."

Feldspar ignored their arrival at the end of the training path. Peter held the dog by the collar as it surged again and again toward the woods, barking furiously. "He's mad for something he saw moving in the trees," Peter said.

"Probably the police," Maeve said bitterly.

Liam shook his head. "It was nothing. A bird, Ma."

"Liam, get some sense into your head. The police are everywhere now. I wouldn't put it past them to be hiding out there watching us. I swear, they'll be following every move you make if you leave the estate. You'll never make it to Amsterdam and onto that ship without them finding out what you're up to."

Liam threw the lead to Peter. "Anything happens and I'm not back by Friday, you run Feldspar in the trials."

Liam stormed off toward the cars.

"Liam!" she called after him. "You're endangering the entire family if you go. Everything we've worked for. You selfish bastard!"

His own mother's words stopped him for a moment; then he got into his car.

Without giving her another look, he drove out the gates. Thirty seconds later, on the road in front of the house, another car turned on its lights and followed him.

# Chapter 10

The excruciating boredom of being in a great city all alone at night in a small bed-and-breakfast room, caring nothing about the bars or plays or restaurants or brightly lit shop windows; not giving a damn for the company of other people, yet feeling keenly the absence of another human being's presence. Michael was pretty certain it was Lydia he missed.

The television was broken and there was no radio. All Michael had were the day-old newspapers he had picked up from the lobby. He already had twice read the news stories, the sports, financial, and entertainment sections, the editorials, and was now working his way through the used-car classifieds. Again. He checked his watch: Midnight was more than four hours away. He smoothed his hair back with both hands, took a deep breath, settled back against the headboard of the bed.

He jumped when the phone rang. "Look, I'm just down the street," Claire Burke said. "I was wondering if I could buy a poor priest a meal."

"You ask all your murder suspects out to dinner?"

"Don't worry; it won't be anything fancy. I won't have a lot invested."

"Emotionally? Financially? Professionally?"

"Michael, you're overcomplicating this."

"I'm not particularly hungry."

"Yes or no? It's been a long day and I need to keep moving."

Michael checked his watch once more. There was still plenty of time. "Tell me where to meet you."

Claire paid for fish and chips at a takeaway on Rathmines Road, extra salt and vinegar for both of them, as Michael got the plastic forks and napkins. They took the brown paper bags outside and talked as they strolled along the sidewalk and ate.

Michael didn't want to talk about Lydia or Danny or himself. Best to get Claire talking about herself. He squeezed a lemon wedge over his cod. "So, you married? Partner? Boyfriend? Girlfriend?"

"Aggressively heterosexual. I'm legally separated."

"I'm sorry."

"It's okay. He's a nice guy, really. John's a banker. Too nice for me. He deserves better. Someone more appreciative of his corporate customer-service skills. He's smooth but very boring." She shrugged. "We gave it five years, and all the while I was moving up quickly in the department. I think that's long enough to give someone when you decided the first year of your marriage that it isn't going to work out. We should have tried living in sin first."

"Life on the police force can be hard on the family. Most people think of police officers' wives as suffering the most, but from what I remember, the husbands had at least as tough a time of it. Most of the problems I saw had to do with jealousy. When your spouse spends an entire night shift riding around the city with someone else, the imagination tends to get overexcited, and not in the healthiest of ways."

Claire stopped walking. "It's easy to forget. You were a detective, too."

"That was another life. Long ago and far away."

"And you're sure the only reason you left the force was your priestly calling?"

Michael wondered if Claire knew more than she was admitting to. The story he had told her about finding the dead twins in the tenement should have been enough to convince anyone of his motivations. It was all true, just not the whole truth. Michael got them walking again. "I told you why I left. My life's priorities changed."

Michael needed to get her talking about herself again. "Where'd you meet?"

"John and I? Over there actually." She nodded to a café across the street, youthful laughter and the smell of grilled meat coming out the front door.

"Ah, this is your old playground." He looked up and down the street. The rush-hour traffic had thinned. The commuter buses were less frequent. There were boutiques and bookstores and lively pubs and ethnic restaurants lining the road. In the first hours of the night, the area was assuming the atmosphere of the village outside the city it used to be before being subsumed into Dublin.

"Yeah, and I went to school right around the corner."

"Convent girl. I know the church."

She watched him eat. "I thought you said you weren't hungry."

"I was just being polite."

Claire pointed to the stoplight. "Let's cross."

They circled back down the opposite side of the street as they finished their supper.

"Have you always worked in Dublin?"

"No. After university and training at the Garda College, I worked in Dublin, then did a stint up in Donegal a couple of years ago. Personnel thought I would gain from the experience of a rural posting, flesh out my résumé."

"And did you?"

"I'd say it gave me a new appreciation for city life. Not just the comforts of civilization. The brutality of the criminals in the countryside is shocking. The violence is so naked, so tribal. The way some of the people live isn't much different from a couple of hundred of years ago. They're closer to death on a daily basis. I saw things done to other humans that I'd never imagined. Perhaps I'm too much of a city girl. The sight of caskets shouldered down the street still makes me think of those small villages, still makes me shudder."

Michael covertly checked the time on the Rathmines Town Hall clock over Claire's shoulder. He was still in no great rush.

"So no children?" Michael asked.

"No, thank God. Can you see me strapping a kid onto the back of my motorcycle?"

"Speaking of which, where is your motorcycle parked?"

"At the office. I didn't want to be drinking and driving."

"You've had a drink already?"

"No, but I thought you might let me buy you one."

She had a hand firmly on his upper arm, already pulling him into the door of a wine bar.

She knew exactly where she had been going.

She was on a first-name basis with the young guy behind the bar. Without her ever having said another word, he uncorked a bottle of wine and set it with a couple of glasses in front of them, left them alone. Michael wondered how many men she had pulled into the place, how many bottles of the dry white South African chardonnay she had shared.

"Did you always want to be a detective?" he asked.

"No. I was a biology major at University College Dublin. I had never had any contact with the police until my last year. Then I was raped by a boy I was seeing at the time. I think I was in denial about what had happened, and probably blamed myself, even though it wasn't my fault. It was fairly rough. My flatmate finally convinced me to report it to the police, but since I had waited and hadn't gone to the doctor, they said that realistically there was nothing they could do, as it was unlikely a case for prosecution could be made. I felt terribly let down. After I had some perspective on what had happened, I decided I wanted to do something for victims. At first I thought of going into counseling, but eventually I decided upon a career in law enforcement."

"I'm sorry about what happened."

"It's just a part of who I am. It's got me where I am today."

"I'm glad for you, then." Michael thought a moment. "The only thing is, something like that can cause real damage to relationships."

"I think I'm pretty much over all that."

"Well, in my experience, a traumatic incident of that sort can have serious implications for intimacy issues later on."

Claire got very quiet.

"Perhaps," he said, "it wasn't your husband who was at fault in your marriage. Did he know anything about the rape?"

"No. He preferred to think of me as a virgin until he met me. What are you saying, that my failed marriage was my fault?"

"Not at all. Women who have been raped often subsequently go to extremes in their sexual lives. Some go completely frigid —" The words were out of his mouth before he could take them back. Michael realized that the wine must have quickly gone to his head.

"I'm not sure where you picked up your psychology, but that's a pretty damned coldhearted analysis. But for your information, I'm in the latter group, the ones at the other extreme. I just can't get enough." She put her hand on top of Michael's and smiled lasciviously.

She finally broke the tension and laughed.

Then she leaned over and kissed his cheek. "You're much better-looking than the shrink I've been paying for the last year."

Michael didn't like what was going on. She was becoming too familiar too soon, yet he didn't want to alienate her by pushing her away quite yet.

142

The wine was good, and got better the more they drank. A lightly jazzed-up version of Irish traditional music played softly over the speakers.

Michael convinced himself that all she really wanted was company. Human companionship without the pretenses of a committed careerist's politics, or a weepy session with her counselor that just left her numb, feeling even worse when she came home to an empty flat. He was a safe, sympathetic man who would listen to her. Not unlike the role he had played with so many of the women he had counseled in his parish.

Their conversation lightened up. They found common ground for laughter. She wanted to talk about Detective Chief Superintendent Brady; he talked about Bishop Ferdinand. Coworkers in garda headquarters; other priests in the parish. Her ex-lovers, both before and after her husband; his girlfriends from before Lydia. The discussion moved again into dangerous territory.

"And how do you find American women different from Irish women?" she asked.

"I'd hate to generalize."

"Oh, go on."

"Well, in my very limited experience, I

think you first have to distinguish between city and country."

"And which do you prefer?"

"I have no preference."

"Which *did* you prefer?"

"If we're talking about my former life, I enjoyed relationships with women from all walks of life. Naturally, I tended to meet city girls when I lived in Boston, country girls when I visited my cousins down in West Cork in the summer."

"And now here you sit with one of those wicked Irish city girls."

"Are you dating now?" he asked, trying to move the focus back to her again.

"Compulsively." Her eyes widened. "How would you characterize your own love life at the moment now, Father? Frustrated? Fulfilling? *Anticipatory?*"

"Aggressively contemplative."

She nodded to the bartender and he opened a second bottle. Even with an eye on the clock behind the bar, he made no attempt to stop her. In a mildly drunk sort of way, he enjoyed her company. But he remained wary.

Claire leaned across him to reach the bottle. He felt the tingle, the warmth of her body that evaporated the musky perfume she was wearing. Her hair brushed against his face.

She took a long sip of wine, looked him directly in the eye. "What does a priest do when he feels the urge to touch a woman? When he looks at a woman and wants her, desires her, must have her?"

Michael smiled but without encouragement.

"And what happens," she continued, "when that priest knows that the woman who is the object of his desire wants him just as badly? How is that conflict resolved?"

Michael's breathing had become erratic, his pulse faster. Better not to answer.

"Ever personally been tempted?" she asked. "I mean, since taking the vows. *Seriously* tempted?"

"Yes, of course."

"I'll hear your confession now, Father Michael. Tell me everything. Was she beautiful?"

"Very beautiful."

"Was she witty and intelligent?"

"She was."

"Did you lust for her?"

"Yes," he said slowly.

"Did she occupy your dream life? Your every waking thought?"

"That might be a bit of an exaggeration."

"When was it, Michael? When did you desire her?"

He said nothing.

"You know you can have her, don't you?" Claire said.

"I do know that."

Claire signed the credit card slip even though he saw she had plenty of cash. "We'll take a taxi," she said.

The short taxi ride was made in complete silence. They sat on opposite sides of the backseat. When his bed-and-breakfast came into view as they took the corner of Belgrave Square, Claire took his hand. She interlaced her fingers with his. Michael felt queasy but didn't resist. He had an agenda, and if this was what he was required to do, so be it. He knew he was partly rationalizing, but justified his actions on a higher moral ground than the priestly prohibitions against allowing a woman to touch him in this way: He would find Lydia's killer, and find the boy, whatever it took. Within some still-undefined parameters.

Inside his room, Claire put her purse on the desk, took off her suit jacket, and carefully folded it over the back of the chair as

Michael drew the curtains closed. Now it was dark, except for the dim bedside lamp. He turned from the window to see her stepping out of her shoes. His first thought: Shorter now, she was less threatening, more feminine.

He hadn't seen a woman move like that for so long, the way she crawled onto the bed. She faced away from him and pulled the pillows out from under the covers. She stretched out, propped her head up on an elbow, and waited for him to join her.

He lay down next to her. Face-to-face. Her hand tracing his jawline from one ear to the other. *My God,* he thought to himself. *Not since Lydia.* Touching his hair. Hand on his chest, holding her breath and closing her eyes, as if to confirm he had a beating heart.

His hand on her hip, the fingertips only. He dared not feel the curve of her waist in the palm of his hand.

She exhaled.

The mottled skin at the top button of her blouse, which he realized she had unfastened. The dilated pupils of her eyes gone violet-blue. Her body was already moving, a rhythmic motion that gently rocked the bed.

They drifted, sharing the same place, the same time.

He instinctively put his hand on her waist, pulled her closer; she arched her back, bent her leg over his thigh. Her hand moved down his body until she found out what she wanted to know. A delicious shiver ran down his spine. She let out a little gasp and closed her eyes again, waiting to be kissed.

Now they most certainly were sharing a commonality of purpose.

*How far am I willing to go?* Michael thought to himself. *At what point do I pull back, at risk of losing someone who can help me?* Not this far, he told himself. Yet he had pressing practical considerations — the need to support himself in Dublin while he continued his own personal investigation — that he still needed to address. God knew in his weakness as a man, he wanted her — wanted a woman — but what he needed was cold hard cash.

Faintly, almost covered by the hum of late-night traffic outside, the Rathmines Town Hall clock struck the hour. Michael heard it; she did not. He had been listening for it.

He sat up. "You're not her," he said. "You're not her," he repeated, shaking his head as he got off the bed and walked to the desk. "I'm sorry."

With his back turned to her so she couldn't see, Michael quickly opened her purse and took the cash. He then parted the curtains enough to let a sliver of light in from the street lamps.

"You can't be here when I get back," he told her. "I'm sorry," he said again, patting down his pockets. "I don't have fare for a taxi home for you."

Claire, stood up, straightened her clothes. "You're just sorry you didn't make love to me. Because you don't know if you'll ever get that chance again. With me, or anyone else."

"Yeah, you must be right."

She put her jacket back on, fixed her hair. She reevaluated him in the new light. "Oh, wait. I think I'm mistaken. You're not kicking me out because of your conscience. Because I know you want it as much as I do. You're going out again, prowling the night, looking for Lydia's killer."

He held the door for her.

"Please don't misinterpret me, Michael. I'm not bitter. Just don't ever forget: You're the priest; I'm the cop. Stay out of the investigation."

# Chapter 11

Michael puzzled over the problem at the Fusiliers' Arch on the north corner of St. Stephen's Green, where the head of the taxi queue formed. A weary horse pulled a carriage and driver with a pair of lovers in the backseat, the last fares for the night.

Inspiration had been nowhere to be found during the afternoon strolling inside the twenty-two-acre city center park itself. Nothing but late-summer straggly begonias in the flower beds, lovers canoodling on the grass, pigeons nosing into empty potato-chip bags, and a few drunks wasted on cheap hard cider lost in the serpentine paths around the pond. The subsequent walk around the perimeter along the busy streets was equally unproductive. Gentlemen's clubs, Georgian exteriors, a grand hotel. Society buildings, an exclusive girls' school, the gaping pedestrian entrance to the boutiques, and street performers of

Grafton Street. No answers.

The dilemma: He needed to find out who had planted the heroin on Lydia. He had a taxi registration number of someone who couriered drugs in the city, supposedly someone connected to the very top of the chain. But did he really want to take that ride to hell, as Fahy had warned? Disappearing into the Dublin night never to be heard of again would do nothing to find Lydia's killer. It was the only lead he had.

The more immediate problem was that a pair of policemen were standing only a few yards away on the sidewalk, paying close attention to the taxis coming and going. Perhaps even waiting for the same taxi he was. It occurred to Michael that they might be posted at that particular position near the taxi rank specifically to observe who was getting in and out of the taxi, on the lookout for drug users, drug runners, drug suppliers. Michael needed to ensure that he stayed above their suspicion. Worse than ending up in hell was never even getting there.

Inspiration was an elusive Muse. After Michael had spent over an hour spent shuffling in the shadows of the Arch, all she offered up was an empty two-liter plastic cider bottle, discarded by one of the park's drunks along the outside of the park's fence.

Michael pounced on the idea, picked up the bottle, messed up his hair, drooped his eyelids, and became another inner-city drunk in the small hours of the morning.

He had to wait until almost two a.m. to see the taxi he was waiting for arrive at the back of queue. Another ten minutes as the taxi made its way to the front. Michael stepped out from under the arch, staggered. He felt as if he had just stepped off the edge of a cliff. He actually stumbled and fell. But the fall was only for show.

The driver saw him approach, anticipated his coming, buried his face in a newspaper. Michael went to the passenger's side, got waved away as a common drunk. With one hand on the car's hood to steady him, he made his way around the car to the driver's side and pressed his face to the glass.

Michael reasoned that the driver dared not refuse a legitimate fare right under the nose of the police, dared not give them a reason to intervene. The driver cracked the window.

"You get sick in here, wanker, and it's a twenty-five-euro surcharge," he said, "plus the fare. Do you even know where you're fucking going?"

Michael pulled the bills from the pocket of his jeans pocket in a wad — the money he had taken from Claire's purse while she was lying on the bed in the near total dark.

"Get in," the driver told him. "Hurry up before the police come over."

Michael checked the registration number again on the laminated license on the dash and confirmed that the taxi was the one he wanted. The driver's name — Dan Murphy — was printed under his scowling picture.

"Where to, cowboy?" He was in a hurry.

"Just drive over to Baggot Street," Michael said.

"Not much of a fucking fare. You could have walked." Murphy eyed Michael in the rearview mirror as he pulled out into traffic. "On second thought, you'd probably never make it."

As they rode, Michael stared out the window at the dark park and asked himself what he was doing in a Dublin taxi, several thousand miles from his church parish, hunting down drug dealers. At that moment he caught a glimpse of the streetlights reflected in the pond inside the park's locked fence. Just as earlier in the

153

day, there was Lydia: reclining on the grass at water's edge by his side, oblivious to the throngs of summer tourists, playing with the stubble on his chin, then pushing him onto his back and kissing him. The police eventually had to run them out as the sun set and the city workers began clearing the rubbish from the grass and footpaths. They folded their blanket together and walked arm in arm back to her place, where they made love until the sun rose again.

Not more than two minutes had passed when Michael pointed down a street. "Pull down there," he said.

"I'll let you off at the corner. I'm not taking any chances going down a dark street with the likes of you." Murphy pulled to a stop under a streetlight and punched the meter to generate a receipt. "That'll be four-fucking-forty-five."

"I didn't say I was there yet." Michael thrust his hand between the front seats, the driver expecting payment. Michael's voice was very sober, very deliberate. "I'm looking for some more of this," he said, showing Murphy the bag of heroin from Lydia's flat. "Top grade stuff. In quantity. Okay?"

"You're the American?"

Apparently word had moved up the chain after Michael had talked to Joel in Dolphin's Barn that someone was asking questions.

"Yeah, I guess I am."

"Everyone's heard there's a Yank snooping around. You got balls, boy. I think there's someone wants to meet you as much as you want to meet him."

The taxi screeched back into traffic. The farther away from the city center, the fewer the cars. Too long after the pubs had closed, too soon for the clubs to let out. Murphy sped through the nearly empty streets, cutting down alleys, taking detours through housing estates, doubling back. If Michael hadn't known better, he would have thought that Murphy was running up the fare. Except he was off the meter now. Murphy was an obvious master of making sure they weren't being followed.

They got stuck once in the new inner-city rail-line construction. Murphy pulled out his mobile phone, spoke in whispers, too quiet for Michael to hear anything over the sound of a pile driver. Another five minutes speeding off the main avenues; then Murphy whipped into the emergency-room entrance of a hospital, the kind of great Victorian brick building still burdened with the urban poor.

"Downstairs and out back around shipping and receiving. Ask for Vincent. He's expecting you. Unless, of course, you want to save your feckin' arse and let me to drive you to the airport now. A plane leaves for Ameriky from Dublin first thing in the morning. Worth thinking about."

Michael threw a fiver onto the front seat as he got out. "Sorry, no passport. Apparently I'm a flight risk."

He passed through the waiting room, pee-yellow walls dingy with city grime, the linoleum floor pocked with cigarette burns and marred with shoe scuffs. Pakistani doctors and Filipino nurses ate a patient's birthday cake at a nurses' station under harsh fluorescent lights.

Up and down the deserted hallways. He must have made a wrong turn. Gynecology or Psychiatry? He couldn't find a stairway down. A palsied old man in a robe moved through a distant corridor intersection like a cheerful zombie, unaware of the time or day. Michael caught up with him and was directed to an elevator by a shaky hand.

Downstairs, in the belly of the bleak building — past the maintenance rooms, the employee lockers, floor-to-ceiling cages with medical supplies — at the end of a wide hallway, he found an office door next to an open loading dock. The sign read SHIPPING AND RECEIVING.

Hand on the doorknob. Locked.

He knocked twice. No answer.

"Damn."

Michael stood in the wide-open door of the loading dock overlooking the parking lot. A power plant hummed nearby, white smoke and steam pouring from its smoke-stacks. The tarmac was flooded with bright lights, making the shadows around the edges of the building even sharper. To the rear of a truck parked in the shadow of the power plant's smokestack on the other side of the lot a cigarette glowed.

He jumped down, walked along the hospital outer wall. He was surprised at all the activity. Voices in the gloom. More cigarettes glowing in the dark, the smell of tobacco and pot. A whiff of beer.

Animal sounds? In the heart of the city? A pack of wild dogs fought over garbage from a spilled rubbish can.

Gradually he became aware of more humans — alone, together, laughing, drinking, smoking, copulating, engaged in sordid activities on their own. The entire night shift must have been outside, hidden in the shadows of the great sooted building.

He was drawn to a faint light illuminating the interior of the back of the truck. On his approach, at just the right angle to a street lamp, he could make out a reflective symbol and the words BIOMEDICAL HAZARDOUS WASTE.

Michael kept to the shadows, well out of sight of the men in boiler suits wearing red rubber gloves. They were throwing bags into the back of the truck from another open loading bay.

Then, without warning, the same sort of thick, cold, pimpled, greasy rubber glove tightened around his neck in a powerful grip, twisting his chin roughly to the side, the contortion of his spine lifting him to his toes.

Now the crook of an arm around his throat, gagging, choking. No more breathing, no crying out. Arms flailing, legs kicking. Ever tighter around his throat now. He felt his eyes bulge as if they were going to pop out of their sockets.

He wasn't sure if the hellish visions flashing before him were hallucinations from the incredible pain or the real-life carnival in the hospital's back lot.

A paradox: In the depths of the night, the darkness became lighter and lighter. A growing buzzing in his head. The darkest shadows became like a dense fog lit by a car's headlamps.

The last thing he remembered for certain before passing out was a flashlight sweeping the ground in front of him and a small feral dog licking something slick and white off the face of a dazed woman lying on wet, trodden-down grass strewn with cigarette butts and beer bottles and condom wrappers.

"Wake up. Wake up, you son of a bitch."

Michael was standing, slumping, against the interior of the truck. His blurred vision began to clear. In the feeble light he saw he was surrounded by a heaping mound of the clear rubbish bags, all stickered as hazardous waste. He couldn't move; his arms were useless; then he became aware that the constriction he felt in his chest was rope securing him to the sides of the truck walls, like a piece of furniture secured tightly to the inside of a moving van.

Gloved hands rested on the hips of the man standing in front of him as he looked Michael over. Michael lifted his eyes into a fleshy red face, certainly that of Vincent.

"Fucking hell," Vincent said to the two other men in the truck. "What are we gonna do with *this?*" He grabbed Michael's face in his hand and slammed his head against the wall.

"Dunno," was the answer from one of them.

"Stick'm," said the other nonchalantly.

"Yeah, stick'm," agreed the first.

"Give me that," Vincent said, jerking Michael's heroin bag out of the hand of the first one. "Where did you get this?" he said, holding it up in Michael's face. "Why are you nosing around asking where you can get more of it?"

Michael had regained enough of his senses to understand that the situation was the exact opposite of what he had planned. The reversal had happened too quickly. He was supposed to be finding out from *them* what the source of the heroin was, not the other way around.

"I was in town just looking to score some good stuff," Michael said.

"Not very likely, I'd say. You don't look like a junkie to me. That means you're either a cop or you're trying to muscle in on our business. Either way, you're in big trouble, fella."

"I'm neither. I'm a priest."

There was some laughing from the three men in boiler suits.

"Look, boy," Vincent said, "I think

you're looking at getting a piece of my action for yourself. Apparently everyone in Dublin but you knows who I am and understands how this works. This here," he said, motioning to the interior of the truck, "is a biomedical waste-removal firm. Hospitals, doctors' offices, nursing homes, dentists pay us big money to take their blood and guts away and dispose of it safely. They don't really care what we do with it, long as they've got a piece of paper from us they can show the government inspectors saying it's been done in an environmentally friendly way. No county councilor in his right mind is going to allow a hazardous-waste dump in his constituency, but there are plenty of poor countries only too happy to see a shipful of garbage bags dumped in a landfill in exchange for a big wad of cash. So we haul this stuff from all across the city to the Port of Dublin, load it onto a barge, and away it goes. Everybody's happy. Until you came along and starting making inquiries.

"It's a dirty business that no one else wants to do. It's legit and makes a lot of money. It also provides us perfect cover for moving pretty much anything around the city, including the likes of this." He tossed the bag of heroin up and down, judging its heft. "When people see our trucks coming, they get out of the way as fast as they can, including the police. As long as it's got one of these biomedical hazardous-waste stickers on it, no one's going to fuck with us. The rare occasion when someone does take a peek into the back of the truck and gets curious about a bag of pills or white powder, all I have to do is mention the words 'AIDS clinic' and they do a one-eighty. Nobody touches our stuff, see? Who's going to go digging through *these* bags?"

Michael took the question as a genuine invitation to speak. "You move drugs freely around the city, and you move drugs freely in and out of the country with the garbage. Very clever."

"You think this is the first time I've had trouble with foreigners coming into the city and hustling my customers? I'm still trying to deal with these goddammed Nigerians and their crack cocaine. How do you compete with something that the users think is a hundred thousand times better than heroin? Not hard to get someone hooked on that kind of high. And the cravings are so much more powerful than smack. Pretty soon these niggers will run me out of business. I'm all for free enter-

162

prise and all that shit, but healthy competition is not exactly welcome. Now you? Don't think so."

Vincent tore open one of the clear bags, dumped its contents onto the floor of the truck. Swabs, bloody gauze, latex gloves turned inside out, a plastic box marked as containing used syringes.

He crushed the container with the heel of his boot, carefully selected one of the hypodermics from among those with shattered chambers or bent needles.

"Shut the door," Vincent ordered.

One of the men pulled the truck's rolling door down hard. It closed with a loud bang.

Vincent held a syringe up to Michael's face, right under his eye. The needle could not have been any closer. Michael held his head perfectly still against the wall, held his breath for fear of jabbing himself on the point.

"Stick'm," a low voice urged.

"Stick'm," echoed the other. "Stick'm."

"So," Vincent said. "Cop or dealer?"

Michael spoke in a harsh whisper: "Priest. I'm a priest."

"If it weren't for the fact that you're American, you'd already be dead. The last thing I need is the heat that killing an American would bring down on us. But you still need to be discouraged, whether you're a cop or a competitor. Cut him open."

Michael dared not move a single muscle, the needle still being next to his face. His wide eyes rolled to either side of him, and he saw the two others opening large knives. Sweat ran down his forehead, over his face, searing his eyes. Where would he feel the first touch of the steel?

They cut Michael's sweater off, tore open his shirt to the waist.

"Ah!" Vincent said. He moved the syringe away from Michael's face. Vincent fondled the crucifix hung around Michael's neck. "A priest!"

Michael panted in sputtering relief, saved after all.

"I don't know what the hell you're doing, whether you're a priest or just pretending to be one to get yourself out of this mess, and I don't give a fuck either way. Stay away from my business. Get out of Dublin. You get one warning," Vincent said, "and this is it."

Michael felt a certain relief, believing that he wasn't about to be cut with the knives. "Thank you," he managed to say.

"Jesus saves," Vincent said, shaking his head. "But not you, boy."

Michael had closed his eyes, was saying a small silent prayer of thanks, had allowed himself to relax for a fraction of a second, long enough not to anticipate what happened next.

At first he didn't feel it, thought it was a twinge. A jab into his shoulder. Then the other. It was happening so fast. Another jab in the arm.

A frenzy now.

"Stick'm."

"Stick'm good."

Not the knives, but the needles. All three of them with hypodermics. Short, hard jabs, up and down his arms, through the material of his trousers. Now he felt the pain.

Faster and louder. *Stick'm.*

Deeper. Plunging quickly in and out of his flesh. *Stick'm.* Through the skin into the muscle.

*Stick'm.*

It would never stop.

Michael thrashed and cried out. Screamed through the pain until there was nothing left but a gaping mouth, his lolling head, eyes rolled back into his skull.

He tried prayer, but that failed. He sank into himself, finally found a place in the depths of his soul where only a blessed ray of darkness could penetrate.

# Chapter 12

Maeve O'Driscoll realized that, for the first time in her life, she felt truly all alone.

She was awake, dressed, smoking furiously, pacing in front of the sitting room fire as the clock on the mantel struck four a.m. She straightened the framed photographs of the children next to the clock, blew the peat dust from the glass. No Liam, no Noreen — no children, no family. She picked up a picture of the three of them taken just after they had acquired the Carnmore estate, only five years earlier: she and Noreen and Liam in front of the stable block in full formal riding attire, ready for the Carbery Hunt. Ten years before that she couldn't even afford the group riding lessons the children had begged for. In the photograph, they sat atop the finest Irish hunt horses a drug fortune could buy.

It had been a long, hard slog from the

damp, unheated terrace house up the hill with a view of the petrol station to the six-million-euro country estate they now occupied. She didn't want to lose it. The great house was everything she had worked for, fought for, killed for. It was her future, her everything. But it meant nothing without her family.

They had been apart before, but this time they were all in different countries. Psychologically, the extra distance between them mattered. There was no telling how long it would be until she heard from Liam, chasing down his heroin shipment in Amsterdam. There was still no word from Noreen, who should have already done what she needed to do to move the American cousins along and returned home. She shuddered, not from the chilly evening air, but out of fear for their lives. And now the police were closing in. Maeve understood what the children were both trying to do: salvage the family business that was falling apart. The family had never been under more pressure. Carnmore, the horses, the dogs, the cars, the boats — their entire empire was on the brink of collapse, and she feared for her family along with it.

Other than the children, there was nowhere else to turn. In the twenty-eight years since Liam's birth, there was still no man in her life. Always the company of men, but never a man. She had raised Noreen never to be reliant on a man, and had set a good example. Even with all her wealth, Maeve still felt like a single mother struggling to raise her family.

She poured herself a large whiskey from the crystal decanter on the drinks table, added a splash of water. She took from the mantel a little booklet, *South of Ireland Tide Tables*.

She looked up the high tide schedules for the day. Of the two high tides along the area's coast, she reconfirmed that the one during the nighttime hours was an hour and a half away.

It being a Wednesday, there would be someone else at a point about a mile down the coast looking up the same tide tables. As had been prearranged for the last two years, subtracting an hour from the high tide time that fell during darkness, both people would know that their rendezvous would take place in half an hour, leaving just enough time to meet and for her contact to take advantage of the changing sea.

It had always been Noreen's job. She had cultivated the contact, brought him into the fold. She had arranged the Wednesday-night meetings, had made the trek over their estate on horseback, up the mountainside overlooking the lake, to the agreed-upon meeting place. It was one of the most important things they did to safeguard their business. With the police moving ever closer to them, it was even more important that the meeting take place. Liam was supposed to have taken Noreen's place, but with both of the children gone, Maeve would have to do it herself.

Maeve took a long swallow of the whiskey and put on her Barbour coat and riding gloves, protection against the gorse thorns and briers. Time to go.

Under a nearly full moon on a cloudless night, condensation from the horse's breath filled the cool air outside the stable. It was bright enough so that there was no need for a flashlight, no need expose herself to anyone who might be watching the hills above Liss Ard. Knowing she would be taking the meeting herself, Maeve had saddled the horse during daylight hours as soon as Liam had fled. She took Noreen's horse, since the mare knew the way better than her own. The horse shook its head expectantly as Maeve mounted her, as if she looked forward to the weekly ride.

Despite her fear earlier in the day that the police were watching them from the woods of her own property, she was certain they would never be able to follow her at night over the rough terrain. The well-worn path the fox took up the hills to stalk sheep was the same one she would take: up the rock at the back of the house, across the lower hills but beneath the crest so her silhouette couldn't be seen against the bright sky, rising up higher to the mountain overlooking the lake in the front of the house, circling the lake to the other side, then plunging down the steep slope leading down to the water. There was no road. The place on the lake was accessible only by walking, or riding a surefooted horse. Or by the sea.

Maeve rode slowly, silently through the rough landscape, all rocks and gorse. The only sounds were the horse's footfalls and the wind through the tall grasses. From that vantage so high up, Maeve could actually see the curvature of the earth on the sea. Of course, her thoughts went to her son, where he was, when he would return home to her.

Down below, the lake shimmered silvery with a fresh breeze and the light of the moon. It was an oddity of nature, by a strange twist of geography and the melted ice sheets that covered Ireland, a rare inland sea lake. At low tide, a small river ran from the lake into the sea, but twice a day when the sea rose high enough to flood the narrow land bridge separating the two bodies of water, the river reversed directions. As a family, they would take picnics to the riverbank, watching for the telltale signs of the sea change, the swards of giant kelp pointing seaward, beginning to stand up vertically, arching their fronds above the silent waters, moments later gently falling over backward, pointing back into the lake. Within just a few minutes, the seawater would regain its frightening speed, the river would reverse, and the ocean would be roaring into the lake.

The mountain became a hill again. Maeve was close enough to the water to see the seals that had slipped over the rapids from the sea to the lake. They dived for fish, swam on their backs, splashed each other with their tails.

Her eye caught the glint of something else breaking the surface of the water. She stopped the horse to take a closer look. Paddles gleaming in the moonlight, a small boat of some sort. In with the seals over the rapids had slipped a one-man kayak, the only other way to that end of the lake other than the path she had just taken.

She dismounted and led the horse by foot the rest of the way. She tied up to a wind-warped whitethorn outside a stone ruin, the remnants of a house built low in the landscape as shelter against the punishing weather that came from the sea, and abandoned over a hundred and fifty years earlier during the famine.

Inside, four crumbling walls. Wind howled through the empty windows. Maeve felt her way around the interior, found the kerosene lamp set on the mildewed table that Noreen had said was there. She lit the lantern, lit a cigarette from the flame, turned the wick down low.

She sat against the window frame facing where the door to the house used to be, smoked, and waited for Noel Hennessy, the athletic young garda, to pull his kayak to shore and make his way up to the ruin.

He was a married man. Maeve had just seen his wife getting shoes for their children in town the week before. There was something in the way the woman looked at Maeve through the shop window as Maeve passed on the sidewalk that told her she *knew*. There was a recognition in her face of the connection between the two families. Did she suspect her husband was on the take from the O'Driscolls, or did she imagine more sinister associations?

Maeve wondered what Noreen exchanged in return for information, for protection. Ostensibly it was as simple quid pro quo — cash for the latest updates on police activity in the area, tip-offs as to where the police would be setting up roadblocks, the best times to smuggle a drug shipment ashore to avoid police detection. He had reliably warned them about every sweep the Criminal Assets Bureau and the elite Emergency Response Unit had been about to make, giving them enough time to move their drugs and cover up their financial holdings, mostly in the form of cash deposited in numbered bank accounts on the Isle of Man. Maeve carried with her in the game pocket of her coat four bundles of fifty-euro notes, enough to satisfy their monthly obligation to the policeman, and then some.

If, on the other hand, it was sex Noreen was bartering with, the man would be very disappointed tonight, indeed.

Noreen had met him, of all places, in the West Cork Choral Singers, an amateur choir made up of local people. When everyone went to the pub for drinks after a weekly rehearsal, a relationship was formed. Subsequently, she enticed him to work for the family, and an agreement was reached for compensation.

The horse snorted outside and a figure appeared in the doorway, dripping wet, clothed in a wet suit and knit cap.

Maeve remained a disembodied voice in the shadow of the window frame. "I hope I don't disappoint you too much, Garda Hennessy."

Hennessy searched the room with his eyes. "I'm surprised, but not shocked," he said.

He shook the water off and stepped inside. He took off his hat and ran his fingers through his thick black hair. "Where's Noreen?"

"Away on business. She should be back soon."

Hennessy nodded. Maeve offered him a cigarette and held the lantern for him to light up. When he stuck his chin out, Maeve could see the sinewy muscles in his neck. In the glow of the lamp she saw how well his body filled out the wet suit. She could see what attracted Noreen to him.

He walked around the ruin with familiarity, making a seat of a broad stone, a lintel fallen from a window to the floor.

Hennessy inhaled the smoke deeply and too fast. He hadn't looked Maeve properly in the eye yet. Was it because he was nervous about something, or did the presence of his secret lover's mother make him squirm?

He stared out the door. "This is getting too freaky," he said. "First a fellow police officer gets killed in that disaster on the beach; then I find myself pulling nails out of the hands of dead men staked to fence posts. That wasn't part of the bargain."

"What the hell happened on the beach?" Maeve said.

"I don't know. There was an Emergency Response Unit sent in from outside the area. Obviously someone in your organization tipped them off. I never heard a fucking thing about it, and it was my job to know. There's a huge surveillance now on the coast."

*Liam*, Maeve thought immediately. Whose life was in peril out on the ocean.

Hennessy said, "I think they're withholding information from me. Memos and bulletins from Dublin are drying up. I'm not even assigned critical duties in the office anymore. I'm definitely out of the loop. They've got me paired up with a rookie, teaching him to shoot the radar gun outside of town. Scares the shit out of me. Makes me wonder if they're onto me."

"I've taken care of the traitor. There won't be any more tip-offs." In truth, the incident on the Long Strand scared her, too. The intervention meant there were powerful state forces outside of West Cork at work. She felt her control over the situation slip a notch lower. "I think you're going to need to be very careful yourself."

Hennessy's hands were shaking slightly, the big muscles in his forearms trembling enough to make it difficult now to hold the cigarette still to his lips. Maeve thought it was not from being cold and wet.

"What do you hear about the country-side murders?" she asked.

"Of course there's a consensus as to who's behind it."

"Who did do it, Garda?"

For the first time, Hennessy met Maeve's eyes. "Don't ask me that," he said irritably. "No one expects any charges to be brought. There won't be any witnesses coming forward, since they know the same thing will happen to them if they talk. So far there's no hard evidence. Which means there won't be enough evidence to send to the Director of Public Prosecutions. No case. It gets filed as an unsolved crime and shoved to the back of a drawer."

"Somehow I doubt that. Your brethren are getting much bolder. They're virtually riding my car bumper every time I leave the estate. They follow me around the inside of the grocery store. I've seen them watching the house from the road with binoculars. I don't have any doubt they are bugging my phones and reading my mail. From what you've told me, you might give some serious consideration to the possibility that they are doing the same to you, as well."

"Fuck. Fuck, *fuck*." Hennessy flicked his cigarette out the empty door frame into the night. "Yeah, and on top of all that, Brendan's girlfriend comes up to me when I'm out for dinner with my wife and kids and says she needed me to set up a meeting for her with someone from the Dublin headquarters. I can't be seen talking to an O'Driscoll in public! What the fuck was that all about?"

"Lydia Jellicoe?"

"Yes. She said she was leaving town later in the week, but would come by the station before she left."

Maeve's mind raced. Her first thought was of when she had called Brendan into the sitting room and given him a forceful dressing-down. Brendan had let slip that Lydia wanted to leave him, taking their child, and move to England. Maeve told him that wasn't possible. No one left the family. She lived with Brendan who, though not personally involved in some of the more salacious aspects of the business, nonetheless knew about everything that was going on. Lydia Jellicoe knew too much.

Her second thought was that if Liam ever found out that Lydia had approached a police officer, he'd kill her himself.

"Why didn't you mention this before?" Maeve said.

"I *did*. I told Noreen all about it here at last week's meeting."

"She never mentioned it to me." Maeve stood and faced the wind blowing through the open window. "So what did you do when Lydia came to you?"

"She never turned up. What happened to her?"

"I don't know. But I'm going to talk to Brendan first thing tomorrow."

Outside, there was the sound of a raging torrent. They both understood the signal.

The tide would have turned, the river reversed its course, rushing back into the sea. Noel Hennessy could now take his kayak back the way he came over the rapids. It was time for the meeting to be over.

Hennessy stood. Maeve took the stacks of fifty-euro notes from her coat and laid them on the windowsill. In her experience, it was always good practice to allow a snitch to pick up his own money, thus assuring his complete complicity.

Hennessy loaded the money into a waterproof pouch. "This will have to be the last time, I'm sure," he said.

"Not if you want to ever see Noreen again, it's not."

Hennessy stopped zipping the pouch closed. The look on his face betrayed his distress.

"The basis for your weekly transactions with Noreen is more than this, isn't it?" Maeve said, lifting the bag.

Hennessy took a deep breath. Maeve reckoned the slight smile on his face was the memory of his last late-night rendezvous with her daughter.

"I like her for a lot of different reasons," he said. "She's good company; she's a gorgeous, talented girl. Even if she is a bit whacked." He thought a moment. "There's this one song we do in choir where the tenors are singing the chorus and the women are backing us up. I really like the way she hums."

"You should consider yourself a very lucky man."

"Believe me, I do." Hennessy put his cap and gloves back on. Maeve handed him the pouch.

She said, "I'm guessing your moral qualms are assuaged by the money, and your fears over how things are getting messy and how you might be suspected of working with us are overcome by the drive to see my beautiful daughter again. Face it, you're an addict, every bit as much as one of those kids shooting up in the alleys behind the pubs. You missed your fix tonight. You're feeling empty, anxious. Don't worry; I'll have her get in touch as soon as she gets back. Discreetly, of course. God forbid you're seen publicly with another O'Driscoll woman."

Maeve lifted the lamp to light Hennessy's way to the door. "I'm just curious," she said.

He turned. "Yes?"

"What does your wife think you're doing out of the house at four-thirty in the morning?"

"She knows how dedicated I am to my job. I tell her I'm getting on top of my work."

"You're a clever one, Garda Hennessy. You'll get along just fine. Safe home."

# Chapter 13

Claire had heard the chatter over her police radio as she was getting dressed just after daybreak. White male, thirty to forty years old, facedown alongside the Grand Canal, a popular dumping ground for Dublin gangland murders. From the contents of his wallet it appeared he was American. That stopped her in her tracks as she prepared her regular breakfast of orange juice and porridge. The first report was that he was dead, and she dropped a glass to the floor. Instinctively she knew it was him. God forbid her ticket to promotion to the corner office was dead. Subsequently, he was determined to be alive, but she never heard that information, as she was already on her motorcycle flying to the scene.

He was being worked on by paramedics when she arrived.

"No, no," one of the paramedics said, "he's just in shock. He's alive. I'm not sure if that's good news or bad."

"Spiked," another of the paramedics said ominously.

At the sound of that word, the blood drained from her face. Claire saw his horrific injuries, was sickened and had to look away.

"I'm riding with him," she insisted as they loaded him into the back of the ambulance.

At the hospital, a facility as modern as the Victorian hospital the night before was dilapidated, she sat on a metal folding chair across from the examining table as the doctors and nurses cleaned the wounds.

Michael regained consciousness, winced at the application of antiseptic.

He suddenly recoiled. A nurse approached with a hypodermic. "What are you doing?" he said in a panic.

"I'm sorry," the nurse said. "We have to draw a sample."

The doctors and nurses held him down.

"Why?" he pleaded. "Not that!" He was still terribly confused by his surroundings. He became aware of Claire's presence. He saw the wounds on his arms and legs, remembered the horror of what had happened, and fought to free himself. In his condition he was no match for the medical staff. He looked to Claire for help.

The nurse exchanged looks with Claire and the doctor. The doctor nodded to Claire.

"Because you've received very serious puncture wounds," she said. "And because there is a chance you've been infected with those dirty needles."

A look of terror crossed Michael's face as his situation became clear.

"I was mugged," Michael told Claire.

"The hell you were. Whoever you were tangling with knew exactly what they were doing." Claire added, "The worst part may have seemed like the pain and trauma of the attack, but the most serious concern now is that you may have contracted an infection. Hepatitis C . . . or worse."

"Oh, my God," Michael said, closing his eyes, yielding to the needle once again.

The nurse finished drawing the first sample, then drew another. "I'm afraid I have to come back in a minute to give you an antibiotic," she said. "Hypodermically," she added apologetically.

The nurse and the doctor left them alone and pulled the curtain for privacy. Michael was shattered.

"I'm so, so sorry," Claire said.

Michael was almost certain he saw her eyes welling with tears. Quite a change from the last time he'd seen her.

"You eejit," she said. "I told you to stay out of this and let us do our jobs."

"I'm sorry about taking the cash from your purse last night," Michael said feebly.

Claire said nothing, only managed to shake her head.

Michael grew apprehensive at the sound of the nurse returning. A hand on the curtain; then it was quickly yanked back.

No, not the nurse.

Chief Superintendent Charlie Brady said, "Sorry to intrude upon such a tender moment. Good morning, Claire. Good morning, *Father* Michael."

"I was just going to take his statement," Claire said.

"I believe your brief is homicide, Detective." Brady quickly glanced at Michael's wounds. He was unimpressed. "He doesn't look dead to me. I'll send someone around from the violent crimes division to record any complaint he might have."

With heroic effort, Michael sat up. "There's an unsolved murder in your jurisdiction, Brady, and a missing child. The longer you wait to do anything about them, the harder it will be to find who's responsible. What's it going to take before you get serious about solving those crimes?"

Brady refused to be drawn in. "Ah, well, I believe we may finally have a suspect, actually, Father Michael; thank you for asking. But as much as we investigators would like to, you just can't rush forensics. My guess is that the lab will confirm my suspicions. I still think we have enough circumstantial evidence to detain you for a while longer." He held up a FedEx package, tossed it to Claire, and spoke to her as if Michael weren't even in the room. Two police officers came into the examining room, flanking Brady.

"Book him," Brady said to her. "On suspicion of the murder of Lydia Jellicoe. See you back at the office."

The pilot of the chartered Gulfstream jet announced they would be landing at the Yeager Airport outside Charleston, West Virginia, in five minutes. Aiden Driscoll folded his reading glasses and put down the financial spreadsheet he was reading. Out the plane window the sun was breaking over the horizon, the great swatches of red and orange on the trees turning colors higher up in the Alleghenies.

As beautiful as the scenery was, Aiden was more concerned with the fact that his commitment to his Irish cousins was being undermined. There was an enormous amount of money on the line — more than he had ever had within his grasp — and the fact that he had given his word to Noreen O'Driscoll that the deal would be done, and quickly. He had been playing it cool, pretending it was a deal he could take or leave. But he wanted it desperately. No one walked away from a quarter of a billion dollars. What should have been a simple transaction had become problematic. Somewhere at the base of that mountain range was a salami-slicing son of a bitch who thought he was a player. Aiden Driscoll and two of his well-tailored associates had come to West Virginia to prove the little shit wrong.

Eddie Martin drove the rental car from the airport, Aiden in the backseat looking at the countryside. Pat Hannity sat up front, navigating with a map in his lap, surfing through the local Christian radio stations. A preacher spoke too close to the microphone, popping his "P"s, ranting about the evils of drink.

"Obviously he ain't Irish," Eddie said.

"Moot point," Pat said. "Most Irish

aren't up this early to hear him."

"Turn that crap off," Aiden said. "Get the CD."

Pat opened a briefcase, retrieved a CD, slid it into the player in the dashboard. It was their traveling music, a compilation of funk and old rock tunes, utterly incongruous at seven-thirty in the morning, but effective in getting the boys' minds off their work and keeping them pumped up.

"Turn it up," Aiden said.

They cruised along two-lane highways, moving into the ruggedly rural eastern part of the state, pushed along by the Ohio Players and Bachman Turner Overdrive. They passed an especially well built girl bent over filling her car at a gas station, and Pat fast-forwarded to "Brick House." Aiden gave them some slack, let them have a laugh, allowing them to enjoy their road trip.

The sun popped over the mountains and they all put their sunglasses on. Lots of wood fires and men lifting a finger off the steering wheels of their approaching pickup trucks as a greeting. An abundance of backwoods clichés: mobile homes with huge satellite dishes in the dirt yard, strip-mined mountainsides, oversize American flags outside shacks, squirrel hides nailed to the side of a barn.

The road got curvy the closer they got to the mountains. They passed the sign for Snapeville. Aiden told them to cut the stereo after Adam Ant finished belting out "Goody Two Shoes."

Dwayne DeVry was tossing a bag of trash into the Dumpster in back of the convenience store when they pulled into the parking lot. If he had any idea who was inside the car, he didn't let on. They sat and watched him for a couple of minutes. He walked the lot, picking up cigarette butts and candy wrappers, got a couple of cases of Styrofoam coffee cups from a storage unit, then headed back inside.

Aiden stuck his foot in the door.

"Nice, tidy place you got here, Mr. DeVry," Aiden said.

DeVry dropped the boxes and ran through the storage room. Aiden let him go, came inside, locked the door behind him.

Pat and Eddie were waiting for DeVry in the front of the store, Eddie blocking the exit, Pat flirting with the cute cashier, keeping her occupied so she couldn't see what was happening. Eddie cornered DeVry at the beer cooler, twisted his arm behind his back, and led him to the storage room. Pat paid for a pack of cigarettes, left the cashier with a wink.

Aiden was sitting in a metal folding chair at a table, arms behind his head as DeVry was led into the room. Pat laid the briefcase in front of him. Eddie shoved DeVry down hard into a chair across from his boss.

"Why are you so surprised to see me?" Aiden said. "Didn't I tell you I'd be here this morning?"

DeVry didn't answer, looked back and forth between Pat and Eddie.

"I'm a man of my word," Aiden said. "Unlike you. You want to try to settle this here and now, or you want to go for a ride in the country?"

"Hey, I just said I was *thinking* about dealing with the other bidder," DeVry said. "I didn't say I'd made up my mind to do it."

"Oh, so now I'm having to *bid* against someone, am I?" Aiden said. He opened the briefcase, unhurriedly got out the contract for sale his lawyers had prepared, took a fountain pen from his inside suit coat pocket, uncapped it, laid it on top of the papers.

"You can't just call me up out of the blue from Boston and demand I sell you my store," DeVry said. "Hell, what kind of a businessman would I be if I agreed to something like that without considering all my options? What makes you different from any other sharp-dressed salesman in a company car offering me the opportunity of a lifetime? Hey, I've got potato-chip brokers coming through that front door every week putting as much pressure on me as you. You wouldn't believe it. So I ask you like I ask them, what's in it for me? Where's the incentive? Where's the one free case with twelve?"

Aiden nodded reflectively. "Who you been talking to, Mr. DeVry? Your accountant? Some lawyer at Rotary?"

"I don't need anyone to tell me that if you're willing to rush down here and pay me two hundred and fifty thousand dollars and push this deal through in such a goddammed hurry that the place is worth a hell of a lot more."

"We had an agreement," Aiden said.

"I never signed anything."

"True. That's why I came here this morning. To expedite the process. I brought copies of the contract. I brought the pen. All we have to do is ride on over to the bank and get someone there to witness your signature and notarize it."

DeVry understood he had something of

value that Aiden wanted. He had foolishly decided not to let go. Upon immature reflection, he had decided that the two parties were bargaining from positions of equal power.

"Tell you what," Aiden said. "I'm going to do you a big favor. I'm going to buy this place from you, pay you some cash under the table, but I'm afraid I'm going to have to deduct ten percent as a hardship fee, and you're going to be happy to do it and trot off to the Sunshine State on the next plane out of here."

"What?"

"You're a dick. I always deduct ten percent when I have to deal with a dick."

DeVry pushed the papers back toward Aiden. "Fuck this shit." He stood up, but the hands of Pat and Eddie on his shoulders rammed him back into his seat.

Aiden sighed. He opened the briefcase, started taking out stacks of hundred-dollar bills, piling them onto the table. Then he took away a pile, handing it to Eddie. "My ten percent," he said.

"I ain't signing anything," DeVry said.

Aiden was unperturbed. "What was it you said when we talked on the phone the other day? Something about *getting things smoothed out at your end?* Yeah?"

DeVry looked at Aiden warily.

Aiden pulled a few bills from one of the stacks, formed them into a tight roll. Pat and Eddie held DeVry in place. Aiden took a hammer out of the briefcase, laid it on the table.

"It's just about impossible to get a gun through airport security these days, even when you fly chartered," Aiden said. "But nothing's stopping me from flying with a jar of Vaseline."

Next, he removed the jar from the briefcase and put on a pair of latex surgical gloves. He removed the lid, dipped the roll of hundred-dollar bills into the petroleum jelly, removed the oily bills, and held them in front of DeVry's face.

"Smooth enough for you? Stand up, Mr. DeVry."

DeVry froze. Pat and Eddie jerked him out of his seat.

"Drop 'em and bend over."

DeVry got panicky, finally realizing what was about to happen. Pat held his arms behind his back as Eddie yanked his trousers to his ankles and forced him to bend over. Eddie pushed DeVry's head down onto the table. DeVry's face was right in front of Aiden's.

"Pucker up your sphincter for Mr.

Franklin," Aiden said.

"Hey, hey!"

Aiden picked up the hammer. "You start signing, or I'll start hammering. Then we'll get things smoothed out at your end, all right. We'll find out how many hundreds you can take up your ass, you greedy piece of shit."

Aiden stood up and walked behind DeVry. Aiden put the slick roll up against the store owner's backside and DeVry bucked furiously, trying to free himself.

"Clenching won't help, DeVry."

"Okay, okay," DeVry said.

Pat let go of his arms. DeVry indignantly gathered up his trousers with one hand signed the documents, threw the pen down in disgust.

Aiden put the papers into the briefcase. "Thank you. We'll take care of getting this notarized; then I'll send you copies. You'll note that the contract requires vacant possession an hour ago."

DeVry finished fastening his trousers.

Aiden capped the pen, handed it to DeVry. "Keep it," he said. "To commemorate the occasion."

The three men from Boston put their sunglasses on and left through the front door.

# Chapter 14

The door to the cottage burst open, flooding the dark interior with sunlight. Maeve O'Driscoll stood in the doorway, looked for signs of life.

"Brendan!" she called out. "Lydia!" No one answered, nothing moved.

The cottage was a typical two-up, two-down, an old whitewashed stone farmhouse that Brendan and Lydia had been renovating over the past few years. Maeve ducked under the low door frame and stepped into a kitchen with an eating space. It was colder inside than out. She saw a woman's touch about the place: spices on the open kitchen shelves, hand lotion on the sink, decorative pottery in the windows. There was also ample evidence of a woman's absence: dirty dishes on the counter, a large number of empty whiskey and wine bottles on the floor around the base of an overflowing rubbish bin, wilted fuchsia in the vase on the dining table. The solid fuel stove was cold to her hand.

A calico cat came in through the open door, rubbed against Maeve's leg, then meowed loudly in front of the refrigerator. Maeve found the refrigerator empty, except for a carton of sour milk.

The disappointed cat pushed through the door to the other room. A battered fiddle case sat on the floor in the doorway, as if pointing to where its owner might be. Maeve followed.

The room was dark and stank of wet fireplace ashes and stale whiskey breath. The cat was walking on the back of the sofa over a lump beneath a coat. Brendan hadn't even made it upstairs. He was still wearing his shoes.

Maeve opened the curtains. The sitting room was just as cluttered as the kitchen. Stacks of old newspapers, ashtrays full of cigarettes, toys pushed over into one corner. On top of the heap was a child-size fiddle and bow.

"Get up, Brendan," Maeve said.

The lump stirred, but only to pull the coat up closer around his neck.

"Get up, you gobshite." She pulled the coat off him. "It's already noon and you're still sleeping off a drunk. You're a feckin' mess. Get yourself together."

Brendan O'Driscoll sat up on the edge of the sofa, wearing rumpled clothes from the previous night. He rubbed his blood-shot eyes, smoothed back his disheveled hair, ran a hand over a close-cropped graying beard while the other hand found a glass of whiskey on the floor.

She waited for him outside and smoked. The cottage was set in a sloping treeless area eight miles outside of town. It was a bleak but beautiful hill with a distant sea view. Close to shore, the sun was dazzling on the water's surface. Farther out, the sky and ocean merged green-gray on the edge of a massive storm front.

Brendan emerged looking even worse in broad daylight. Without saying anything he went into one of the outbuildings and returned with a bucket, slamming the door behind him. He let the chickens out into their yard, kicked at them a bit, and threw grain over the ground from the bucket.

"I hate Lydia's feckin' chickens," he said. He threw the grain harder, slung the entire contents of the bucket, then bashed it against the side of the henhouse. He squatted on the ground, buried his face in his hands, and wept.

197

"I warned you to keep her under control. Where is she?"

"I don't know. She left and took Daniel with her over a week ago. I haven't heard a word since then."

"Jesus, why didn't you tell me?" Maeve said crossly.

"I was afraid to."

Maeve flicked her cigarette butt to the ground. A chicken pecked at it, ran away with its prize. "Didn't you tell her she can't just quit us like that?"

"I told her everything you and I talked about. You know Lydia. She's always had a mind of her own. What you said just made things worse."

"I think she's gone and done something really stupid," Maeve said. "I just found out she approached the police. It must have been after you talked to her."

"Oh, God. How do you know she did that?"

"You know a lot, Brendan, but you don't know everything."

He stood up, shaking his head. "She threatened to start talking about everything she knew if I didn't let her go. She was desperate, fed up living a life with an O'Driscoll. She didn't want Daniel growing up in a crime family. It was either

I leave with her or she was taking Daniel without me. I left one night for a session at the pub, and she was gone when I came back home."

"I'm not sure you were as forceful as you needed to be."

"No, Maeve, really. I pleaded with her. I begged her. I didn't believe she'd do it. I can't believe she took our son." He hung his head, tipped the bucket upright with his foot.

"She's put herself in a great deal of danger."

"What did she tell the police?"

"I don't know. Apparently she was trying to set up a meeting with a detective in Dublin. I can only imagine what for. Rightly so, she didn't trust the local police."

Maeve decided it was better not to let Brendan know anything else until she had had a chance to talk to Noreen.

"Do you have any idea where she is?" Maeve said.

"She took some cash we had around here. I checked with the bank, and our account there hasn't been touched. We don't have credit cards, so she can't have gone very far. I know she wanted to go back to England, but there's no way she could have made it. The first place I thought of was her mother's flat in Dublin, but I never got an answer when I phoned there. I just assumed she'd be back in a few days." His eyes welled up. "Maeve, I miss her. I miss my boy."

He was a long way from being sober. "So why didn't you leave with her?" Maeve asked.

Maeve followed Brendan into the henhouse. He started filling a used egg carton with eggs the hens had laid.

"What am I supposed to do?" Brenda said. "You think a fiddler can make a living playing sessions in the pub a couple nights a week and giving group lessons to schoolkids? I have two people to support. At worst, I figured I could send Lydia money if I had to. If it were just me I'd barely survive. I'm in no position to walk away from the family business."

"I'm glad to hear that. I wouldn't want to lose you either. You perform a very valuable service to the organization. Especially if you can stay reasonably sober."

"It's just this week, Maeve. It's been hard. You have my word I won't let it become a problem like it did before."

Brendan led them back outside. As they walked to the front of the cottage, a wall of wind knocked them hard. Maeve looked to the sea and felt herself sinking. If Liam had been able to take over the ship, he was somewhere out there. There were so many things happening all at the same time, so many lethal pitfalls threatening to destroy everything that she valued. All she could do was keep moving ahead, addressing each problem in turn.

"I've been thinking. There's a job I need you to do."

The clouds had moved in very quickly. Suddenly the sky burst open. They moved to the shelter of an open stone cowshed, voices raised slightly against the sound of rain pounding on the corrugated metal roof.

"What is it?" he said.

"We were almost ruined by someone informing on us about that last shipment on the beach, but we took care of that. I think we've got a much more serious problem now. You teach Noel Hennessy's kids, don't you?"

Brendan was perplexed. "The garda?"

"Yes."

"Yeah, I teach them, why?"

"He's ours. We bought him last year. I suspect he may lose his nerve and turn on us soon, and we can't let that happen. We need to do something quickly, before Noreen returns."

"What do you need me to do?" Brendan said apprehensively.

"He's going to be extra cautious about letting anyone get close to him. He and his wife know you. They don't know you're involved with me. They think you're just a fiddle player, right?"

"Yes."

"All I need you to do is set up a scenario so he lets his guard down long enough for a couple of the lads to get close to him."

Brendan was hesitant.

"This will help Lydia," Maeve said. She knew it was a lie. "He knows too much, and Lydia could get sucked in, in ways she never imagined. Who knows, she might even be implicated if we all go under. If she has qualms about you being involved in the business, she'd be mortified to be led away in handcuffs herself. What would happen to Daniel? I don't think you want to take that chance."

"No." After some reflection: "Maeve, I've always been on the periphery. I've never had to take anyone out before."

"Don't worry; you don't have to actually do anything. It'll be quick and simple. Easy-peasy."

"Easy-peasy," Brendan repeated. He drew a breath. "I'm doing it for Lydia and Daniel, okay?"

"This is the Republic of Ireland, Father Michael, not the United States," Chief Superintendent Charlie Brady was saying. "We can arrest and detain you for questioning without charging you for up to six hours and I can personally authorize another six hours if I want to. We don't need probable cause. All we need is probable hunch. Of course, we can rearrest you, as necessary, anytime any new scrap of evidence comes our way. Or, legal counsel advises me, we can place you in indefinite protective custody. It wouldn't be hard to make a case that someone is out to get you, Father. You see, we have options."

Michael sat bandaged at a table in an interrogation room at Dublin Garda District Headquarters on Harcourt Street. On one side of him sat Brady, on the other Claire Burke.

"I'll do whatever I have to do to find Lydia's killer," Michael said. "If my being here and answering your questions will help, then I'm happy to do it, though I've told you everything I know already."

Brady emptied the contents of the

FedEx envelope onto the table. "What about the inquiries to his past employers?" he asked Claire.

Claire reviewed her notes. "The Tucson diocese confirmed his graduation from seminary and subsequent employment. I spoke to the bishop myself. He had only highly positive things to say."

Michael lowered his head, closed his eyes. He could see the look on Bishop Ferdinand's face when he had received the phone call from the Dublin police informing him of his involvement in Lydia's murder investigation.

"But now we have a surprise package from the Boston Police Department."

Michael tried catching Claire's eye, but she refused to look at him. It was apparent that she had read the report in the FedEx envelope.

"Very, *very* impressive," Brady said, reading the cover letter attached to a stack of documents. "I didn't realize you come from such an illustrious family, Father. Perhaps we don't always follow the American regional news the way we should. Does this look familiar to you?"

Brady showed him mug shots. The defiant man was nothing like the sickly father he had last seen. "As a courtesy, the

Boston Police Department has sent along information on your family, as well as yourself. Brian Driscoll. Served twenty-four months of a six-year sentence for running illegal bookmaking operations. Again another year served for receiving stolen goods from a series of warehouse burglaries. And a brief stint for assault and battery in connection with beating up a loan shark. Also indicted for attempting to affect the outcome of various horse races, but the all the witnesses mysteriously disappeared so the case had to be dropped. The Feds nailed him on tax evasion and he did another year for that. Apparently he got out of the business just before the government could prosecute him under the racketeering statutes; otherwise he'd still be in jail."

Michael sat stoically listening to Brady read from the Boston Police Department's report. Each new paragraph was a stab at his family pride.

"Your brother Aiden has rather a fiery temper, doesn't he, Father?" Brady showed him another mug shot, this one of a youthful Aiden sneering at the camera. "Virtually demolished a bar and smashed the face of a nightclub bouncer. He pleaded that one down and got probation, but then got himself caught beating up some young woman's ex-boyfriend. That cost him three months. I see the last date of his arrest was seven years ago, before he went to college. Ah, well, perhaps he has reformed. Or, in theological terms, at least been redeemed.

"Now this other brother, Kevin. He's the lucky one, I'd say. Four arrests for various violent acts, but no convictions. Again, it's hard to prosecute a case when the witnesses suddenly get a case of the stupids and can't recall what happened, or suddenly end up as part of the flotsam in Boston Harbor. A dysfunctional family if ever I did see one. No wonder you got the hell out of Boston."

"Brady," Michael said, "in nontheological terms, you're a prick."

"I don't believe I've ever heard a priest use that word before in that context." He was flipping pages, skimming. "Now, let's see. Yes, yes, yes. Now we're coming to the really interesting bit. Not in a sensational way, of course, but relevant to our present investigation."

Brady took a few moments to read the pages to himself. He tried catching Claire's eye when he finished, but she was staring vacantly at the floor.

Brady flipped back a few pages and read aloud: " 'Lt. Michael Driscoll, Detective, Special Investigations Division. Last assignment, prior to suspension, liaison officer with FBI's organized crime unit, Boston office.' " Brady threw a photo onto the middle of the table of Michael in his police uniform. " 'Lieutenant Driscoll was subject to internal investigation relating to the death of fellow undercover officer Clarence Darby. Due to sensitivity of the evidence and individuals involved, responsibility for investigation subsequently assumed by Office of the Attorney General, State of Massachusetts. Conclusion: Although the department's internal inspector general's report found evidence confirming the allegation that Driscoll alerted organized crime figures in his own family as to Officer Darby's identity as a police department plant in the Driscoll family criminal enterprise, thus resulting in Officer Darby's death by an alleged member of the same organization, the attorney general's office determined the evidence to be inconclusive and declined prosecution. Lieutenant Driscoll elected to take early retirement, without prejudice. Pensionable.' "

Brady threw the report in front of Claire,

addressed Michael. "These findings are purportedly, officially, conclusive, but to me still seem rather ambiguous. So did you or didn't you tip off your own crime family to the existence of a police plant in their midst?"

"The attorney general's office was completely correct," Michael said. "There was a vendetta against me once certain people higher up discovered who my family was. Then I became an easy scapegoat to cover up an especially bad instance of managerial incompetence. Clarence Darby didn't die because I tipped anyone off. He died because a drunken police commissioner was shooting his mouth off at a bar one night and bragged about having someone on the inside of a major . . ."

"Go ahead and say it, Father. 'Crime family.' *Your* family."

"My mother was no criminal, Brady," he said bitterly. "I don't dispute that some of my family were involved in criminal activities. I certainly don't approve of it. But I was never a part of it. The fact that I happen to be the son and brother of two people who went to jail has no bearing whatsoever on the murder investigation."

"What are we supposed to think? You rush over here after getting a phone call from a woman obviously mixed up in drugs, and now we learn that you are from a major East Coast crime family. The circumstantial evidence is beginning to mount up, or at least cause us to start looking more closely at this man who appears to be closer to the heart of the crime than he cares to admit. Anything else you want to tell us about, Father?"

Michael looked at Claire. Her face said nothing. He thought he had lost her.

"I believe him, Charlie," she said. "My gut tells me he didn't kill Lydia or Daniel. I see no reason to detain him."

"Thank you," Michael said.

Brady snapped, "I don't think it's such a good idea to be discussing legal strategy in front of an interviewee. I'd strongly advice him to seek legal counsel, but I'd prefer it not be someone from inside my own department."

"I don't need legal counsel, Brady. I have nothing to hide, and I'm willing to talk to you or anyone else and help in any way I can."

Brady ignored him and talked to Claire. "From what I've seen today, it's obvious to me that you lack enough detachment from this *suspect* to continue as the chief investigator in this case. Take him downstairs. Photograph him, measure him, fingerprint him; I already have the proper authorizations. Then turn over your notes to me. This case is being reassigned."

# Chapter 15

"We know Daniel was here because we found this in his pocket."

Michael and Claire stood on the ground floor of a Victorian menagerie, a vast room filled with glass cases of stuffed mammals and sea creatures.

Claire opened the palm of her hand to reveal a small rubber monkey. "Just the kind of silly thing a five-year-old boy would pick out for himself," she said.

Michael turned it over. The label on the bottom read *Irish Natural History Museum.*

"The clerk at the gift shop confirmed that Lydia bought it for him the day she was murdered," she said.

Michael took the toy, cupped it gently in his hand. Daniel — Lydia's son — his own son with her had held the same toy in the same place only days earlier. He imagined how it must have filled the small boy's hand.

They walked beneath a stuffed basking shark suspended from the ceiling. The wooden floor creaked. Michael wore his coat over his shoulders. The doctor told him it would be at least another day before the pain from the puncture wounds would allow him to put his arms through the sleeves.

"We now know that they left here together in the late afternoon," Claire said. "Interviewing people working in the businesses up and down the surrounding streets, we discovered, however, that at some point he and Lydia became separated. Daniel was seen by a waiter at an outdoor café on Kildare Street being led off in the direction of the university in the company of two men. After that, we lost the trail."

Michael nodded appreciatively. "I apologize. You *have* been working the case."

"I can only imagine how difficult this is for you."

High school students were scattered throughout the museum, sitting on the floor in front of display cases, drawing tablets on their knees, charcoal in their hands. At the back of the gallery was a section devoted to ocean life. Michael and Claire unobtrusively watched a girl turn her pad so she could shade the underside of a nautilus.

"The latest theory we were working on was that Daniel was somehow lured away from Lydia while they were out that day, then used as bait to draw her out of hiding."

"Why didn't you tell me this earlier?"

"Michael, I couldn't. I was the investigator and you were the suspect."

"Now you aren't the investigator and I'm no longer a suspect?" He didn't expect a reply. "Go on."

"We were working on the assumption that they were both in her flat when the attackers came there. I've had a hunch, though. I think they were staying somewhere else, and Daniel was taken to her flat first as bait for Lydia. We found signs that the lock had been picked."

"Which means that whoever Lydia killed knew about the existence of the flat."

"And, therefore, must have had some personal knowledge of Lydia," Claire said. "That's why Brady was pumping you so hard about your knowledge of Lydia's personal life. On the surface of it, the case can convincingly be made that you are a prime suspect."

"Except that she was killed before I even

got to Dublin. Remember?"

"There are dozens of ways you could have slipped in the day before, then flown back to the States before you caught your flight into Dublin. The bishop and your housekeeper can vouch for you only up to a certain point. Your whereabouts aren't adequately accounted for over the crucial twenty-four-hour period prior to your getting on that plane in Tucson."

They climbed the stairs to the next floor, a room lit by a frosted-glass ceiling. An enormous fin whale from West Cork dominated the air above them. They walked farther up to the first of two mezzanines overlooking the heads of great horned beasts hung on the wall over display cases. An art teacher squatted down, directed a student shading the neck of a pheasant with a green pencil.

"I thought you believed I wasn't involved?" Michael said.

"I still think that. Listen, I'm just telling you how it looks from the outside. To be honest, my opinion is based on my gut instincts, not the facts."

Michael stopped, irritated. "Perhaps Brady was right in taking you off the case."

"It's to your own advantage, Michael. Don't you see how it frees me up? I can be of more help to you now that I'm no longer taking direction from Brady on how to pursue the case. That's why I wanted to get you out of the office. I needed to talk to you alone, and we couldn't do that at headquarters."

"How much more of Brady am I going to have to take?"

"Unfortunately, he'll keep trying to wear you down, keep hauling you in for more questioning. If he decides he has enough evidence, he won't let you walk like he did this morning. The fingerprinting today was all about humiliation, the process of breaking you. Same with the arrest."

"I guess now I really am one of the family. My very own arrest record. Fingerprints and mug shots."

"At least you weren't wearing your clerical collar."

They finished walking the perimeter of the floor and took a flight of steps to the narrow mezzanine on the third level. There was barely enough room for them to walk side by side. Glass models of basic lifeforms. Michael lifted pieces of canvas covering wooden frames. Underneath, sponges, jellyfish, fluke worms, round worms, bristle worms. Bugs on stickpins under glass.

"Why has there been no mention of her murder in the press?" Michael asked.

Claire looked around to see if anyone was within earshot. A lone security guard on the other side of the mezzanine watched them, but was too far away to hear. "Now that I'm no longer on the case, I can tell you," she said. "It all goes back to the heroin found in Lydia's flat."

"Yes?"

"The lab analyzed it and found it to be uncut. That was surprising, considering it was such a small amount. Not surprisingly, though, it matched exactly the heroin coming from the country's biggest distributor. No one in this part of the country should have his hands on anything that pure. Stuff like that comes only from outside the city, up from the south. Brady is afraid that if there's media coverage, the press will somehow find out what we know about the heroin in Lydia's flat and the importers will be tipped off. He's stalking bigger quarry than some spotty-faced dealer, or even a Dublin distributor. He aims to put the gang that's bringing about ninety percent of the heroin imported into the country out of business for good. By investigating Lydia's background and tracing her connections he thinks he can move to the heart of the heroin gang."

Michael lifted more canvas squares over displays as he walked through the gallery, giving him time to turn over the clues Claire had handed him so far. Most of it he had figured out himself. Someone close to Lydia had killed her, most likely someone connected with a heroin importer. The finding that Daniel was used to lure her to the apartment wasn't news. As was the fact that the drugs were from somewhere outside Dublin.

"I'll tell you where Brady is taking the interrogation. He sees you as a link to the gang, through Lydia."

"I don't follow you."

"The heroin gang is in West Cork." She stopped and watched his reaction closely. "Beginning to sound familiar?"

"No."

"The O'Driscolls. Tomorrow he's going to start pumping you for information about your West Cork cousins. Michael, he knows who they are. You've got major criminal connections both sides of the Atlantic. Charlie Brady is the master of deception; don't ever forget that. You don't get to his level without at least a few people calling you a son of a bitch. He doesn't really care if you killed Lydia. But he's going to play you as if you did, hoping to sweat some details that will allow him to move closer to the drug barons."

"Brady will be very disappointed. I don't know anything about what they do down in West Cork."

That much was completely true. There had been hints as to what their business was, but during his high school years when he visited them in the summers it seemed never to encompass more than a loose organization engaged in a bit of ducking and diving, petty crime in the local area. Later, there were rumors of armed heists, hijackings of trucks offloading container ships in Cork City. The O'Driscolls had extensive contacts in the shipping industry through their fishing business and could easily have found out which containers held valuable merchandise that could be stashed in secret warehouses until it could be sold in the big working-class estates in the city.

"He thinks they are involved in the murder?"

"It looks like in-family fighting to him. He thinks the pressure we've been bringing on them is beginning to yield results."

Michael said angrily, "How long have you known about the West Cork connection?"

"A few days."

"Is a woman being murdered and her child missing the kind of *results* you're proud of?"

Michael stormed off toward the stairs, followed closely by Claire.

"Michael," she said as they headed back down. "It's ridiculous to think I could give you confidential information on an investigation. You were a detective once. You should know."

He turned quickly on her on the steps. "I'm seeing things clearly now. You've been messing with me. You don't care anything about solving Lydia's murder. All you want is information from me that you can use to nail the O'Driscolls." He hurried down the staircase.

"That's not true," Claire said on his heels. "Maybe that's what Brady wants, but not me. You know I've been helping you. To the point that I got myself thrown off the case. Stop," she said. "Will you stop a moment?"

They were back on the ground floor. "What?" he snapped.

"Maybe I made a mistake and got too close to you, okay? You're going to have to trust me, Michael. Now that I'm no longer under Brady's thumb I can work both sides of this. I'll make sure Lydia's killer is caught and punished. Give me some credit, okay? I clued you in as to what Brady's up to. Just play along with him, stall for time, and let me handle things through the back channels. Stay away from the investigation. You just about got yourself killed trying to go it on your own. I care, goddammit; can't you see that?"

Back where they began, Michael stood in front of the museum gift shop, studying her flushed face. She was looking small and vulnerable, like when they had lain together on the bed in his room. She was either the world's best liar, or falling in love with him. He was satisfied he knew which.

Michael squeezed the toy he had been carrying around with him inside his fist, thought maybe it had given his son a small measure of comfort as he had been led away.

On their way out, they passed a gibbon monkey, standing erect in wired rictus. Their footfalls shook the wooden floor, rattling the display. The monkey's bared teeth chattered as if he were alive and mocking.

Michael and Claire walked outside the station together. On the steps, her cell phone rang. She listened, told the person she'd be there right away. "You're going to have to take a taxi or bus back to your place. I have to go."

"Everything okay?"

"I just need you to go to the B-and-B and wait for me."

Michael felt that the phone call had somehow involved himself. "Does it concern me?"

Claire had already strapped on her helmet. She threw a leg over the motorcycle. "Michael, go and wait."

"What's so urgent?" A disturbing thought passed through his mind. "It's Daniel, isn't it?"

Claire turned the ignition, revved the engine, and was about to speed off. Michael grabbed on to her jacket.

"You're not going without me."

"Damn it, Michael!" Her shoulders heaved. "All right, climb on."

The motorcycle was flashy and it was fast. She gripped the machine tightly with her legs and leaned down low. He held on to her waist as she weaved in and out of Dublin rush-hour traffic, riding up between two lanes of cars halted at stoplights, darting through intersections, cutting up small side streets. When a large Guinness truck blocked her way in front of a pub, she took the sidewalk to get around.

"Where are we going?" Michael asked again. He knew they were generally heading in the direction of the city center, not too far from Lydia's flat, but he was unfamiliar with the exact back roads she was taking.

"Almost there," she said.

Rounding a sudden sharp corner off a busy commercial street, the motorcycle leaned heavily, and he held on to her tighter. He saw the sign for a dead end as a blur. She accelerated toward a half dozen police cars and an ambulance filling the cul de sac.

"Wait here," Claire told him as they dismounted.

"The hell I am," he said.

"I'm only trying to spare you needless worry. Please stay here," she said firmly.

She joined a group of uniformed police officers gathered around a large paper-recycling Dumpster near the back bay door of a department store. Even with a clear blue sky above, the surrounding buildings blocked the sunlight and made the alley gloomy and cold. Tenants and workers leaned outside windows to see what was happening in the street below.

A powerful camera flash filled the shadows of the alley, turning Michael's trembling hands silver-white, the pupils of his eyes to hard pinpoints.

Michael took a few steps closer, trying to hear Claire talking to the police officers; he saw her body stiffen, her face harden. She was helped to the top of the Dumpster, where the photographer was standing, shooting downward. More photographs into the abyss. She nodded to the paramedics, their gurney already assembled in front of the ambulance. Claire directed the officers to help.

Michael was already at the base of the Dumpster when Claire ordered that the scene be sealed off until the technical examination team could sift for clues. From a heap of flattened cardboard boxes, a dozen pairs of hands sheathed in latex carefully lifted the body of a child onto a gurney.

Thick tufted streamers of colorful shredded packing paper clung to the hair, became entangled in tiny rigid fingers.

"We can't be sure," Claire warned Michael.

"Get out of my way."

Michael pushed through the police to be with the child on the gurney. The paramedic gently pulled the thin paper strips from the face. It was a boy, blue in the face, eyes and lips delicately closed. The head seemed at a peculiar angle, as if the neck might have been broken. Michael looked closely at the dark hair. The chin. The eyebrows. The distinctive cheekbones. He looked nothing like Lydia, everything like an O'Driscoll.

"It's Danny," Michael said. He made the sign of the cross, motioned as if he were going to touch the boy, but Claire stopped his hand midmotion.

"Don't," she said. "You don't want to contaminate the evidence."

The paramedics started to move the body.

"Wait!" Michael said loudly. He pulled from his inside coat pocket a prayer book.

"Wait for a priest," a voice said.

"I *am* a priest," Michael said.

Michael held his hand just over the boy's head and read the last rites.

Michael withdrew and bowed his head, caught himself checking a sob as the child was loaded into the back of the ambulance.

Claire looked back and forth between Michael and the dead boy, but said nothing.

The ambulance left without a siren. Michael sat on the curb with his head buried in his hands as Claire finished talking on her mobile phone out of earshot.

She sat down beside him. "That was an interesting bit of news," she said dully.

"What?"

"I didn't want to say until I was absolutely certain, but it confirms an earlier suspicion of mine. The lab just reported that there was no trace of heroin found in Lydia's body."

Michael sat up. "What about the track marks on her arm?"

"Oh, they found even more injection sites. Not just on her arm, but on her thigh, mainly on her thigh, actually."

Michael thought back to his days as a street cop. "So what? Sometimes users inject there so other people can't see they're shooting up."

"The first clue was that she wasn't mainlining, not injecting into a vein. All the shots were into the subcutaneous fat. Injections there, especially in the thigh, are where someone would inject herself if she wanted a slow release of a drug. Opposite what addicts crave. The forensic team didn't find any corroborating evidence at the crime scene, but I knew as soon as I saw a copy of her medical records I'd ordered faxed from her doctor in Skibbereen. She was a type-one diabetic."

"How could that be? There was never

any indication of that when we were together. I would have known."

"Apparently it started out as gestational diabetes, when she was expecting Daniel. It's fairly common. Then later it developed into type one and never resolved. It's not very common when it progresses like that, but it does happen."

"So the heroin found in her flat . . ." Michael wanted to compare the police read on that subject.

"Planted, I'd say. And by someone who knew her fairly well. Knew they might just get away with making it look as if she had a heroin problem."

"And was in over her head with a dealer," Michael added. "Well, obviously whoever killed her had some drug connection."

Michael's old detective instincts kicked in. *Think like a criminal.* Everyone knew someone. Connections. Linkage. Who did *he* know in Dublin?

Claire drew a breath. "I don't want you going off and doing something stupid, just to try to prove that you aren't the killer."

"Difficult proving a negative."

"You should know that Brady is beginning to question whether or not you should still be considered the top suspect in Lydia's murder."

"Oh?"

"Your DNA sample was no match for any evidence found on Lydia's body."

Michael was confused. "I don't recall ever giving a DNA sample."

"I'm afraid it's yet another instance of my boss's feigned uninterest in you as a suspect to put you off your guard. I want you to believe me when I tell you I knew nothing of this."

"Tell me."

"The glass of water he offered you during your talk . . ."

"It was an interrogation, not a talk."

"He gave it to the lab afterward and they took a saliva sample from it. When he helped you with your coat back on, and brushed the lint from your lapels and shoulders, he was taking hair samples. He was just pretending that he thought it was a mere drug-related crime."

"And now he doesn't have a priest who killed his lover. Imagine what the tabloid headlines could have been. But it's back to a *mere* drug-related crime. How unsexy. How unlikely to attract any media attention to himself. How unworthy of his time. How about you? Is it worthy of *your* time?"

"I can push only so far without his sanction. You know I want to find their killer. Perhaps since there's a child dead now, I'll be able to have more resources assigned to the case."

"Perhaps," Michael echoed bitterly.

Claire saw his anger and laid her hand on his arm to comfort him, but Michael pulled back angrily.

"Taking another sample?" he said.

Michael felt violated. Not only was he a suspect in the murder of a woman he had loved and left his parish for, but the police were playing games with him, taking samples without his consent or knowledge. His mind was filled with profanities the likes of which hadn't crossed his mind in years.

"I see it on your face," Claire said. "Don't say what you're thinking. It isn't becoming of a priest."

"How about of a *man* — a man who has just lost the only woman he's ever truly loved?" he shouted. "How about of a man who has just seen that woman's baby pulled from a Dumpster?"

"I understand," she said calmly. "You need some time alone."

*You're dammed right I need some time alone.*

But he wisely kept his own counsel and let her ride off without him.

# Chapter 16

Declan O'Driscoll's office on the seventy-eighth floor of the Nash Building had an unobstructed view down Forty-second Street. The lines of the broad avenue intersected in a dusky vanishing point of taxi brakelights and neon signs.

The information technology department of Whitehall-Cogburn was an open, contemporary design, organized around a large central fluted column, a postmodern IT god rising up from the center of the room to the ceiling, cleverly hiding wires and cables from the rows of computer workstations. Declan sat in comfortable anonymity among two dozen other programmers sipping Diet Cokes and coffee as they toiled over accounting software problems.

He pushed aside a Styrofoam box, the remains of a greasy chicken vindaloo. Lunch was still unsettled in his stomach two hours afterward. Breathing fire, he swore again he'd never go back to the takeout across the street, but he was addicted to their curry sauce. Another week and he'd forget all about that queasy feeling.

He gazed out the window down at the flashing lights running in circles around the sign of the Indian restaurant across the street. They looped endlessly, like the error in the computer program he had been deconstructing all day.

The company receptionist buzzed him. He had visitors in the main lobby.

Two sharply dressed men greeted him as he exited the elevator, introduced themselves as Eddie Martin and Pat Hannity. Aiden Driscoll had sent them to pick him up.

Declan led them to a corner. "Guys," he said. "I can't just blow out of here in the middle of a business day."

"Oh, yeah, you can," Eddie said. "We've got a private jet waiting for you at LaGuardia."

"I've got books, files, CDs, notes I need back at the apartment."

Eddie stared at him. Pat scanned the lobby to see if anyone was watching.

"Plus," Declan said pointedly, "tonight's my laundry night."

"We'll drive you to your place to pick up your things. Let's go. Now."

Declan could see they lacked a fundamental sense of humor. "Lead on."

Aiden Driscoll eased back into his seat and dialed a number on the Gulf stream's telephone. Noreen answered.

"I want you to know I am personally delivering Declan to West Virginia," he said. "I concluded negotiation for the store today. I'll see Declan gets set up; then Kevin will come down to oversee the operation until we are ready to push the button. I have to get back to Boston to wrap up another deal there. Everyone happy with that?"

Noreen had been waiting in Boston at a hotel near Logan International Airport. She had vowed not to leave the city until Aiden had delivered on his promise.

"Very," she said. "Thanks a million, cousin."

"Go home," Aiden said. "I don't want anyone discovering you are anywhere near us, or what's going down in West Virginia."

"I'm flying out this evening," Noreen said. "Kisses."

Aiden hung up. Sitting across from him, Declan quietly read a computer magazine and ate peanuts. Pat and Eddie sat on the other side of the plane.

"What do you need?" Aiden asked Declan.

Declan didn't look up. "A couple of personal computers, the fastest, most powerful you can get. Printers, miscellaneous electrical supplies, cables, the kind of stuff we pick up at a Radio Shack. Better get three or four TVs. It's essential I have reliable, high-speed Internet access. Case of beer. That ought to do it. For now."

"There's plenty of beer where you're going," Aiden said.

Pat Hannity said, "I'll take care of everything else, boss."

Aiden scrutinized his youthful cousin slouched in the seat across from him, his feet propped up against the side of the cabin wall. An unlikely candidate for boy genius if he ever did see one. Hard to believe he had thought up the scheme they had just embarked upon. True, it was Noreen O'Driscoll who had understood the significance of the idea when Declan had been talking about his work over a beer, and all the vulnerabilities he saw in his role as an auditor of state government computerized accounting practices. And it had been up to Aiden to determine that the proper access could be had. But every-thing would come down to whether Declan could really execute what he had promised was theoretically possible.

Declan was not oblivious to Aiden's scrutiny. "Don't worry," he said casually, without peering over the top of the maga-zine. "I know what I'm doing."

Claire had departed on foot for her of-fice after leaving Michael on the steps of the museum, declaring she wanted to brief the person taking over Lydia and Daniel's case so her successor could get started without delay. Michael agreed to her offer to pick him up the next morning for his next interview with Brady. He showed her the prescription for painkillers he was told he should fill as soon as possible. She made him promise he would return to his room to get a full night's sleep. He watched her walk out the gate and down the street in the direction of police head-quarters.

Michael crumpled the prescription and threw it into a trash bin as soon as she was out of sight. The last thing he needed now was to be moving through the fog of pain-killers.

Drawing upon his undercover-detective

skills, he followed her at a safe distance, observed her from the opposite side of the street, making use of doorways and the crowded sidewalks to hide himself as she stopped and looked in his direction before crossing streets. Curiously, she crossed, then recrossed at several points along her route, as if she were trying to throw someone off her trail. Heading toward Grafton Street, she passed the Nubian statues guarding the main entrance to the Shelbourne Hotel. At the corner of the building, rather than continuing toward her office, in a move that almost lost him, she abruptly turned down a side street. He sprinted to see where she had gone, just in time to see her quickly ducking into the side door of the hotel.

Michael waited across the street for a minute, trying to decide what to do. Several people in waiter uniforms entered what looked to be an employee entrance. Just as a waiter inside was closing the curtains against the dusk, Michael saw Charlie Brady seated at the bar, standing to welcome Claire with a broad grin.

With a considerable amount of pain, Michael put his coat on and primped in the dark glass of a shop front. He figured he was just far enough on the other side of scruffiness to prevent being denied admission to the swank landmark hotel.

He assumed a look of unchallengeable confidence, entered through the main doors and cautiously walked past the front desk and dining room. He had been in the hotel many times before and knew the layout well. Down the corridor on his left was a sign for the Shelbourne Bar. That was where he needed to be. She had lied to him. He had to find out what the hell she could possibly be telling a man whom only ten minutes earlier she had denigrated as a deceptive son of a bitch.

He took a step down the hall, then stopped. He'd learn nothing by confronting them. He needed answers, not satisfaction.

He retraced his steps back outside around the corner of the building. Filing in with more of the waitstaff, he entered through the employee entrance.

Someone had left some clothes in the men's changing room. He found a pair of glasses on the bench. A knotted black tie on a doorknob. There was a waiter's black jacket hanging up. It just about fit. Michael wet his hands, slicked his hair back. It was the best he could do.

To the kitchen, avoiding anyone's eyes. A

waiter pushed through the door, affording Michael a glimpse of the room filled with the after-work crowd.

"Take those," someone rushing by directed, pointing to a tray of glasses just taken from the dishwasher.

Michael took the tray and pushed the door to the Shelbourne Bar open with his hip.

The door from the kitchen led to the space behind the bar. Michael kept his back to the room as he unloaded the glasses from the tray onto the counter in front of a mirror that spanned the wall. He began wiping the glasses dry, then set them upside down on a rubber mat ready for the bartenders to use. From his position he could easily watch Claire and Brady talking at the other end of the bar. He could make out the timbre of Claire's voice over the buzz in the bar, but couldn't hear what she was saying.

Brady nodded seriously, but looked pleased. Claire spoke rapidly, her face and hands animated. He had to get closer to find out what they were talking about.

He slowly worked his way closer to them, his back always facing the couple sitting on bar stools. He took a quick look around. So far no one from the hotel had questioned his presence, but that wouldn't last for very long. He kept busy wiping down the counter, straightening the condiments and utensils, inching to within ten feet of where they sat.

He could almost read their lips now in the mirror. He had to take a chance. He slid a few feet closer. He picked up a paring knife and began cutting lemon wedges. They were directly behind his back. He could hear everything they were saying.

"Hero's not too strong a word," Brady was saying. "At the very least, there's a promotion in it for you and me. This could be my elevation to Assistant Commissioner. The main thing is, we can't have him screwing things up for us. We have even greater successes ahead of us. Do you think he suspected anything?"

Claire finished sipping a glass of wine. "Nothing, not a thing. I'm sure he doubted my sincerity, but after that ruse about kicking me off the case, he bought it all."

"You didn't have to sleep with him, did you?"

"Jaysus! The last thing I need is another lover! Especially some man who hasn't made love for several years. I have to draw the line somewhere, Brady."

Brady laughed. "I'm not sure I feel comfortable being put into the same category of lover as a priest. Or perhaps you changed your mind? You were thinking maybe we'd spend the night together upstairs? Frankly, if I had known this, I'd have booked us into someplace a bit more . . . economical."

"Feck off, Brady, you cheap bastard. Either way, the answer's still no. It'll always be no." She rolled her eyes, laughed.

Claire finished her glass of wine and slid it toward the back of the bar. "Well, it's not like he didn't do it."

"Of course he did it." Brady took a long drink of lager, drained his glass. "You know what's better than forensics, or even witnesses? A suspect who committed the crime. Once you know you have the right man, the truth will come out eventually. Evidence will percolate to the top. I'd rather have the murderer sweating it out in jail than all the DNA and eyewitness evidence in the world and no living being."

Claire nodded. "Speaking of which, we can't take the chance of him being on the loose another day. I told him to put up with you a bit more, but he's not going to take being jerked around indefinitely. When's that file going to be ready to hand to the Director of Public Prosecutions?"

"Midmorning, latest."

"Good. I didn't take any chances of his not showing up. I got him to let me bring him in myself. Tomorrow when he's here for an interview, rearrest him. This time not just for questioning."

"Agreed, totally."

"Then we can move on to even bigger stuff down in West Cork."

"Much."

They clinked glasses.

Michael felt hot with anger. Even though he had never completely trusted her, she had played upon his emotions, his sensitivity about finding Lydia and Daniel's killer. The worst part was that if they truly believed he was the murderer, they would stop putting resources into finding out who the true killer was. Added to that, they were going to arrest him, and charge him with murder.

Brady added, "We need to charge him in the murders and make sure he's not bailed. After we give the DPP our file showing he's from an established crime family with connections on both sides of the Atlantic, there won't be any question of his getting out and skipping the country."

Michael saw all his options slipping

away. He'd never be able to continue the search for the real culprit.

"Excuse me, could we order another drink?"

Michael froze.

"Excuse me . . ." It was Brady, talking to *him*.

He kept his head down, looking at the counter, flicked his eyes up once to the mirror. In that brief instant Claire saw him. Startled recognition was on her face. It was her gasp he heard.

A fast walk back to the kitchen became a run. Brady was short but quick. Michael heard a stool tipping over, and knew that Brady was scrambling over the bar.

He knew his way back out through the kitchen better than Brady, running through the employee room and out the back door. He tore off the jacket, flinging the glasses and tie as he ran. He ran across the path of a city bus, leaving the chief inspector looking desperately for where he had fled.

As he scrambled down the sidewalk, losing himself in the crowds on Grafton Street, he silently cursed himself for almost being suckered into believing the detective. He also cursed *her*, for thinking she could take advantage of some weakness that was consequent to his being a priest. Just because she was a woman and he had wed the church, she thought he would lack the clarity to see through her ploy.

*She was wrong, wrong, wrong,* he said to himself, pumping his arms in rhythm to make the bus pulling away from Nassau Street. He didn't even know where it was going. It didn't matter.

Puffing hard, he slumped deep into a seat. The bus roared over the Liffey.

Michael couldn't get the words out of his head: *deceitful bastard.* She had been right about that.

But if Charlie Brady was the master of deception, then Claire Burke was his willing mistress.

# Chapter 17

Maeve O'Driscoll stood in the bay window of the sitting room and watched the big quarried slates from the roof flying through the air, and getting stuck vertically in the green lawn. The worst storm to hit the south of Ireland in a decade was trying its best to tear the great house apart. All the outside shutters had been closed, except for the bay window overlooking the front of the house and the entrance gate beyond. The cut limestone walls were thick and solid, and the house was otherwise unmoved. As she waited for Noreen to pull into the gravel drive, she listened to sounds she had never heard before — a haunting melody in the fireplaces throughout the house, harmonic distortions of the wind blowing over the tops of chimney pots.

She had also instructed Brendan to report to her as soon as his job was done. She had given him the rest of the week, and knew he had a fiddle lesson with Garda Hennessy's children after school sometime in the next day or so. The mother dropped them off, and Noel Hennessy picked them up on his way home from the garda station. Brendan said he wanted to get it over with as soon as possible, certainly before Lydia returned.

Noreen at last arrived. Maeve welcomed her with a grateful mother's embrace.

"The sea is over the road at Tragumna," Noreen said. "I had to take the long way home." Maeve helped her off with her rain gear, set it over a chair near the fire to dry. "They've shut down the airport. I think my flight was the last allowed to land at Cork."

"I'm relieved you're home, daughter." Maeve placed her hand against the window, felt the tremors from the storm. "I'm sick with worry about Liam. He left for Amsterdam to pilot a ship after the skipper refused because of the weather forecast. I've heard nothing for three days. If he's out there in that, he's going to be in massive trouble. I just wish he would radio us he's all right."

"That was pretty stupid of him," Noreen said, disappointed rather than critical.

"There was nothing I could do to stop him. Nothing!"

"All we can do is wait, and pray," Noreen said, more of a chant than a true belief.

"Just as women have always done when their kinfolk have gone to sea." Maeve closed her eyes against the possibility of anything happening to her son. Surely his fate was not that of Noreen's father, to die in a storm out at sea, the ship lost, all hands lost, never to be given a proper burial. She shuddered to realize that she was even thinking in those terms. She should be thankful, at least, that her other child was home safely.

Maeve led them to the chairs in front of the fire. "What news of our American cousins?" she asked. "Was Aiden cordial?"

"He threatened to pull out of our partnership if we pressured him too much. I don't doubt that, given the opportunity, he'd cut us out."

"Begrudgery," Maeve spat.

"Anyway, he sends his regards. I got him straightened out. He closed the convenience-store deal and by now he should be with Declan in West Virginia. Everything appears to be working out. It's all up to Declan at this point."

Maeve was genuinely pleased that their business venture was making progress, yet she had more troubling issues at the fore-front of her mind. Self-preservation of the family was paramount. Besides her son's life being at risk, there were still the looming threats of police.

"There's something I need to ask you about," Maeve said.

"Yes?"

"Since Liam ran off to Amsterdam, I met with Noel Hennessy the night before."

"Oh?"

"Noreen — daughter — he told me about Lydia Jellicoe approaching him. Why didn't you tell me?"

Noreen shifted uncomfortably in her chair. "I assumed Brendan was taking care of Lydia. You had that talk with him and got him straightened out, right?"

"Brendan discussed it with Lydia *before* she talked to Hennessy. She wasn't going to listen to Brendan or me apparently. She's taken Daniel and left him. He hasn't seen her for over a week."

"For fuck's sake," Noreen said, exasperated. "She knows about everything Brendan's been involved in and, through him, knows about everything *we* do."

"That includes West Virginia. I asked him, and he admitted she was aware of the plan."

"This is a very bad situation," Noreen said.

Maeve found it hard to believe her daughter wouldn't have mentioned such an important piece of news that she had heard from Hennessy. But she could understand how Noreen would have assumed Brendan could control Lydia better than he did.

"Another thing," Maeve said. "Hennessy thinks that Dublin is onto him. I'm afraid he's going to find himself under so much pressure soon that he'll crack and give them everything he knows about us. All that plus his contact with Lydia makes him a very dangerous man. He's no longer an asset, Noreen. I had to make a decision in your absence. Brendan is going to help a couple of our men do the job. Do you understand what I'm saying?"

Noreen stared into the fire. "Yes."

"You get so obsessive about your men. You need to learn to maintain a certain detachment, especially when it concerns the family's business."

"I don't need a lecture on men, Ma."

The sound of a door slamming hard in the hallway startled them both. In a moment, a storm-drenched Brendan entered the room.

"I didn't expect to see you so soon,"

Maeve said nonchalantly.

Brendan's hands were shaking. He was dazed and out of breath. She thought it was the look of a man who was really not suited to kill, but did it out of necessity, and still couldn't believe he had done it. Doubtless, he had seen Death.

"The Hennessy children had a lesson today," Brendan said in a vacant voice.

"Ah." Maeve waited for him to tell her more. It was done. Noreen knew it, too, and couldn't look at her cousin.

Brendan said, "They never showed. I heard the news picking up a newspaper on the way home."

Maeve looked at him quizzically.

"He's dead," Brendan said. "He drove out to Baltimore this afternoon, climbed to the top of the beacon, and hung himself. I just got back from out there. The police have the area blocked off, but you can see still him from the other side of the harbor. They can't get him down because of the storm. It may be days."

A strange yellow-green-gray sky in the east, a sunset like veined agate. Huge billows of sea foam blew up from waves crashing at the base of cliffs at the place where the full fury of the Atlantic storm

247

met landfall. Atop the cliffs at the entrance to Baltimore harbor, Garda Hennessy hung at the end of a rope by his neck from the pinnacle of a thirty-foot-tall white-washed medieval tower. His battered body flapped like a banner in the force-ten gale.

A contingent of Hennessey's fellow officers were finally convinced by the attending priest to quit the scene for their own safety, abandoning him to twist cruelly through the night, a deadweight dashing against the bloody stone.

No one was in any doubt as to what they would find upon their return the next day.

Early morning on Dublin Bay. Michael stepped down from the commuter rail car at the Clontarf Road DART station, two miles from the city center. Almost everyone else was headed to jobs in the other direction.

Haggard and unshaved after a week of physical and psychological punishment and a sleepless night spent hiding out in the streets, Michael was nonetheless more determined than ever to get to the root of the great crime in which he had become entangled. It was clear that the answers were no longer to be found in the city. He had to go south, and had to do it soon.

The police would be watching the train and bus stations. A bulletin would be issued for taxis and intercity buses and rail. He figured he had at most another three hours to make his escape. He left the rail station and picked up his pace, headed in the direction of the seagulls hovering at the other end of town.

The waves came dangerously close to crashing over the seafront walk. The rain had stopped but the wind had abated only marginally. The ocean swells rose to frightening heights. Cat's-paws covered the water's surface as far as he could see. There were no ships under sail. He realized it was the first time he had smelled the sea in years.

After half an hour's walking he saw the sign for the Clontarf Yacht and Boat Club, but the gate was locked. Not surprising, he figured, considering the atrocious weather.

Next door was a hotel, and inside a large nautically themed bar. He sat and ordered a pint of Guinness. He asked about the yacht club next door and was told it was open only on weekends at this time of year. The young bartender didn't know anything about crewing opportunities with club members. Michael checked out the room: heads stuck in the morning newspapers, a few people lounging sockless in their deck shoes and chinos. It could have been an extension of the club next door. No one seemed to pay him any attention.

Michael saw a notice board on the wall. Race events. Regattas. Sailing lessons. Boats for sale. He was still reading for what he had come for when he heard a voice behind him.

"I overhead you at the bar," a man said to him in an English accent. "Looking to crew?"

"Yes, I am, in fact."

The man standing with Michael was the most unlikely-looking of sailors. He wore all the right clothes, but was too pale to have spent much time skippering on deck, too thin to convince Michael he had undertaken much strenuous work with sails and lines.

"Where you going?" he asked.

"I'd like to sail south, ideally down to West Cork."

The man thought a moment. He extended his hand. Michael was unimpressed with his handshake. "I'm Thomas Reed. You know the waters down there?"

"I know the area from Baltimore up to Youghal, and down around the Beara Peninsula very well. I sailed there every summer for several years."

Reed was assessing Michael as he spoke. He seemed to have made up his mind. "I have to get my thirty-two foot Contessa to Schull, but maybe I can pick up some more crew down in Cork. My problem, though, is that I sold my boat, and if I don't deliver in the next three days the deal's off. And, frankly, I can't afford that. I've been holed up here waiting for this storm to pass and to find crew. Since I'm so late setting out, we'd have to leave today. The weather is supposed to break by this afternoon, but it's still going to be rough. I suppose I can get us down as far as Waterford and a little beyond. You still up for it?"

Michael thought of how dangerous the sea had looked as he came into the club. But he knew that before he had jumped on the train to Clontarf. Under normal circumstances he'd never set out in weather like that. But these were anything but normal circumstances.

"I'm your man," Michael said.

"Then I'm your skipper," Reed said. "We sail at noon."

# Chapter 18

They motored out of Dublin Bay under clearing skies. The sea was still very choppy, but the boat, named *Kiss the Quaker* — the shortened name of an Irish reel, it was explained — was capable, and it was fine sailing from Dun Laoghaire to Arklow, where they stopped for diesel. They pushed hard throughout the night, taking turns at the helm while the other slept below in three-hour shifts, then anchored off Kilmore Quay south of Wexford. They both slept until midmorning; then Michael cooked a meal of steaks and fries.

Thomas Reed was more interested in talking about himself than in asking Michael probing questions. That was fine with Michael. From what Reed had said, Michael read between the lines and determined he had recently lost a business in Manchester, then lost his house and wife. Reed's wife had taken up with a blocklayer working on the extension to their former home.

"She and her solicitors don't know about the boat. I kept it in Plymouth for years. I'd take various girls out for weekend trips."

Michael thought Reed an unlikely candidate for a paramour. The sleek boat and the smarmy promise of a day of Asti Spumante and sunshine under sail was the more likely attraction.

"She found out I was sneaking off to the coast with a couple of birds from the office, but never discovered the *Kiss the Quaker*. Basically, she wiped me out. This was the only asset I owned by myself that was of any consequence and could be turned into cold, hard cash. Some German in Schull saw the ad on the Internet two weeks ago and wired me half the money sight unseen. I'm practically giving it away."

Michael could not be all that sympathetic to an adulterer who seemed to be getting his just deserts. But he was a working guest on board, and remained polite. "Sounds like a desperate situation," Michael said. "I'm sorry."

"I'll tell you how exactly desperate it is. I'd never done a channel crossing before last week. I did it alone, and it scared the hell out of me. I can't tell you how many times I just about got run down by one of those enormous container ships."

"The shipping lanes are treacherous. You're lucky to have made it, especially considering the storm that blew in."

"I had no choice. I'm pretty sure my ex still has a private detective investigating me. I got the feeling that if I didn't leave when I did, he'd find out all about the boat and they'd get a court order to have it seized."

They weighed anchor after they ate and trimmed sails to take advantage of the prevailing west-southwesterly wind. By nightfall they passed Dungarvan. Michael was below, listening to weather reports on Irish Radio One. He called Reed down to look at the maps.

"We might have a problem," Michael said. "That big storm spun off another low front out in the Atlantic, and the forecast is for another major gale." Michael flattened the map of the eastern Atlantic with his hand. "They're predicting the storm to consolidate here." He pointed. "If so, it will sweep up across Ireland from the south and reach maximum strength by morning. We're right in its path. If we don't get out of its way, we'll be pushed back all the way to Dublin — or worse. I know that part of the coast, and there are plenty of stretches where there's no protection. I think we should run like hell to Cobh, where we can get a mooring and wait out the storm."

Reed's tone changed from anything Michael had heard in the last two days. "We can't do that," Reed said. He stabbed at the map. "We can beat it to Schull if we keep the sails up and stay under full motor."

"There's no way we'll make it to Schull by then. That's another two full days if the weather were in our favor."

"We'll just have to push hard. I lost valuable time sitting on my arse in Dublin waiting for that last storm to blow over. Maybe with one hand on deck it would be too much, but that's why I took you on as crew."

"Reed, you're just wrong. Look at the map!"

"I'm not stopping until we get to Schull. Period."

Reed went back up top without saying anything else.

Michael lay in his berth, listening to the radio. Each weather report was more ominous than the last. The scope of the storm was becoming even more massive than originally predicted. The barometric pressure gauge started falling quickly. Michael was unable to sleep.

When it was Michael's turn at the helm, Reed declined to go below. He clearly didn't trust Michael. Reed looked at the charts until the wind became too strong to reasonably read. Near the end of Michael's shift Reed made coffee for himself and fastened his safety harness to the cockpit. He was ready for the next three hours, or so he thought.

"Get some rest," he told Michael.

At dawn, Michael was awakened not by the light but by the violent rocking of the boat. He scrambled up the steps. Passing just off their bow was the Roscoff-to-Cherbourg ferry heading into Cobh. The *Kiss the Quaker* had almost been swamped.

"Reed!" Michael yelled.

Reed was motionless, sitting in the cockpit chair, though slightly slumped over. Michael shook him. His body was held upright at the shoulder by the safety line. He had fallen asleep.

"You almost got us killed!" Michael said.

Reed finally realized what had happened.

"It's okay, it's okay," Reed said. He roused himself, gripped the wheel tighter. "Everything's all right."

"No, it's not."

Michael looked at the pennant on the mast. The wind was singing in the rigging. He checked the wind speed — forty-eight knots. The boat was flying through the water, tacking into the wind. Reed had set the autopilot.

"You can't fall asleep under these conditions," Michael shouted over the wind. "The weather's too bad and we're crossing a shipping lane."

Michael tried to take over the wheel.

"Fuck off," Reed said, elbowing him out of the way. "It's my ship, and I'm the skipper."

"You're going to get us both killed and lose your ship. Then where will you be?"

Reed wiped the sea spray from his face. He didn't have the kind of experience to be sailing in a force-ten gale. Anyone with experience wouldn't put himself or a boat through that kind of punishment.

"Reed, have you even looked at your fuel gauge? You've been running the engines flat-out all night. If we turned to shore now, we might just make it back to Cobh. In any event we have to take on more diesel."

Reed reluctantly looked at the fuel gauge, then cut the engines. He squinted at an approaching squall.

"Cobh, Reed. You're just about to get blasted off the face of the earth. That's the leading edge of a monster storm front."

"Make us some more coffee," Reed barked.

"Diesel, Reed, not coffee. Your engines don't run on caffeine."

Reed was red-faced. "I said we're not stopping until we make Schull, and I mean it," he spat like a madman.

Michael thought the situation had become too heated too quickly. He drew a breath and checked his temper. The storm actually was aiding their speed considerably. At the rate they were going, they would be passing Kinsale in only a couple of hours. Between the two of them, they ought to be able to handle that much. It was enough time to reason with Reed and make him see the insanity of what he was trying to do. Kinsale was now their only bet for a sheltered harbor.

Michael made coffee for them both, then strapped himself in alongside Reed. The waves grew and the wind slammed them hard as they met the squall. The sails were trimmed as tightly as they could be. They sailed without a word between them, the radio squawking below deck. They caught snatches of more dire shipping reports for the southeast.

Michael consulted the global positioning system device and calculated that they were less than five miles from Kinsale. The ship was becoming highly unstable. Michael climbed out of the cockpit. "It's time we take down the mainsail," he said, not asking permission.

"No!" Reed said, grabbing Michael's arm.

"Reed, you idiot. You don't know a damned thing about sailing in a storm. You have to bring down the mainsail or we'll be blown down. There's more than enough sail in the jib."

Reed let go. Michael carefully climbed on hands and knees to the mast and began the slow process of bringing down the mainsail in the heavy winds. Several times he was hit by a wave breaking over the bow and saved himself from being washed overboard by grabbing on to the safety line around the edge of the deck.

A quick glance at Reed as Michael made his way back to the cockpit. Reed was studying the charts and checking the GPS device himself.

Michael swung down into the cockpit, completely exhausted. He wiped the salt water out of his eyes.

"Take over," Reed said.

Michael opened his eyes. With one hand Reed held on to the wheel, with the other a revolver.

"What are you doing?" Michael said.

"I'm making sure we're not going to be turning to Kinsale. I can read a map as well as you can. Both hands on the wheel. I'll navigate."

Reed was crazed enough to use the gun, Michael figured. He would just have to do the best he could under the circumstances.

The next six hours were pure hell. The prevailing wind shifted as the storm picked up intensity. Michael tacked back and forth to make headway. Reed sat behind him with the gun draped over his knee.

"We haven't moved ten miles from when you took over," Reed said. "I think you're deliberately holding us back."

Michael lost his temper. "Don't you think I want to be out of this as much as you do?"

"Just get us there."

"I'm doing everything I can. If you don't like it, why don't you take over?"

Reed lifted the gun.

"Shut up."

Michael noticed that some of the steel had gone dull in Reed's voice. The skipper had gone over two days without any real sleep, and had been battling the sea for all that time. He was beginning to weary. The adrenaline was no longer enough.

Michael didn't have access to the charts anymore, but he knew the coastline. He hugged the shore as best as he safely could and saw them pass in succession — Timoleague, Glandore, Castlehaven — playground ports of call of Michael's youth. How many times had he and Lydia sailed into their harbors, anchored for an afternoon lazing on deck, followed by dinner ashore, then back to their cozy cabin on his ship to make love?

The churning sea wouldn't allow him more than a moment to let his concentration slip. The gale was now blowing sea spray off the tops of the swells. The boat pitched, became lost in a wave's trough. Several times he wondered if they could possibly withstand another wave breaking over them. They held on and rolled. If they were dismasted, would he call a lifeboat for help? Would Reed let him? Wouldn't they discover who he was and turn him over to the police, thus making a waste of all he had done to get this far? Michael wouldn't allow that to happen.

As they rode the tops of the waves, Michael started looking for ever more familiar landmarks. Castle ruins, a field with trees of a certain configuration, a bright blue fisherman's cottage overlooking the ocean. They were getting so damned close. Reed picked up on what he was doing.

"Don't even think about it," Reed said. "We ain't pulling into Baltimore."

Michael stared ahead. He looked to the shoreline only when they were tacking in that direction.

The cliffs finally came into view, one of the most rugged coastlines in all of Ireland. It was the entrance to Baltimore Harbor. Out of the corner of his eye Michael saw that Reed had lifted the revolver off his leg and was holding it straight toward him.

"Reed, look at the charts. We need to hug the shore and sail through the Carbery Islands, not out on the open sea. It's the most direct route to Schull. Technically we have to pass through Baltimore Harbor to get there."

Reed studied the maps. "Okay," he said. "But I can read a chart just as well as you can. Straight through to Roaring Water Bay."

There were hundreds of islands just off the coast, some small, some large. Michael was in his home territory now and knew every rock under the water, even though they couldn't be seen. Michael steered them between Sherkin and Reengaroga. Baltimore was behind them.

Michael gave orders to Reed to tack to avoid the rocks. At first Reed was reluctant to pocket the gun; then he saw they were in real danger of running aground, back and forth, the wind shifting directions. Michael increased the pressure on his skipper, kept him busy with the lines. The maneuvering became frantic as they passed between Turk Head and Hare Island. Reed wasn't up to the task and resented taking orders.

"If you think you can do better, you take over the helm!" Michael shouted back at him. "Look out there." He pointed to the open waters of the bay. "We'll be destroyed if we don't work together to keep the boat together."

Reed struggled to properly set the sails. He was so close to Schull. He was at the bow hanging on to the bucking ship, spotting rocks under the waves, shouting directions to Michael.

He was concentrating too hard, just as Michael had planned. Michael turned the wheel sharply so that the sail caught the wind from the backside and the boom swung violently. The boat keeled over and Reed was unable to maintain his grip. He fell overboard. Michael straightened the boat and it quickly passed Reed; then the slack in his safety line stiffened. Reed was being dragged behind, trying to shout for help, but being silenced by the force of the water slamming into his body.

Michael turned the boat back toward Baltimore. He pulled alongside the pier and tied up. Exhausted from the ordeal at sea, he still managed to pull Reed aboard.

Michael knelt next to Reed lying on the deck and patted him down to make sure he no longer had the revolver. He found it in his pocket and threw it over the side. Reed would never make the yacht's delivery now and would be a ruined man. But he was alive.

And Michael had arrived. He trudged up the hill from the pier and set out to thumb a ride to get him the few miles from Baltimore to Skibbereen.

# Chapter 19

Maeve and Noreen O'Driscoll left the Carnmore compound knowing the police would follow them wherever they went. The Garda Síochána did not disappoint. A white, unmarked car tailed them without pretense along the coast road. It dropped out at a crossroads and another took its place.

Maeve had not seen the devastation of the countryside for herself that Brendan and Noreen had inadequately tried to describe. The weather that came through with the second front was even more atrocious than the first. The torrential rain from the first storm had soaked the ground and weakened the root structures of the great trees, some of which had stood for more than a hundred and fifty years. The gales of the second storm easily knocked them down, leaving hundreds of beeches and oaks lying across the fields. County work crews with chain saws and tractors were already clearing the public roads.

The extent of the police surveillance along the coast was even worse than Garda Hennessy had implied. Police strategically placed at key points on promontories scanned the water with high-powered binoculars. Noreen pointed out a helicopter battling the wind and rain off the coast.

The police obviously knew more than Maeve did. The saturation surveillance indicated they had received word that Liam's ship was somewhere close by. During the previous night, Maeve had picked up a weak transmission on the frequency they used to coordinate their drug runs. With Noreen's help, they had plotted coded coordinates and determined that Liam was waiting just outside the twelve-mile Irish territorial limit. Something must have alerted him as to what awaited him.

Maeve parked her car and set the brake hard on a steep slope at a lay-by overlooking an expanse of shoreline. "It's a setup," she said. "I wouldn't be surprised if the Dutch skipper who was supposed to sail the ship here was compromised by the police over there. I'll bet the Irish police told them that Liam would probably come to take over the ship himself, because everyone knew there was only so much time until the port authorities started snooping around the ship in dock. There was no choice but to set out to sea. It's a trap to catch Liam."

They sat in silence a few moments watching the roiling water. Maeve slipped her hand into her coat pocket and fingered her rosary beads.

"If he stays out there, he will surely be sunk, and he dies at sea," Maeve said.

"If he comes in he will be caught, and he dies in a prison cell," Noreen replied. "He's crossed too many people. I think I know which one Liam will choose."

"He's not suicidal, just stubborn."

"Mum, there's nothing we can do."

Something in her voice reminded Maeve of when she was a little girl.

"Is he like his father like that?" Noreen asked.

The question shocked Maeve. They never discussed the man who had died at sea. All the children really knew was that he didn't leave Maeve when she had become pregnant with Liam, then later Noreen, though for some unfathomable reason they never married.

"Liam is my son," Maeve said. "His father has no bearing on him or what is happening now."

Noreen knew to push no farther, though her mother's cryptic answer should have prompted only more questions.

"I'm sorry," Maeve said. "I don't mean to cut you off on this subject again. All you need to know is that I loved your father very much." Maeve turned her head to look out the window and said to herself, *And loathed Liam's.*

"I am completely helpless to save him," Maeve said out loud to the rain beating against the window. "There's no worse feeling for a mother. I'm not ashamed to admit I've been praying for a miracle."

Michael found clean, dry clothes at the farmers' co-op on the edge of town. He took a path up above the main street and emerged near the sports center, where he paid two euros for a hot shower. Afterward, he settled into a small library nearby for several hours, feeling like a vagrant hiding at a table in the shelves with a stack of local newspapers and gardening magazines. He felt anxious, ready to make a move, but knew there was nothing he could do until dark.

At dusk he bought a chicken burger at a takeaway and hiked to a hill overlooking the town. Just like the last storm, the rain stopped, but the wind seemed to blow even harder. He sat against a large rock and imagined what the lives must be like of the people in the houses below. The stars and planets appeared; then a large moon rose between the hills cut by the River Ilen. Under a bright sky he could see Friesians grazing in the fields on the other side of town.

Michael closed his eyes and slept until the cold of the stone woke him.

Nighttime showed how the market town had become more gentrified in his five-year absence. Smart store window displays, an upscale coffee shop, well-tended flowers in window boxes and hanging baskets. New teak windows and doors and fresh paint on town houses hinted at new money.

There were over forty pubs in the town of only twenty-five hundred. Each had its own peculiar décor and clientele. Typical for a weeknight, there would be only a half dozen men staring into their pints at the bar. Most had televisions tuned to a soccer match. Only one pub displayed a hand-lettered sign in the window announcing, *Trad Music Tonight*.

Most gigs started around ten o'clock. Michael waited an extra half hour just to be sure, then walked to the alley at the rear of the Crosstown Bar and entered the back door. Coming in that way rather than the front meant the musicians sitting in the corner just inside the front door wouldn't see him entering.

A hallway led to another door. As soon as he opened it he was enveloped by the music. The pub was packed, people seated and standing, facing the musicians. No one saw him enter or paid him any attention except for the woman working the bar. Michael signaled for a pint of Murphy's and leaned against the wall. He was just another nameless blow-in come to town for a drink and a bit of music.

Michael counted five fiddles, two Irish flutes, a button accordion, a guitar, and a set of uilleann pipes. The ensemble was in full swing, playing "*John Brosnan's Polka.*" It was definitely a cut above the usual Irish traditional music session. The players seemed to be of professional quality.

The musicians finished to applause. Michael paid for his drink and made his way closer to them as they talked among themselves before the next tune. The pub filled with a buzz of soft conversation. Michael got a good look at the fiddler occupying the place of honor on the bench in the corner. The man finished smoking a hand-rolled cigarette and took a long drink of water. As the others in the circle were talking, he lifted his bow to his fiddle and started playing something Michael recognized from his many nights spent in the pub as a double jig, "*The Humours of Ballyloughlin.*" Someone sitting at the bar shushed the small talk in the pub and everyone got quiet. The fiddler tapped his foot on the wooden floor, closed his eyes, and gave an astounding virtuoso performance.

The fiddler accepted congratulations as he rose and made his way to the bar. Several offered to buy him a drink, but he declined. Finally someone set a bottle of Coke in front of him. He looked up into Michael's face. Michael's week-old beard threw him at first; then recognition showed on the fiddler's face.

"Michael!" he said.

Michael kept his voice low. "Brendan. How are you?"

Brendan was genuinely happy to see him, if a bit confused. "Not too bad, and you?"

"Not too bad, Brendan."

It seemed as if neither of them really meant it, though.

"What are you doing here?" Brendan asked. "I didn't know you were coming to Ireland."

"I came to see you."

Brendan was even more confused. "Me?"

"When do you finish?"

Brendan looked at the clock on the wall. "They pay me to lead the session till midnight. Don't run off."

"I'll just hang out till you're done."

"Good." Brendan turned, then hesitated. "Please tell me you didn't bring your feckin' spoons."

"God as my witness, I haven't played the spoons since I was thrown out of the pub the last time I was here. But if you insist —"

"You show your spoons in here, boy, and there'll be a murder out back tonight."

They laughed.

"Finish up and we'll have a talk," Michael said.

Brendan took his drink back to the corner and settled in for some more music. The pipe player gave them the opening measures; then the rest joined in.

Michael found an empty seat at a table near the rear and spent the next hour absorbing the music. He didn't realize how much he missed it. This was the real thing. For an hour Michael let the music fill his head, pushing out all thoughts of why he had come.

The barkeeper dimmed the lights, signaling last call just before midnight. Brendan packed up his fiddle and brought a couple of drinks over to Michael. Some of the other musicians continued to play.

"It's great to see you again," Brendan said. He flicked his eyes to Michael's collarless neck. "You didn't get kicked out, did you? Steal a few bob from the collection plate?"

If only Brendan knew, Michael thought. "No, I didn't get kicked out. I'm taking a sabbatical."

"That's what they usually say about priests who are under investigation for fondling a parishioner." Brendan elbowed him.

"Sorry to disappoint you. That's not the case at all." Michael took a long sip of his stout and looked hard at his cousin. "So how's life?"

"Not too bad, Michael. We've just about got the cottage fixed up. I've done all the work myself. Lydia's done a great job decorating. You'll have to come over. Hey, you haven't even seen Daniel, have you?

Here . . ." He got his wallet out and showed Michael a picture. The boy was balancing on a piece of playground equipment, Brendan on one side, Lydia on the other.

"She takes Daniel to the Irish-language playgroup," Brendan said. "Isn't that the look of a happy family?" Brendan smiled, but his eyes were dull.

"Brendan, I know there's a problem with Lydia."

"Lydia?"

"She rang me to say she was in trouble."

Brendan tossed his head back. "Oh, shite. What the hell is she phoning *you* for?" he roared.

Brendan would have been sensitive to the thought of his partner telephoning her old lover. He and Brendan had always been friends. Brendan's relationship with Lydia had begun only after Michael left the scene, so there was never any jealous rivalry.

"I was going to ask you the same thing," Michael said. "How long's it been since you've seen her?"

Brendan grew somber. "Over a week. What do you know? Have you seen her?"

Michael wasn't ready to answer that yet. "I never talked to her since I've come over." A necessary tinting of the truth for the moment, both to spare Brendan and to find out what he knew. "What were the circumstances under which she left?"

"We had a fight. I thought it was just one of the usual."

"What was it about?"

Brendan looked to see if anyone was listening. "She wasn't happy about the work I've been doing for the family. She kept threatening to leave me and take Daniel. She finally did it."

"I'm sorry, Brendan."

Brendan finished his water and considered the empty glass. "Hang on," he said, rising quickly to go to the bar.

Michael grabbed him. "Wait."

Brendan tore loose, made it to the bar, and loudly ordered a double whiskey.

"Don't do this," Michael said upon his return.

"I'll do what I damned well please." He swallowed a mouthful of whiskey. "Is Lydia the only reason you came back to Ireland?"

"Yes. She sounded desperate. I had to come. Brendan, you've always been able to trust me. Is there something you're not telling me?"

"No."

Brendan's quiet reply told Michael there was more.

"I just want Lydia and my boy back," Brendan said, his voice cracking. "Where is she?" he asked. "Where's Daniel?"

"Where do you think they are?"

"I don't know." He lifted the whiskey to his lips.

"When was the last time you were in Dublin?"

"Months ago. A fiddle festival in March, I think."

Michael held on to his arm. "Listen to me," he whispered harshly. "There's something I need to say, and I want you to be very clearheaded when I tell you."

Brendan set the drink down. "Tell me. She's never coming back to me, is she?"

Michael summoned all the courage he had. "Lydia and Daniel have been killed. I got to Dublin too late to help. They were murdered."

"Please, God, no." Brendan's face and body went slack.

In his capacity both as a parish priest and a cop, Michael had broken the news of a death in the family many times before. He knew there would be denial, then shock. Brendan would need time.

"It's my fault," Brendan muttered,

shaking his head, then knocking back the rest of the whiskey. Tears ran down his cheeks. "I'm responsible. I'm sorry. It's all my fault."

Michael wondered if it was really true.

"Give me your keys. We can talk about it on the drive home."

Pat Hannity directed the UPS deliveryman to wheel the handcart full of computer components into the back room of the Snapeville convenience store. Eddie Martin was there overseeing a technician from the cable company installing a high-speed Internet connection. Aiden sat on the edge of the checkout counter with a cup of coffee watching Declan trace and label wires running out the bottom of the other side.

"How long you think this will take?" Aiden said.

"If everything checks out and we can get the PCs up and going, I should know in a couple of days."

"That's enough time?"

"Barely. It's either going to work the first time or not."

"We need to get this store reopened ASAP so there's no suspicious discontinuity on the records in selling everything."

He tapped the machine that dispensed lottery tickets. "Especially this."

"Understood."

A car pulled up outside. Aiden unlocked the door. "Welcome, brother."

Kevin strode into the room, hands on his hips. "So this is your prime real estate acquisition?" He checked out the merchandise in the savory snack section, toggled the drink dispenser. "What's the thinking — convert it into a Louis Vuitton boutique? Nice addition to the investment portfolio, bro." He ejected a straw from the dispenser, and stuck one between his teeth like a hick. "What the hell are a couple of Boston boys like us doing down here?"

Hidden from Kevin's sight under the counter, Declan flicked his eyes up at Aiden. He stood up, clutching a fistful of wires and cables.

Aiden put his arm around his cousin. "Kevin, you remember Declan?"

"Sure I do," Kevin said, shaking his cousin's hand. "How the hell are you?"

"Great."

Kevin searched Aiden's face for answers.

"Declan is going to be helping us out, isn't that right?" Aiden said.

"Yep."

"We've reached an agreement with our

country cousins," Aiden said. "An exciting business opportunity, right here in the middle" — he gestured expansively — "of nowhere. And it doesn't involve designer luggage or handbags. Declan, I'm going to take Kevin for a ride; then I'm headed back to Boston. If there's anything you need, Kevin will get it for you. I leave you in his well manicured but capable hands."

Aiden had Kevin drive them to a scenic overpass he had spotted on the way from the airport. They walked to the middle of an abandoned railroad viaduct that spanned a steep gorge.

"I'm here because you told me it was urgent," Kevin said. "But I'm not staying unless you tell me what this is all about. Everything."

Aiden jammed his hands into his pockets and began slowly walking the length of the bridge. "Fair enough. A month ago a courier from Cork brought me a package — some Clonakilty blood sausage and a proposal from Maeve O'Driscoll. Declan works as a computer analyst in the auditing department of a major New York accounting firm. While he was with a team in West Virginia earlier this year to evaluate the integrity of the state's lottery program, he came across a security flaw in the system's computer program. He patched it, but at the same time he didn't reference it in the audit report. The other thing he didn't do was mention the fact that he also wrote a back door into the program, a subprogram that allows him access back into it — from a remote location."

"Brainy kid."

"Yeah. So, as he's a good Corkman at heart and returns to his roots every Christmas, he's having a chin-wag with naughty Noreen, who has sense enough to understand what he's talking about; then she has a word with Auntie Maeve. To protect himself, Declan set the back door up so that it's self-erasing after a period of time, so when the system is later audited by someone equally as thorough, it won't be found. The problem is, it took Maeve several months to make up her mind that it was both necessary and beneficial to bring us into the deal, since they are being watched so closely by the Irish police. The patch is due to self-destruct in only two weeks. We've got to use it or lose it."

"We don't want to lose it."

"No, we definitely do not." Aiden rocked

back on his heels and looked out over the mountains as if he were surveying his own personal kingdom. "And it gets better."

Aiden pulled his hands out of his pockets and gave Kevin a folded piece of paper.

"What's it say?" he asked Kevin.

"State of West Virginia lottery."

"What else?"

"Multistate Powerball."

"West Virginia is one of about two dozen states that participate in the Powerball lottery. On a good day, if you win the West Virginia lottery, you're talking a couple of million dollars. Be the only lucky son of a bitch to pick the correct six numbers in a Powerball draw, and you're looking at a two- or three-hundred-*million*-dollar payout. Or more."

Kevin was catching Aiden's excitement. "Yeah, yeah."

"Whereas the state lottery is held every Wednesday and Saturday night, the Powerball is only once every three months. There's only one more Powerball before Declan's back door expires. That's a week from today." Aiden bent over, picked up a stone, and threw it over the side of the bridge. It took a few seconds to hit gorge bottom.

Kevin's eyes were gleaming. "Who else is in on this?"

"Maeve swears to me only herself, Noreen, Liam, and Brendan, who was the courier bringing me the particulars of the deal."

"And our side?"

"You're it. No one else needs to know the full scope of the plan, though we'll have to start clueing some of the others in."

"This is all kind of last-minute, isn't it?"

"Put it down to Maeve's greed. If she hadn't waited a couple of months trying to figure out how to do it without us, we wouldn't be in the crunch we are now."

"That must have been Liam's influence."

"I agree. Stay here and babysit Declan. Make sure he's doing what he's supposed to do. Keep him comfortable and happy; don't piss him off too much. He likes playing cards; let him win. Hell, what's a few hundred compared to a few million, ya know?"

Aiden checked his watch, then took a final deep breath of cool mountain air. "Never, ever forget he's one of *them*. I don't trust Maeve, but right now Declan is the man in the driver's seat. I want two of you with him at all times. You and Pat and Eddie can sleep and take a dump in shifts.

Do *not* let him out of your sight."

On his way out of the Corner Bar, Brendan had tried paying for a bottle of whiskey with his evening's meager earnings, but Michael wouldn't let him. Michael paid for it himself, intending to use it as a truth serum. At the cottage they finished it off together. Afterward, Brendan found half a bottle of sickly sweet Bailey's Irish Cream hidden by Lydia among her homemade herbal oils. The only truth elicited was that the woman they had both loved was forever gone.

They got very drunk and cried. First Brendan, as he was prone to emotion, but then Michael when he saw his cousin's tears and heard his voice cracking as he told about the day when Lydia had presented him with their son. That was when Michael lost it. Since the nearest maternity hospital was in Cork City, an hour and a half away, and since the birth was not expected to be difficult, a midwife was on call.

"I was waiting downstairs — where we're sitting — listening to Lydia's birthing pains up there, completely unaware that my son had died. He was stillborn."

Michael felt his own heart stand still.

"The midwife resuscitated him. It wasn't but a few seconds, but technically he had died."

Since he'd been off the drink for so long, the alcohol affected Brendan more than it would someone who had been having a moderate amount all along. He began slurring his words, spilling his glass.

There was something that Brendan wanted to say, but couldn't. Finally he threw his head back and took a deep breath. His eyes were filled with tears when he blurted out, "He's your son, too."

Michael wasn't sure he heard him correctly. "What do you mean?"

"Lydia gave him to me and I raised him. But you are his father. Did you not know, Michael?"

"What?"

"Lydia would never have told me, but she had to say something when the doctors were talking about Daniel and the parents' blood types for a possible transfusion. For fuck's sake, surely you had some idea."

Michael sat shaking his head, listening in stunned silence, except for the sobs he could no longer contain.

"I loved him as my own," Brendan said. "He was part of Lydia, and I loved them both the best I could."

Michael buried his head in his hands. "Oh, God."

"She loved you enough not to wreck your new life, Michael. If she had told you about the boy, you'd have never stayed in the priesthood. She loved you that much. But she needed a father for her baby, and I loved her. We were a family, Michael."

That night, after Brendan had fallen asleep on the couch, Michael climbed the narrow circular stairs to the boy's room and slept in the antique steel bed where Lydia had given birth to their son, Daniel's babylike scent still on the pillow, the perfume of Lydia's hair beside his face.

# Chapter 20

The tenor bell at the Church of Ireland was tolling as Michael drove Brendan's car to the car park on the edge of town. He left behind a sleeping fiddler at the cottage. Brendan had mentioned Garda Hennessy's big funeral in town during their long conversation. The family would be represented among the mourners as an act of defiance to the police. The O'Driscolls were never far from death.

Before getting out of the car, he took a moment to gather his thoughts, to wipe a tear shed in mourning for the death of his own son. There was a mob filling North Street, overflowing past the town square, down Market Street and Main Street. Shopkeepers stood in the doorways of their shops. Schoolchildren in uniforms bunched together with their teachers at the bottom of the steps of the procathedral of St. Patrick. The town had come to a standstill.

Michael made his way through the crowd toward the funeral home on North Street. A coffin was being shouldered out the door by six uniformed men of the Garda Síochána. A woman dressed in black followed the coffin. She was holding the hands of two children. The whole of the town turned to watch them walk the hundred yards through the street toward the cathedral to the funeral Mass.

Michael touched the arm of a mourner, one of the many women in black dresses shuffling along. She must have thought it was a bump in the crowd.

"Noreen," Michael said.

Noreen O'Driscoll turned, not comprehending. Her eyes were red and swollen from crying. It took another moment for recognition to register on her face.

"Michael!"

They were forced to talk in whispers as they walked, the crowd silently surging toward the cathedral.

"What are you doing here?" she said.

"I've come to ask your help, and your protection."

"Are you in trouble?"

"I might be."

Noreen wiped the tear streaks from her cheeks. She caught her reflection in a shop window and quickly fluffed her hair. They were surrounded by people on all sides.

"We can't talk here," she said. "It's not safe to be seen with me. I'm certain I'm being watched by the police."

Michael looked at the houses and buildings lining the street. Faces in the windows, plainclothes police standing deep in the doorways talking into two-way radios. Michael suddenly felt very self-conscious. He lowered his head, pretended to be one of the mourners, and avoided anyone's eyes.

"After the funeral, meet me," Noreen said. She thought a moment. "Where are you staying?"

"At Brendan's."

"Perfect."

"Noreen, I can't meet up with you if you think the police will be following you."

"The police won't bother following me, there, since it's just my cousin and you can see the whole countryside from his place." She looked at him quizzically. "Exactly what kind of trouble are you in?"

Michael felt the eyes of the police bearing down on the two of them as they talked. The last thing he needed was for the Dublin detectives to find out he had escaped to West Cork. "I don't feel comfortable talking now, but I'll explain later. I think I should go."

She took his hand and gave it a squeeze. "So good to see you again, Michael."

Noreen let go, and Michael stood in place as she was caught up in the sea of mourners flowing to the cathedral and disappeared.

Michael heard the car and peeked from behind the net curtains in the kitchen. He pulled the sitting room door shut. Brendan hadn't stirred on the couch.

The car trunk closed. Michael watched Noreen sitting on the bumper taking off her shoes and pulling on a pair of Wellington boots. He met her outside.

"Where's Brendan and Lydia?" she said.

"Brendan's sleeping off a drunk and Lydia's not here."

"Oh." She said it without much surprise. She looked around to see if anyone was watching. "Let's go for a walk."

The crooked, narrow road leading from the cottage around the back of the hill was lined with a row of fuchsia hedges. The purple and red blooms were still hanging on to summer. The only sound in the air was from fat bees on the flowers.

"I was absolutely floored to see you," Noreen said.

"It's a bit of a surprise to myself that I'm back."

"You said you're in trouble. I see you've lost your collar. Something to do with your parish in the States?"

"No. It's the law."

"You?" She laughed. "Let me guess, you knocked over a bank to distribute money to the poor." She playfully grabbed his arm and pulled him to her. "You forgot it was a crime."

Michael noticed she had reapplied makeup since he had seen her earlier. She had brushed out her hair.

"I'm afraid it's a bit more serious than that."

His tone prompted a change in her own mood. "What is it, Michael?"

"What do you know about what is going on with Lydia Jellicoe?"

"You come all the way to Ireland to ask me about Lydia?"

Michael had not seriously considered the possibility that a woman like Noreen would give a damn about a lost conquest from so many years ago. Up through the high school years, Noreen had been interested only in making out in the boathouse, with nothing more emotional than that. Until she had graduated to the more intense and personal pleasures of the flesh. He had given her no satisfaction either way, which had made her mad as hell, though he suspected his brother Aiden had satisfied her, despite the fact that they were second cousins.

"Forget the past. I'm asking for your help. When did you last see Lydia?"

"I don't know. Two, three weeks ago."

"What were the circumstances?"

"I don't recall exactly. It was probably just passing on the street. It's not as if we have a lot to talk about. The only thing we ever had in common was you, and frankly we've said all there is to each other on that subject. She could be a real bitch."

"I really don't want to hear that. She wasn't like that at all."

"Wasn't?" She looked at him oddly. "Through your stained-glass colored lenses perhaps. Sometimes people do change, and sometimes it's for the worse."

"I had no idea you would still be so vindictive after all these years."

"You flatter yourself too much, Michael. Have you ever considered the possibility that how I feel about Lydia has nothing to do with you?"

Michael actually considered the possibility for the moment, then rejected it.

"What it was you saw in her," Noreen said, "obviously wasn't enough to maintain your interest. Well, at least that's what I thought. Here you are once again — even as a priest — in search of your dear Lydia."

"Let's start this from the beginning, shall we?"

"Fine with me."

"Lydia and Daniel are dead."

Noreen held them up walking. "What?"

"I got a desperate call from her about a week ago. By the time I got to Dublin, she and Daniel had been murdered."

"Why hadn't I heard anything about this?"

"The police weren't disclosing details of the murders. They didn't want to tip off the killer that they were on to him."

"Do they know who did it?"

"They *think* they do."

"Who?"

"Me."

Noreen looked at him carefully.

"But I didn't. That's why I need your help. If they think it's me, they'll stop looking for the real killer."

Noreen got them walking again.

"Does Brendan know?"

292

"Yes. As you can imagine, he's not taking it very well."

"How did you come to be involved?" she asked.

"Well, from the police perspective, I'm a convenient suspect. There's my past relationship with her, I suddenly appear at the crime scene from the other side of the world, and they know about my family's business. There's also a drug connection with the murder."

The mention of that seemed to worry her, though she said nothing. Just like the Dublin detectives, he'd withhold information unless it was absolutely necessary. Michael had decided not to mention the fact that the police had drawn a specific connection to the O'Driscolls. Better to keep his cousins off guard as he went about looking for his own clues.

"I'm telling you because it could be only a matter of days until the fact and some of the circumstances of the murder become public knowledge. After it became apparent I've fled Dublin, the news would likely have been released to the media."

"That's a very dangerous situation," she said. "For you and us. Your being here could put us in a very uncomfortable position. We've already got too much attention as it is."

"I understand. I just need a few days to figure out what I'm going to do."

They reached a crossroad. "I don't know, Michael."

She was hesitating too long to think.

He pleaded with his eyes, saw her drop her guard. "I need you," he said. "Please help me."

"This is why I still hate you." She made a fist as if she were going to beat his chest, then put her head on his shoulder. "You'll need to talk to Ma. The decision is hers."

Maeve received a coded text message on her cell phone saying to meet at one of the several prearranged sites they had devised in case of emergencies. All during the drive into town she had worried there would be more bad news at the end of the trip.

She was, of course, followed. But there was no way the police could anticipate that she would turn up the wrong way of a one-way street and disappear into an alley. She walked briskly to a door in the wall facing the street, unlocked it, and hurried through a garden to emerge at the back of the Church of Ireland's manse behind the church.

Out of sight of anyone outside the church grounds, she climbed the steep metal steps on the outside of the church tower. The narrow door at the top was left cracked open.

Noreen was sitting on a bench inside the belfry. A man with his back to her peered out over the town through a small window. He turned at the sound of her stepping inside. Even when Noreen told her who it was, she did not believe it until she heard his voice.

"It's a good thing you couldn't recognize him," Noreen said. "Maybe the police will have just as hard a time." She went on to explain Michael's predicament, how he got to West Cork, and the news of Lydia's and Daniel's deaths.

Maeve checked out the windows to confirm that no one had followed them, wiped the pigeon dung from the windowsill off her hands. "This is a bit much to take in," she said.

Maeve paced the eight-by-eight-foot room, fitting the pieces together in her mind. There was too much going on, too many coincidences. It would be foolish to rush.

"What contact have you had with your family in Boston?" she asked.

"We exchange cards at Christmas and on birthdays. No, come to think of it, no one from home sent me a card on my last birthday. But there's still Christmas."

"When was the last time you were there?"

"My mother's funeral, about four years ago."

"Phone calls? E-mails?"

"No. I think you can tell I'm not very close to them anymore."

Maeve felt she had to keep pushing.

"Are you aware of any joint ventures between the two families?"

Michael grasped lightly at the bell ropes around the room's perimeter. "Last I heard, my father and brother wouldn't breathe the air from the same room as an O'Driscoll, much less have to split the profits with you on some deal."

Maeve queried Noreen: "Have you talked to him about our business?"

"Of course not."

Maeve nodded thoughtfully. "Noreen may be too polite to you to say it, but I will. Despite the regrettable situation you find yourself in and our inclination to help you as someone we've always liked, you *are* from the Boston side of the family. Without going into details, I can tell you we have had some violent disagreements recently with Aiden on how to proceed with our new business arrangement. The level of trust between us is very low. So you won't take it personally if I tell you I don't altogether trust you and I find your sudden presence here disturbing."

The floor creaked under her feet. Minute holes in the timbers, fine dust on the floor. The place was about to collapse from woodworm. Liam had treated the floor joists in Carnmore House when they first moved in. The thought of her son stranded on the open sea in the terrible storm flashed through her mind, took her breath away. An idea occurred to her.

"You say you want us to hide you and protect you. That's a highly risky proposition for us. If, however, you were to prove yourself useful to us, in effect prove your bona fides, I am sure we can work something out."

"What do you want me to do?"

"We have an immediate problem, and you can help. Apparently you lost none of your skills at sea." She cut her eyes to Noreen. "As Noreen has explained to you, Liam is in a desperate situation himself, life-threatening. He slipped out of Amsterdam between those two monster storms, and now that he realizes the police are waiting for him here, he refuses to come in, and he refuses to dump his cargo overboard."

"Do I even want to know what the cargo is?"

"It's a medium-sized, commercial fishing boat. Just like hundreds of others. I'd assume he has a hold full of Atlantic cod, wouldn't you?"

Michael understood.

"None of the fishermen's wives will let their husbands take on the job of sailing out beyond the territorial waters into this storm. If you want to help us and prove yourself, I need you to go out there."

"What good will that do?"

"I don't know how the hell you'll do it, but the only way to get Liam in here is to get him off that boat. But he'll never abandon it unless he's convinced it and its contents are going to make it safely back as well."

Michael seemed to be thinking the problem through.

"You've only got until tomorrow morning to make a decision. After that, he will have to find his own safe passage out of West Cork. Unless you are willing to risk your life for us, we are not willing to risk ours for you. Bring Liam back alive, and I'll consider you as my own son."

Maeve and Noreen both watched Michael closely. He was fixated on the bell ropes.

"I think I know what I need to do," he said. "If you can't arrange for any of the fishermen to go out with me, can you at least get me the use of one of the larger fishing boats?"

"Yes, that can be arranged."

Michael nodded. "The other thing I'll need is a half dozen Friesians."

"Cows?" Maeve and Noreen exchanged glances.

"Yes. If you can promise me you'll have good milk cows at the Baltimore pier at first light tomorrow, I will give you my answer now. I'll bring Liam back to you."

# Chapter 21

Michael stood at the controls of the motorized winch on the whitefish shipping fleet boat. When the two lads from Carnmore had wrapped the sling around the great belly of the last cow on the pier, Michael moved it slowly through the air into the ship's hold, where another two men secured the cow to the wall. The whole procedure had taken less than half an hour, and Michael was sure no one suspected anything.

After everyone else was off the boat they untied the lines and he reversed into Baltimore Harbor. He had helped out his cousins many times on their fishing boats, and it wasn't long before he felt comfortable again piloting the ship.

Michael had Liam's coded coordinates from Maeve and had plotted a route to Liam that required him to head off at first in the opposite direction once out of Baltimore Harbor, then circle around to the back of the ship from the eastern side so that the police would not be aware of his presence.

The sea was still just as treacherous as it had been a few days ago, but the fishing ship was much more seaworthy than the sailing yacht. He also had the advantage of much stronger diesel engines. At first running with the wind behind him, he was flying through the water. Inevitably he had to start making the wide arc toward Liam. His progress slowed by almost half as he was now fighting the current, the wind, and the waves.

Even from his vantage high in the pilot-house, visibility was limited by the sea spray coming off the top of the monster waves and the squalls that swept across his path. He was navigating by instruments alone. He checked his global positioning and readjusted the rudder for the final run to his cousin.

Michael got to the rendezvous point but Liam was nowhere to be seen. Michael reckoned where he might have drifted if he had been unable to hold his position. At first nothing; then he saw dim red and green running lights pitching wildly off the bow. Michael got only a few meters closer, afraid they would be pushed into each other. He set the engines and rudder to hold him as steady as possible.

Michael turned on a powerful handheld searchlight and flashed it at Liam's ship. Now he could see what had become of the trawler. There was a tangle of lines over the side. Metal equipment boxes welded to the deck flapped open and shut. Though it was hard to tell in the wild sea, it appeared to be listing as if it had taken on a lot of water. The pilothouse was dark. There was no response to the light from Liam.

Despite security worries, Michael had no choice but to try to raise Liam on the two-way radio. He tuned it to the channel Maeve and Liam had used. "Mike check," he said. He waited a few moments, then tried again. "Mike check." Then he gave the code word Maeve had instructed him to use so that Liam would know he was a friendly.

Still nothing. He turned the volume up on the receiver and strained to hear anything at all. He flashed the light across the ship again. Hissing white noise, but now there was a voice coming through like a ghost trying to make contact from the other side.

Michael thought he saw movement in the pilothouse. There it was again: a hand wiping condensation from the windows. Now he was sure it was a voice, but even though they were only fifty yards apart, the signal was weak. Michael squinted into the mist between them and thought he saw the radio aerial snapped off.

Michael fiddled with the fine-tuning on the receiver, maxed out the upper-end noise filter. There it was. "Do you read me?" he heard clearly, though still more distant than the reality of their proximity.

"I read you."

"I turned the engines off this morning to try to conserve enough fuel to make it back in. I'm keeping the lights off and bailing the water by hand so I don't run the batteries down. I lost my aerials last night."

Michael turned the searchlight on himself and gave Liam a thumbs-up.

"By the way, who the fuck are you?" Liam said.

"Your savior," Michael answered. He turned on all the lights inside his own pilothouse so Liam would be sure to see who he was.

The signal was so weak he wouldn't have to worry about the police overhearing them.

"Set your course so you are running with

the wind, rather than against it," Michael told him.

"Goddammit, I'm not leaving my ship."

"Yes, you are. I promised your mother to get you home safely."

"You go can to hell. I've been here this long, I can wait this out. You try to board and I'll blow you away." Michael saw him wave a handgun.

"Your ship won't last another twenty-four hours. All this has been for nothing if it sinks. I'm not going to allow both of us to die out here. There's a way, Liam. If you can stabilize your boat, I am going to pull alongside and get you off."

"No way."

"Just listen," Michael barked. "Then I'm going to take over your ship. We're going to switch. You sail straight into territorial waters, get boarded by the police. They'll search the hold and find six of the finest Friesians in the county. You tell them you were exporting them to France but got caught in this storm and had to turn back."

"They'll never believe that."

"Of course not. But what can they do? You tie them up once you get close to the coast with a good chase, and give me time to sail your boat into a cove beyond Baltimore."

Nothing but static on the receiver. Liam took his time thinking about the proposition. "What's to stop you from just getting me aboard and then setting this boat adrift?" he said.

"I swear to you I won't do that."

Another few moments' silence.

"Would a priest lie?" Liam said. He laughed. "Just in case, I'll fucking murder you and dump your body into the sea if you cross me. I don't care if you are family or a priest."

In raucous seas, Michael positioned his boat alongside Liam's. He needed to be close enough to extend the arm used to winch goods from one ship to another, but not so close that they would collide.

Liam climbed outside, moving along the treacherous deck. Michael set his ship's rudder and engines to hold a steady course, and prayed a rogue wave wouldn't slam him into Liam. He made his way along the perilous deck and threw Liam a thick line. Liam secured it to a halyard, tested its strength, then gave Michael a thumbs-up. Now their fates were connected.

Michael watched how the ships interacted. They rose and fell alongside each other. When the wave broke to the port side of Liam, but starboard of Michael, one boat veered away from the other and the rope was snapped tight. It wouldn't take that kind of punishment for very long. When the wave broke opposite across the bows, the ships were forced dangerously close.

"We'll be crushed," Liam shouted over the storm.

"We're not going to allow that to happen."

Michael worked the controls of the mechanized arm used to get the cows aboard, extending it just over the edge of Liam's deck. He lowered the winch. Liam watched the rise and fall of the arm relative to the ship, gauging when he could safely move close to it.

"More line!" Liam called out.

Michael let more line out, knowing how dangerous it would be. The wind caught it, maniacally whipping the weighted end around the deck. Liam struggled to hold on to the ship as he covered his head with his arms. The clasped end smacked against the pilothouse window, shattering it. Liam waited for an opportunity, saw the line go slack for a moment, and pounced on it, but in the process had to let go of his handhold. The ship dipped in a trough, a furious burst of wind knocked Liam off his feet, and for a moment he was suspended in midair hanging on to the line. Michael saw his hands slipping. A second later Liam slammed onto the deck and somehow managed to hold on.

"Hook it! Now!" Michael shouted.

Just before the line was ripped from his bloodied hands, Liam managed to fasten himself to the winch. Michael immediately pulled the levers back and lifted Liam off the ship. He retracted the arm and set Liam down near a safety line. Liam wrapped his legs around it and freed himself, then fought his way against the bucking ship and waves to the pilothouse, the end of the winch in hand.

Liam embraced Michael. "I could kiss ye," Liam said.

"No, thanks, I'm celibate."

Michael looked at the line between the two ships tensing, felt the shudder as the two boats pulled against each other. "No time to waste," he said.

Michael handed the controls over to Liam. "Get me onto your ship, then get the hell out of here. Don't be too quick to let the police catch up with you. Considering the condition that boat's in, I'll need as much time as you can give me to make it back."

"You have just enough fuel to motor in if you can make the sea work for you."

Michael shook his hand, then hooked himself up to the winch. He opened the door. "See you back in town."

"Safe home," Liam said.

"And you."

# Chapter 22

"It makes me nervous when you watch me like that," Declan O'Driscoll said without shifting his eyes from the computer monitor.

Kevin stuck his nose back into a copy of *Hustler*. He and Eddie were working their way through a stack of magazines they had gotten from behind the counter in the front of the convenience store. Pat had been manning the front counter with only a bare minimum of competency ever since they had gotten the store up and running again after Declan had finished connecting all the wires from his laptop to the lottery system. Some especially grating Irish trad blared from Declan's computer speakers, a primary school class playing on tin whistles.

"I don't see much happening," Kevin said.

"Just because *you're* not doing anything doesn't mean nothing's happening." He licked orange fingers, wiped them on his trousers. "I'd like some more Cheez Puffs."

Kevin kicked Eddie's feet off the table. "Go get him some more Cheez Puffs."

"What?"

"Go get him some fucking Cheez Puffs. And bring in another carton of Marlboro Lights."

Kevin flicked his lighter several times without success. He threw it into the trash can across the room. "I need a new lighter, too."

"And some gum," Declan said. "Anything but spearmint."

Eddie sulkily threw his magazine down onto the table and left. Kevin got up and walked over to where Declan was seated in front of two PCs. Now he had all the equipment he had requested installed, set up on large, folding banquet tables arranged in a "U" shape, himself in the middle. A multicolored graphic pulsed on one of the computer monitors.

"What's that?" Kevin said in a low voice so Pat and Eddie wouldn't hear.

Declan looked up at the mirror in the corner, surely covering a security camera to monitor employee shenanigans in the back room. Satisfied Pat wasn't paying attention, he explained: "I'm using a hacking program to probe the ports of the state's computer systems. I'm looking for weaknesses I can use to get in. All these bars sliding up and down on here tell me if anything interesting has been found. This part shouldn't take that much longer."

"Can't they trace you doing that?"

Declan shook his head. "First of all, I'm connected to a proprietary Web site that allows me to send it encrypted signals from here, so the Internet service provider we're using can't tell what I'm doing. Then the hacking program uses five different proxies, and every time it sends out a probe it changes to a new combination. See this?" he said, pointing to the screen. "This shows how the proxies are queued up. Right now I'm connected to a server in Russia that's connected to one in South Korea, then Poland, Mexico, and Argentina. There's no freakin' way I'll be traced. Trust me."

"There was something else I was wondering," Kevin said. "When you break into the state computer, aren't they going to see that you've picked and printed the winning ticket after the drawing?"

"You think I'm stupid? When I was auditing their computer program, I inserted a subprogram that allows me to set whatever time I want on the numbers we enter into the main frame from here, so it will look like the winning ticket was bought the previous day."

"Got it. Sort of."

Eddie returned with a bag, tossed it to Declan.

"Hey," Declan said. "These are Chee•*tos*. I said Cheez *Puffs*. Tos, Puffs, get it?"

Eddie was about to say something but Kevin stopped him. "Here, let me have them," he said, taking the Chee•tos. Kevin nodded with his head to go back into the store.

"Seriously, do we really have to listen to that fucking music?" Eddie called out as he left.

Declan said, "Tell him there's information I need encrypted on the music file. Plus the music covers up our talking, in case we're being bugged." He raised his voice over the music and shouted to the store. "Then tell him to go fuck himself."

Kevin laughed. "You're a funny guy, you know that?"

"Yeah, well, you go fuck yourself, too. I'm doing something important here."

Instinctively, Michael knew the cove near

Whitehall was too shallow to enter any farther. He put the boat's engines into neutral just inside and threw a light anchor over to check the depth. The line barely went thirty feet below the surface. The cove would be silted up, and there was no use testing any closer. Just as he was setting the main anchor, the engines spluttered and died. He had exhausted the fuel supply.

*What a ride,* he said to himself.

Michael saw a familiar car parked on the road at the end of the cove. It flashed its headlights; then a figure got out and stood beside it. Michael recognized Brendan and waved to him.

Michael went into the ship's hold. He moved a pile of cod around with a gaffe until he found Liam's precious cargo hidden underneath. Eight boxes carefully wrapped in black plastic garbage bags and duct tape. A rough estimation told Michael it would have a street value of five or six million dollars.

He filled the dinghy with the boxes and lowered it to the water. He got in and paddled to shore.

Brendan was sitting on the hood of his car, the front door open and the radio playing. There was no one else around in the secluded cove.

"Jaysus," Brendan said, helping Michael pull the dinghy ashore. "You're a wreck."

Michael fell exhausted against the side of the small boat. "I've had enough of the sea to last me the rest of my life. Get me back to the desert."

"Come on," Brendan said. "We need to get this stuff loaded into my car before anyone wanders down here."

Michael wearily waved a hand. "They're all chasing Liam. No one's going to bother us."

"All the same, I think I know a bit more about this than you do. I'm not taking any chances. Let's go."

Michael forced himself to his feet and started loading boxes into the trunk of Brendan's car.

They traveled in silence, listening to traditional music on the Irish-language radio station. The music stopped on the hour and the announcer read the news in Irish.

Michael started to say something, but Brendan stopped him. Brendan turned up the radio and listened intensely.

Michael noticed a change in his cousin's demeanor: His face was visibly reddening and his grip tightened on the steering wheel. Without warning, Brendan pulled the car over to the side of the road and slammed on the brakes.

"What is it?" Michael said.

Brendan pushed the search button on the radio. He skipped over commercials and music until he found another presenter reading the news in English: "The main story . . . Gardai have released the name of a suspect in the murder investigation of a woman and child in the Dublin area last week. An American, Michael Driscoll, is being sought in connection with two deaths. Last seen in Clontarf, Dublin, he is considered dangerous, and police caution the public against making contact with the suspect. It is thought he may be traveling to West Cork. Anyone with information concerning his whereabouts is encouraged to contact their local garda office. . . ."

The first thought in his mind was of Claire Burke. She would be on his tail soon. Then he saw the look on his cousin's face. "It's not me, Brendan; I swear it. I was going to tell you all about this. The police —"

Brendan turned in his seat and threw an awkward punch at Michael, who stopped it with his arms.

"You were too drunk to talk about it sensibly!" Michael said.

Brendan took a swing at him, but Michael had anticipated it and moved out of the way.

"I didn't do it, Brendan."

Brendan tried hitting him again, but Michael restrained him.

"Stop and listen to me!" Michael said, as Brendan struggled to free himself.

"You son of bitch," Brendan shouted. "They wouldn't name you as a suspect if they didn't think you did it. You *did* do it!"

"That's *not* true!"

Brendan wrestled out of Michael's grip. He panted, his eyes filled with hate, his hands clenched on the steering wheel. He smashed his fists onto the top of the dashboard. "God damn you!"

"Brendan, I need your help. I've been set up. I left Dublin because I found out they wanted to pin the murders on me, and if I'm sitting in jail I wouldn't be able to find the real killer. It's not me. I wasn't even in the country at the time."

"I don't believe you."

"You have to believe me; otherwise Lydia and Daniel's killer will get away with murder. Brendan . . . the killer is someone in the family. I want you to help me find out who it is."

Brendan took a deep breath, relaxed his

arms. "That's crazy."

"It's not. Someone from down here planted heroin on Lydia. The police know it came from this part of the country. It must have come from the family."

"I'll kill whoever did this with my bare hands," Brendan raged, making fists in the air.

Michael couldn't help but wonder if that same furious temper could have swung the walking stick that killed Lydia. Or even broken Daniel's neck.

"No, don't, Brendan. Don't bloody your hands. I want the person who did it punished as badly as you do. No more bloodshed in the family. Please. I vow to catch whoever it is, no matter what it takes. We have to keep things quiet or we'll tip them off as to what we're doing. Together we can do it."

Brendan's whole body shook with anger, but his face was full of fear. "Of course I'll do anything to help you find the killer."

Instead of turning at Ballydehob toward the hills up to Brendan's cottage, they drove straight through the village. The silence between them for the twenty-minute drive told Michael that Brendan hadn't completely accepted the fact that Michael wasn't responsible for the deaths. At the same time, Michael wasn't totally convinced that Brendan wasn't somehow involved, despite his display of apparent grief and outrage.

"You missed the turn," Michael was finally forced to say.

"We're not done yet. Maeve wants you to finish the job."

"I *am* finished."

"She wants to be rid of this stuff before Liam gets back so he doesn't have to put himself at risk again for his drugs. You're going to have to get it far away from Liss Ard."

"Let me guess: And I'm just the man to do it, right?"

"Right."

"That wasn't part of the deal. I promised to get Liam back alive, not run heroin up and down the country. It's not right. I don't want any part of it."

"Well, sometimes we do what we must, rather than what we want. Plus, as Maeve said, Liam isn't home safely yet. The alternative is that you take your chances and catch the next bus out of here. I'm just following orders. I was told to drive you to Skibbereen and let you out at the petrol station near the river. I'll drive around for half an hour while you do your shopping."

"What shopping?"

Brendan pulled a wad of fifty-euro notes from his pocket. "Get yourself down to the men's clothes shop. You'll be wanting something flash. Nice suit, fancy shirt, designer shoes. High-fashion stuff. Then go next door to the jeweler and buy a chunky gold necklace. The way Noreen put it to me, just imagine yourself the prince of the Regency Palace."

"Sorry, I don't follow you."

"Didn't you and Lydia ever go there? Downtown Cork? The Regency Palace is an old art deco movie theater that was converted into a dance club. Oh, yeah, Noreen said it'd look good if you trimmed your hair and beard. You definitely want to look the part. You're going dancing tonight."

# Chapter 23

At the point where traffic naturally slowed and split between the bypass and main route going through the town of Clonakilty, Michael saw the reflective coats of the Garda Síochána standing in the middle of the dark road. It was a police roadblock, the first of several he would encounter on the drive between Skibbereen and Cork City. As it was explained to Michael by Brendan, once the police realized they had been duped by the O'Driscolls and discovered the boat laden with heroin that Liam had left Amsterdam on was not the same one they boarded, the word would be out in the countryside that there was a large drug shipment on the move. Despite the extreme danger of his mission, he was convinced he wouldn't be discovered. The car he was driving had been "borrowed" by one of the O'Driscoll gang from a farmer known to be holidaying with his wife in Lourdes; then the boxes from

Brendan's car had been transferred into the trunk. The police would have been actively searching for any of the O'Driscoll cars that were under surveillance, including Brendan's mud-caked Ford Fiesta.

The matter of his being wanted for murder was far more serious, but he gained confidence from having almost fooled Brendan with his new look. Michael had startled him midbow in front of the cottage fire on his way out the door. The vision of the stranger in his house in his high street clothes, slicked-back hair, and devilish goatee was enough to make Brendan put down his fiddle and shake his head. At Clonakilty, and again in Bandon, the police dutifully checked his the car registration and insurance details posted in the corner of his windshield, took one look at his costume, and waved him through in the direction of the city.

Michael had been instructed to park on MacCurtain Street. Shortly after midnight, Michael locked the door and set out on foot down the steep hill, then across the bridge over the River Lee to the heart of the commercial district of the city.

Once on Patrick's Street, Michael turned to get his bearings and look where he had come from. The residential part of the city climbed from the river, rows of terraced houses on ridge above running along the river, rising and falling on top of each other like an arpeggio.

Farther down the street, the lights of the Regency flooded the sidewalk and street in front of the old theater. A group of girls tarted up for the night spilled out of a taxi. Young people noisily approached the area. He wasn't the oldest person going to the club, but he wasn't the youngest by far.

Michael joined the back of the queue waiting to get into the club, listened to the stories of those around him. Football matches rehashed, clothes bought on sale compared, sexual conquests plotted.

In his amazement, he wondered, *How far is this from my desert church in San Xavier de Bac?*

The queue moved quickly. Michael climbed the steps to the second floor, paid his admission, and got the back of his hand stamped.

He stepped through the door and was at once enveloped by the music, the cigarette smoke, the lights, the smell of pheromones and perfume in the heavy air. Instinctively he made his way to the bar. As always, too many people vying for drinks, not enough bartenders. He squeezed through the crowd, secured a place at the zinc bar. As he waited to catch a bartender's eye he found himself surrounded on all sides by several very friendly women in their early twenties moving to the music, waving money to get the bartender's attention. None too discreetly they checked him out, from his designer shoes to his neatly trimmed hair. Evidently they liked what they saw. In the interest of appearing to be an engaged participant in the night's carnival, he charmingly returned their lascivious smiles. The woman in front of him got her drink, turned sideways, and brushed against him provocatively.

The club was divided into two parts. In the main room a deejay entertained the dancers with house music. In the foyer another deejay played hip hop and R & B, joined by another guy on decks, drum machine, and sampler.

Most of the male patrons seemed to be buying American beers. Michael followed suit and paid for a bottle of Budweiser. He made his way back through the crush of people ordering drinks and staked out a prominent position between the bar and the doorway to the foyer so he could watch the action in both rooms.

The message had come from Noreen

through Brendan. All he had been told was that someone would find him; all he had to do was look as if he fit in.

Michael caught his reflection in the mirrored wall. Who was that man caught up in a swirl of colored lights, jostled by dancers, stern face flashing in a strobe light? If he could fool himself, he could fool the undercover police who he was told would be prowling the club.

But why, he wondered, of all the club patrons, might he be singled out for observation? Brendan speculated that it was just another precaution in case their operational security had been compromised. Brendan spoke as if he had lots of experience in such matters, but Michael didn't probe further. He assumed Brendan was more enmeshed in the O'Driscolls' crime ventures than his cousin let on.

He circulated on the periphery of the dance floor with drink in hand. He felt as if he were on undercover duty again, though the venue was much more upscale than most of the seamy Boston nightclubs he had prowled. He looked for likely contacts, likely undercover cops. He knew to ignore what people looked like, what they were wearing, and watch their eyes, study their movement through the club. Who was paying him close attention? When he moved from one part of the club to another, was anyone following him?

Yes, there was someone who raised his suspicions. A couple, actually, whom he had first seen at the bar, and who seemed to be tracking him. Every time he discreetly checked on them, they were engaged in a passionate kiss, or having a good laugh. But they were a constant presence wherever he went.

Michael tested his hunch. He moved rapidly from the main room to the foyer. Decidedly more intense music, a more intense crowd. The couple followed him as far as the steps, then stayed at a comfortable distance. Was the man talking into a hidden microphone when he turned his head away from Michael?

Good tailing technique dictated that he be handed over to another surveillance team at that point. If it hadn't all been in his imagination, there would be someone else tracking him now. Turning slowly as if he were just taking in the dancers, he scanned the room for who might be watching him now. Too many people to know for sure one way or the other.

His predicament: He wanted to avoid detection by the police, get the job over with, but needed to make himself available to his contact. Though he was virtually certain he was under police surveillance, he had to assume his contact understood the dangers and would know what to do.

Michael finished his beer, bought another, decided to keep circulating. In dark corners of the club, lovers intertwined, drugs were all but openly bought and sold. Club security in their distinctive jackets and two-way radio earpieces were more concerned about lager louts spoiling everyone's fun and scanned the crowd for fights about to break out.

Michael felt the swirl of bodies pumping in the dense air as he plunged into the middle of the packed dance floor, felt the concussion of the bass in his chest from the huge speakers. He couldn't help notice how gorgeous the women were, even more beautiful than the ones at the bar or on the periphery. Their bodies were moving seductively, breasts swaying, belly tops riding up to reveal bare midriffs over hip-hugger jeans or microskirts. He had never seen so many thongs on public display.

In the flash of the strobes he searched faces as he pushed through the crowd. Most either had their eyes closed, swaying to the beat, or were staring rapturously into their partners' faces. Ecstasy was definitely on offer tonight.

Another brilliant burst of strobes exploded like hot white fireworks in sync with the drum machine. Something he saw caused him to stop. What was it? A woman danced alone, her eyes open, looking directly at him through a mass of bobbing heads, a glint in her eye like a quasar spinning out a beacon in an otherwise dark galaxy.

He took a roundabout route to her. Slightly older than the other girls, more worldly, less overtly sexual in what she was wearing, yet somehow more exotic. Perhaps it was her waist-length hair or seeming self-absorption. She knew he was coming. As soon as he entered her orbit she put her arms around his neck and danced. She made him move, made him put his arms around her. He felt her body, let his hands run up and down her sides. It all happened so fast. *This is all part of the act,* he reminded himself.

He pushed aside all the reservations looming in his mind and forced himself to play the part, his fingers running through her hair, pulling her head to him, kissing her deeply as the fronts of their thighs pressed against each other. Her hands were in his back pockets, pulling him in, crushing his body against hers. Only for a fraction of a second did he ever consider the possibility that this was not the one.

Anyone watching the way they kissed would think nothing other than that the next step would be lovemaking in the back of a car, if they could even wait that long. He experienced physical sensations and had unpriestly thoughts he hadn't had in years. For the sake of his mission, he completely got into the moment.

As they kissed, their hands were all over each other. His hands on her bare hip, riding up inside her open blouse, cupping her breasts as he kissed her even harder. She tugged at his trousers, ran her hands down over his backside, up along the inside of his leg.

*She is so, so close.*

He felt extremely self-conscious, and quickly glanced around the dance floor to see who might be watching. The couple he thought might be police was no longer visible. Then in the strobe light he saw a face he swore he recognized. A momentary panic set in as he thought Claire Burke was among the dancers in the middle of the room, albeit heavily made-up. Surely she hadn't tracked him to this venue. Another burst of strobe light and whoever she was had disappeared. He dismissed his fears as paranoia.

Then the woman ran her hand down his shirtfront, down inside the front of his trousers.

He flinched, but let her.

For the first time he heard the woman's voice, speaking closely in his ear above the music: "That's very nice, but not what I'm looking for," she said. She pulled at his belt buckle. "For fuck's sake, where are your car keys?"

Michael kissed her once more, for effect, he told himself. "Inside coat pocket," he said.

She ground herself into his hips and kissed him in a way he was sure he had never been kissed. Her hand was inside his coat, retrieving his keys.

She smiled, held his goateed chin with the crook of her finger. "Mmmm, yummy. Thanks, lover. Give it another hour, then check under the wheel well."

# Chapter 24

Even in the dark, the Traveler's Inn glowed eerily under the moon in one of those violent West Cork colors that the pubs and houses were often painted, in this case Pepto-Bismol pink with dark green trim. At three in the morning the outside lights finally went out, the heavy curtains were closed, and the front door locked. It was as forbidding a place as the vast moorlands in which it was situated.

After hours, the pub was one of the last remaining O'Driscoll safe houses outside Liss Ard. It was so remote that the police could not approach it without being seen for miles away.

Cars now assembled in the car park to the side, figures walked silently across the gravel to the back door. The proprietor, a trusted distant relative and one of Liam's fellow greyhound enthusiasts and business partner in the pub, had banked a coal fire and gone to bed upstairs.

Michael was the last to enter. There were framed photographs of champion dogs on the walls, trophies on shelves behind the bar. Maeve and Noreen sat on one side of the fire, Brendan on the other. Liam was behind the bar, merrily filling drinks. He smiled broadly at Michael. "My hero," he said.

Michael leaned against the bar. It was the first time he'd seen his cousin since rescuing him from the boat. Liam pushed a pint of stout toward Michael. All eyes were on Michael as he took a large drink.

Noreen made room for Michael next to her on the bench. As the others talked among themselves, she said quietly, "Thank you for what you did for Ma. And for Liam. I love my brother."

"You're welcome."

"Fair play to you," Maeve said. "You did great a job."

"Thanks."

Brendan laughed. He seemed a little drunk. "A great job on Dervla, I'd say," he said, a bit too loudly. "I understand she felt you up pretty good."

"From what I hear, it was the other way around," Liam said. He cut his eyes over to Noreen to see her reaction.

Michael felt himself blush. He felt Noreen's glare.

"Ah, leave him be," Maeve said, coming to his rescue. "He was only doing our work." She and Noreen were having hot whiskeys. "He's proved himself." She raised her glass to him.

"*Slainte*," Brendan said. Everyone repeated the toast.

Liam explained: "Dervla is the girlfriend of our main distributor in Cork. She took your car keys and they got the merchandise out of the trunk while you had another beer after she left you breathless on the dance floor."

Noreen, who had been silent up till now, finally spoke. "I vote we make him an honorary member of the family. But you'll have to start putting the 'O' in front of your name again."

"That would certainly raise some eyebrows back home," Michael said.

"Like we give a shit what anyone there thinks," Liam said.

"You've got to choose between us or them," Noreen said. "At least while you're staying here."

"All this antagonism between the two families seems ridiculous," Michael said. "All because of something that happened thirty years ago. Can someone explain to me what exactly happened?"

All eyes were on Maeve. "It may seem ridiculous to you," Maeve said. "But people here have long memories."

"That's not much of an explanation," Michael said.

"It will have to do," Maeve answered.

"But we're all great friends now," Brendan blurted out. "Us and your family, aren't we? See how things change? Business partners now, even."

Maeve shot him a withering look and grabbed his drink roughly from his hand, spilling it. "Can't you keep your mouth shut for once? Ever?"

The self-congratulatory mood around the fire was poisoned. Brendan wiped his wet hands on his trousers, sat with his head on his chest.

"What's he talking about?" Michael asked, wondering what could have provoked such a violent outburst.

Liam looked at his mother to see how she would respond. Noreen stared into the fire.

Maeve said, "Recently we've come to an agreement with your brother on terms for a joint venture. Frankly, it's a business matter and doesn't concern you."

"I thought you said I was one of the family now. I just risked my life to save your son, broke the law, and broke my priestly vows to deliver your drugs to Cork. That should count for something."

Maeve put her hand on Michael's arm. "As head of this family, I've made a decision that certain things need to remain confidential. I'd ask you to respect that. When and if the time comes that you need to know, we'll address that then. That in no way diminishes my gratitude for what you've done for me and the family. Now then," Maeve said, signaling that she was finished with that topic, "We need to figure out what to do with you. I promised I'd hide you and protect you. There might even be something useful you could do. I was thinking earlier today about the fish-processing plant. Liam and I have decided to use our own drivers to haul the fish from the boats to the plant on Marsh Road, then from there to port in Cork."

"The Irish still consider fish penitential food," Noreen explained. "Almost eighty percent of everything coming out of Marsh Road gets shipped overseas. You can't run a business selling products only at Lent."

Maeve said, "Our problem is we've been using independent haulers, but I'm afraid undercover police may be driving the trucks as a way to get close to our businesses and keep tabs on us. I want someone we can trust coming in and out of our places. This town is full of blow-ins. I want you to drive for us. Start off by making local deliveries. No one's going to take special notice of a new man at the wheel. Plus you can be our eyes and ears as to what's going on. You see something suspicious, you can phone in a coded message to Liam in the office. Otherwise, I think it's best you keep your distance from Liss Ard. Why don't you just stay with Brendan?"

"Sure."

"Good. Everyone clear on what's going on?"

Brendan wanted to say something. "What about Lydia and Daniel?" he asked meekly.

"What about them?" Maeve said.

"I can't just leave them up in Dublin."

Michael explained calmly, as he had done before, "Their bodies won't be released for a while. They've done autopsies, but they will want to keep them until they've made a case."

Brendan looked hard at Michael. "Frankly, cousin, they've already made a case. It's just that their prime suspect is on the run."

Everyone assumed it was the drink talking. Maeve interrupted him before Michael could say anything. "I'm not going to listen to that nonsense. Michael has explained to me exactly what has happened."

What Michael had told Maeve was that he had been framed upon showing up to help Lydia. He had not revealed everything else he knew about the case.

"The farther we stay away from that situation, the better," Maeve said. "We will bury the dead when the time comes."

Michael was afraid that Brendan, in his drunkenness, was about to divulge Michael's own theory about how he thought it was one of the family who had committed the murders. Or maybe Brendan was just putting on a good show for everyone, pretending they were still antagonistic toward each other. It occurred to Michael that one of them sitting around the fire could have done the deed. Killed his beloved Lydia and the son he would never know.

Liam saw Michael watching him light up a cigarette. He held the pack out. "Smoke?"

"No, thanks."

Michael happened to glance down at the cigarette package. He tried not to show how hard he was jarred when he saw the brand name Carabello printed on the outside.

"I get them every time I go over to Amsterdam. Damned hard to find over here."

Michael thought of the Carabello cigarette butt he had taken from the fireplace at Lydia's flat. He was right. The murderer was someone in the family. Now he had a specific suspect.

"It's done like this, dear. You take the tip of the knife, slide it up the gullet. One slice downward; then you lay open his guts. Now you try."

It was Michael's first day driving the truck for Carbery Islands Seafood. He had met Damien, the man in charge of packing and shipping, who gave him a quick tour of the place. Michael was introduced as a Canadian friend of a friend who had just moved to the area and had experience driving trucks for the fishing industry in Nova Scotia.

The central work area consisted of rows of stainless-steel tables where women wearing chain-mail gloves to protect their fingers from wickedly sharp knives cleaned fish. At the end of each table was a tub for the waste. Two men constantly wheeled around to each of the work stations trolleys of fresh fish brought in during the last twenty-four hours, then removed the waste. The chilled air reeked of blood and offal. Tom Jones sang love songs over the speakers.

Betty, one of the more senior women cleaning fish, was giving Michael a demonstration.

"How long have you been doing this?" he asked.

"How old are you?"

"Thirty-six."

"I filleted my first cod for a wage before you had teeth in your head to chew."

She finished cleaning the guts out of the fish, washed it off, and slid it into a container of thick cod fillets. She pulled another from the box of undressed fish.

Michael pulled on a pair of the safety gloves and picked up a heavy butcher knife.

"Give it a good whack, dear," she said. "Just like I showed ye."

Michael brought the heavy knife down, removing the head.

"That was handy," Betty said. "Remember what I told ye about the tail. No waste."

Michael chopped the tail off, leaving some meat on it. That would be cleaned later and sold as a cheaper cut. He got a fillet knife and skillfully opened up the fish, cleaned it, then slid it into the container with the other fillets ready to be packed for market.

Betty winked at the other women. "What do you think, girls? Put him to work on the line?"

The other woman laughed and nodded.

Michael saw Liam and Damien come out of the office. Liam handed him a clipboard.

"Here are your assignments for the morning," Liam said. They went outside the back of the building to a small fleet of trucks and vans painted with the company's name.

Michael clenched his jaw when he noticed that Liam was smoking his Carabellos again. Having his cousin as the prime suspect in the murders allowed Michael to concentrate his efforts on one person.

"You'll be driving the big reefer the lads finished packing out," Liam said. "This morning you'll just be making deliveries, first to the local shops, then up to Cork to the English Market. On your way back, I want you to pick up a load of fish from Union Hall that came in last night. Here's a mobile phone to keep in touch. You let me know if you see anything coming our way, like we talked about. All right?"

"Yeah, I'll get going right away."

The truck was a large refrigerated unit, about half the size of a tractor-trailer rig, easy to drive and maneuver, even in the tight streets running through villages on the way to the city. He stopped at a half dozen supermarkets and butcher shops, chatted with the amiable men working the forklifts, then moved on to Cork.

He found the address on Grand Parade and followed the signs to the service entrance at the back of the English Market. It was a large Victorian produce and meat arcade in the city center that catered to the wholesale trade in the area as well as selling fresh goods to many of the shoppers who lived and worked in the city. While Michael waited for the pallets of cod to be offloaded, he wandered through the market and bought himself lunch at a deli. The truck was empty and ready to go by the time he got back.

Liam had told him to keep his eyes open for any obvious signs of a police presence, especially driving back through the villages close to Skibbereen. He had been so intent on watching the roadside and streets off the main road that he failed to notice the silver car that had been following him ever since Bandon, less than half an hour on the journey back. How long had it been on his tail?

From his sideview mirror Michael tried to see who was in the car, but couldn't get a clear look because they were keeping their distance. There seemed to be two heads above the dash, but he wasn't sure. They were driving awfully slowly, he thought. Maybe they were waiting for a safe passing point to get around him, he thought. He moved into the outside lane when the road split briefly from two to four lanes on a hill and slowed to thirty miles per hour, giving the car behind him ample opportunity to pass. Still the car remained behind him.

The proof of their intentions would be at the turnoff from the main road to Union Hall. The chances of both vehicles going to the small fishing village were minuscule. Michael signaled the turn and stopped in his lane to allow oncoming traffic to pass. He turned, keeping his eye on the mirror. The other car followed.

The drive into Union Hall was up and

down hilly terrain with lots of curves. Just when Michael thought he was no longer being followed, he caught a glimpse of the other car rounding a bend.

He crested a hill and saw the sea out on the horizon. The sun was shining and he could see the whole countryside laid out before him. It was a stunning view, but not one he had time to appreciate. Somewhere over the next series of hills was Union Hall. Michael knew the area well. Could he lose the car behind him before he got to the coast?

Michael stomped on the gas. The diesel engine was sluggish but powerful, and the back of the truck was empty. He gradually built up speed. He was flying down hills, throwing the truck around tight curves. It was taking the car behind him longer and longer to make the same maneuvers. Finally, on a straightaway, Michael saw that he had gained at least fifty yards on the car that was still twisting and turning down the hill.

Now Michael was taking the narrow road and its curves at an insane speed. With every sharp turn he thought the truck was going to be thrown off its center of gravity and tip over. He prayed he would meet no one coming from the other direction, since there would be no time for either to respond. He was hurrying ahead, trying to get to a turnoff he remembered before the people behind him realized he had made the turn. Ahead he saw a familiar outcrop of rock. Not bothering to slow down, he turned the steering wheel hard, putting the truck into a sideways slide on the loose gravel on the road, and cut the corner. He accelerated out of the turn, the branches of whitethorn trees screeching loudly against the side of the truck.

He hurtled down the road, needing to get far enough away so the passengers in the car wouldn't see him as they passed the road he had just taken. He took another series of quick turns, all the while mentally calculating where the car would be on the other road, laughing to himself at the thought of having fooled them.

But just losing them wasn't enough. He wanted to know who was chasing him.

The road came to a "T" intersection and water appeared in front of him. It was a finger of the ocean contained by steep rocky hills. Michael took a left and drove along the water, fairly certain he knew where the road would emerge. Another quarter mile and the road took a sharp bend rounding the tip of the finger; then he was driving on the opposite side of where he had been, in the opposite direction.

He saw a flash of metallic silver through the trees, the glint of sunshine on glass. He was going to win the race the people in the other vehicle didn't even know they were in.

There was a hundred-yard-long, one-lane bridge spanning the ocean finger at this point that was a shortcut for getting around the inlet. In the middle of the bridge was a narrow passing point, barely large enough for two medium-size cars to get around each other.

Michael braked before he emerged from the pine copse on the side of the road. He watched the driver hesitate on the other side of the bridge, as if he were trying to make up his mind what to do, where to go. After a few moments the car slowly began crossing the bridge.

Michael waited until the car was a quarter of the way across the bridge, then whipped out from his hiding place. He quickly got the truck onto the bridge. He put the truck into second gear and pushed the accelerator all the way to the floor, aiming directly at the person behind the wheel in the car ahead of him. It was apparent from the jerky movement of the car that the driver couldn't decide whether to back up or try to make it to the passing point.

The car made the wrong decision and raced Michael to the middle of the bridge. He knew what the other driver didn't: There was no way both of them could fit through. Michael kept accelerating. The car driver got there first, realized he had made a mistake, saw the truck wasn't going to stop. Michael shielded his face from the driver's view as he approached at seventy miles per hour, setting up a vibration that shook the whole bridge. With only seconds left, the passenger scrambled out of the car and jumped up onto the bridge rails just in time to watch the car being sideswiped by a fish delivery truck speeding by at a horrific speed.

The car spun wildly and wedged tightly between the bridge posts. It wasn't going anywhere.

Michael flicked his eyes into the sideview mirror to see who the driver had been, but they were already out of sight.

Michael picked up the crates of fish at Union Hall and returned to the processing plant in Skibbereen. Liam was busy on the phone. By the time the truck was unloaded it was after four o'clock, too late in the day to make another run, so he got to work cleaning out the back of the truck. The women from inside waved to him and giggled as they passed him on the way to the car park after work. The two men from inside who had been pushing the trolleys around hosed down the floor and squeegeed the water outside. Everyone was finished for the day, and soon only Liam's car was left.

Michael went into the office and hung the clipboard up on the peg for the truck he had been driving. In the designated spaces, he wrote down the date, mileage, and locations visited, then signed it.

He was just about to punch the time clock at the far end of the wall when something caught his eye. Michael checked in the business office, but Liam was gone. Michael looked through the window in the door leading to the processing area. Liam was fiddling with a scale on the far side of the room.

Each of the clipboards corresponded to a different company vehicle. What had grabbed his attention was the highly recognizable signature of someone he knew — Brendan. Michael lifted the clipboard and examined the log sheet for the company van. Interspersed among the other drivers' entries were several dates the vehicle had been taken out by Brendan over the past few weeks. Apparently his cousin had also been doing some driving for the business. The log showed several trips to local stores, and a couple to Cork, likely making the same trip to the English Market that he had just completed. Michael did a quick mental calculation of the mileage records. Something wasn't adding up.

The anomaly was an entry for a run to Cork City. The math was right, but the distance traveled was all wrong. Whereas all the other entries for a round-trip to Cork were about 160 kilometers, this particular notation indicated almost seven hundred kilometers. Even allowing for long side trips to any of the other villages between Skibbereen and Cork, it didn't make sense.

Michael heard noise coming from the processing room — Liam walking toward the office. He quickly deciphered the date scrawled for the entry: September fourteenth — the same day Lydia and Daniel had been murdered.

Michael heard Liam's voice and hung the clipboard back up on its peg.

Another speedy computation in his head: to Dublin and back would have been about 600 kilometers.

He turned around just as Liam entered the room, talking into his mobile phone. Liam nodded and said good-bye.

"Ma wants you to come over for dinner tonight so we can discuss strategy," Liam said. "I'm to smuggle you in the backseat of my car. You can spend the night and I'll bring you to work in the morning."

Michael thought for a moment. The only thing on his mind was getting back to Brendan's cottage to confront him about his apparent trip to Dublin.

"I really should be getting back to Brendan's."

"Ma insists."

Liam wasn't going to let him go.

"Okay, sounds good."

They went outside together. Liam happened to glance at the truck Michael had been driving, and saw the gouged paint on the back panel.

"What the hell happened to this?"

"I had a bad scrape with the law."

"What do you mean?"

"Someone was following me back from Cork. I'm pretty sure it was the police in an unmarked car. I had to lose them."

Liam studied the damage, ran his finger along the chipped paint. "You're probably just being a bit paranoid."

"I don't think so."

"Well, I suppose someone who's on the run from a murder charge can't be too careful."

"You know damned well I didn't do it."

Though it seemed more likely that the car following him was someone keeping an eye on the O'Driscoll gang's activities, the thought that the Dublin police might have tracked him to West Cork unnerved Michael.

"Let's go see what Ma's cooked up," Liam said.

# Chapter 25

Liam dropped Michael off at Carnmore, then drove back into town, saying he had forgotten to pick up some more whiskey for his mother. As they all waited for his return, Michael helped set the places at the long pine table in the kitchen.

Michael noticed that Maeve seemed especially fidgety. Noreen, however, was in a playful mood, chastising him for mislaying the silverware. She seemed never to miss an opportunity to be close to him. He thought Maeve would be embarrassed or annoyed by her daughter's antics, but she was too distracted.

After Liam's return, everyone helped himself to food off the Aga cooker: slices of smoked back bacon, roast potatoes, mashed swedes. Liam and Michael drank pint glasses of whole milk; Maeve and Noreen sipped tea. For dessert, Noreen distributed bowls of custard.

There was an awkward silence. Maeve and Noreen kept eyeing each other. Liam scraped the last of his custard with his spoon and seemed oblivious to anything that might be going on. There was a small amount of speculation about who might have been following the truck in the mysterious car. Dinnertime with his cousins years ago had always been a boisterous affair, a smaller house, smaller kitchen, bigger noise. But that was when they were children, and before they had become a great crime family. He wondered if their self-absorption during meals was now the norm. Or if it was his presence.

In the sitting room, Maeve poured herself a large whiskey and slumped into an armchair. Noreen joined Michael on the couch. Liam lit a cigarette, then a fire.

Michael took a deep breath and realized it wasn't the sweet-smelling ash in the fireplace he detected. Michael was closely watching everything Liam did now. It was apparent that what Liam had lit wasn't a cigarette at all, but a joint. Liam took another long draw on it and walked it over to Noreen. She took a drag, held it in her lungs, exhaled, then offered the joint to Michael.

"Pass."

"I think you need to mellow out a bit," she said. She scooted closer to him until their legs touched. She put her arm playfully around his neck, offered up the joint to him again. "Go on."

"Not for me, thanks."

Noreen accepted the refusal in good humor. She and Liam traded smokes on the joint, got higher. Finished with it, she sat back deeply in the couch, but kept her hand behind Michael's head. She twirled a strand of his hair. He tried moving away, but she persisted.

"Noreen," he admonished.

Liam reclined in his stuffed chair by the fire, a stupid look on his face. Maeve took a large drink of her whiskey.

Michael again tried getting them to talk about his day's problem. "I'm not sure it's safe for me to be out so publicly. Every garda in the country has got to know these are your trucks I'm driving."

"You worry too much," Maeve said. "The important thing is that it gets you away from here. Better for you to be out if the police decide to pay us a visit or raid us here at the house or at the plant."

Liam added, "Your taking the trucks out might distract them from what we're doing here. I, for one, don't mind wasting their time chasing you around the countryside. It takes some of the heat off us."

It suddenly hit Michael why they wanted him driving the trucks. "Oh, I see now," he said angrily. "You're deliberately using me as a decoy!"

Maeve shrugged. "Just one of the trade-offs for sheltering you," she said.

"You call that sheltering me? You're putting me at higher risk. I thought you were finished with all this drug business. Now what are you trying to cover up?" Michael looked around at Maeve and his cousins slouched in their chairs. "You can all sit here and get stoned tonight, but I'm not. In fact, in light of what I just learned here tonight, I'd like to go back to Brendan's. I may need to reconsider my position with my new *family*."

The truth was, he was anxious to get back to Brendan to find out what he had been doing the day of Lydia's death.

Liam smirked. "We don't treat you any feckin' differently from anyone else in the family. That means once you're in, you can't leave. And if you stay, you keep your goddammed mouth shut." The intent was serious, but the words trailed off dreamily.

"Right," Noreen added in a detached

voice. "Shut your gorgeous goddamned mouth."

Michael stood up. "I'll walk into town, then thumb a ride back out to Brendan's. Good night."

"Sit down, Michael," Maeve said sternly. "What you need to learn is that in this family no one is greater than the whole." An even harder edge crept into her voice: "*No one.*"

The sudden change in her tone startled him.

"No one walks out on me or the family," she said. "That includes you, Michael. Same goes for Lydia Jellicoe or Brendan."

"Why do you bring them up?"

"Everyone in this house knows they were having problems," she said.

Liam yawned loudly. "Long day," he said. He rose groggily from his chair and left.

"You'll have to learn to trust me, Michael," Maeve said. "Do you think the reason I asked you here tonight was for us to have dinner together?"

"What *is* the reason?"

"Ma knows," Noreen said in a raspy, far-away voice. "Ma knows everything. Ma's a good ma." She laughed to herself.

"I'll go prepare the guest room for you,"

Maeve said with finality.

Maeve put the screen in front of the fire, then turned out the lamps, leaving Noreen and Michael sitting in the glow of the burning wood. Michael felt an urgent need to escape — not from the house as much as from the woman sprawled on the big couch cushions. He didn't want Noreen to embarrass herself any more.

"Good night," he said gently, rising from the couch. "See you in the morning, okay?"

Noreen reached out and took his hand. "Don't go. Please."

Michael looked down at her. She stretched her arms upward and smiled seductively. Her lips glistened. If he weren't a priest and she weren't his cousin he would definitely have been tempted. The truth was, in a detached sort of way, he *was* tempted. But his heart and his mind overruled the most carnal of desires she had aroused in him.

Her eyes were slits. "Please?"

Michael lifted her to her feet with his hands. Noreen played with his hair, his face, put her hand on his chest, leaned in and tried to kiss his mouth, but he turned to the side.

"Come to bed with me," she said.

Michael shook his head. "Noreen . . . it's the pot talking."

"It's me, Michael. Me talking. I want you. I'd do anything for one night with you. Make love to me tonight. God, I need you so badly. My whole body aches for you."

"I believe you," he said tenderly. When she tried kissing him again, he pushed her away. "Go to bed," he said. "Without me." He kissed her on top of her head. "Good night."

He left her standing in the room all alone — a desperately unfulfilled woman facing the prospect of another night not spent in the arms of a man, he thought.

Whether out of curiosity or kindness or the need to reassure himself, Michael made the mistake of turning on his way out. She was shameless: the mouth slightly open, eyes closed, the way she tipped her head back and shook her hair, the heaving breasts, pert nipples showing through her tight top. She ran her hands up and down her sides. He had never seen a woman more intent on lovemaking. He decided *lovemaking* was too polite a term for what she wanted.

Michael climbed the wide stairs to the next floor, where the family had their bedrooms. The guest room was at the end of the hall.

He was surprised to find Maeve sitting on the edge of the bed, waiting for him. "You're not sleeping with her?" she said.

"No," he said firmly.

Maeve nodded. "You're stronger than most."

"She makes me weak. She would take all my strength away from me. She takes; she has nothing to give me. She never understood that."

"She has wanted you unlike she has ever wanted any other man."

"She wants me because she can't have me. After she had me, then I'd be just like any other. I'd be left broken. She'd stand laughing over me."

"She's got issues. She's a good girl."

"You're her mother. You have to say that."

"Yes."

After some reflection he said, "You don't mind them getting stoned like that?"

"I don't mind if they want to relax a little bit. Especially Liam. He doesn't say much. He keeps a lot in."

"Hard day of tinkering with the fish scales. It's exhausting work, I'm sure."

Maeve shook her head sorrowfully. "This

is what I'm talking about. You have no idea what we have to do." She took a deep breath.

"Tell me."

"I do want you to understand the real reason you're here tonight. Liam didn't go back into town to get me another bottle of whiskey."

"No?"

"No. Brendan had a serious accident. We didn't want you walking in on it."

The horror of what she had said took a moment to set in.

"What's happened to Brendan?" Michael demanded.

"Please keep your voice down. Noreen doesn't know — yet. I'll tell her to-morrow."

"I don't give a damn about that; what happened to Brendan?"

"He was distraught over Lydia and Daniel. He drank too much. He was de-pressed that he hadn't made anything of himself professionally. Anyone can under-stand why he killed himself. When the po-lice find that shotgun by his side, then they'll also have found the murder weapon used to kill those ten men a couple of weeks ago. They can neatly wrap up that investigation."

"That's just a little too neat . . . Auntie. They were all spiked to fences and savagely beaten. Brendan couldn't have done that by himself."

"There's something else I think you could consider, especially given your own position in relation to the law. It wouldn't surprise anyone — least of all me — if it turned out Brendan were the person responsible for killing Lydia and Daniel. The Dublin police will eventually make the connection. It was a crime of passion. You understand passion, don't you, nephew?"

Maeve watched Michael closely for a reaction. He couldn't hide the fact that he had considered Brendan's involvement a real possibility. She wouldn't know he had factual basis for that belief. It occurred to him that if the Dublin police actually concluded that Lydia's and Daniel's killer was dead, they would back off their investigation. He wondered if this was part of Maeve's plan — to have the Dublin murder cases closed. If that was true, it was yet another indication as to the family's involvement.

"Makes sense, doesn't it?" Maeve said. "You can understand how his grief at killing his own partner and child would only add to his depression. He reached his breaking point and killed himself."

Michael could let her go only so far with her conjectures. "That's complete nonsense. Liam did it, didn't he?" Michael insisted.

Maeve refused to be drawn out. "Liam's a good son. I'm sure he was a comfort to his cousin."

"Why?" Michael pleaded. "Why?"

"You heard him yourself. He can't keep his mouth shut."

"Where does it end? When does the killing stop? What's going to be left of the family?"

"I know you and your father and brothers have always looked down on us. We may share a bloodline, but when your father's family left for America, he left behind a way of life that you frankly are unable to fully comprehend. Do you know how miserably poor this nation was until just a few years ago? This rural ideal that the Germans and Dutch and English flocked to for a pastoral retreat among Europe's peasants? Ireland was a third-world country until we prostrated ourselves to the European Community. It's our struggle, Michael, not yours. To pretend to understand is arrogance. On a more personal level, there is our business, and there is our love for one another. Our business is crumbling, the police are closing in. Times are tough for us. We do what we have to do to survive. All we have is each other now. We're not so very different from any other family, are we?"

# Chapter 26

"What the hell are you doing?"

Kevin Driscoll had sneaked up to look over Declan's shoulder as he sat at one of the computers. Declan ignored his question for the moment, pounded the keyboard rapidly with his thumbs and index fingers, and concentrated on blasting another Space Invader off the monitor.

Kevin said, "Is this what you've been doing all morning?"

Declan kept playing until he lost his last battleship. Game over. He entered his name as winner of yet another high score.

"It's taking longer than it should because you guys bought junk components," Declan explained. He hit the escape key, and the program he had shown Kevin the other day was still working away, apparently still probing for open ports in the state of West Virginia's mainframe.

"I thought you said it would just be a

362

couple of days. Me and the boys been sitting on our asses waiting for you to break into their computer. I thought we were under some strict deadline?"

Declan reached under the desk and pulled up a handful of loose cables. "See this chrome shit? I told you before that I needed nothing but gold-plated connections. This is highly sensitive work I'm doing here. I'm getting too much data loss. If this thing fails, it's your personal fault."

"Well, maybe we need to find some way to get our hands on some *gold*-plated cable connections." Kevin slid a piece of paper across the desk to him. "Write down what you need and I'll send Eddie out to get it."

"That's what I did last time and he fucked up."

"Jesus," Kevin said irritably. "What do you want me to do?"

"Let's go shopping. I'm tired of being stuck in here all day with you guys anyway."

"Aiden told me not to leave here."

"Your call," Declan said dismissively. He hit another key and the game popped up on the screen. He started it over again, jabbing at the keyboard.

"Okay, okay," Kevin said. He stood, thinking what to do. He punched a number into his cell phone and listened. "Shit." He hung up. "It went directly to Aiden's voice mail. All right, where to?"

"I saw a Wal-Mart on the way in. They should have what I need."

"If we're going, let's do it."

"Let me save this."

Declan kept an eye on everyone as he worked. Eddie was leaning back in his chair against the wall snoozing. Kevin gave him a kick and woke him up. "Go get the car ready," Kevin told him.

In the front of the store, Pat was watching a small black-and-white television with a coat hanger as an antenna. "Wuss," he said to the TV. He laughed. "What a fuckin' idiot."

Kevin entered from the back and saw Pat was talking to some pathetic defendant on *The People's Court.*

"We're going out," Kevin said. "Sell a zillion lottery tickets while we're gone, will ya?"

"Sure, boss."

Kevin went back into the room with Declan. Kevin flicked through the channels until he found the local noon news. "See this?"

Declan looked up from the computer. At the bottom of the TV screen was a

Powerball logo and a running total for projected winnings of the national lottery. "Yeah. Turn it up."

Kevin increased the volume so just the two of them could hear the reporter.

"Already the Powerball lottery jackpot has grown to over two hundred million dollars. People from all over the state are flocking to stores like this to buy lottery tickets. With only a few more days to go, this could easily turn out to be the largest jackpot in Powerball history."

"Don't forget," Kevin told Declan, "we're in this together."

Declan gave him a wink and an enthusiastic thumbs-up as Pat returned. "Two minutes," he told them.

Kevin and Eddie made small talk across the room. The story about not being able to get into the big mainframe was another lie. Declan was in already. He had broken through within an hour of his hacking that first afternoon, because he knew exactly where he was going, exactly what he was doing. Hadn't he already laid a path for himself when he was auditing the state's lottery accounting programs?

Declan pulled up another program he had been secretly running in the background. He hadn't been playing Space Invaders all morning. That was just a ruse to fool anyone who happened to walk by while he was exchanging e-mails.

Declan had probed Kevin and Pat and Eddie on their knowledge of computers and knew they'd believe just about anything he told them on the subject. The truth was, gold-plated cable connections didn't make a hell of a lot of difference in what he was doing. What he needed was a subterfuge to get out.

They bought his technical mumbo-jumbo. *Suckers*. Declan had already classified them into neat columns. He was smart; they were dumb. Seemed a pity to be splitting three hundred million dollars with dumb people.

Declan typed a sentence in the word-processing program on his PC. As a matter of course, he always encoded sensitive or confidential communications. This was one of the most sensitive, most confidential notes he had ever sent. He highlighted the words, right-clicked on the mouse, and ran it through a strong encryption program he had downloaded from the Internet. He copied the encrypted message into an outgoing e-mail template, typed the address, hit the send key.

Now all he had to do was run the clock

out. *Only four more days.*

Kevin was getting impatient. "We going or what?" he said.

"Yeah, yeah, yeah," Declan answered.

Just before he wiped out his original message, he read it over to himself one more time and smiled:

*I am in, baby. Come to me.*

Eddie and Kevin looked like pharmaceutical sales reps crossing the Wal-Mart parking lot. Declan threw his head back in the sunshine, soaked up the rays.

"Grab a cart," Kevin ordered Eddie on the way in the front door. Declan heard him tell Eddie in a low voice, "Keep your eye on him."

They went straight to the electronics department. Declan loaded the cart up with computer components.

"Happy now?" Kevin said.

"Almost." He threw a handful of music CDs in.

"What the fuck?" Kevin said.

"I work more efficiently with some good music."

"Whatever. Just get your shit and let's go." He took control of the cart and steered it to the checkout in the department.

Declan moved the cart out of line. "We need a few things on the other side of the store."

Kevin rolled his eyes, motioned for Eddie to follow as Declan pushed the cart.

Declan grabbed things off the shelves as he cruised up and down the aisles.

"You guys are beginning to stink," Declan said. "Here, try some of this." He tossed a can of deodorant to Eddie. Kevin shook his head, warning Eddie. Eddie looked at the can, shrugged, put it into the cart.

He led them through housewares, office supplies, automotives. He finally stopped in hardware.

Declan said, "I love power tools, don't you guys?"

Eddie nodded, squeezed the trigger of a power drill. Declan ran his thumb over the blade of a circular saw.

"Put it *down*," Kevin said.

Declan pretended to be looking for some piece of equipment he needed for his work back at the convenience store. "Let me see, where is it?"

Declan surreptitiously checked the ceiling and the aisles once more. With Eddie blocking the view of the store security cameras and Kevin blocking the view of anyone looking down the aisle, he reached over and pulled a package of large alligator clips off the pegboard display, quickly ripped them out of their packaging, slipped them into his pocket. Cables, CDs, computer components he could explain away to Kevin, but alligator clips were taking a chance. He *really* needed the alligator clips.

Kevin had lost all patience. "Come on!"

Declan said calmly, "I think I've got everything I need. We can go now."

# Chapter 27

Maeve fixed a full Irish breakfast — bacon, fried eggs, sausages, black pudding, toast and tomatoes; then Liam and Michael left for the fish plant. Liam gave him a route to drive consisting of deliveries to smaller grocers in the nearby towns. The van was loaded and he went off by ten o'clock.

He drove first to Clonakilty, a half-hour trip, then circled back to Skibbereen via a stop in Leap. After lunch he made a delivery to the boating village of Schull. On the way back to the office he stopped for fuel in Ballydehob.

He filled the van with diesel and went inside the shop to pay. The woman working the till looked at the van through the window as she made change.

"You're with Carbery Islands Seafood?"

"Yes." Her question made him nervous.

"I was expecting to see Brendan. He always comes here on Wednesdays to fill up the van, but in the morning."

"I did Clonakilty first today. I suppose I'm working his usual route backward."

"Brendan can't drive afternoons, since he teaches fiddle to the kids after school on Mondays and Wednesdays. My daughter, Deidre, is one of his students."

"Oh?"

"You don't know what's happened to him, do you? I took Deidre to her lesson today and he wasn't there. He's never missed a lesson before."

Michael knew. He imagined someone finding his cousin's body — a neighboring farmer, the postman, the man who had to come inside to read the electric meter. After several days it would not be a happy discovery.

Something occurred to him. "Hang on. You said he's never missed a lesson?"

"Not in four years. He's a great teacher. You should hear Deidre play."

Michael was thinking about the day Lydia died, the day he had signed out for the van, a Monday. "Week before last, the fourteenth. He made that lesson?"

"Oh, yes."

"You're sure?"

"I'm positive. Deidre turned eleven that day. Brendan had the whole class play

'Happy Birthday' for her."

"Right."

The woman handed him change and a receipt. "I prepaid for lessons for the whole term. You see him, tell him he owes me for one."

Behind the plant, Michael hosed out the back of the van. The employee car park was still full, the official end of the workday another hour away.

Upon his return, Liam had told him to do an extra good job of cleaning the vehicle inside and out. Michael got a bucket, began filling it with water. Liam approached, pulled a rolled-up newspaper from his back pocket, and handed it to Michael.

"Just came in," Liam said. It was a copy of the *Evening Echo*, the late Cork newspaper.

Michael opened the newspaper to the front page. He was startled to see a picture of himself, his old passport picture, alongside a police artist's drawing of what he might look like with a beard. The likeness of the drawing was almost dead-on accurate for when he had had a full beard before he had trimmed it for the disco.

Liam pointed to the accompanying article. "There's a reward for you now. Ten thousand euro might not seem like a lot to you and me, but it's a hell of a lot to someone who cleans entrails from fish for hourly wages." He nodded toward the employees tidying up the premises. "Your presence here is too dangerous. Finish up as usual, don't rush off, so you don't attract any more attention; then clear your stuff out and get back to the house."

Michael skimmed the article. There were enough lurid details about his supposed murderous acts to make him an easily reviled person that no one would have any reservations about turning in to the police — reward or no reward. Farther down the page he saw Claire Burke quoted as the lead detective on the case. "I've made it my personal mission to track this heinous criminal down so he can never harm a woman or a child again," she told the newspaper reporter. She was grabbing all the publicity she could get. Michael thought back to what Brady had said during his last interrogation — confirmation that Brady's saying the case was being reassigned was a complete sham.

Michael avoided eye contact with anyone as he vigorously scrubbed the inside walls of the van. He wanted to get away from all the people at the plant as soon as he could, but considered prudent Liam's advice on maintaining a low profile until the end of the day. As he worked, he considered the implications of what he had learned from the woman at the petrol station. It seemed he was wrong about his Brendan's involvement in Lydia's and Daniel's murders. If Brendan had definitely been in Skibbereen the day they were killed, why had he signed out for the van? And if he didn't take it, who did?

Michael rinsed the inside of the van and left the doors open so it would dry. He filled the bucket with clean water to wash the van's exterior but found that the detergent bottle was empty. He went inside the building.

The cleaning supplies were in the storeroom. On his way back outside he ran into Betty, the woman who had shown him how to properly gut a fish.

"How are ye?" she said.

"Doing great." He tried to hide his nervousness. "You?"

"Not too bad."

Michael's first reaction was to move on quickly, but he needed an answer. He pulled her aside. "Betty, I wanted to ask you something. Brendan O'Driscoll had a regular route to drive for the plant, didn't he?"

"Oh, I'd say so. For the last few months anyhow."

"I was clocking out yesterday and noticed something I was a bit curious about. I saw that Brendan had signed for the van a couple of weeks ago, but I happen to know that he didn't have it out for the whole day. Do you have any idea what that could have been all about?"

Betty thought a moment. Then she looked around to see if anyone was listening. "I heard he liked his drink," she whispered. "Wouldn't surprise me in the least if he had taken the van out and ended up sitting in front of a pint for the rest of the day."

Even with Brendan's history with the bottle, Michael thought that explanation unlikely. He had never heard of an instance when Brendan had let his drink interfere with his work. The responsibilities of fatherhood had at least sobered him up during the day. There must be another reason for the discrepancy.

"Thanks, Betty."

"No problem, dear."

Michael walked around the corner toward the back door and nearly ran into Liam.

"How's it going?" Liam said.

Michael held up a new bottle of detergent. "Just need to wash the outside." Out of the corner of his eye, Michael could see a small group of employees looking at a newspaper together. He was certain it was the *Evening Echo.* And that they were looking at him.

"Don't panic," Liam said. "In fact, you need to act naturally, as if nothing is any different. Take a look under the hood, why don't you? The engines can get pretty dirty driving to Cork and back every day." Liam reached over to a trolley and got a towel, threw it to Michael. "Just give it a good wipe-down."

"No problem."

"Okay. See you in a bit."

On his way back to the van, Michael realized that something about Liam's demeanor might have suggested he had overheard his conversation with Betty. Michael wondered if he was just feeling more paranoid, since his picture was in the paper and he knew that Claire was on the case.

Michael finished washing the van. He wanted to run, but wiped the vehicle down with the towel then popped the hood. Liam was right. There was a lot of grime built up from riding the rough West Cork roads. First he took a screwdriver and knocked off big chunks of mud that had flown up from underneath. He wiped the wires and cables, cleaned the battery. He licked his finger and tested the greasy manifold to see if it was too hot to work on. The wet finger sizzled.

He stood with his hands on his hips, looking at the engine. Even though he was mainly killing time until the other employees left for the day, he wanted to do a good job. He thought about it, then went back inside the building into the supply room where he'd seen a spare chain-mail safety glove.

Michael put the glove on. It must have been one of the women's, since it just barely fit. At least he could work on the hot engine without fear of burning his hands. He turned the dirty towel inside out and stuck his head back under the hood to give the engine block a swipe.

He never heard the footsteps crossing the tarmac behind him. His only warning was hearing the lunge, the swish of clothes as an arm thrust toward him, grabbed him around the neck. Instinctively Michael grabbed at his throat, just as one of the fish-gutting knives flashed past his head. He caught it in his hand — in the hand covered with chain mail.

A powerful arm exerted almost unbearable pressure with the knife. Michael felt the wickedly sharp blade nicking the skin on his hand through the tiny gaps in the metal glove. If it weren't for the glove, though, his fingers would have been sliced off as cleanly as he'd sliced open the cod's belly. Then his throat would have been neatly cut from ear to ear.

Now that he had the knife in his hand he battled with everything he had to hold on to it. The attacker must have been surprised that he hadn't let go already. If the man ever managed to extract the knife, Michael was dead for sure. A couple of quick cuts across his own belly, his guts spilled onto the ground, then a thrust into his back through his heart. Michael fought even harder, curiously aware of his environment. Birds were singing in the trees; traffic buzzed on the road in front of the building. A horn blasted.

At first the attacker didn't seem to notice it, but then the vehicle sounded as if it were approaching down the business driveway, the driver continuously honking the horn, as if trying to get someone's attention.

Michael took advantage of the fraction

of a second's hesitation in the assailant's resolve to utilize his police academy training. He grabbed the wrist and was about to twist it under, forcing the knife to drop, but his maneuver was foiled. The attacker knocked the brace holding up the hood with his elbow, causing it to come crashing down hard on Michael's head. Michael lost his grip and was momentarily stunned, trapped beneath the heavy hood of the truck. He prepared himself for a slash of steel.

Instead he heard footsteps running away. By the time he freed himself, the assailant was gone. There was also no sign of whomever had been blowing the car horn.

Maeve brought bandages into the kitchen, where Noreen was gently dabbing at Michael's bloodied hand and applying antiseptic. Michael saw Liam's car pulling into the driveway. Liam got a large bag out of the trunk and slung it over his shoulder, then walked to the kennels at the back of the house. The dogs barked wildly at his arrival. After a few minutes he took the steps two at a time to the kitchen door.

"What's this?" he said.

"Michael was attacked at the plant," Maeve said. "Where the hell were you?"

"I was getting dog food at the co-op."

"Michael just about got killed! We can't allow strangers to come onto our premises and rough people up!"

"What do you want me to do? Call the police?"

"People are getting bloody bold," Noreen said. "First they chase our van; then they try to kill someone at our place of business."

"You notice anything in common with those two incident?" Liam said. He cocked his head toward Michael. "And now this!" Liam threw down the *Evening Echo* onto the table.

"Oh, Jaysus," Maeve said.

"He can't stay here," Liam said. "He's a major liability. I wouldn't be surprised if someone from the fish plant hasn't already phoned the police."

Maeve shook her head as she thought. "I suppose it could have been a robbery attempt," she said. "There are some Travelers in the area again. My guess is that Liam was the intended victim. Someone saw Michael leaning over the engine and attacked him thinking it was you. This just confirms something I had been thinking about earlier. We need to be even more careful when we leave Liss Ard. Liam, you're not going to like this, but I've decided it's too risky for you to go to the greyhound trials tomorrow."

Liam completely lost his temper. "Nothing is going to keep me away from there. I've been working Feldspar all year. Clonakilty's the last big meeting before Clonmel. If he doesn't run Saturday, everything I've done will have been a waste. There's no way I'm not going."

Noreen said, "I think she's right. If it's not the police, it's whoever attacked Michael this afternoon thinking it was you."

"Feldspar's already registered," Liam said. "I'm there. That's final." Liam glared at his mother and sister.

Michael broke in. "I'll take him," he said.

"*You'll* take him?" Maeve said.

"How's that going to help?" Noreen said.

"Get another car for the day that can't be traced. It shouldn't be too hard to make it look as if he's still here while we sneak out. It worked when I drove to Cork. It can work tomorrow, too. I'll cover up so no one will recognize me, either. I guarantee you."

Maeve said, "I don't imagine I'd have any more success in keeping him from the greyhound coursing than I did keeping him from getting that ship in Amsterdam. I suppose if he is hell-bent on going, it would be better if he were driven there secretly by Michael. We can leave Liam's car out front in a prominent position so the police will think he's at the house. One of the lads can get you off the property somewhere out of town where you can pick up a car."

"I still think it's too risky," Noreen said.

"It'll be fine," Michael said. "I got him back here safely before; I'll do it again."

Liam smiled broadly. "Thanks, cousin."

The phone rang and Maeve answered it. "Just a second," she said. She took the phone out of the kitchen.

Noreen finished bandaging Michael's hand. "Be right back," she said, taking the medical supplies away.

Behind the door leading to the dining room, Maeve spoke on the phone in a raised voice, though Michael couldn't make out what she was saying.

Liam rolled up his sleeves and washed his hands at the sink. Michael turned quickly and caught a glimpse of Liam's arms as he was buttoning his sleeves. Even after washing up, his forearms were raw, black, abraded.

"Nasty bruise," Michael said.

"Yeah. The dogs get a bit overexcited." He hung up the towel, clapped Michael on the back.

Maeve returned, hung up the phone. "Bastard," she said. She called out for Noreen to come back into the kitchen.

"Who was it?" Liam asked.

"That was Michael's brother. Threatening to cut us out of the deal if we didn't up his take on the deal to seventy-five percent."

Noreen was incredulous. "What? How can he do that?"

"He said he's got Declan, and he's in control of the venue. He must think we're desperate." She looked to her daughter.

"I don't know where the hell he got that impression," Noreen said.

"He must have sensed fear when you were in Boston. It's something you can't hide, not from a man like that."

Michael interjected, "Don't you think it's about time you let me in on what's going on?"

Maeve smiled. "I was just thinking the same thing."

"Ma — " Liam started.

"No," Maeve said. "He's proved himself over and over to us." She turned to Michael. "And it's only fair, considering we have another job for you."

Michael was wary about throwing himself into more danger before he had completed the work he had come to do. "What kind of job?"

"I don't trust Aiden and he doesn't trust me. He said he's on the way over here and wants to meet tomorrow night. Funny that he wants to come all the way over to tell me to my face to go to hell. If I know him, he isn't coming alone, and there's no way I'm going to meet him by myself. So what do you think the real reason is that he's flying over?"

The clear implication was that Aiden was coming to West Cork with a gang of thugs to forcibly pressure the O'Driscolls to go along with the new terms.

"So what is it you want me to do?" Michael said.

"Aiden wants to meet one-on-one. I'm afraid I'd antagonize him if I went. He'll be expecting me, but you're going to act as our emissary. A sort of family reunion, like. You need to convince him how stupid he is to try to change the terms of our agreement. You need to let him know in unambiguous terms that if he persists with this kind of talk, there's going to be a bloodbath. And he's at the top of the list to go. I thought you'd have an interest in saving your own brother's life."

It seemed to Michael that he had no choice. If he refused to act on Maeve's behalf, she would cut him loose, or worse.

"Take Liam to his greyhound coursing; then you can meet Aiden afterward."

"Okay," Michael agreed. "But first I want to know everything about this venture with my brother." Michael saw the worried looks on the faces of his cousins. *"Everything,"* he repeated.

# Chapter 28

Michael had made subtle but important changes to his appearance. No longer the scruffy West Cork blow-in or sharp-dressed man ready for the disco, he had donned a well-worn Barbour coat, tweed cap, and Wellies and looked now like an established member of the Anglo-Irish landed gentry.

Michael drove another car "borrowed" for the day, this time a painter's utility truck cleared out of brushes and buckets and paint cans. They had thrown a couple of blankets into the back to try to make the dog as comfortable as possible for the forty-five-minute journey. Michael heard Feldspar's weight shift and slide as he turned off the highway down a rutted country road east of Clonakilty.

"Easy," Liam warned.

Liam read a copy of *The Sporting Press* as they bumped along the rutted road. He scanned pages listing draws for the greyhound coursing at various meetings across the country, which dogs would be paired against each other. "Keep on this road until you see someone selling programs," Liam said.

As he drove, Michael considered all that he had learned the previous night from Maeve about the Powerball scheme. At first he had thought that Lydia had become another casualty of domestic violence. Then he had concluded that preservation of the O'Driscolls' drug empire had somehow been at the root of Lydia's murder. Now the most likely motivation seemed to be in keeping secret the scheme behind scamming the richest lottery in America. After announcing the results of the Irish national lottery, news on the radio had reported the Powerball jackpot in the States as already topping $300 million. Michael was even more certain that one of the O'Driscolls was responsible for the deaths, with Liam clearly the prime suspect. All Michael had to do was stay alive and avoid the police long enough to find the evidence to nail his cousin.

It was surprisingly cool even for an early fall morning. The grass in the fields was still wet with dew. Another quarter mile later they passed a farmyard where a couple of men holding a stack of programs stood blocking the middle of a dirt road. They saw Feldspar pacing in the back, recognized Liam as a fellow greyhound owner, handed them a couple of free programs through the window, and waved them through to a large field where cars were parking on the grass.

Liam had been explaining how the greyhounds were raised and trained for coursing. "You buy the puppies from a breeder when they're around twelve weeks old. You get them in pairs and rear them together. If you get one by itself it just becomes like a house pet and it's too docile for coursing. Training starts when the dogs are about fifteen months old. I usually get males, since you can't run bitches in season because of extra fat around the heart," he said. "Lots of owners use the services of a professional trainer, but not me," he said with pride.

They got out of the truck, leaving Feldspar in the back. There was no sign of police anywhere. The easygoing atmosphere of the countryside venue made Michael feel for the first time since arriving in Ireland that he could let his guard down a bit. Liam nodded to other greyhound owners milling around the backs of their cars, some of whom had early races and were already rubbing the dogs down with liniment. Michael kept his hat pulled down low over his eyes and his coat collar turned up. Liam pointed to a pair of dogs being exercised. "Depending on the predetermined position in the program, a dog is fitted with either a red or white collar, indicating whether he's starting out running on the left or the right. Those are special coursing muzzles they're putting on them so they can't bite the hares. Well, that's the idea, at least."

The length of the coursing field was defined by chicken wire nailed to wooden posts. Next to the fence near the field's entrance was a snack van, its generator humming, a queue forming for coffee and curried chips. Bookies stood on overturned milk crates near the fence taking bets.

"You ever been to a coursing event before?" Liam asked.

"No."

"Let's go down to the other end so you can see how they're slipped."

On the far right end of the field inside the fence was what Liam called the slipper's shed, inhabited between the events by a man in a red coat.

Liam said, "After an announcement of the event over the speakers, the two owners bring their dogs over here, where the steward checks their registration cards against the tattoos in the dogs' ears. Then the slipper takes over and buckles them into their slips side by side."

Michael and Liam watched as the first brace of dogs was summoned to the slipper's shed. After the dogs were buckled into their slips, the slipper strained to hold them back.

"Keep your eyes open," Liam told him. "The hares they use are caught in the surrounding fields a couple weeks before meeting and are trained to run the course. They're kept in a pen together behind the slipper's shed."

The slipper gave a signal and a hare was released. It shot out of a chute and ran in front of the dogs, who were barely controllable after they saw him. Once the hare had a head start of about twenty yards, the slipper released the dogs at the same time and they tore off side by side after the hare, which frantically raced toward the opposite end. The hounds thundered by on the turf. Spaced out on both sides of the course every ten yards or so were men shooing the hare so it wouldn't run off to the side, thus spoiling the event.

Michael and Liam shielded their eyes from the sun so they could follow the action at the end of the course. As the hare got closer to the end, one of the dogs closed in. A judge on horseback wearing a red coat ran parallel to the hare to get a closer look at which of the two dogs would be the first to "turn" it, causing the hare to turn off course. Eventually the dog wearing the red collar turned the hare just before it ran into the "escape" at the end, under which the dog could not follow. The judge reached into his coat pocket and pulled out a red flag, indicating which dog had won the event.

"That was pretty exciting," Michael said.

"You liked it, huh?" Liam was trying to determine Michael's frame of mind. "Maybe one day you and I can go in on rearing a couple of dogs together. Form a syndicate. Buy up all the best puppies for a whole season. Start a dynasty."

Michael read him: Liam had no intention of ever rearing dogs together.

"Sure, we can do that," Michael said.

Feldspar didn't run until late in the afternoon. They stood by the fence, and Liam showed Michael how to mark up his program to keep track of the winners and losers of each run. As the time came closer for Feldspar's event, Liam got noticeably more jittery.

"I've got a bad feeling about this," Liam finally said.

Michael and Liam walked to the slipper's shed with the dog between them on a lead. Liam was so nervous he couldn't talk anymore. Michael left him alone until the run was over.

Perhaps it was a premonition on Liam's part, but Feldspar lost to a greyhound he had beaten on every previous occasion. They collected the dog near the escape. "Look at the results," Liam huffed as he thrust his program in Michael's face. "Eight out of ten of the winners wore the red collar! Of course, today of all days I had to draw white!"

"Unlucky," Michael said.

Liam nonetheless patiently groomed and watered Feldspar before putting him into the back of the truck. He spoke lovingly to the dog as he rubbed his muscles down with liniment again. He opened up to the animal in a way Michael had never seen him relate to a human being.

Liam had planned on going to the nearby pub after the meeting and told Michael they would be staying for the day's full schedule of events, but after Feldspar's loss, he sullenly told Michael it was time to pack it up and go. Even so, it was late enough in the day that the sun was just beginning to set over the hills.

Other dog owners and members of the public milled around the cars, looking over the dogs. A burly man stopped to talk.

"American?" he said.

Michael felt his cheeks flush.

"I heard you as you were leading the dog to the slipper," the man said. "I have a sister in Boston. Where you from?"

Liam cut his eyes to Michael as he groomed the dog.

"New York, actually," Michael finally answered.

"Good town. I don't know it as well as Boston. My uncle lives in Queens." The man was looking at Michael's clothes, trying to reconcile them with his background. "What brings you over here?"

"I'm on holiday," Michael said.

"Really? What do you do back home?"

"I work for a pharmaceutical company."

"I'm a retired garda. I just moved down here from Dublin."

He was looking closely at Michael's face, as if he recognized him, but wasn't exactly sure from where. Michael saw Liam getting as nervous as he himself felt.

The garda's mouth opened, then closed, his eyes narrowing, as if he were checking himself from saying what he was thinking.

Liam quickly got the dog settled and closed the car up. "We'd better be moving on," he said. "Nice to meet you, though."

The man watched Michael and Liam as they sped off across the field toward the gate. Michael looked into the wing mirror. "He's writing down something, probably the car registration number."

"Jaysus, that was close," Liam said. "Too feckin' close. They know you're here now. We've got to get you out of here as soon as you talk to your brother."

They rode mainly in silence the rest of the way, Liam offering occasional assistance in negotiating the back roads in the growing gloom. Michael drove them back to the Traveler's Inn. A car was waiting there to take Liam and the dog back to Carnmore.

"Good luck," Liam told him. He looked Michael squarely in the eye and shook his hand, seeming to snap back to life. "See you back at the house."

Declan O'Driscoll reattached the cable running into the lottery ticket printer. He took a small screwdriver from his pouch of computer tools and started tightening the screws that prevented the cable from accidentally pulling out. Kevin hovered over him in the front of the store, more to relieve boredom than out of any particular interest in the technical side of what Declan was doing. Pat was telling the person at the front of the line that the lottery machine should be fixed in just a moment. The crowds in the store had been growing all day.

"You're blocking my light," Declan said.

"Sorry." Kevin backed off. He stuck his hands in pockets and walked up and down the aisles of the store, checking out the merchandise.

"Damn," Declan said. "Wrong size screwdriver. I need to get another one from the other room, okay?"

"Sure."

Declan went into the hallway separating the front room from the back. Instead of going to retrieve his tools, however, he quietly opened the door to the back of the walk-in cooler. From inside, he watched Kevin and Pat through the glass doors of the cooler past the six packs of beer on the wire racks.

He quickly got to work. From his pocket

he pulled the big alligator clips he had stolen from Wal-Mart. Out of his trousers he pulled a couple of lengths of electrical wire. He connected the wires to holes in the clips, then attached the business end of the clips to the wire racks where the beer was stored. He had a small flashlight that he turned on and stuck into his mouth. He cautiously pulled the large circuit breaker for the cooler. As careful as he was, the lever still closed with a loud snap, though the sound was muffled by the insulation of the room.

Kevin, who had been toying with merchandise in the office-supplies section out front, looked up from a pen he had been clicking and testing its ink flow, but seemed not to notice that the interior cooler lights had gone out and the compressor, which was always going on and off, had stopped.

Declan worked as quickly as he could. First he reached over the shelves and pulled out all but two six packs of Budweiser, and hid them behind some other beer. He attached the bare ends of the wires to an electrical outlet, and flipped the circuit breaker back into position.

The cooler light came back on and the

compressor kicked in. He put away the flashlight as he stood back and admired his work. His handiwork was neat, the wires barely visible.

He went into the washroom. He attached the hose the employees used to wash down the workroom, ran it down the hall to the cooler, and flooded the floor, all the while nervously watching Kevin and Pat in the front room, Eddie in the back. He let the water rise to just below the wires running along the wall.

He heard Kevin calling his name. He coiled and replaced the hose, and shut the cooler door just as Kevin came into the hall looking for him.

Aiden had told Maeve that he did not consider the Traveler's Inn to be a neutral meeting place. Maeve in turn had told him to suggest someplace, and he had come up with Noonan's Pub, an old favorite drinking place of his well out in the country, several miles off the Ballydehob road.

Michael passed the lay-by overlooking Roaring Water Bay. A large yellow moon rose over a calm ocean, casting deep shadows onto the rugged landscape. Several miles off the coast, the beacon from the Fastnet Rock lighthouse swept over the water.

Michael took the next turn, a sharp left leading down the peninsula. A signpost indicated he was headed toward Turk Head, the promontory beyond Lisheen. Something slid along the floor of the passenger side. He reached over while he drove and picked up a wallet, laid it on the dash so he wouldn't forget about it. Liam must have been so distracted by his dog's defeat that he had dropped it and forgotten about it.

The pub was supposed to be closed to the public. The elderly owner had died a few months earlier and the family was still haggling over who would take it over. Until they settled their dispute, the beer signs and outside lights were left unlit at night. Aiden had been a favorite of the old man's and knew the chink in the stone wall outside in which he kept the key hidden.

Michael found the pub completely dark when he parked by the front door. There was already another car there, but no one was to be seen inside the pub or out.

He opened the truck door and the dome light came on inside, which caused him to see the wallet on the dash he had forgotten about. He opened it to confirm it was Liam's. There was Liam's driving license, several credit cards. Out of idle curiosity he rifled through the various compartments. A few hundred euros of mixed denomination. In between the bills several slips of folded paper, credit card receipts for petrol.

Michael unfolded them, read each one in turn, laid them on the passenger seat. He ignored the amount filled and paid. He was reading for store locations and dates. Skibbereen, Bantry, Ballydehob.

He opened the last one — a station near a roundabout just south of Dublin. The date was the same as when the van from the fish plant had been taken on the six-hundred-mile journey. The day Lydia was murdered.

Michael saw a light flick on inside the pub.

# Chapter 29

Michael found the front door to the pub unlocked. He cracked it open an inch and listened without looking first: three light thumps on a far wall, the sound of someone walking across the floor a few feet, a moment's hesitation, then three more thumps.

Aiden Driscoll didn't bother turning to look when Michael stepped through the door. Supremely confident, he took aim with a dart, threw it, sighted another. All scored within a tight circle.

Michael looked into the corners of the room while he approached his brother as the final dart was thrown. The chairs were turned neatly upside down on the tables. The beer spigots were covered with tea towels. In front of the mirror behind the bar, a spider fell on a thread to the counter.

Aiden studied the dartboard, then pulled out the darts. Still not realizing who had come to meet him, he said, "So are you going to shoot me now or you really going to listen?"

"How about I'll talk, *you* listen," Michael said softly.

Aiden looked up, clearly shocked at Michael's presence. "You?"

"Welcome back to West Cork, brother."

Neither had seen the other for several years. Aiden looked fit, self-assured, prosperous. Aiden held his hand out and Michael shook it. They hugged quickly, awkwardly.

"What the hell are you doing here?" Aiden said, still confused, suspicious.

Michael leaned against a bar stool. "Tonight I'm here to see you. But I'm in West Cork to find out who killed Lydia Jellicoe and her son." The full story about Daniel would have to wait.

"Lydia?"

"She and her son were murdered in Dublin last week. She wanted me to help her. I got there too late, and then the police tried to pin the murders on me."

"That would probably explain why I got a call from the FBI wanting to know where you were. I told them you were in the Arizona desert. I thought it was a joke. Or an excuse to make a contact with me. I figured they were trying to test out a tapped line or get a voice print off me. I had no idea they were hunting you down for murder."

"I fled Dublin and came to West Cork because I found evidence an O'Driscoll was responsible for the murders. I'm pretty sure I just figured out who did it." Michael pulled Liam's wallet from his coat pocket, took out Liam's driver's license, and threw it onto the bar so Aiden could see the picture.

"Liam? Are you sure? Why would he do that?"

"Because of this lottery scheme you and Maeve have cooked up. I know all about it, Aiden. At first I thought it was just their drug business, but now the O'Driscolls are so desperate and the stakes are so high, they'll do anything to protect their huge payoff. Three family members have already died, and no telling how many others, to keep your plan a secret. There's been too much bloodshed. I'm here to tell you enough is enough, Aiden."

Aiden pulled a stool out and sat down. "Did you come here alone?"

"Yes, of course."

"Who else in the family was killed?" Aiden said.

"Brendan."

"If anyone in the family were to get killed, it doesn't shock me it was Brendan. We all knew he was dangerous in the way he drank and talked. I warned them they had a security problem."

"Maeve sent me here to tell you she's not going to accept a penny less than what you agreed to on the Powerball scheme. Fifty-fifty. But I'm here to try to put an end to all the killing."

"She's hardly in a position to be telling me anything."

"She'll fight you, Aiden. She has nothing to lose. Don't push her on this."

"Why do you want to help out a family who you say has killed Lydia? You sound as if you're on Maeve's side."

"I'm on no one's side. I'm stuck in the middle trying to do the decent thing."

"Then come back to the States with me. Come back into the family. Be a comfort to your father before he dies. I can find a way to smuggle you onto my private jet."

"I'm not leaving Ireland until my job is done and I've nailed Lydia's killer and cleared my own name. Tomorrow morning I'm going to the police with what I know."

"Forget Lydia."

"I tried, and it didn't work."

"Your own father is dying and you refuse

to visit him, yet you can't get over here fast enough when Lydia calls. Brother, where are your priorities?"

Michael said nothing.

"Maeve O'Driscoll and her organization are over," Aiden said, looking at his watch. "As of about an hour from now. You don't want to be here when things start getting rough."

"You didn't come here to talk, did you?" Michael said.

"I brought six of my best men with me," was Aiden's answer.

Michael shook his head, stood up, and walked over to the window at the back of the pub. He pulled open the curtain. The magical view of the moonlit countryside had been blotted out by the thick clouds.

"You know I'm not a superstitious person," Michael said. "But I can't help thinking about the stories we used to hear about the O'Driscoll family banshee. How the ghost of a long-dead O'Driscoll female ancestor would appear and wail as a warning that someone in the family was about to die. I imagined I heard her in my parish church right before Lydia phoned me and was killed. Maybe I'm spooked, but I thought I heard it again on the drive over here. And now I'm afraid, if you are right, I am going to have a whole chorus of banshees screaming in my head." He stared out the window at the emptiness. He pleaded with Aiden: "Don't do it."

Aiden walked over to join Michael at the window. He put his hand on Michael's shoulder and they both looked into the black night.

A cloud shifted and the moon shone briefly on the landscape. Something moved.

Aiden stiffened. "I thought you said you came alone."

Michael was squinting out the window trying to see what it was before he answered.

"You set me up!" Aiden said. "Traitor!"

"No!"

Aiden ran to the front door, flung it open, ran toward his car. Michael heard the scuffle outside, heard his brother utter something unintelligible. There was a flash of guns blazing. Men shouting. More shots.

Michael slammed and locked the front door, cut the light, looked out the front window. The glass was old and wavy and he couldn't make out anything clearly. The moon shadow lifted again and he saw a figure running frantically over the rough grass in the field across the road from the pub. He heard another shot and the figure fell.

A band of men followed their quarry like a hunting party into the tall grass of the field. Something thrashed in the grass. A final shot put the wounded animal out of its misery.

Now he could see. Liam O'Driscoll pointed toward the pub and they began running in his direction. Someone else pounded hard on the back door. They were coming from both directions.

The groan rising up in Michael's throat was terror, grief, an unarticulated prayer — for his dead brother, for his family, for his own life, which had never seemed so fragile as at that moment.

Aiden had forewarned Maeve that he was bringing several security men with him to Skibbereen. It was no big deal, he had said, just the normal precautions when traveling overseas. At the same time Michael was meeting with his brother, Maeve had arranged for Aiden's men to meet at the Corner Bar with several of her own crew. She and Aiden agreed it was best if they kept an eye on one another.

Peter O'Sullivan had bought the last

round of drinks for the group. Aiden's men were led by Tom Parsons, several years senior to Aiden and the most experienced with a gun. Tom had selected the five others accompanying them on the trip, all with substantial backgrounds in enforcement. At ten-thirty at night in a small-town pub, the boys from Boston were unflinchable but overdressed.

"You guys need to relax," O'Sullivan told Parsons. "Don't you ever take off your coat and tie?"

Parsons smiled, loosened his tie. "Better?"

O'Sullivan laughed. "West Cork is as casual as it gets. We only wear ties for funerals around here."

Parsons nodded and took a long drink of lager, never taking his eyes off his host.

Over the course of a couple of hours the two groups of men drank, seemed to bond.

"I know what we need to do," O'Sullivan suggested at one point. "There's a spectacular night view over the town that you gotta see. Just across the street, up in the Church of Ireland belfry. I know where the key's hidden. How 'bout it?"

Parsons was feeling friendly, probably the beer. "Sure, why not. One more round?"

"Excellent idea."

After finishing the next round, a dozen boisterous men left the pub and crossed the street. They passed a grocer's shop closed for the night.

"Everybody grab a couple of milk crates so you can see out properly," O'Sullivan said.

They climbed the open metal steps outside the back of the church, each with a pint of lager in one hand, a milk crate in the other. O'Sullivan unlocked the door and let them in. He pulled on a large block of lead attached to a rope that counterbalanced the weight of the heavy trapdoors that covered the window slats to keep the pigeons out when the belfry was not in use. The bell ropes hung loose in the middle of the room. The Skibbereen men showed their guests where to turn their crates over on the floor around the perimeter of the wall so they could stand on them and see out over the town through the slats. They stacked them two high to get an unobstructed view.

The Boston boys were taking in the sights around the four walls. Maeve's men stood behind their guests on the crates in the middle of the floor and pointed out areas of interest. On two of the sides was a nice vista of the surrounding countryside — the River Ilen shining in the light of the moon, the mountain over Lough Ine. From the other sides Parsons was admiring Skibbereen landmarks — the cathedral, the town hall, the Famine History Museum.

"Beautiful, isn't it?" O'Sullivan said.

"Yeah, nice."

"Look closely," O'Sullivan said. "Can everyone see them cows out there on the other side of the river? You don't see a lot of those in Boston, I'll bet." Then, as a prearranged signal, he said, "Those aren't just any cows, city boys," he told them. "Those are *Friesians*."

Aiden's men all focused their attention on finding the cows in the distance. At that instant O'Sullivan and his men quietly, quickly lifted the ends of the bell ropes with their specially knotted hangman's nooses and threw them over the heads of their visitors. Without a second lost, in unison they kicked out the crates from underneath the men and Aiden Driscoll's finest fell hard three feet before their necks snapped. At the same time the bells swung down from their standing positions, clanging and clashing dissonantly. The heavy bells tolled out over the town, a death knell for Aiden Driscoll and his band of Boston sharpies.

O'Sullivan and his men scrambled down the belfry steps even as the limp-bodied men in their suits bobbed.

A block away on Bridge Street, where she had been parked, Maeve O'Driscoll listened to a melancholy waltz on the traditional Irish music radio station and smoked. She turned down the volume and cracked her window. She heard the bells — music to her ears. She started the car and headed back to Liss Ard to await news of Aiden and Michael Driscoll's deaths.

# Chapter 30

"How 'bout getting us a nice cold Bud?" Declan said to Eddie.

Eddie was mesmerized by another television show. Judge Judy was laying into some poor guy who'd trashed his girlfriend's apartment after he found she had been sleeping with his best friend. Now the girlfriend wanted compensation. "Get it yourself," Eddie answered without emotion.

Kevin, who was cleaning his gun, stared at Eddie until he looked up at him. "Yeah, yeah, okay."

Declan secretly read again the two-word he had just received: *Go now.* He wiped the message and closed out his e-mail account. It had been only in the last two minutes that the store had been emptied of customers. The demand for lottery tickets had been relentless, but finally there was a brief break.

Eddie muttered to himself about the precious geek at the PC issuing orders as he went to the walk-in drinks cooler. He yanked open the door and went inside. He looked at the rows of beers on the wire shelves until he found the Budweiser, Declan O'Driscoll's favorite.

In the back room, Declan checked the big digital clock on his computer. He'd give himself another minute — not so long that Eddie's absence would attract attention, hopefully long enough for his plan to have time to take effect.

In the cooler, Eddie stepped into an inch of water on the floor. "Oh, hell," he said. His shoes and socks were soaked right through to the skin. He found the shelf tag for the Budweiser. There were only a couple of six-packs left at the far end, so he had to reach up and over to get to the beer. As soon as he touched the wire shelf, ten thousand volts surged through his body and his brain was instantly fried.

The lights in the store dimmed momentarily. Kevin and Declan looked up at each other.

"Brownout," Declan told Kevin. "This dirty electricity out in the country is hell on computers. Thank God for surge protectors. Going to take a piss."

Kevin looked around the room, hesitated. "Whatever," he said. "Make it quick."

Declan headed off to the rest room, but went to the cooler instead. Eddie was already lying on the floor in the water. His body was shaking in violent spasms, not because he was still alive, but because his hand still touched the base of the wire shelving.

"Dickhead," Declan said.

Declan got a mop from the hallway, used the handle to knock the semiautomatic handgun out of the back of the holster in the waistband of Eddie's trousers. He hit it through the water over to the door and into the hallway. He wiped it dry on his shirttail, turned the safety off, and put the gun into his pocket.

"Hey!" Declan called out. "We've got a problem in here!"

Kevin came running into the hallway, Pat from the front of the store.

"Holy shit," Pat said, seeing Eddie's body. He took a step into the cooler, splashed into the water, convulsed and fell to the floor.

Kevin stood back, understanding what the problem was. "Help me get him!" he yelled at Declan.

Declan pulled the gun out of his pocket,

aimed it at Kevin. "Fuck you and your family. And I mean that."

"Wait," Kevin said, backing up. "No, wait . . ." Then realizing his only chance of saving himself was to rush the gun, he lunged.

Seeing another customer pulling off the road into the store parking lot, Declan squeezed the trigger, three quick shots to his cousin's midsection. Kevin's momentum carried him forward to the cooler door, where he fell.

Declan switched the current off in the back room and the bodies stopped convulsing. He shoved Kevin's body into the cooler with the other two, shut the door, and padlocked it.

He adjusted the thermostat to take the temperature down inside the cooler. The bodies wouldn't start smelling in the chilled air until well after the Powerball draw. By then, he'd be long gone and very rich.

Declan walked to the front of the store and helped himself to a pack of cigarettes and a new lighter decorated with an American flag. "Land of opportunity," he said in his old West Cork accent. "You got that right."

He sat on the counter and lit up.

Looking through the six-packs of beer behind the glass cooler doors on the other side of the room at that particular angle, he could just barely see the eyes of the three dead men staring out through the bottles.

A customer pushed through the front door. Declan hopped down from the counter and stood behind the cash register.

The man walked directly up to Declan, handed him a twenty-dollar bill and a lottery form already filled out with numbers. "I want the winning Powerball lottery ticket," the man said jovially.

"Don't we all," Declan said. He took the money, made change, and handed the customer his ticket. "Good luck."

The banging on the back door of Noonan's Pub wouldn't stop. Now someone was beating on the front door with something like a large timber. Glass in the windows began breaking behind the thick curtains, first on the front, then on the side of the pub. Michael stood in the middle of the room in the dark, not knowing which way to turn.

It suddenly got quiet.

Michael could hear his heart beating in

his chest as he turned his head from side to side, trying to hear what was happening outside.

Another ten seconds of dread in the silence. Through the broken window he heard the cocking of a gun. He dropped to the floor just as gunshots blazed through the curtains. He crawled toward the back of the pub, since all the firepower was coming from every direction but that one.

He heard shotgun shells being reloaded as others continued to fire inside. Against the back wall where there were no windows, he knocked over a heavy table and got behind it for protection from the bullets and shotgun blasts.

Unexpectedly, the back door suddenly burst open. He closed his eyes and said the shortest prayer of his life as he cringed and prepared to be blown away. Instead he felt a hand grab him roughly by the collar and yank him up.

"Let's go!" the person whispered harshly to him in the dark. "Now!"

Michael saw the figure in a full helmet and bulky clothes run to the back of a shed, then wheel out a motorcycle. The ignition turned over, the engine revved.

"Get on!"

Michael hesitated.

"What are you waiting for, you eejit?"

Michael jumped onto the pillion as the motorcycle spun out in the gravel. They roared off, crashing through empty beer kegs and crates of bottles, ducking gunfire until they were around the first bend in the road.

Michael held on tightly as they raced through the countryside taking back roads he didn't even know existed. Mixed with the smell of cordite and motorcycle-jacket leather, something pricked at the back of his neck.

That perfume, he thought.

Maeve and Noreen stood quickly as Liam rushed into the library at Liss Ard. He was breathless, bloodied.

Maeve looked at him with horror. "Jaysus," she said. He must have pulled the trigger at close range. She took hold of his face in both hands, smudged the fine droplets of blood from his cheeks with her thumbs. The same fine spray was on the front of his coat and his trousers. "We need to burn these clothes straightaway."

"We got Aiden, but Michael escaped," Liam said.

"How could that happen?" Maeve said.

Noreen showed him a text message on

her mobile phone. "It's okay. Everything's going to be all right. Declan just confirmed he took Kevin and his minders out. And Tom reported in that he got all of the men Aiden brought with him."

Maeve shook her head. "How could he have gotten away?"

"He rode off on the back of a motorcycle. It must have been one of Aiden's accomplices."

"This worries me — a lot. Michael knows everything about us — our drug business, the lottery scheme. He's not going to let us get away with killing his brother and carry on about our business. I'm sure Michael didn't have any trouble figuring out that we used him to lure Aiden over here."

"Don't worry; we'll find him," Liam said. "We'll hunt him down and take him out."

Maeve was unconvinced.

"Look," Noreen said, "we've accomplished almost everything we set out to do. We've completely decapitated their organization. With Aiden and Kevin gone, there's no leadership. And now Declan is absolutely free to execute the Powerball plan for us. Michael won't be able to get very far, since he's a wanted man. Liam will get him."

"Where is everyone now?" Maeve asked.

"They're combing the countryside for Michael," Liam said. "Other than those we'd planned on going with Noreen over to the States, I've gotten every man out."

Maeve nodded, still distracted by the fact that Michael had gotten away.

"Ma," Noreen said, "the lads are leaving in the morning and will be in West Virginia by the end of the day. Declan is into the mainframe. All we have to do is keep him safe for a few more days so he can get on with his work. Payday is Monday, Ma. Then everything will be okay. The money will be all ours. No one will be able to touch us. We'll never have any worries again. We'll leave Ireland and go someplace sunny. Isn't that what you want? Spain? The Costa del Sol? We'll all be fat, tanned, and rich."

Maeve had been thinking. "That all sounds fine, but we still have a plan to execute. We can't get lazy, take anything for granted. First we kill all the traitors, then their sympathizers, then the indifferent. Show me that Brian Driscoll's last son is dead; then I'll know for sure we're almost there."

Claire Burke took off her riding gloves

and laid her motorcycle helmet on the table. She shook her hair out.

"By the way," she said, "you'll be happy to know that you tested negative for HIV and hepatitis C."

"To be honest, I've had my mind on other things. I just saw my own brother being killed." Michael hung his head in disbelief.

Claire remained silent until he looked at her again. "I'm sorry," she said. "There's something else you probably should know. I had a hunch about it, but the DNA analysis confirmed you are Daniel's father."

"I know. All this killing. My own family. It's too much." He was overcome by anger. "What are you going to do to stop these people?" he shouted.

"That's why I'm here, Michael."

"If you don't mind me saying so, you're doing a pretty lousy job of ending this madness."

She explained that they were in a safe house that had been used by undercover police in the area to monitor the coastal drug trade. The house was in a hidden cove well off the main roads. On their way in, Michael had seen a dirt road leading to a pier jutting out into what must have been Roaring Water Bay. The house was rough, unrestored. There were four cots in the sitting room and a table with chairs. An assortment of police equipment sat on the table — two-way radios, nylon handcuffs, binoculars. The fireplace was full of cigarette butts. Across the hall was a simple kitchen with cheap appliances that had started to rust in the damp.

"You'll be safe here," she said.

"Really? In the way someone can feel safe being locked into a prison cell?"

"I know I have a lot of explaining to do."

"Don't bother. I wouldn't believe a word you told me."

"Okay. I know that you overheard my conversation with Brady at the Shelbourne Hotel bar. Michael, I swear to you — it was all talk. I was just telling him what he wanted to hear."

"For what? Your career? At the expense of me?"

"I still don't believe you murdered Lydia or Daniel. I've always been confident of catching the real killer."

"How long have you known my whereabouts?"

"I assumed you might be making your way to West Cork after I connected you to your cousins down here. I've had you under observation pretty much since you arrived."

"So why have you allowed all this to happen? Why have you been tracking me if not because you think I'm the killer?"

Michael followed Claire into the kitchen. She filled the electric kettle with water and turned it on.

"Michael, there's something big going down here in West Cork. Bigger than drugs. Bigger than anything any of the organized crime gangs in Ireland have ever undertaken. We picked up intelligence that the O'Driscolls are involved in something that will allow them to get out of the drug trade permanently. That's pretty impressive, considering they earned an estimated ten to fifteen million euros last year. Those bastards killed my partner right in front of my eyes. Not to mention that I'm over thirty and my career needs a boost. I don't plan on working for Charlie Brady the rest of my life. I need a win, Michael. This is going to be it."

Michael, of course, knew what she was talking about — the Powerball scheme. Given his experience with her, he was saying nothing. He had ideas of his own about how to fix that situation.

"I'm a leg up on your career ladder," he said. "You allowed me to be named a murder suspect to cover up your other undercover operation."

"Michael, a crime's been committed. Or about to be. If the O'Driscolls are willing to kill this many people to protect it, it's something that needs to be stopped."

"If you want to make yourself a hero, why don't you go arrest Liam O'Driscoll right now? He's the one who killed Lydia and Daniel."

"Where's the proof?"

"I *know* he's the one. It's circumstantial, but I know he's involved."

"You and I both know you're going to have to do better than that."

Claire rinsed two cups from the sink as she waited for the kettle to come to a boil.

"I am grateful to you for rescuing me from the pub back there," Michael said.

"It's not the first time, you know."

"I didn't. How so?"

"The other day when Liam almost cut your head off outside the fish plant. I was watching you from across the road. As soon as I saw him attack you I laid on the horn and rushed over as fast as I could."

"Apparently it did the job. Thank you at least for that. And I assume that was you following me in the silver car over to Union Hall?"

"I thought you were pulling a runner on

me. I was afraid I was going to lose you."

"I did."

"True, but at least you didn't leave the area."

"I came to do a job."

"So did I."

"And I'm not done yet. I have to stop Maeve and Noreen and Liam."

"I do understand, but I'm sorry, Michael; I can't allow you to do that. You're no longer useful here anymore. Not to me, nor to the O'Driscolls. They want you dead. Plus, I saw everything that happened at Minahane's tonight, even though I was powerless to stop it. Another person has been murdered."

"Not *just* another person, but my brother! And yet another you don't even know about! You can find Brendan O'Driscoll's body at his house."

"All the more reason for me to be closing this operation down. You'll have to return to Dublin. I've phoned for a couple of uniformed police officers to drive you back while I stay here to tidy up."

Claire's mobile phone rang. She answered and listened. She spoke cryptically so Michael couldn't understand what she was talking about.

She said when she had rung off, "You're

definitely on the way out of here tonight. Six of your brother's men were killed in Skibbereen tonight. There were two groups of Liam's men — one to kill you and Aiden, one to wipe out Aiden's security. Now they're all out looking for you. Your escort has already left the Skibbereen garda station and is only five minutes away."

Michael knew if he went back to Dublin he would be paraded in front of the cameras in handcuffs before being locked away. He already had a name in the media as a multiple killer. Brady and the legal infrastructure would have too much political capital invested to admit they had made a mistake and allow him to walk free. There was no way he could let the police take him away.

Michael slowed his mind down. He needed to think. He watched Claire going through boxes of tea bags in the cupboard. He walked casually into the other room. He sat back against the table as he talked to Claire in the kitchen.

"What's my choice?" he said.

"Regular or herbal."

Keep her busy, keep her talking, he told himself. "Regular. Any milk?"

As she bent over the refrigerator he

joined her in the kitchen again.

"I don't see any," she said.

"That's okay. I've changed my mind about the tea."

Michael quickly grabbed her arms and pulled them behind her back, slipping over her hands the nylon handcuffs he had taken from the table in the other room. He cinched them tightly onto her wrists.

Claire spun around furiously, her face red with rage.

"You're not getting away with this!" she said fiercely.

He turned her back a bit roughly to face the wall, took another set of handcuffs, and secured her through the first pair to the oven door handle.

"I don't want you to think I'm ungrateful for what you did," Michael said. "However, I must go."

Michael took the binoculars and police radio from the table. He reached up and pulled a key from among several on hooks, the one labeled *outboard.*

Out the front door he heard Claire calling his name as he ran down the road toward the pier.

He jumped into the small fishing boat and tried the key. It fit, but was sticking in the lock from the corrosive effects of being left out in the open sea air. He finally got it to turn and the engine sputtered, then died. He primed the carburetor, checked the battery connections, and tried the key again. The engine turned over, the pistons fired; then it died again.

Michael heard a sound in the distance. He looked up and saw the headlights of a car winding down the road toward the safe house. That would be his police escort.

He frantically tried the engine again and again. He smelled the petrol and knew he was flooding the engine. He turned the ignition off and fiddled with the engine settings. The approaching car was almost to the house now. One more try: The engine wanted to start, but didn't.

A deep breath. *Okay, I can do this.*

This time the engine turned over, sputtered, hesitated, then roared to life. Michael revved the engine, untied the boat from the pier, and raced off into the dark waters of Roaring Water Bay at full speed. He was already too far along the coast to see the police freeing Claire Burke. He knew they would not be far behind him.

# Chapter 31

Three cars with darkened windows arrived in front of the Driscoll office building at twilight. Four men in the front car got out quickly, surveyed the area, and rushed up to the building to unlock the front door and go inside, where they carried out a security check of the premises. Four others from the rear car got out and flanked the doors to the car in the middle, waiting to be given a signal from one of the men inside that all was safe. They opened the back car door and shielded a confused old man as he stepped out onto the sidewalk, then hustled him inside.

Ger O'Keeffe pulled the chair out from behind Aiden Driscoll's desk as Brian Driscoll entered the office. The old man shuffled into the room, started to sit in the guest chair across from the desk.

"Here, boss," O'Keeffe said.

Brian sat in the chair. His ancient tweed jacket gapped, revealing pajama tops tucked into baggy trousers. The lamp on the desk cast deep shadows on his unshaved face, made his rheumy eyes glisten. Even in the midst of a crisis, the men who had served Aiden Driscoll moved effortlessly in starched shirts, unrumpled suits, perfectly knotted ties.

He hadn't sat on that side of the desk in almost four years. It felt odd to be in charge again. He looked around Aiden's office. Pictures of the family on the credenza, computer on the desk, a phone with a bewildering array of lights and buttons. A neat stack of spreadsheets, books on finance and the equity markets. Incomprehensible words leaping off the pages of the *Wall Street Journal*s that had accumulated in his son's absence.

He was utterly lost, but was too hungover to know it. He shuffled some papers left on the desk, glanced at file folders in the in-box. There was nothing familiar in anything he looked at. He felt the eyes of Ger O'Keeffe and four of his men on him.

"Where's Kevin?" he said. When no one answered him, he asked again more irritably, "Where's Kevin?"

"He won't answer his cell phone," Ger said. "Neither will Pat or Eddie."

"Do they know?" Brian asked.

Ger had been trying to make sense of the old man all afternoon, but his speech had been slurred, his conversation illogical, confusing.

"Does he know his brother has been killed?" Brian yelled. "What Maeve O'Driscoll has done to my boy and to the others?"

"I don't know, boss. If we can't get in touch with them in another hour I was going to send someone down to West Virginia to see what's going on." He paused for thought. "If that's what you want us to do."

The whole reason they had come to the office was to get out of the house so they could talk and so he could make decisions. After Ger had brought him the news of Aiden's death, he was told he had to take over the family until Kevin could be found and a decision made as to who would run the organization.

"No," Brian said. "Later. Kevin can take care of himself. I don't even know what the hell he's doing down there, or for that matter what Aiden was doing in Ireland. I want you to get a team together to go to West Cork. I'll give you the name of someone in the area who used to run guns for the IRA. He should still be able to get you whatever you need. My son will be avenged."

"Should we lease a jet from the company Aiden uses?"

Brian's head was beginning to clear a bit. He was able to think through things more easily now. He shook his head. "Split everyone up. Half of you leave from Boston; the other half leave from New York. Schedule yourselves on different flights in case the police over here or over there are watching."

Ger was emboldened by the old man's resolve.

"Maeve O'Driscoll will not get away with killing my son," Brian said.

"Do you want her taken out?"

"No," Brian said emphatically. "Let her live the rest of her days mourning her son, just as I will spend the rest of my days mourning mine. Everyone else . . . they are dust."

Michael knew the countryside between Skibbereen and Ballydehob almost as well as did the O'Driscolls who were hunting him, and certainly better than the police whose helicopters flew up and down the coast. Though they probably would not have found the small fishing boat he had flooded and submerged, they would have figured out that he had fled on water and abandoned the boat at some point to flee on foot.

He cautiously walked along a country road toward the lights of a farmhouse. A hundred yards away he used the binoculars to check for any signs of activity but saw none. He hiked closer, circled the farmyard to see if anyone was tending to some late-night cattle emergency, but saw no one outside. All the lights were off inside. Michael crept close to the outbuildings, made his way to an unloved blue car caked in mud and cow shite parked on a steep hill on the side of the house. In light of his own situation, it seemed ironic that West Cork was free enough from crime that many of the farmers still kept their keys in their tractors and even cars.

The car door was unlocked, the key in the ignition. Michael got inside and closed the door as quietly as he could. He released the handbrake and let the car roll backward to the bottom of the hill and out onto the road. He cranked the engine without revving it unnecessarily, riding with his lights off until he was well away from the farm.

Michael assumed the major roads would be blocked by the police. He bypassed the familiar route up above Ballydehob in favor of a barely used track up into the hills.

There were no lights on inside Brendan's cottage when he arrived, and the path around the outside was dark. He kicked something as he walked to the house. He bent over and picked up a dead chicken. Inside the chicken yard he could make out lots of feathers — more dead chickens. The fox had come and gotten to the chickens left out overnight. It was a sign that Brendan had been killed before the end of the day, when he normally would have closed the chickens up into their shed. The fox had killed them all and probably taken only one away. The mess outside made Michael wonder what kind of a mess he would find inside.

The body was gone, but the smell of decayed flesh lingered. No one had come to clean up the bloodstained rug and walls. On closer inspection the couch, the table and chairs, the books, the fireplace — everything in the sitting room was covered in blood. There were obvious drag marks leading from the sitting room to the outside. There was no telling where Liam had taken his cousin. Michael couldn't bear to be in the room any longer.

The fiddle case was where he had last seen it — on the floor between the kitchen and the sitting room. He picked it up, closed the sitting room door, took the fiddle into the kitchen, and put it on the counter. He opened the case. There was a dusting of sticky rosin on the face of the instrument. The bow hair was loose; he didn't even know how to tighten it. He just hoped no one would ask him to play it.

Michael went up to Brendan's bedroom. Brendan and Lydia's bedroom. He hadn't been in that room before. A record of her daily existence. Five years — day after day after day — and not one spent with him.

He went through the dresser drawers first. It was more personal than he could bear. Lydia didn't own much, but what she had was good stuff. A lot of it he recognized from their time together. He clutched to his face a large silk scarf she used to tie around her neck in a continental style. Like the day they had walked to the grotto above Lough Ine.

He pulled out the drawers of a small desk. This was Brendan's stuff: extra strings for his fiddle, an old rosin cake, foreign coins worthless with the introduction of the euro.

He still couldn't find what he was looking for. The bedside table fooled him — no knob implied no drawer, but he pulled an edge out from underneath and it moved. He took Brendan's wallet, and was happy to find a driver's license and several hundred euro. He dug through the papers to the bottom of the drawer and found Brendan's passport.

On the shelf below the mirror in the bathroom, Michael propped the passport open to the photograph. He cut his hair in a similar style, changed the part from right to left like Brendan's. He lathered his face with shaving foam and changed the shape of his beard to conform to the one in the photograph. He washed his face, dried it, turned his head from side to side, studying himself in the mirror.

They shared the O'Driscoll profile — nose, mouth, cheekbones, eyes. It was damned close. He changed into Brendan's clothes. He could pass for the dead man, no problem.

There were ways to get to the Cork road without going through Skibbereen or Ballydehob and the awaiting roadblocks or squads of O'Driscolls that would be roaming the area. Up and over the mountains for half an hour, crossing the Bantry road and continuing across country through rough grazing along roads not marked on most maps. Some he knew; others he didn't. If he maintained his bearings and was able to keep moving east, he would eventually get to where he needed to be. It would not be easy at three in the morning.

He made excruciatingly slow progress. Several times he got lost and discovered he had been driving in an enormous circle, ending up where he began five minutes earlier. He eventually made it to roads outside Drimoleague and Dunmanway.

It was already four-thirty. He was worried about the time, and as soon as he got around the towns he felt he was far enough away from Skibbereen to safely get back onto the main highway into Cork.

The road from Dunmanway to Bandon was virtually empty, and he drove fast. The farmer's car shook as he pressed above sixty miles per hour, and the brakes squealed loudly when he tapped them on the curves. But the engine was good and he found he could accelerate even more. The fiddle case slid in the backseat as he fought the car to stay on the road.

On the seat next to him the police radio he had taken from the safe house squawked. Michael turned up the volume. Chatter between police cars cruising the roads. The signal was strong.

Just as he was about to round a bend, Michael was surprised to see several hundred yards ahead the reflective strip of a police car with its lights off on the side of the road. He slowed the car. It didn't seem to be a roadblock as such, but from the conversation on the radio, he determined there were police cars spread out along the road out of Skibbereen. They were specifically looking for anyone suspicious who might have been involved in the killings in Skibbereen.

Michael checked the time again. Four-forty. He couldn't delay getting to Cork any longer. It was too risky being stopped and questioned, but the only way in was past the police car in front of him.

Michael cut his lights and the road in front of him went inky black. As his eyes adjusted to the dark, he was actually able to see the faintest reflections of the star-light in the cat's-eyes embedded in the pavement. He picked up speed — thirty, forty, fifty miles per hour as he closed in on the position of the police car pointed in his direction.

He was afraid the garda would see the interior of his car, so Michael turned off the dashboard lights.

He could no longer see his speed, but he kept accelerating. The moon had fallen below the horizon, and the mud on the dark car would absorb any incidental light. He was virtually invisible, hurtling down the road like a Stealth Fighter. Michael held on and put his foot all the way down on the accelerator.

Michael figured he was just shy of a hundred miles per hour when he zipped past the police car. At that moment he took his foot off the accelerator to diminish the sound of the whining engine, then floored it as soon as he was past. If the officer had blinked, he would have missed Michael completely. If he were looking straight ahead at the road, Michael would have registered as nothing more than a dark blur — a flock of birds migrating by starlight, a speck of dust in his eye.

# Chapter 32

Michael stood in the area in front of the ticket desks at Cork Airport and read the upcoming flights off the departure boards. There were three early-morning flights leaving before seven a.m. One left for Dublin, the other two for London. He knew either route would get him a connecting flight back to the United States.

Michael had already checked out the security situation. A single dozy airport security officer stood outside the front entrance to make sure no one parked illegally. Upstairs, another security officer was checking passports and boarding passes, while two more ran carry-on luggage through an X-ray machine. The stolen car wouldn't be found in the airport car park for several days.

At five-forty-five a.m. the airport workers were just coming on duty. It was still dark outside and there weren't many people in the check-in area. He selected the British Airways desk, since it was the quickest way out of the country. "Does your six-thirty-five to London Gatwick connect with anything to Boston this morning?" he asked the reservation clerk.

She typed the city information into her terminal. "You're into Gatwick at eight-oh-five, departing British Air for a non-stop to Boston at two-fifteen p.m."

"No good. I've got to have something this morning."

"Let me see." More typing. "I can get you a connecting flight with American Airlines that leaves Gatwick at eleven-oh-five a.m."

"That's better."

"Your name, sir?"

"Brendan O'Driscoll."

"Return?"

Michael thought for a moment. "One way," he finally said.

"I might point out that it's cheaper to just buy a round-trip ticket and throw the return portion away. Officially, I'm not supposed to tell you that, but that's what I'd do myself."

"Okay, that's what I'll do."

"And how will you be paying for this?"

Michael paid for the ticket with the cash

in Brendan's envelope. It took all but twenty euro.

"Any checked luggage?"

Michael patted the fiddle case. "Just this, carry-on."

The clerk took quickly checked his passport, made some final notes in Michael's record, and printed his tickets. "Boarding is in twenty minutes."

Michael took the escalator up to the next floor and went to the security checkpoint. No problems getting through.

"Give us a tune?" the guard manning the X-ray machine said as Michael lifted the fiddle case.

Michael made a sick face. "Late session at the pub," he said. "I'm wrecked. Next time," he said with a wink.

There were only a few dozen passengers in the departures lounge. A couple of bored people waited for the duty-free shop to open.

Michael sat in a chair in the middle of the room so he could see everything going on, including the people coming out of the hallway from security. He picked up a newspaper that had been left on the next seat. It was a copy of *USA Today*. He skimmed the front page. The news didn't interest him very much; then he saw a reference to a feature article in the *Lifestyle* section: "Powerball Lottery Jackpot Heads Toward $300 Million."

As he was flipping through the paper to the article he heard a group coming down the hallway. Peering over the edge of his paper he saw six men coming in his direction. They all looked very serious and spoke in low voices. He recognized them immediately as members of the O'Driscoll organization.

He hid behind the paper as they came in his direction. Were they looking for him? Of all the places he could have been, how could they have known he was at the airport?

They passed him by. They were carrying tickets. He caught sight of one of their boarding passes. They were on the same flight to London that he was.

He considered the possibility that the O'Driscoll gang was breaking up, leaving the country because the pressure had become too much. But if that were the case, where were Maeve and Noreen? One thing he knew for certain: He wasn't about to ride on the same plane as the O'Driscolls.

Michael waited until they had taken seats near the gate and walked quickly back to security. "I've forgotten something," he told them.

"The airport pub's not open yet," they told him.

He laughed with them.

"Better hurry or you'll miss your flight," the man running the X-ray machine said.

*That's the point,* Michael said to himself as he ran back downstairs.

There was now a long line at the British Airways counter. Michael got at the back, checking and rechecking his watch as the line slowly moved forward.

Another position at the counter unexpectedly opened up, and Michael ran to get to the front, much to the irritation of several people who had been waiting a much longer time.

"I'm sorry, sir, that's nonrefundable," the clerk told him.

"I just paid cash for this ticket and it's completely useless to me now," he said. "I have to get my money back so I can buy a different ticket."

"The best I can do is apply the amount of the fare to another ticket bought for a trip on British Airways."

"I don't need Brit Air. I need to change my flight to Boston via Dublin on Aer Lingus."

"I really am sorry. There's nothing I can do."

Michael stared at her blankly for a moment as he tried to figure out what to do. He saw her looking over his shoulder at the growing queue. She wasn't going to budge. If he were traveling as a priest, he could have asked for some sort of professional consideration, but that wasn't possible. "Okay, listen," he said. "Don't you make some kind of bereavement concessions for family members in cases of emergency?"

"We'd have to have a copy of a death certificate."

"I'm on the way to the funeral. Please — it's a family emergency."

She looked at him dubiously, then started typing changes into her computer. "You'll have to send us a copy of the death certificate."

"Thank you."

She gave him his new tickets and boarding passes. "The Aer Lingus flight to the flight connecting to Boston is just about to close their gate. If you run, you might just make it."

# Chapter 33

Three nearly identical Cadillacs pulled into a dusty truck stop near the Huntington, West Virginia, airport. The six O'Driscoll gang members had paired off into three rental cars. Peter O'Sullivan jumped out of the passenger side of one of them, walked to a public phone in the parking lot, yanked a yellow pages book off its chain. He got back into his car and started flipping pages.

"Pawnshops," he said, running his finger over the page. "Look at all the fucking pawnshops in this town." He cross-checked the addresses with the map he had picked up from the Avis counter. "There are several up and down the same street. Get going; I'll navigate."

They got to the first address, and Peter directed the others how to get to the nearby pawnshops. They went in pairs into the stores, casually made their way through aisles of junk to the gun counter. Through the glass counter, they looked at the hand-guns, a wide assortment of revolvers and semiautomatics.

"No waiting for period for hunting guns," the clerk told Peter as he slipped behind the counter.

"What qualifies as a hunting gun?"

"Depends what you're shootin'."

"Snipe."

"Never heard a that. Not to be rude, but where you from, anyway?"

"New Jersey."

"Ahh," he said knowingly. "That explains the funny accent. Shoot lotsa snipe up there?"

"Bagloads. How about that right there," Peter said, pointing to a hunting rifle on the wall.

The clerk took the gun down, ran his hand over the stock. "Great deer-hunting gun. I'll throw the scope in for free."

"That's for my buddy. I'll need one, too."

"I wouldn't have anything else as powerful as this one. I've got twenty-twos for shootin' at beer bottles and I've got some nice shotguns."

"He'll take a nice shotgun and cartridges, if you've got them."

The clerk reached under the counter and

got a couple of boxes of shotgun shells. "Two boxes enough?"

"Perfect."

"You'll be needing some ammo, too," he said. He rummaged beneath the counter until he came up with two boxes of cartridges for the rifle. "Anything else?"

"That ought to do it."

Peter paid cash. "What have you got to stick these in?" he said.

The clerk offered black plastic garbage bags.

"That'll work," Peter said as he cinched the yellow ties at the top of the bag. His partner nodded agreement and they headed out the door with the guns under their arms.

Declan O'Driscoll sat with his chin in his hand at the computer desk as he repeatedly hit the enter key. He watched the blur of numbers on the monitor as the computer program ran through a simulation of picking the winning number for the Powerball lottery. Along with the new number, the program generated a figure for the resulting hypothetical payout. The amount a single winning number would get had only in the last hour topped $300 million.

He glanced through the door to the front of the store. He was highly irritated. How the hell did they expect him to keep the store open by himself and do all he had to do with the computer program? Every time the front door chime rang, he had to jump up and man the counter. Where was his help? Hadn't they said they were on the way? He left the desk and had sold another thirty lottery tickets before he was able to return to his computer.

With each lazy tap of his index finger every few seconds, the figure rose by increments of over ten thousand dollars. Beneath the Powerball lottery icon in the corner of the screen were two figures: one that corresponded to the payouts Declan's own program was generating, another for the time left to buy a Powerball ticket. At that rate, the jackpot would be worth well in excess of $350 million.

*More than a third of a billion dollars,* Declan thought. Up to now the scheme had been executed in the abstract. It had been all computer programming and messing with numbers. Now the reality of the plan caused a burst of adrenaline to surge through his bloodstream, made his heart race, his palms sweat. The sums he contemplated were almost unfathomable.

Just as he was getting excited about the prospect of joining the ranks of the idle rich, he was startled by the sight of five well-dressed but tough-looking men coming inside. He picked up the handgun he kept beside the computer.

Declan minimized the computer program on the screen, and a screen saver popped up to hide his work. He stuck the gun in the back of his blue jeans and walked into the hallway separating the back room from the front to get a better look.

Without warning, he felt something hard against the back of his head.

"Good fucking thing we got here before someone else did," a voice behind him said in a thick West Cork accent. Declan lifted his eyes up to the convex security mirror at the ceiling and saw a man standing behind him with a shotgun to his head.

"Well, fuck you and the donkey you rode in on," Declan answered.

The man behind him lowered his gun. "Where is everyone?"

Declan turned, shook Peter O'Sullivan's hand, then stuck his thumb out toward the walk-in cooler. "Chillin' out," Declan said.

Michael simply took a taxi from Logan

International Airport to the house on Boston's South Side and walked up to the front door. He had made it all the way from Skibbereen to Cork, to Dublin, then through U.S. Customs and Immigration with no problems, so he expected none at his own brother's house. He saw the curtains in the windows at the front of the house twitch. He stood at the front door holding the fiddle case and rang the bell.

"What's in the case?" was the first thing the man who answered the door said to him. Michael recognized him as Ger O'Keeffe, one of the older members of the family's organization.

"A fiddle."

The man didn't know whether to believe Michael or not. It was obvious Ger had no idea whom he was talking to. "Open it."

Michael patiently opened the case, producing the fiddle and bow. The man checked the pockets and compartments of the case, found nothing but a chin rest, extra strings, a rag, rosin.

"Ger," Michael said. "Tell my father that Michael has come home."

Ger suddenly realized he was talking to Brian Driscoll's son. "Michael," he said. His face softened. He embraced Michael. "I'm sorry. Come in."

Ger left Michael standing in the hallway of his old family home. Michael hadn't set foot in the house since his mother's funeral. He put the fiddle case down and walked into the living room. The couch, the chairs, the end tables, the rugs were the same as before. Everything was clean but seemed a bit dated and shabby now. Framed pictures on the wall were slightly askew. He lifted the top of the upright piano his mother used to play. He played a few of the yellowed ivory keys.

Ger walked softly down the carpeted steps. "He's asleep," he almost whispered.

Michael stopped playing and closed the lid. He nodded.

"Why don't you come upstairs? Jeff is getting him up."

Michael followed Ger upstairs. Outside his father's bedroom door, Ger knocked softly, then again when he didn't hear a reply. The door opened and Jeff Roche let them in. Another man Michael recognized as Frank Hearns was helping his father sit up in bed.

Michael walked slowly across the room to the bed. The old man wheezed. Jeff was holding a coffee mug of something for Brian to drink. Michael took the mug from his father's trembling hands and smelled it.

The whiskey fumes burned his nostrils. He set the mug on the bedside table.

Michael hardly recognized his father. The hair had thinned; the face had sunk. His vacant eyes were red and watery.

His father looked at him, squinting. "Where's your collar?" he said. "Where's my son?"

Jeff and Ger discreetly left the room.

Michael bent over and put his arms around his father, but felt no warmth.

Brian cocked his head, heard voices that didn't exist, spoke to people who were no longer alive: "You said you were coming back. You promised me. Tell your mother what you told me. Go on, tell her. I want her to know. I never trusted Maeve O'Driscoll and her bastard children. But your brother told you to go over there. I told you not to go, so it's not my fucking fault. I'm not responsible for both my sons dying. Tell her." His voice rose to an angry shout: "Don't you leave me here by myself!"

"I'm here, Dad," Michael said. "I'm your son. I'm your son, too. I'm back."

Ger had a hard time keeping up with Michael as he walked down the hallway outside the bedrooms.

"It's too late, Michael. I wish I could have explained about what's going down. Your father doesn't speak so clearly now. The dozen men he ordered to Skibbereen were given instructions not to come back until they had finished the job."

"It's never too late!" Michael said angrily. "How could you allow him to give orders like that?"

"Michael, with all due respect, you know nothing about what goes on here. With Aiden dead and Kevin missing, the old man's calling the shots. Everyone listens to him. Once he gave the orders, that was it."

"Get someone on the phone. I'll call them back myself."

Ger looked at his watch, shook his head. "It's a done deal by now."

Michael opened the door to Aiden's bedroom. He went straight into the walk-in closet, ran his hand over suit coats, felt finely tailored material between his fingers, examined the labels of the silk ties hanging on pegs. Ger stood at the door a respectful distance away and watched.

"They sure as hell will listen to me," Michael said. "My father has lost his mind. I'm taking over. I'm in charge as of this moment."

"Michael —"

"Shut up and listen! I'm not allowing Maeve O'Driscoll to get away with killing off my family. But we're going to handle this my way. I need everyone you have. How many men are left here?"

"I can pull together ten or so."

"Fine, then do it. *Now.*"

# Chapter 34

Noreen O'Driscoll pulled her car up in front of the cathedral. Maeve and Liam looked at the people walking to Mass. Now more than ever, it was important that they show the townspeople and the police that everything was normal. As soon as anyone sensed fear or desperation, the O'Driscolls would be done for and the neighbors and shopkeepers who only the previous day had called out to them across the street in town cheerfully would turn on them, turn in every scrap of useless gossip they could remember to ingratiate themselves with the police.

Maeve had told everyone in the organization to show up for Saturday-night Mass, which accounted for the streets already being filled with cars double-parked up and down North Street. Noreen would have to drive on up toward the sports center to find an empty space.

Noreen's mobile phone beeped, indicating a text message. She read it, checked the rearview mirror as a car honked behind her.

"Ma, I need to run back to the house. Declan says he's got a coded e-mail for me. It might be important, so I'll just drop you two off and come back later to pick you up after Mass."

Maeve and Liam got out of the car, joined the crowd filing up the steps into the cathedral.

Back at Liss Ard, Noreen fired up the computer in the study and got into her e-mail. She decoded the message from Declan. It was a brief note just to let her know that the West Cork lads had arrived and they had secured the store. Not that urgent a message after all.

Noreen looked out the window behind the computer. Something was different in the yard behind the house. A rake that had been leaning against the wall of the kennels was lying on the ground; a watering can was tipped over. A length of rope kept on the wall was missing.

She stood up so she could see the other end of the kennel. The door was swinging open. It was *never* left open. Liam always checked to make sure the latch was set before he left the house, and she had seen him do it before they had left for Mass only half an hour earlier.

Noreen went outside and walked to the back of the house. The kennel door repeatedly slammed against the wall in the wind. She closed it, made certain it was secure. She started to go pick up the rake and watering can, then realized the dogs were making no sound. They normally would have heard her and started barking.

She opened the kennel door. It was absolutely quiet. She stopped and listened. No, there was a creaking sound, as if there were weight on the timbers in the joists above. Someone walking in the loft? She took a step inside and switched on the lights.

She screamed with fright. Both of Liam's prize greyhounds swung by the neck from the ends of ropes thrown over the roof beams.

"Sweet Jaysus!"

She ran outside directly to her car, jumped inside, and cranked the ignition.

"They're back," she said to herself in a panic as she raced down the driveway.

As usual, many of the men waited outside the cathedral during Mass as the women attended worship inside. Some sat in their cars and others stood around the steps and smoked. Liam leaned against the rail and chatted quietly with Peter O'Sullivan and ten of their finest gang members.

They could hear the priest through the open side door beginning his homily. It was his annual appeal for the youth to consider a religious vocation, a life as a priest or a nun. His words were a buzz against the men's conversation about Irish football, plans to build houses, fantasies of holidays in Spain during the upcoming winter.

The cathedral was high on a hill overlooking the north end of town and the countryside beyond. A pair of swans dived for food at the bottom of the River Ilen. Everyone's attention was drawn to a vintage Rolls-Royce driving down the Cork road and passing in front of the cathedral.

As they were distracted, a dozen men slipped out of the side doors of the cathedral, rushed up to the back of the O'Driscoll men, and quickly shot them execution style at the base of their skulls with silenced handguns. The dead men fell in place on the steps.

As the priest asked the congregation to join together in the Lord's Prayer, the assassins quickly looked over the dead to make sure they had killed everyone. The lead assassin rolled a body over with his foot and saw that Liam O'Driscoll was dead, his blood pooling, running down the steps. Liam's body jerked. The assassin pulled off another shot to the forehead just to make sure; then they fled in cars waiting to drive them out of West Cork.

Noreen stopped her car in the middle of the street, blocking traffic in both directions. Car horns blared. She ran screaming up the cathedral steps as Mass was letting out and the women and children were just finding their dead.

Wails filled the air; shrieks echoed off the cathedral walls.

Maeve found Liam before Noreen got to him. She cradled his head in her lap and rocked back and forth.

"My boy," Maeve said. She smoothed back his curls. A dark stain spread on her dress, wet with Liam's blood. Noreen held on to her mother and cried.

A woman Maeve knew only from seeing her in town pointed a finger at her and yelled, "You killed them!"

Another woman shouted as she wept bitterly, "It's all your fault! You've brought all this onto us!"

Maeve cringed, repeated quietly to herself, "It wasn't me; it wasn't me. I wouldn't kill my boy."

"No, Ma, you wouldn't."

"My boy's dead!" Maeve screamed.

But her complaint was lost amid the other women and children crying for their dead.

At Logan International Airport, a car drove past the hangars filled with private jets to a Gulfstream idling on the runway. Ger O'Keeffe climbed down the steps from the jet to greet the car and open the back passenger door.

Michael emerged from the car wearing one of Aiden's finest suits, a starched shirt, and an exquisitely knotted tie. He had shaved, changed his hairstyle back to the way it was, but with a touch more style. With his sunglasses on, he could have easily passed for his brother.

"We're ready to go," Ger told him as Michael bounded up the airplane steps.

"And they understand my instructions?"

"Yes."

"And they agree with them?"

"They will do it because you tell them

460

to. They've lost brothers, cousins, friends. They want revenge. And they know that's what you want as well."

Michael let the comment pass.

The rest of the men already seated on the jet stopped talking when Michael came on board. First a cop, then a priest, and now Aiden's replacement as head of the Boston Driscoll organization. They looked at him in amazement.

"All right, listen up, everyone," Michael said forcefully. "I told Ger there is to be no more bloodshed. We'll use our brains, not our guns. If you can't go along with that, you can get off this plane right now."

They looked to Ger for guidance. He looked dubious, but shook his head in agreement.

"Good," Michael said. "Buckle up; we're taking off."

# Chapter 35

Three of Maeve O'Driscoll's gang members occupied the inside of the Snapeville convenience store, two manning the front room and one in the back with Declan. The other three were outside, trying to look inconspicuous as they sat in their cars at the front and back of the store. They communicated with each other in clipped phrases using cheap two-way radios. All day long and well into the night they watched a steady stream of muddy pickup trucks and SUVs pulling into the parking lot. Most people returned to their vehicles carrying nothing heavier than a lottery ticket. Some came out with a fistful of tickets, feeling especially lucky, or buying numbers for coworkers.

Declan sat playing poker with his minder, a big red-faced, blue-eyed man with small teeth. He wasn't real bright. Under genetic assessment Declan was sure he'd test positive for inbreeding. He had known Tadgh since they were kids in Skibbereen. Unlike Kevin and his two brutes, Tadgh never intentionally gave up a game of cards. Declan was over twenty dollars in the hole and they were only playing quarter ante.

Declan was losing because he had his mind on his work. So far everything was going according to plan. He had successfully been running endless simulations against the West Virginia lottery system. For five days he had inserted a hypothetical winning number after the simulated cutoff for selling tickets, fooled the mainframe into thinking that it had been picked and printed the previous day, and printed the winning ticket out in the front of the store.

Less than twenty-four hours left. Then they could claim their prize.

Bye-bye Snapeville, West Virginia; hello, Monaco. He had already swiped a bottle of sunscreen from the store and stashed it in his briefcase.

Well after the sun had set, Ger O'Keeffe slowed his car as he approached the entrance to the convenience store on the outskirts of Snapeville. Michael sat on the passenger side.

"There they are," Michael said.

The parking lot was lit up. Michael was certain he saw a rifle in the hands of a man sitting in the back of one of the cars facing the parking lot entrance.

"There'll be another one at the back," Michael said. "And look over there," he said, pointing to another one of the cars parked out front. "There's a silhouette of a head in that one. He's slumped down low in the seat, see? Stop here."

Ger pulled to the side of the road.

"Go change the tire," Michael said.

"What?"

"We need to give the others a chance to sneak to the back through that field. I told them to make their move in ten minutes. We need a diversion. Go on."

"Jesus, I'm too old and too fat for that."

Michael lowered the window and raised his voice. "You stupid son of a bitch, get out and change the tire!"

Ger got hot and started to respond, then checked himself.

"Don't hold back," Michael said in a low voice. "Let's give them a real good show. You drunk."

"Fuck you," Ger said.

"Louder."

"Fuck you!" Ger yelled.

Michael reached into the backseat and got a couple of cans of beer from a bag. He popped the top, took a good swallow, then flung some on Ger.

"You fucking idiot," Ger said angrily. He snatched the beer from Michael, took a large drink, then threw the can out the window. He opened the car door, got out, slammed it hard.

Michael popped the trunk open before he got out. Ger walked wildly to the front of the car, bending down as if checking out a flat tire. Michael got a tire iron from the trunk, and knelt beside Ger. He pushed Ger and he fell over.

Ger got up swinging. Michael lifted the tire iron over his head.

"Don't you dare!" Ger roared, then swung again, missing.

Michael slurred as if he were drunk, "You were driving; you get down there and fix the tire!"

Behind the convenience store the sentry got out of his car and walked around the corner to see what all the commotion was about. Satisfying himself that it was just a couple of drunks, he turned back and was punched so hard it knocked him out.

The rest of Michael's men ran from the shadows in the field behind the store. They had parked their cars a half mile away and hiked through the countryside. They bound and gagged the West Cork gangster and dragged him into the shadows. At the same time someone found a ladder on the side of the store leading to the ventilators on the roof. He was joined by another man pulling tools out from his big Swiss army knife — a screwdriver, pliers.

The other held a flashlight as the first unscrewed the top to the ventilator hood. "Yeah, that's it."

"First we override the power so we don't electrocute ourselves. Then all we have to do is switch these two wires, you reverse the polarity of the motor, and the fan runs in the opposite direction." He switched the motor back on, held his hand over the vent, felt the air being drawn in from the outside. "Got a match?"

"You must have your mind on something else," Tadgh said as he scooped up his winnings. "Or maybe you're just having a run of bad luck."

Declan frowned, glancing over his shoulder at the computers. He was overcome by an uneasy feeling. "Yeah. Maybe I just need to go check on something."

Declan left Tadgh counting his winnings.

He leaned over the back of his computer chair, and cleared the screen saver on the monitor. The computer program was running automatic simulations now. He looked closer at the screen.

"That *can't* be right," Declan said.

Tadgh sniffed at the air. "Hey, what are those guys smoking in there?"

"Dunno," Declan answered distractedly.

Declan watched as the computer program ran through the simulation exercise.

He stared at the words on the screen: *No winner.* The amount of winnings was calculated as $0.00. The same thing happened three times in a row.

"Hey," Declan uttered.

"What?" Tadgh answered.

"Never mind, not you."

Declan sat down in his chair and stopped the automatic simulation. He changed the setting to manual and tapped the enter key. *No winner.*

He hit the key again and again, and got the same result — no winning number selected, zero earnings. The program he had written wasn't able to insert a random number representing a simulated draw, then send it to the printer. Something was terribly wrong.

"This can't be right," Declan said to

himself. Then to Tadgh, "Has anyone been messing with my goddammed computers?"

"Nope, not me."

"Holy shit." Declan stopped the simulation, closed the program, and started it over again, hoping to clear some unknown corruption in the system. He hit the enter key for a manual simulation: *No winner.* He banged the key harder and harder, getting the same result each time. "Fucking hell!"

Over the two-way radio they heard one of the men in the front say, "Just letting everyone know we may have a problem out here."

Tadgh was ignoring him. "Hey, hey — we gotta problem *here.*" He was standing up, looking all around the room. Smoke was pouring in from the vent in the ceiling.

One of Michael's men stood on the ground at the back of the convenience store and threw another empty plastic motor oil bottle from the garbage up to one of his associates on top of the roof. His companion on the roof held a lighter to the bottle, then dropped it onto the ventilator before it flamed. He motioned for more bottles. The burning plastic and burning oil created an especially acrid smoke that got sucked into the building.

The last two customers ran out of the store and sped off.

He pointed to some electrical wire sheathed in plastic lying on the ground outside the back door. They threw him a few coils and he added that to the small controlled fire he had going.

In the front parking lot, Michael led Ger closer and closer to the store as they traded insults and threw punches. Michael swung wildly at Ger with the tire iron, swung again, then smashed the rear window of one of the parked cars.

The man who had been slumped behind the wheel watching them fight rushed out of his car. "Hey! What the fuck do you think you're doing?"

"Leave him alone!" Ger said.

The man guarding the front door came over to assist his associate in throwing the two drunks off the property.

Michael became even more belligerent as he was grabbed by the lapels and shoved backward away from the cars.

"You can't do that to him," Ger said, lunging at the man who had been sitting in the car.

The front door man raised his rifle and

aimed it at Ger. "You're not going to get another warning. Get the hell out of here," he said.

The man in the other car joined his companion. "Leave now," he said.

"Sure," Michael said.

Michael and Ger kept their eyes fixed on the two men in front of them so as not to betray what was taking place at the store: a fire on the roof, four men with a couple of bread crates just about to wallop the hell out of Maeve's men standing in front of them.

The Irishmen moaned senselessly on the ground.

"See? No guns, no blood," Ger said.

Michael looked them over. "A little bruising, but no blood. It's a start." He eyed the roof fire. "Come on, take up positions around the doors."

Thick black smoke filled the top foot of the back room.

Declan took the CD out of the computer and gathered his notebooks.

"Where you going?" Tadgh said.

"I'm not going to die in the back room of a fucking convenience store in Snapeville, West Virginia. That's an electrical fire! Can't you smell it?"

"Shit, okay. Let's go. I'm going to grab the guys on the way out the front."

Declan wasn't listening. He was already pressing on the security bar on the back door. Out into the fresh night air, into the waiting arms of Michael Driscoll.

Three more men were surprised fleeing through the front door, subdued, and bound and gagged like the others as the small fire was put out on the roof.

"Cousin," Michael said, pulling Declan's head back hard by the hair. "What have you done with my brother?"

# Chapter 36

Liam O'Driscoll was laid out in a small, musty room in the funeral home. Maeve and Noreen sat with their heads bowed in front of his coffin, listening to the sound of traffic passing in the wet street. A large truck rumbled by, rattling the window.

Mortician's putty filled the wound in Liam's forehead, but the makeup used to smooth the work was that awful shade of orange used to effect a winter tan. The hair had been washed and dried, but the part was on the wrong side. Maeve had taken a comb from her purse and fixed it.

After dark, the priest slipped in through a side door for a hurried visit. He rushed through prayers for the dead, and informed them unapologetically that there would be no funeral Mass. He told them what the funeral home owner would not: The townspeople wanted Liam O'Driscoll buried so they could get on with the funerals of their own dead. If Maeve insisted, he would perform a private ceremony at the cemetery. She curtly rejected the offer.

There were no other mourners during visitation. When the town hall clock struck ten, Maeve stood and kissed her son for the last time on the lips. She put a copy of the program from the Clonakilty greyhound coursing on top of Liam's crossed arms and shut the coffin lid herself.

Midmorning the next day, Maeve and Noreen returned to the funeral home. A less than adequate crew from the funeral home struggled to load the coffin into the back of the hearse. They shoved the oak box hard to the front against the chrome pegs and slammed the rear door shut.

Dressed in black, Maeve and Noreen walked behind the coffin as it drove slowly through town. Surprisingly, shopkeepers and the town's residents stood on the sidewalk to await the passing of the hearse. There were hundreds of people lining the streets silently, just as they did for the removal of other prominent town residents.

But as they approached a crowd at the town square, Maeve realized what they were doing. People were turning their backs to them as they passed.

"Head up, my dear," Maeve said.

Outside town, the hearse shifted into lower gear as they made the final turn up the hill to the cemetery. There they came to what had become the eternal view of the dead — the prickly gorse in brilliant second bloom on the barren rocks overlooking the River Ilen.

A cemetery worker leaning against his shovel beside the grave saw them enter the gate. He took a last, long drag on his cigarette and threw it into the hole.

"Where's the key?" Michael demanded of Declan.

Michael yanked the lock on the walk-in cooler door. It wouldn't budge.

"I don't know."

"Hang on," Ger said, leaving the hallway.

He went outside and returned with the tire iron. "Stand back," he said. He bashed the lock three times until it popped loose.

Even before Michael opened the door Declan was saying, "I swear I didn't have anything to do with this, Michael."

Michael saw three lifeless figures on the

floor. He recognized two of them, but the third was on his side. Michael knelt and rolled Kevin's body over just enough to see his face.

"I swear, Michael," Declan said, "I had *nothing* to do with this."

Michael closed his eyes. A second dead brother. Another unhappy family reunion. He had never been particularly close to either of them, yet the grief was almost debilitating. He had lost his entire family.

"You had *everything* to do with it," Michael said, now unable to control his anger. "If it weren't for you, none of this would be happening now."

"I'm just a computer programmer."

Michael grabbed Declan by the shoulders and slammed his head hard against the cooler door. "No!" he shouted. "You're going to take responsibility for this mess. You and the rest of your family! I'm holding you all to account!"

"Michael, it's your family, too," Declan said.

Michael raged, slammed Declan's body against the door again and again, then realized what he was doing and stopped. He breathed hard. All eyes were on him. He took a deep breath.

Michael said, "We're here to take over the Powerball lottery. You and the O'Driscolls aren't going to be pulling this scam off."

"I'm glad to hear that, because there's a problem," Declan said softly.

"I'm not in any mood to hear about problems, especially yours."

"You need to know, though: Just before you got here I noticed that the simulation I was running wasn't working."

"What's that mean?"

"It means as of this moment I can't break into the lottery system. We can't beat the Powerball game."

Michael said, "You say you're a computer programmer; then fix it." Michael looked at the television showing the countdown to the lottery. The cutoff for purchasing tickets was only fourteen hours away. "Fast."

"I thought you just said you weren't going to let it go forward."

"I said I'm not allowing *you* to let it go forward. The O'Driscolls will never see a penny from your scheme."

"Why should I help you? Am I getting a cut? It was my idea, after all. And how do I know you won't kill me when you're done with me?"

"You don't. But the alternative is that Ger does to your head now when he just did to that lock."

Michael surveyed the carnage inside the cooler. "The dead can wait one more day. I have no intention of getting the authorities involved at this point. Right now, get the smoke cleared out of here and let's open back up for business. I want to see those lottery tickets flying out of here." He addressed Declan. "Isn't that what we need to do? Keep selling tickets like every other convenience store so no one will suspect anything?"

"That's right."

Michael jabbed a finger into Declan's chest. "Take him into the other room and sit him down in front of his computers. Make sure he isn't communicating with anyone outside. He *will* fix whatever problem he says he's having. If you need to resort to a bit of smacky-face to get his attention, just don't let me know about it."

Noreen O'Driscoll palmed the wheel of her car and hung up her cell phone. Maeve looked at the countryside on the way out of town. "No one is responding to my phone calls or e-mails," Noreen said. "I haven't heard anything from Declan since last night. I'm afraid something's gone horribly wrong."

The two women were still in black, their shoes and dresses splattered with mud from walking the two miles behind the hearse to the cemetery.

"We've lost control of everything," Maeve said. "Everything."

"We did everything we could, Ma. I felt it today. Our luck just ran out."

They parked in front of the house.

"I've been thinking," Noreen said. "What we need is a holiday. We need to get out of here. Maybe we won't even come back."

"Maybe."

Maeve looked at the great house, the lake, the hills and the mountains that were Carnmore. She felt it, too. She knew it had slipped away. She just wasn't ready to say it out loud.

"It would be nice to have a round of golf without being followed by the police. Someplace far away."

"True."

"I was thinking earlier, there's a really nice facility and course at the Greenbriar."

"What's that?"

"A mountain resort in the States. In West Virginia."

"Daughter," Maeve warned.

Noreen feigned ignorance. "What?"

"We both know that's where Michael probably went. That's why we haven't heard anything from Declan."

Noreen held her head back to keep the tears welling in her eyes from rolling down her cheeks.

"You have to let go," Maeve said. "He's destroyed our family. Don't let him destroy you. Give him up."

Noreen shut her eyes hard and screamed as she pounded the steering wheel, "I'll never give him up!"

"He's just a man, daughter. You need to clear your mind of him."

"We can't let him get away with this!"

Maeve sighed deeply. "How far is the Greenbriar from Snapeville?" she asked.

"Couple of hours, maybe less."

Maeve exhaled, felt the tension flow out of her whole being. She felt as if she had been holding her breath for years. Now she was resigned to everything that was about to happen. There was no more future and no more pressure.

"Not too bad a drive, then," Maeve said. "Let's get packed."

"It won't take me long. All I'm taking is my golf bag and what I've got on," Noreen said. "I won't need anything else."

# Chapter 37

Michael returned to the back room of the convenience store. "They're lined up outside the door buying tickets."

Ger caught his eye and shook his head. Declan still hadn't found a fix to his computer problem.

"What's up?" Michael said.

Declan ignored him, continued his frantic efforts to fix the computer fault.

Michael turned up the volume on the televisions. It wasn't just the local media hyping the Powerball lottery. The national networks had live feeds from all the states participating in the big draw. With less than two more hours to go until ticket sales would be cut off, lines grew around the country. There was no possible way the people standing at the back would make it to the front in time to lay down their money for a chance at what had become a projected jackpot of just under $400 million.

One network ran a piece on what various people would do with their winnings if their lucky number came up. Almost all said they'd be keeping their current jobs. Most said they'd give away some of the money to charity. Sons were getting mothers new cars. New houses with swimming pools were near the top of everyone's wish list.

It was obvious that most of the bettors were from less educated, less well-off families. Lots of single mothers and recent immigrants. But the hype was now such that a broader cross-section of society was getting in on the act. Computer salesmen, graduate students, nurses, high school teachers, and even a few accountants were interviewed standing in line.

Michael had decided they were all losers.

Declan glanced up from the computer monitor with annoyance. "Do you mind?"

Michael turned the volume down. "Speak to me," he said.

"I swear . . . this was working fine just before you got here."

"Sorry, you can't blame that on me."

"Yeah, yeah, yeah."

Declan was in a world of his own. He was editing the program he wrote, loading it, connecting to the West Virginia lottery

481

system, running a simulation again. Michael looked over his shoulder: *No winner.*

"Goddammit!" Declan said.

"You say it was working just before I got here. You're serious about that?"

"Absolutely. I had been running successful simulations of inserting the winning number for the past three days."

"What's the key thing that makes your program work?"

"Besides the genius who wrote it?"

"Yes, besides that."

"The subprogram I wrote that allows me to insert the winning numbers into the mainframe from here after the numbers are announced. I can't figure out why the mainframe isn't responding to my instructions."

Michael thought about what he had said. "Let's get some fresh air. Behave yourself, got it?"

"Sure."

Michael signaled to Ger to go with them. He wasn't going to take a chance of Declan making a run for it.

Outside, Michael said, "You're connected to the Internet and to the lottery system through the cable system, right?"

"Yeah."

Michael pointed to a wire running from

a pole across the parking lot into the convenience store. "That wouldn't be your cable, would it?"

"It could, why?"

"You might want to climb up on the roof and take a look at the connection. I'll just bet one of the guys knocked it when we were smoking you out. Could be costing you a few nanoseconds. What do you think?"

"I think you're a son of a bitch for not telling me this earlier."

Michael nodded toward the ladder at the side of the store. "Give you a hand up?"

"Yeah, yeah, yeah," Declan said. He tapped the enter key to run the simulation. Up popped the winning number combination along with the associated jackpot that had just topped $400 million. He tried it again and again, each time the computer generating the winning number and higher level of payout. He had control over the mainframe computer program again.

"We're back in," Declan said triumphantly.

Michael was standing behind him. "Good thing. Ger here thought you were faking having a problem. You can thank me he didn't start breaking your fingers one by one until you got smarter about finding a fix. You sure this is going to work?"

"I didn't design it to fail."

"Okay, so what's left to do?"

"Now that the mainframe seems to be responding to me, I'd like to have a final trial run of printing out a hypothetical winning ticket after a hypothetical draw. I want to make absolutely sure we can fool the system into thinking the winning number has been selected."

"What happens if someone else has actually picked the winning number? That will cut our take by half, or more if there's more than one winner."

"It's happened only once before that more than one person has picked the same winning number. Out of the last six Powerball draws, there's been only one dual winner. The odds are in our favor."

"We've got less than an hour till the draw. If we're going to do a full-scale simulation, including printing a valid-looking ticket, we need to do it now."

Michael sat down, tapping the arms of the chair as he thought. "No."

"No?"

"I haven't made my mind up yet."

"I thought you had already made a decision to go ahead with this?"

"I'm going to reserve making a final decision."

"Why?"

"Because I may want to find out what it's like walking away from four hundred million dollars. And watching your face as it slips away."

"Michael, don't do this out of revenge."

"I'm calling the shots now. I'll do it or not for whatever reason I want."

"If you're not going ahead with this, don't tease me. Let's just shut this down now and walk away."

Michael tapped the chair arm more frantically. "Remind me again," he said. "What are the odds of winning the jackpot?"

"One in about a hundred and twenty million," Declan answered.

Michael thought another few moments. "Run it," he finally said. "Show me it's going to work."

A broad smile spread across Declan's face. "One winning Powerball lottery ticket coming up, boss."

# Chapter 38

Maeve and Noreen O'Driscoll cleared U.S. Immigration and Customs in Atlanta, then caught the shuttle train from the international terminal. For two women embarking on a fabulous holiday at an expensive resort, neither had much spark. They stood on the crowded train hanging on to the poles, looking blankly at the faces of the other people around them, a mixture of Americans returning from vacations and foreigners like themselves coming to America for business or pleasure.

An automated voice announced they would be arriving at Terminal A.

"This is where we part, daughter," Maeve said.

"No, Ma. We don't get off till Terminal B."

"I was studying the departing-flights schedule after we arrived. I've decided to attend to some business before I join you."

"What kind of business?"

"I want to pay a call on my cousin Brian in Boston while we are over here. He's not been in the best of health, you know. We're the last of our generation."

The train was slowing.

"Ma . . ."

"Shhh. Not here. There's not time. It won't upset our plans. I won't be but a day later. You can get some good practice in on the driving range. Who knows, maybe you'll even hook up with a cute golf pro."

"Ma . . ."

The train stopped, the doors opened.

Maeve kissed Noreen's cheek, her forehead, and hugged her. "Forgive me; I'm just feeling sentimental. Don't forget I love you," she said, then dashed off the train. She was lost in the crowd swarming at the foot of the escalators as the train pulled out.

Maeve had never been to America before. Before the disasters that had befallen her family, she had been envied, feared, admired, respected among the people of West Cork. She was Maeve O'Driscoll, the namesake of the queen of ancient Ireland who led her warriors into battle. Here at the Avis rental car desk at Logan International Airport in Boston she was less than a nobody; she was Irish.

Her name, her accent, her "country of origin" — as the forms in front of her read — were a mark against her. She felt like the Paddy she was, even more so for her thick West Cork brogue. One of millions of quick-witted, silver-tongued drunkards who visited the United States every year. Their reputation preceded them. Those who didn't head straight to Disney World and the beaches of Florida fanned out to stay with relatives in New York, Boston, Chicago, San Francisco. Most would leave at the end of two weeks wearing Gap baseball hats and carrying a bag full of cheap CDs. On their way home they'd stock up on liquor at the duty-free shop. A few would stay and find jobs in the underground economy working construction sites and bars.

At least, that's how she felt.

She got a map and directions from the desk attendant and drove straight to Brian Driscoll's house. It was late afternoon by the time she turned the corner onto Manor Street. She pulled the car next to the curb and stopped. She sat for a moment to get the feel of the neighborhood.

So this was what it was like for an

Irishman of Brian's generation to come to America and do well, Maeve thought. Late September and people were still in short-sleeved shirts. The oak trees were so tall, the yards so expansive and green. She heard the sound of sprinklers ratcheting over the lawn, splashing the sidewalk, saw fat robins bathing in their spray, digging worms in the sodden turf. Children's voices came from screened-in front porches of the large clapboard houses, bicycles and toys in the driveways. A light breeze blew through the trees; American flags hanging outside many of the front doors along both sides of the street fluttered.

She checked the address, rang the doorbell. No one answered. She walked to the back of the house, tried a white-painted wooden gate and found it open. Well-tended flower beds, a barbecue pit, an empty hammock. Was it the right house? On the steps was a hurley and ball. Hanging on the clothesline was a child-size Munster jersey. She walked over to the hammock, picked up an old wool flat cap lying on it, turned it over. The label inside indicated it had been bought in Tragumna, a woolens shop just outside Skibbereen. It was the right place.

The back door was open, too. Inside she passed through the kitchen into the central hallway. A gallery of portraits: photographs of Aiden Driscoll and his family. Group wedding shots, first confirmation, wife and kids at Disney World. Brian Driscoll and his wife seated in front of a fiftieth wedding anniversary banner.

She checked the rest of the floor and found no one around. Back in the kitchen she opened drawers until she found a sharp knife short enough to fit into her purse.

The steps upstairs were carpeted, and she hardly made a sound until the creak on the landing. All the bedroom doors except one were open. She put her ear to it, heard nothing. She slowly turned the doorknob, opening the door enough to stick her head inside.

Brian Driscoll was sitting up in bed, holding a revolver in his shaky hand pointed toward the door. "What do you want?" he demanded.

Maeve was at first startled, then smiled at him. "Brian," she said. "It's Maeve. Maeve O'Driscoll."

He was hard of hearing, blind without his glasses. He cocked the hammer of the gun. "Who is it?"

Maeve slowly walked into the room.

Brian squinted harder. "Stop or I'll kill ye."

"Brian. It's your cousin Maeve from Skibbereen."

Brian let the tip of his gun droop. Maeve sat in a chair next to the bed. Her feet accidentally kicked something glass under the bed. A bottle of Jameson whiskey rolled out from underneath. Maeve handed him his glasses from the bedside table, then slid the coffee mug with his dentures closer to him. He had been soaking them in the whiskey. He put the gun into the folds of his bedcovers, put the glasses on, exercised his mouth to properly set the dentures.

"Did you see Michael?" he asked.

"Yes, in West Cork."

Brian looked extremely confused, then, as if finding enlightenment: "Aiden and Kevin are dead. I sent my men to kill your family, but I told them to let you live."

"I know. I came here to thank you."

He acknowledged her with his head. He was slightly drunk, but his confusion was more than just an alcoholic daze.

"So how are ye?" Maeve said.

Brian thought about that a moment. "Not too bad altogether."

Maeve could see it in his face, hear it in

his voice. He was losing touch with reality, slipping back into his past. He was a lad in West Cork. The more they talked, the thicker his accent became.

"You remember how we used to sit together on the Rock above town?" she said.

He was *there*. Cows grazing behind stone walls, the fragrance of freshly cut hay, bales of silage, pink and purple foxglove at the edge of a field, the cathedral bells striking the hour for suppertime.

He closed his eyes. "You had such pretty, long red hair. Freckles in the summer. And on your lovely white breasts."

"Brian, where is everyone?"

"Gone to market."

"When are they coming back?"

"No, that's not right. Katie's gone to meet her sister in Hingham."

"Are you sure?"

"No, I beg your pardon. I was wrong. Katie's gone to market, then to pick up the kids from school. I told her if she ever served me anything but Clonakilty sausages again I'd throw her out of here."

"It's her house, too, Brian."

He became indignant. "It's *not* her feckin' house!"

"Okay. Where's Michael?"

"He went somewhere."

"He's been here?"

"Yes, he was."

"Where is he now?"

"Did you know they stopped the train service to Skibbereen?"

"Yes, I did. That was almost fifty years ago. Did Michael say where he went?"

"He went to Virginia."

"West Virginia?"

"I'd say so. You didn't see Aiden or Kevin, did you?"

"No, Brian."

"Ye sure?"

Maeve took a deep breath. "Brian, you killed my only son. Why did you do that?"

"You're the bitch who killed *my* boys, aren't you?"

"Who told you that?"

"Aiden's wife, the one I'm throwing out. As soon as she gets home with my sausies. Well, after she makes me breakfast."

"Brian, it was all business until you murdered my boy. You didn't have to do that."

"He's a no-good bastard."

Maeve slipped her hand inside her purse and grasped the knife handle. "You're weren't demented enough not to understand what you were doing when you sent your gang out to kill Liam."

"Aiden always said your boy was a no-good bastard, and I believed him. Aiden's smart. I haven't seen your boy for donkey's years, but I do know for a fact that he was a bastard. Everyone said so. I mean, if he weren't a bastard, where's his father? Dead at the bottom of the sea, I'd say. What's that make his mother?"

"I'm his mother, you eejit. And *you're* his father. You've killed your own son."

"Oh?"

Maeve heard a car door close outside. She parted the sheer curtains and looked to the yard below. Aiden's wife was getting her hands around bags of groceries. A boy and a girl unbuckled themselves from the backseat and sprinted across the lawn directly into the sprinkler. The boy picked up the sprinkler and hosed down his sister. Katie Driscoll labored with the bags down the driveway toward the back gate.

Brian looked to the ceiling as he figured the relationships. "Then that would make you the little bastard's mother," he said, "and me the little bastard's father. That's the problem with small villages. Was it the cider got you drunk and we shagged up behind the Rock?"

"No, Brian. It was simple rape."

Maeve pulled the knife from her purse,

raised her hand over her head and brought it down swiftly. An instant before the point of the blade penetrated Brian Driscoll's chest, a gunshot tore through the bedsheets, blowing Maeve backward out of her chair.

Katie Driscoll yelled desperately from the kitchen in a panic. "Brian! Brian!" She was running up the stairs.

"Fuck all," Brian Driscoll said. He put the gun to his temple and pulled the trigger.

# Chapter 39

Michael paced back and forth in the convenience store between the front room and the back, checked his watch against the countdown clock on the television screens. Ten-sixteen p.m. Forty-three minutes to go until the Powerball draw.

"Well?" he said.

Declan typed instructions into the computer keyboard. "Hang on." He copied numbers down on a scrap of paper, scooted his chair back. "Let's go see."

Michael followed him to the checkout counter in the other room. "C'mon, spit it out," he told the lottery ticket machine.

The printer dutifully obeyed. Declan checked the numbers against what he had written down. A perfect match. He handed the ticket to Michael. "See? It's working perfectly again. The ticket is dated from yesterday afternoon. All we do is run the same sequence the moment the Powerball draw takes place and it's all ours. Satisfied?"

Michael examined the ticket.

Declan said, "I put this whole thing together. It was my idea. I wrote the program, hacked into the Powerball mainframe, set up all the electrical systems. What's my cut going to be, Michael?"

Michael crumpled the ticket, letting it fall to the floor as he walked down the hallway. He opened the cooler door. "Your cut is you don't end up like that," he said, showing Declan the dead bodies. He slammed the door shut hard.

At the instant the door closed loudly Michael heard another sound outside. Something was striking the side brick wall, a small *tock*. It hit the steel security door to louder effect, hit the roof, the wall again, then smashed the tempered-glass window, which cracked spectacularly but didn't break.

Just as suddenly, the assault stopped.

The whole crew gathered at the windows, trying to determine the source of the attack. "I'll go check it out," Ger said.

Michael stopped him with his hand. "Wait." He had seen something in the dark of the field behind the store. "Stay with

Declan. Make sure his work isn't interrupted. I'm going out."

"I really don't think you should do that," Ger said.

"Lock the door after me."

The parking lot was fully lit by lights outside the store, lights high up on utility poles. Outside, Michael shielded his eyes against the glare as he walked across the blacktop. He could see nothing beyond the perimeter of the store's property.

An object sailed over his head, hitting the Dumpster on the side of the store behind him. He crouched. He wasn't quick enough to see what it had been, but had a good read on where it had come from. He cautiously walked in that direction, just over a hump in the landscape.

More missiles flew over his head as he crested the hill. Hidden from view of the store but illuminated by the lights on the utility poles, Noreen O'Driscoll rolled a golf ball into place in front of her with her foot. A dozen or so golf balls lay on the ground beside a golf bag.

Noreen acted as if she hadn't noticed his arrival. She lined up a shot with a golf club, took a couple of practice swings. She swung again and the ball arced over the hill. A couple of seconds later came the sound of it striking glass.

"What are you doing?" Michael said quietly.

"Working on getting out of the rough."

"What are you doing *here?*"

She rolled another ball into place, lined up the shot, swung. A divot landed near Michael's feet.

"If you hadn't got involved, none of this would be happening," she said.

"What's happening?" Michael said patiently.

"Your family, mine. You, me."

"There is no you and me."

As they talked, Noreen kept setting up more shots, firing them over the hill.

Her arms were shaking. "You should have stayed in your desert parish, Michael. This whole business was between the families. It had nothing to do with you. People started dying as soon as you showed up. What's a priest doing getting involved in our kind of business?" She looked at the way he was dressed now. For the first time they made eye contact. "At least, you *were* a priest."

"No," Michael said vehemently. "You're wrong. People died before I got involved. That's the only reason we're having this insane discussion out in the middle of a cow pasture in the middle of nowhere. A friend called on me for help. If Liam hadn't killed Lydia and Daniel, I would have never gone to Ireland and gotten involved."

Noreen had hit all the balls she had. She leaned on her golf club and listened to Michael. Her face was completely devoid of emotion.

Michael said, "I happen to know Liam was in Dublin on the day Lydia and Daniel were killed. Why do you continue with the pretense of protecting your brother? He's dead; what's the point?"

"Yes," Noreen said. "Liam was in Dublin that day. And so was I. And I can tell you with absolute certainty he didn't kill them."

"No? Then who did? What lowlife did you two recruit from the streets to do such an awful thing? I saw Lydia. I saw Daniel. I know what happened to them." He shuddered. "You disgust me," he said as he turned back toward the store.

"Don't you walk away from me!" she shouted. "I came all the way here to talk to you!"

Michael turned quickly around, pointing a finger at her. "We are finished!" he yelled back. "I'm sending someone out to take care of you until I'm done here. The law's the same in Dublin as it is here. Recruiting a killer for hire is a capital offense. You're going to be doing time. Same for your mother."

Noreen and Michael stood facing each other in the strange bright lights in the immense field.

Noreen jutted her chin out in a superior way, making Michael think she knew something he didn't. "Have you talked to your father lately?" Noreen said coyly.

"*What?*"

"Ma was saying how much she regretted the families not getting along. She was thinking a trip to Boston would sort things out."

Michael punched a number into his cell phone. The phone didn't even ring twice. Aiden's wife answered hysterically.

"What is it, Katie?" Michael said.

He could barely make out what she was saying. "Your father's been shot!" she said. "Maeve O'Driscoll got into the house while I was making the school run. He's dead, Michael. They're both dead." She was sobbing hard.

"Katie, call an ambulance. . . ."

As Michael was talking on the phone, Noreen lifted the golf club over her head as if she were going to take a swipe at the ground, then let the club fly out of her hands toward Michael, hitting him hard in the back of his head. He staggered, dropped the phone, lost it on the ground. He stumbled and fell, Katie's tinny voice bleating somewhere close in the high grass.

Michael was disoriented, his eyes unfocused. He felt the wetness at the back of his head, his fingers bloody. He saw Noreen reaching into the golf bag to pull another club out. He had to get to his feet, push himself off the ground. She rushed to where he was struggling to get up and lifted her hands over her head again. She brought the club down hard, barely missing him.

Through his mind flashed the realization that her weapon wasn't a golf club, but some sort of heavy wooden stick. She took aim and swung again, a direct blow to the head until he caught the stick in his hand. He let out a groan at the pain that shot up his arm. He fell to his knees to keep his grip on the stick as Noreen tried to pull it loose.

In the flurry of the struggle the black-painted shaft he was holding on to gleamed in the light. Noreen unexpectedly jerked it hard out of his hand, lifted it over her head, and was able to strike him hard in the chest. He reeled, managed to grab the end, felt its roughness, and knew at that moment what he had in his hands.

"You!" he shouted.

It was his old walking staff, the stout length of blackthorn from which the ram's horn that had been used to bash Lydia's skull in had broken off.

Michael said, "You were in her flat. You killed her, didn't you?"

Noreen took a step back, glaring at him. "She knew too much, Michael," she said, panting. "You brought her into the family from outside. That was your fault. Then after you left she stayed, and that was her fault. But she was never one of us. She was going to the police to tell them everything about the Powerball scheme. It was business. A sort of a murder, like, but nothing personal."

Michael used the opportunity of Noreen's backing up to stand and brush himself off. "Killing another human being is always a personal act," he said. "And I don't imagine my relationship with Lydia made it any easier to kill her, did it?"

Michael took two steps toward her and grabbed the staff from her hands. She let him. He looked at the length of it, drew a deep breath.

Noreen said, "If you had given me the chance, I would have loved you better than she did. I would have never let you go. I'd have given you a son; then you wouldn't have run off to the Church."

"I *had* a son," Michael said bitterly.

Noreen didn't understand. Then she did.

# Chapter 40

Ger handed Michael a towel to clean the blood from his face and hands. "She's locked into one of the storerooms outside separate from the others," Ger said. "She's mad as hell, but at least can't do herself or anyone else any harm. Nothing but Styrofoam cups to beat her head against."

Michael propped the blackthorn walking stick in the corner behind the televisions. The Powerball countdown clock showed only three minutes left. Ticket sales had been cut off two hours earlier. The final tally flashed on the screen. The payout for a single winning number had indeed surpassed all previous records. Some lucky ticketholder might be claiming a jackpot of $413 million.

"Are we ready to go here or what?" Michael demanded.

Declan kept his eyes on the computer monitors, checking and rechecking that his programs were running smoothly. "All systems go," he said. "T minus three and counting here at Snapeville mission control."

Two of the gang talked quietly between themselves. "I heard that if you bought fifty tickets a week, you'd win the jackpot on average about once every thirty thousand years."

The other said, "I heard if you had to drive ten miles to buy a lottery ticket that you'd be sixteen times more likely to be killed in a car crash on your way to buy the ticket than you are to win the jackpot."

Michael stood in front of the television screens with his arms folded. A commercial ended and the Powerball presentation was about to begin. As the others came in from the front room to watch the draw he said quietly to Ger, "Maeve O'Driscoll went up to Boston to kill my father, but he shot her first, then turned the gun on himself."

"My God. I'm sorry, Michael."

"That's my two brothers and my father dead because of *this*." He gestured to the televisions as the camera focused on the actual piece of machinery that would cough up the colored balls with their numbers. Michael didn't even mention the fact of Lydia's and Daniel's deaths.

"Can I ask you a question?" Ger said.

Michael nodded.

"Why are you doing this, anyway? I mean, with everything that's happened, plus your being a priest and all."

"It has nothing to do with my being a priest. We can't stand by and allow evil to triumph when we have the power to stop it."

"But you're *not* stopping it," Ger said.

Declan hushed them before Michael could reply. "Turn it up," Declan said.

Michael turned the volume up on the TV with the remote control. The Powerball show host had just started going through the usual spiel about the draw being supervised by a major accounting firm, whose representative was standing beside the machine that would spit out the colored balls with their numbers. The firm was Whitehall-Cogburn, Declan's employer.

Declan smiled. "Thank you, Whitehall-Cogburn, for making this all possible."

There were two Beitel Criterion drawing machines. One contained fifty-three white balls from which the first five numbers would be drawn. The second contained forty-two red balls from which the sixth and final ball would be drawn, the "Powerball." The presenter flipped a switch on the machine and the hard rubber balls dropped into plastic drums and started tumbling over each other.

Declan nervously tapped his finger on the sides of the keyboard. "Okay," he said, and pressed the enter key with special emphasis. "I just switched the program over from manual to automatic operation. All I have to do is type in each number drawn and after all six numbers are entered, my computer will take over from there."

Declan sat with his fingers over the numbers on the keyboard. "Call them out to me the moment they pop up so I don't waste a second having to look up from the keyboard or wait to hear the draw announced."

The moment had finally arrived. They weren't wasting any time on TV. The selection process began and the first ball fell through to a display rack. Michael could see the number even before the zoom lens had focused on the ball.

"Thirty-eight," Michael called out.

Declan repeated every number as he entered it to make sure it was right. "Thirty-eight."

"Six."

"Six."

"Thirty-two."

"Thirty-two."

"Forty-four."

"Forty-four."

"Seventeen."

"Seventeen."

Just one more number to go. The selection moved to the second machine filled with red balls for the final draw. Declan anxiously drummed his fingers on the keyboard and bounced his leg up and down as he awaited the final draw.

"Eight."

"Eight!" He talked to the computer. "Go, go, go!" He moved his face closer to the screen. "No duplicates!" he yelled out.

"What's happening?" Michael said.

"No dupes! No one else picked all six of those numbers! Hang on . . ." He craned his neck to watch the program doing its magic. "C'mon, c'mon!" he shouted impatiently.

"What?" Michael wanted to know.

"Just waiting for confirmation that the program was able to insert the winning number into the pool of selections and have it credited to this store."

"*Well?*"

Declan shot out of his chair. "*Yes!*"

Declan ran to the checkout counter in

the front room. Everyone else followed. The lottery ticket dispenser was already printing out a ticket. Declan's eyes widened as the printing neared completion. He tore it off, examined it, saying aloud each number: 38-6-32-44-17-8. "This is it. Damn."

"You're sure?"

"I'm positive. A perfectly legitimate ticket. Bought by some lucky redneck at two-fourteen in the afternoon in this very store. See for yourself." He gave the ticket to Michael.

The ticket dropped as it was being passed. Michael caught it in midair. Declan gave him a warning look. He took the ticket into the back room and checked the numbers against what he saw on the TV.

Michael's whole look changed. Almost, but not quite a smile now. Was it satisfaction? For thwarting the people who had murdered Lydia and his family? For the knowledge that he held over $400 million in his hands?

"You'll want to be taking care of that," Declan said.

"You're right."

Michael reached over Declan's pile of books and notes. He pushed them aside, looking for something. He picked up a lighter. He flicked it a couple of times until it lit. Michael kept the flame going.

"What are you doing?" Declan said, alarmed at how close the fire was to the lottery ticket. No one breathed as Michael brought the flame just underneath the slip of paper.

Michael released the button and the flame died. He told Ger, "Have your men put Declan and Pat and Eddie into the cars. We'll take them back to Boston with us on the jet. I'm not going to have their deaths sensationalized by the local cops. Let Maeve's gang go free, but we'll take Noreen with us. Lock her up at the office, feed and water her until I tell you what to do with her. Then destroy everything before you go: the computers, the televisions, Declan's CDs and notes. Any evidence that would link any of us to this place."

"There's no way we're going to be able to clean up all our fingerprints in here," Ger said.

"Fine." Michael tossed the lighter to Ger. "Then burn it."

"Declan's stuff?"

"The whole damned place. The entire world is going to know where that lottery ticket was bought by tomorrow morning.

They'll find their temple of greed in ashes. We'll start a rumor that some disgruntled customer torched the place for not selling him a winning ticket."

Everyone watched Michael carefully fold the lottery ticket and place it into his wallet.

Declan had been waiting for something.

"Leave now," Michael told him curtly.

"Shall I wait for you to be in touch?"

"You could be waiting a very long time."

Michael walked to the other side of the room, picked up the blackthorn walking stick, and left through the front door. He almost stumbled on a golf ball outside. He picked it up and flung it into the night sky.

# Chapter 41

Ger O'Keeffe heard voices from inside the den of the house on Manor Street. He stuck his head in the door. Michael was sitting in an armchair watching the news on television. He wore another one of Aiden's tailored suits, a black one with a white shirt and black tie.

Michael didn't notice Ger standing outside the door. He was staring at the TV screen, watching a news story about the Powerball lottery. After three days, still no one had come forward to claim the $413 million prize. All that was known was that the winning ticket had been sold at a convenience store in Snapeville, West Virginia, on the day of the draw. When the television cameras and reporters had shown up to film a segment on the business that had sold the ticket, they were surprised to find that the store had burned to the ground. Rumors were already circulating that it had become an arson case. Police were investigating loose talk at local bars about unhappy ticket buyers who had sunk hundreds, thousands of dollars into what they were sure was a decent shot at winning the lottery.

A professor at a nearby community college interviewed on local television blamed a failed education system for the innumeracy. A Baptist preacher blamed the Devil.

Michael turned the television off and Ger quietly backed away.

Michael hated attending funerals. When he had officiated as a priest, he was able to maintain some emotional detachment. He could stand in front of the weeping family and friends and speak from his prayer book about the resurrection of the dead and life everlasting. When he was sitting shoulder-to-shoulder with the bereaved he wasn't afforded that out. He grieved just like everyone else. He had seen enough of the dead, shed enough tears. He wasn't ready to lead the mourners at a triple funeral.

He had already said good-bye to his father, Aiden, and Kevin. Not to their faces, because he hadn't wanted to see them that way in the funeral home. Instead he had gone through his brothers' childhood rooms, maintained as guest rooms and not much changed from when they had all grown up in the house. He was instinctively drawn to the icons of a more innocent age: baseball gloves, Boy Scout sashes with merit badges, old high school textbooks. In Aiden's old room, a photograph of the three of them, arms around one another's shoulders on one of those summer holidays in West Cork, sailboats on Roaring Water Bay, the humps of the Carbery Islands in the background.

He sat in the den that was his father's shrine and felt he finally understood. The man wanted success in America too much. To return home to Ireland a failure would have been worse than starving.

The only reason Michael went to the funeral Mass was for Aiden's and Liam's wives and kids. He sat between the two widows on the front pew of their local Catholic church and put on a brave face as the new patriarch of the family. As they left for the cemetery, he let his hand touch the breast of his suit coat, felt that his wallet was still in the inside pocket.

Such a bright day. At least it wasn't raining. Burials in the rain were so depressing. At the brief graveside ceremony, he assembled the wives and children

around the three coffins. He had given instructions for Ger to tie up any loose ends
having to do with insurance and business
interests. The widows would be well pro-
vided for. His familial duty was done.

During the last prayers while everyone
had their eyes shut, he slipped to the back
of the group. He could still hear the
priest's solemn words as he wound through
the gravestones.

He put his sunglasses on and simply
walked away.

# Chapter 42

A week later, in her Dublin office, Detective Inspector Claire Burke received a long, cylindrically shaped overseas express package from the United States. Inside were an envelope and an object carefully covered in bubble wrap. Attached to the bubble wrap was a warning note: *Evidence — Do Not Touch.*

She opened the envelope and read the letter.

*Hello, Claire.*

*I hope that your allowing a murder suspect (me) to slip from your fingers will be more than compensated for by the fact that you now have in those same slippery fingers the evidence that can be used to help convict the person responsible for the deaths of Lydia and Daniel. You were right; I was wrong about Liam O'Driscoll. All I had was partial information about him that did not exclude any other suspects. I suppose he could be considered an accessory to the murders, as he was present, but he is dead and it is, therefore, a moot point.*

*My fingerprints, of course, are all over the enclosed walking stick from which the ram's horn was broken, as it is mine. You should, however, also find the bloody fingerprints of Noreen O'Driscoll. You can find her at the Boston address listed below. If she won't confess, I am sure you can connect the dots yourself. You will get your O'Driscoll after all, it seems, even if you were never able to solve the great crime you were hoping to use to further your career. Last time I saw him, Charlie Brady was showing classic signs of hypertension, and at the rate at which he smokes there may yet be a vacancy in the department before you know it, for which I am sure you are well qualified.*

*I know this may be pushing my luck — all things considered — but I wanted to ask a couple of favors. . . .*

It was not such an unreasonable request, Claire thought.

She typed a memo to Charlie Brady recommending withdrawal of the file from the director of public prosecutions naming Michael Driscoll as the suspect in the murders of Lydia Jellicoe and the boy Daniel O'Driscoll. Although it was a bit premature, she set into motion a formal notice to Interpol that Michael should be taken out of their database as a wanted man so that he could travel freely again.

Then there was that other matter. *That* would require her to stretch the rules about as far as she dared, call in a few favors of her own, but Michael had already been proved to be the boy's father, and Lydia his mother.

Claire reread the last lines of the letter:

*Lest you believe I am bitter about what happened, I just wanted to let you know that I think you are nothing if not a great talent and a prodigious beauty. You flattered me, you seduced me, you tempted me, you betrayed me. For my part, I have snatched from you the great crime you sought to solve. I am sorry, but know I am doing the right thing.*

*I forgive you. Can you forgive me?*

*Please don't waste your time trying*

*to find me. I refuse to be found. Nice Dublin city girl like you — you don't want to go where I'm going anyway.*
*Very sincerely,*
*Michael Driscoll*

Consuela, housekeeper to the priest of San Xavier de Bac, was in the church kitchen cutting homemade bread into little cubes to be used for communion when she heard the jeep driving along the road fronting the church. A horn honked twice. She put down the knife and wiped her hands on her apron.

The postman in the jeep who brought the mail was gone in a cloud of dust by the time she got to the mailbox. She retrieved the mail, read the addresses, and sorted letters as she walked to the church office.

She came to a stop in the courtyard. There was a letter addressed to her. No one had ever sent her mail in her own name to the church before. She didn't recognize the block print. The stamp was funny, with the word *Eire* printed on it. The postmark indicated it had been sent a week earlier.

Father Douglas, the priest filling in during Father Michael's absence, was out for the morning calling on parishioners and visiting patients in the hospital, so the office was empty. She put the parish's mail squarely on the desk, then tore open the letter addressed to her.

Consuela was old, and it was dark in the room, and she didn't notice the small piece of paper that fell out between the folds of the letter onto the floor when she took it out of the envelope.

She held the letter to the light of the window. The writing was the same block print, consisting of a single line: *Gracias, para San Xavier de Bac.*

Consuela wondered why someone would send her a letter saying that. She looked inside the envelope but saw nothing. How curious, she thought.

Her thoughts were interrupted by the sound of a door opening, then slamming shut. At first annoyed by the disturbance, she was gladdened by the sound of children running down the hallway. Three small children, just let out of the Papago Indian reservation school, burst into the office. They were the earliest of the children who came to the church in the afternoons for the after-school program that Father Michael had begun.

They ran up to her, hugged her skirt, called her Grandmother. She was Grandmother to all the children of San Xavier de Bac. They had smelled the bread in the kitchen and wanted her to feed them. They tugged on her skirt and begged her until she finally agreed to take them.

Consuela stuffed her letter back into the envelope. On her way to the door, the youngest of the children saw something on the floor. She stooped and picked it up, handed it to Consuela.

As she had just cleaned the office earlier that morning, Consuela immediately figured that the piece of paper must have slipped from the letter addressed to her. As the children rushed ahead to the kitchen, Consuela took the paper back over to the light of the window to examine it.

How nice, she thought. Someone had sent the church a lottery ticket. It wasn't the first time that had happened. Usually the tickets were accompanied by a letter explaining how the sender was making a donation to the church and swearing off gambling. The especially nice thing was that since the church was a charity, the entire amount of the donation was tax free.

Consuela stuck the ticket in between the pages of the Bible on Father Michael's desk for safekeeping. As soon as Father Douglas returned in the afternoon, they could make a phone call and find out if the ticket was worth anything at all.

First, there was a brief visit to the grotto above Lough Ine.

His coat zipped up tightly to his neck against a stiff breeze, Michael Driscoll parked at the lake and hiked up the hill to the small shrine. Though it was windy, the sky was cloudless and the sun bathed the hill in brilliant light.

Mary's robes shone bright blue through the ferns. Some pilgrims had left scraps of paper with prayers, weighted by stones. Others had left tokens of devotion — a doll, a photograph in a Ziploc bag, even an empty whiskey bottle. None of it meant anything to him except for the placid face of the Virgin. Her outstretched arms embraced him, pulled him back to her, comforted him.

Michael knelt on one knee and said a prayer: *"Please, God. No more dead, no more wailing O'Driscoll banshees."*

Then he said a prayer for himself. He was alive. Now he needed to live.

Michael had found a boat with a skipper for hire in Baltimore. Michael told him he just wanted to go far enough out so he could see the open ocean from the bay.

A fifteen-minute journey in the direct sun had warmed Michael enough so that he needed to unzip his coat, revealing his clerical collar.

When they got to the right place in the bay, Michael hung over the side of the boat, opening the urns Claire had managed to have waiting for him at a pub in the village. He discreetly spread the ashes on the water so that the skipper, a superstitious island man, didn't know it had happened.

It was just a matter of moments until Lydia's and Daniel's spirits were lifted up, and the dust that they had become was swallowed by the sea.

Michael stood and watched the water churn.

"Where to now, Father?" the skipper said.

Michael took an envelope from his coat pocket, examined the return address — Lima, Peru. From the envelope he pulled a note in Spanish with the letterhead of an urban mission church, and a group photograph of smiling but dirt-poor children amidst the squalor of the *barrios*.

"What are the odds of getting this boat

to South America?" Michael asked.

The skipper looked to the open sea and seemed to seriously consider the question for a moment, then shook his head. "Not a chance."

# About the Author

**David Compton**, born in Atlanta, Georgia, was a marketing executive with several Forture 500 companies before he turned to writing. His first novel, *Executive Sanction*, was a national bestseller.